LET ME LOVE YOU

REAL AMERICAN COUNTRY
BOOK 3

JENNIFER CARR

Edited by
ASHLEY ANDREWS

To the survivors—

Your strength is immeasurable, your resilience inspiring.

This story is for you, a reminder that even in the darkest moments, there is light, love, and hope waiting to guide you forward. May you always know your worth and find the courage to reclaim your joy.

You are not alone.

LET ME LOVE YOU PLAYLIST

If you like to listen to music while you read, there's a Spotify playlist curated specifically with a song for each chapter of *Let Me Love You.*

Scan this QR code to list on Spotify

FOR YOUR MENTAL &
EMOTIONAL WELL-BEING

This book contains depictions and discussions of domestic violence, emotional trauma, and recovery. While the story ultimately centers on healing, resilience, and love, it includes moments that may be triggering for some readers. Please proceed with care and prioritize your well-being.

PROLOGUE

Kensi

The silence of the penthouse pressed in around me. It was like standing at the summit of an ivory tower, high above New York's ceaseless pulse. The city stretched out beneath me, twinkling lights and shadowed streets humming with life—a harsh contrast to the sterility enveloping me. I had once thought this view would be a dream; now it was like looking through the eyes of someone else—someone who didn't exist.

The walls, lined with art pieces whose worth I couldn't begin to comprehend, mocked me with their silent judgments. I knew wealth. I'd been born into it, lived with it, enjoyed it. This life, however, had been forced upon me.

At first, I'd been a willing party. I was doing what had been expected of me since birth. My responsibility to toe the line for the sake of my family had been called into play. And I was happy to do it because I thought there would still be freedom to live my life. But I had been wrong.

My bare feet whispered across the cold marble floors, the chill seeping into my bones as if the stone itself were siphoning the warmth from my body. Each step was a reminder of the grandeur that caged me, the wealth that bound me tighter than any chain could.

This place was supposed to be a home, our home. But it was nothing more than a glorified display case. A place where Luka could showcase his latest acquisition—me, Kensington Rose Romano Solinas, the wife who completed his image of prosperity and power. But no amount of gilded frames or priceless vases could fill the emptiness that echoed through any of the vast rooms.

There was a time when I'd been naïve and doe-eyed when it came to the marriage I was now trapped in. It didn't take long for all of that to change. Luka's expectations became clearer day by day, each one carving away at whatever hope I had for a life of my own. The moments of kindness I once believed were real turned out to be just another layer of the mask he wore.

That's when the doors started to close, one by one. It started with little things: the way he locked his study, keeping certain parts of his life under lock and key. Then it became the silent rule that he would dine alone if he was working late, the stinging implication that my company was somehow distracting or unnecessary. Finally, I realized I was merely one part of his world—a polished, expected part, but separate all the same. We existed in the same space without touching, two lives side by side but barely overlapping.

And so, one day, he'd suggested I take my own room. The words were perfectly courteous, but I couldn't mistake the chill beneath them, a silent nod to the growing distance between us. He'd made it sound like a kindness, like an invitation to carve out my own space here, as if it was a gift. But it was a tacit acknowledgement of what we both knew: this marriage was a partnership in name alone.

When I moved into my own room, I expected it to feel like a victory, a tiny piece of independence. But here I was, pacing the walls, suffocating in the opulence, more isolated than ever.

I walked to the floor-to-ceiling windows, my hand resting on the cool glass that separated me from the world below. How many people out there were living their truths, breathing in the freedom that coursed through the city's veins? And here I was, perched high above them all, suffocating in a life that was never truly mine.

The penthouse was a crown atop one of the architectural kings of the skyline, a symbol of wealth and affluence. As I watched the city breathe beneath me, the weight of a diadem that symbolized not royalty, but captivity suffocated me.

Turning from the cold embrace of the night sky, I faced the towering mirror that stood like a silent sentinel in the corner of the room. Its frame was a masterpiece of carved mahogany, but within its confines, I saw not the wealth it was meant to reflect but the hollow gaze of a woman I scarcely recognized. At twenty-three, the woman reflected in the glass was a stranger, her eyes shadowed by the bruise of a recent blow and the invisible chains of a year spent in silent, gilded captivity.

The bruise on my cheek was an ugly splotch of violet against my pallid skin, an artist's careless drop of paint on a whitewashed canvas. It throbbed with a rhythmic reminder of Luka's temper, each pulse syncing with my heartbeat. I reached up, fingers trembling, and gently traced the edges of the discolored flesh. Pain flared at the touch, but beneath it, something else flickered—a spark of defiance that had long lain dormant.

For the first time in months, I held my own gaze in the mirror, refusing to look away from the emptiness that had taken root in my eyes. Beneath the surface, I saw something else—a memory, a glimpse of the girl I used to be before this life hollowed her out. I thought back to a small rebellion from my childhood. When I was eight, I had cut off a lock of my hair, just to spite my father's obsession with a perfect image. His fury had been immediate, but there'd been an odd satisfaction then, like I'd reclaimed a tiny part of myself. Now that same spirit—untamed, reckless—stirred again, fighting to rekindle.

I allowed my mind to drift back to the day I exchanged vows with Luka Solinas. It was heralded as the perfect union, the joining of two dynasties. The press had clamored for photographs, capturing every orchestrated smile and staged kiss. But what did they know of the contract signed in whispers, the promises made not out of affection but strategic alliance?

Tonight's conflict had escalated with terrifying speed when my return home after my weekly Pilates class was delayed. The session itself had concluded on time, but as I was leaving the studio, I unexpectedly ran into a girlfriend from high school. Our chance encounter turned into a spontaneous catch-up, the years melting away as we stood chatting on the sidewalk, oblivious to the passing time.

I arrived home to silence—a deceptive calm that veiled the tempest awaiting within the penthouse's walls. Luka's silhouette was a dark stain against the soft glow of chandeliers, his posture rigid, a foreboding omen. The air crackled with his anger, a storm cloud ready to burst.

Before I could explain the innocent delay, accusations were hurled my way. He was convinced of an infidelity that didn't exist, his anger boiling over into a fury that could not be quelled by reason or truth.

"Where have you been?" he asked, his voice deceptively soft, yet laced with poison. My explanation, truthful and innocent, crumbled against the fortress of his jealousy.

"Who is he?" Luka demanded, the words sharp as shattered glass. His accusations, wild and unfounded, pierced the remnants of trust we might have once shared. I could only watch, hollow, as the man who vowed to protect me became the very thing I needed protection from. His hands, which had once held mine in a dance of pretense, now struck with a force that branded both my skin and soul.

This bruise wasn't the first, and I knew it wouldn't be the last. As I traced the angry mark on my cheek, the painful reminder settled into a simmering anger I could no longer suppress. Something within me had shifted, solidified into resolve, like the crack of ice forming over a still lake. My pain, this constant bruise of betrayal, was now inseparable from my anger—a fuse sparking to life.

The face staring back at me was both familiar and foreign. Even my name, Kensington Rose Romano Solinas, taunted me, a constant reminder of the life I was bound to—a life meticulously designed by others, leaving little room for my own desires or identity. My father had insisted on calling me Rose, suppressing my mother's family name, Kensington, a legacy that symbolized independence and strength—qualities he'd never wanted me to embrace. My marriage to Luka, once celebrated as the perfect union, had rapidly unveiled its true nature: a meticulously constructed cage designed for control and subjugation, not unlike the manipulation I had experienced under my father's influence.

Outside, life flowed freely, unconfined, alive. I pictured myself slipping unnoticed into the crowds below, a face among faces, unknown and unburdened by the legacy of a name.

Just Kensington. Not Solinas. Not Romano. Just...me.

That thought—the idea of a life beyond these walls, free of both Luka's bruises and my family's grip—kindled something hot and defiant in my chest. A question formed, small but unrelenting: If I can imagine that life, could I someday live it?

1

KENSI

Six months had passed since I found myself staring at my bruised face in the mirror. My resolve to escape had only solidified in the days that followed, each act of rebellion, no matter how small, a stitch in the fabric of my newfound courage. Yet, my first attempt to flee was a failure and a reminder of the fortress I was trying to escape.

It happened on an otherwise ordinary day, under the guise of an afternoon at a local art exhibit—one of the few outings Luka allowed his wife to attend 'alone.' Of course, I was no longer allowed to be truly alone. There were always enough people present who would keep an eye on my every move from a distance. My plan was simple: slip away from the exhibit and meet Marco, who would take me to Newark, where I'd board a train as far from New York as I could get.

I'd met Marco through one of the Solinas family's philanthropic facades that they called a charity. It was a homeless shelter where reformed criminals who had committed "victimless crimes" served community service hours—a benign enough cause that wouldn't raise Luka's suspicions. Yet it was through this unlikely avenue that I found the ally I needed.

One afternoon, during a scheduled group meeting, the heavens opened, unleashing a torrential downpour that cleansed the city's streets with its fervor. As I arrived at the shelter, I struggled with a stubborn umbrella that refused to open, oblivious to the fact that the rain had soaked through my sleeve and displaced the carefully applied concealer, revealing bruises in the shape of fingertips on my bicep—evidence of Luka's latest bout of fury. It was one of the volunteers, Marco, who noticed, his observant eyes catching sight of the mark as I finally wrestled my way into the building, drenched and defeated.

Marco approached me with a concern that was unexpected in the world from which I came. He was soft-spoken yet serious, his voice imbued with a gravity that demanded attention.

"If you ever need help, I can make problems go away," he said softly, his gaze flicking between my face and my arm, ensuring I understood the gravity of his offer. He spoke with the conviction of someone who had faced his own darkness and drawn hard lines against it.

"There's a line between power and cruelty," he said quietly, almost to himself. "And I won't stand by while someone crosses it." His words settled around us, a shield against the casual violence of my world.

Marco became my lifeline, procuring the fake documents I needed: a new birth certificate, a driver's license, and a passport, all bearing the name Kensi Morrow. The transactions were made in cash, no questions asked, the secrecy of our dealings paramount.

However, on the night of the art exhibit, Luka's surveillance was more extensive than I had anticipated. Before I could even reach the sidewalk, his men intercepted me. I concocted a cover story about feeling faint and disoriented, claiming I needed to step outside for air. The bodyguards allowed me a few minutes of air before suggesting I finish the gallery tour or be taken home. I spent the next hour staring at art through unfocused eyes, counting down the minutes until I could disappear into the safety of anonymity.

Luka, though skeptical, accepted my explanation—but not

without consequence. The punishments that followed any action he deemed an indiscretion were severe, leaving me with injuries that were harder to conceal. Cradling my wrist, now encased in plaster, his words echoed in my mind.

"Remember your place, Rose," he had whispered venomously, the menace in his voice a dark melody that promised further pain if I stepped out of line again.

That was when my resolve turned to steel. I also knew that my next attempt had to be my last.

The setback of my failed escape attempt was disheartening, yet, in the shadow of this failure, an unexpected opportunity presented itself—one that would ultimately work in my favor.

Several days after the incident, Luka left early for a meeting, leaving explicit instructions that I was not to leave the house for any reason. He had been more paranoid than usual, which had caused me to wonder exactly what kind of meetings he had been attending, though I didn't dare ask. That morning, I found myself in need of important documents for a charity gala I was reluctantly hosting—another guise for Luka's networking. The only silver lining was that I was finally using the degree in Hospitality and Event Management that I'd worked so hard for.

Navigating the meticulously organized chaos of Luka's office, I found the folder I needed tucked away in a cabinet labeled "Events." Amidst the mundane—budget breakdowns, catering menus, agreements with entertainment, and décor rental invoices—I stumbled upon another folder nestled inside the one I had been searching for. Just as I was about to close the drawer, a name caught my eye: Minetti.

Compelled by fear and an insatiable need to know, I opened it and found records of transactions that blurred the lines between legal and illicit, alongside names I'd only heard whispered in tones of both respect and fear. The documents painted a clear picture of Luka's involvement in activities far removed from the legitimate business fronts he paraded in public.

My heart raced as I considered the significance of what I'd discovered. This evidence could be my ticket to freedom. Yet, holding onto it filled me with dread. If Luka discovered what I'd found, the consequences would be far worse than any punishment I'd endured before.

I couldn't get caught. Not now. My mind raced with the possibilities. These documents could secure my passage away from this prison. But who could I trust? Luka's reach was extensive, his connections spanning the legitimate and shadowy corners of society. Involving the FBI was a logical option, but the risk of involving law enforcement was monumental. I would become a target—not just for Luka, but for anyone implicated in these documents. Could I survive the fallout?

Acting quickly, I used the scanner behind Luka's desk to make copies. The machine whirred quietly, its hum amplifying the pounding of my heart as I stole evidence of Luka's duplicity. I tucked the copies under my shirt against my back, a makeshift hiding place that would have to suffice until I could deliver them to the authorities.

As I scanned the event documents, my palms grew clammy. Every second spent in this office was a risk, each faint click of the scanner ratcheting up my anxiety. I barely managed to return the files and close the cabinet when Luka's voice, sharp and commanding, cut through the silence from the hallway outside. Panic seized me, a visceral reminder of what would happen if he found me here, uninvited.

Luka stormed past, too engrossed in his phone conversation to notice me slipping out of his office. My heart raced as I retreated to the relative safety of my own space within the penthouse, the documents a physical reminder of the dangerous game I was now playing. This accidental discovery, though terrifying, offered a sliver of hope —an opportunity to tilt the scales in my favor, using Luka's own misdeeds as leverage in my quest for freedom.

That night, the flashbacks returned—of a time before I fully understood who my family really was. Despite its veneer of respectability, the Romanos had deep roots in organized crime. I remembered gatherings where men with cold eyes and dangerous smiles spoke in hushed tones, their conversations punctuated by the clink of expensive glassware.

I thought back to the year I was set to graduate from college. My father, a key figure in this underworld, had brokered my marriage to Luka Solinas—a move to unite two powerful families in a bond sealed not with love, but with the promise of power.

Trying to shake the memories, I inhaled deeply and conjured the image of a beach. The imagined sound of waves calmed me, lulling me to sleep.

When I jolted awake, my breaths came in short, panicked gasps, as if I were still fighting for air, struggling against an unseen force that sought to drag me under. In my dream, I'd waded into the ocean's cool, gentle waves. But suddenly, an undercurrent seized me, pulling me away from the shore with terrifying strength. I fought, but the current was relentless, dragging me under. Panic set in as I struggled to breathe, the surface—and my escape—growing further out of reach.

Abruptly, I was awake, my heart still racing. In an effort to ground myself, I reached under the bed and carefully pulled the copied pages from between the slats. The texture of the paper was grounding, each word and number a tangible proof of Luka's duplicity.

These documents, hidden so carefully, were my silent rebellion against the life that had been chosen for me. They were proof of my determination not just to survive but to reclaim the life that had been stripped away from me on my wedding day.

The discovery of these documents hadn't just been a stroke of luck; it was a sign, a turning point. I couldn't allow myself to be caught in the undercurrents of Luka's world any longer. The pieces were all in place: the evidence of Luka's crimes, my secret communications with Marco, and the fake identity that promised a fresh start. All that remained was to seize the right moment. The risk was monumental, but the thought of another day under Luka's control was infinitely more terrifying.

As I hid the documents once more, a silent vow settled in my heart. I would not wait for rescue; I would be my own savior. And when the moment came, I would be ready to leave Rose Solinas behind and step into the world as Kensi Morrow, free and unburdened by the shadows of the past.

2

KENSI

The shelter, bustling with activity and constant foot traffic, provided the perfect cover for discreet communication. Assigned to the kitchen, Marco and I worked amid the sounds of chopping vegetables and simmering pots, our whispered exchanges hidden by the ambient noise.

Marco found a moment to pull me aside, under the guise of needing help with a supply inventory in the pantry. It was a secluded spot, away from the prying eyes of the other volunteers, the shelter's patrons, and any other eyes Luka may have had on me.

"I waited for you," he began, his tone full of concern but laced with caution. "What happened?"

I hesitated, acutely aware of the risks involved in even this whispered exchange. Still, Marco was my only lifeline, and I needed him to understand. "The timing was bad," I admitted softly, my eyes not meeting his. "Luka's bodyguards... they were watching closer than I thought. They caught me before I could even reach the sidewalk."

Marco's jaw clenched momentarily, a ripple of frustration crossing his features. He shifted slightly, glancing at the door before smoothing his expression back into practiced neutrality. "Are you going to try again?" he asked, his voice hushed against the backdrop of clanging pots and the murmur of voices. His eyes flickered from corner to corner, ensuring our privacy in the cramped room stacked with non-perishables.

I edged closer to him, my fingers tracing the ridges of a dented can on the shelf as if it were the most important task at hand. "Yes," I whispered back, the word barely escaping my lips, a confession filled with determination and dread. "But I need something first." The urgency in my veins was a tangible force, pushing me forward despite the tremors of fear that danced along my spine.

Marco's brow furrowed, a testament to his concern, but the set of his shoulders told me he was already bracing for whatever reckless plan I had concocted.

"The name and address of the FBI agent who arrested you," I said, my voice so low it was nearly swallowed by the shelter's background noise. The plea hung between us, bold and nearly unthinkable—a request that could change everything.

Marco's eyes widened, the stark surprise etched into every line of his face as if my words had physically jolted him. I could almost hear his thoughts churning, rapid-fire, as he processed the gravity of what I was asking—no, pleading—for.

For a moment, I feared I had overstepped, asking too much of someone who had already risked a great deal by aligning with me. Yet, after a brief pause, he nodded slowly, the effect of my plea reflected plainly in his expression.

He discreetly pulled out his phone, his fingers moving swiftly as he searched for the information. The tension between us was palpable, a silent acknowledgment of the dangerous path I was choosing to walk.

Finally, Marco stopped, his gaze locking onto whatever information he had unearthed. He reached for an old can of beans, its label peeling at the edges, and tore a strip from the paper. The pen he produced appeared between his fingers as if by magic, and he scrawled something in a hurried, cramped script. His hand trembled just the slightest bit as he extended the makeshift note towards me, offering the inked salvation with a caution that conveyed more than words ever could.

"Are you sure you know what you're doing?" The question slipped from his lips, so faint it might have been mistaken for the sigh of a ghost. It hung in the air, delicate and fraught with implications.

Meeting his questioning gaze, the strain of countless sleepless nights and the conflict of my own internal debates pulsed behind my eyes. The glaring reality of my situation left no room for doubt or second-guessing; the course was set, the dice already tumbling mid-air. As if channeling a strength not my own, I prepared to step beyond the point of no return.

I grasped the strip of paper between my fingers, its edges frayed and the ink slightly smudged. "What choice do I have?" I asked, my voice resonating with an unfamiliar firmness that bounced off the pantry walls.

As I stared at the scribbled words, a chill of trepidation clashed with a surging tide of determination; Marco had already ventured into dangerous waters by aiding me, and here I was, diving deeper into the abyss hoping I didn't pull him too far down with me.

The truth was staring back at me in black and white—the name and address could lead to salvation or ruin. But the documents I'd stumbled upon were more than a lifeline; they served as indisputable proof of Luka's wrongdoings. With each beat of my heart, a sense of obligation grew—this wasn't just about my escape. It was about taking apart Luka's empire of darkness, brick by brick.Marco watched me, his own conflict etched in the lines of his face.

I slipped the paper into my pocket. The scent of simmering stew from the kitchen wafted toward us, a reminder of the world outside our bubble of conspiracy. Yet within that small, concealed corner of the shelter, we acknowledged the reality: the future was fraught with hazards, but the shackles of dread that had bound me were breaking.

"Thank you," I whispered, barely audible above the hum of the shelter's daily routine. Our eyes met one last time, allies in the shadow of the unknown. I walked back into the shelter's din, his question echoing in my mind: Are you sure you know what you're doing? But I already knew my answer. There was no turning back.

3

KENSI

The locker door clicked shut, the sound louder than I expected, echoing through the space and amplifying my own heightened senses. I folded my gym clothes slowly, steadying my breaths, feigning calmness despite the adrenaline coursing through me. Outside, the guard stood stiff as a statue, his gaze occasionally flicking toward me, feigning disinterest but watching all the same.

Yet, within the stifling confines of my surveillance, Marco and I crafted a plan, a glimmer of hope in the unrelenting darkness.

Each week, under the pretense of generosity, I carried small bags filled with clothes or toiletries in my large tote bag of a purse with me to the shelter.

The morning air heated my cheeks as I hefted another bag into my arms, its familiar bulk oddly comforting.

"Just a few things for the shelter," I said to the guard who had become my shadow, offering him a practiced smile that didn't quite reach my eyes. He scrutinized the bag with a cursory glance and nodded, his suspicion momentarily appeased by the routine.

In reality, the larger bag contained pieces of my go-bag, a careful accumulation of essentials for the moment I would seize my freedom. And each time I dropped off a bag at the shelter, I left behind a fragment of the fear that had been my constant companion.

"Kensi, can you take this out?" a volunteer asked, nodding toward the overflowing trash bin. It was the out I'd been waiting for.

"Of course," I replied, my voice even despite the adrenaline surging through me. I pushed the bin before me, navigating through the narrow hallways until I reached the back door.

I glanced around, ensuring no prying eyes followed, then slipped out, letting the door close with a soft click behind me. The smell of the city at night filled my nostrils—exhaust and garbage mixed with the distant aroma of street food—as I made my way to the car.

Marco's car sat where we had planned, the trunk barely open but enough for me to notice. My fingers trembled as I lifted the lid, verifying the space he had cleared for me. With a quick look over my shoulder, I climbed into the cramped darkness, pulling the lid down and sealing myself inside.

The suffocation hit immediately, the air thick and still around me. I fought the claustrophobia, focusing on the steady beat of my heart and the reason for my discomfort. This was the cocoon from which I would emerge free.

An eternity later, the engine roared to life, the vibrations coursing through the metal and into my bones. As the car moved, the world outside unknowing of the cargo it carried, I allowed myself to breathe a little deeper. Ahead lay uncertainty, yes, but also the sweet promise of liberation.

When the car finally halted almost another hour later and the trunk opened to reveal Marco's concerned face in the dim light of an alleyway behind a hotel, a wave of relief washed over me. I was sweaty, nervous, but an overwhelming sense of happiness flooded my soul.

"Are you OK?" Marco's voice was laced with worry.

"Almost," I murmured, my voice stronger than I really was. That single word echoed with my longing for what lay just beyond reach— the precipice of freedom. He offered his hand. I grasped it, allowing him to help me out of my temporary confines. My legs were stiff, my clothes wrinkled, but none of that mattered now.

Marco didn't waste time. From the depths of his coat, he produced a manila envelope, worn at the edges from the many times he must have checked its contents. "Everything you need is in here," he said, passing the package to me with a solemnity reserved for moments of great consequence.

My hands shook as I took it from him, feeling the gravity of what it represented. I peeled back the flap and pulled out a fresh driver's license. The plastic was cool against my fingertips. There beneath a photo of a woman with light in her eyes, was a name I had chosen but never spoken aloud: Kensi Morrow.

Tears pricked the corners of my eyes, not of sorrow but hope. Here was proof of my new existence, tangible evidence of the life waiting for me. And though the road ahead was fraught with uncertainty, this small card provided a sliver of possibility.

"Thank you," I whispered, the words inadequate for the gift he had given me. With a surge of emotion, I stepped forward and wrapped my arms around Marco. His body tensed in surprise before he reciprocated, a brief embrace that spoke volumes of the risks we'd taken. We separated quickly, understanding the need for caution, yet in that fleeting contact, gratitude and solidarity were exchanged.

"Go, before anyone sees," Marco urged. "You'll be safe now," he stuttered, pointing towards the front of the hotel. "The train station is just across the street."

I clutched the envelope to my chest, the papers inside more valuable than any currency. It was time to step into the unknown, to allow Kensi Morrow her first taste of the world.

I had one last request, a favor that came with risk. "Can you do one more thing for me?" I asked, my voice tinged with the gravity of what I was about to ask.

He hesitated, the lines of concern more pronounced on his face. But at my insistence, he listened as I asked him to contact the FBI agent, to alert him to be on the lookout for some important mail. It was a bold move, implicating Luka without ensnaring Marco in the web of consequences that would inevitably follow.

"I assure you, it has nothing to do with you," I said, hoping to alleviate his worry. "But it could be crucial to keeping my path clear for a while."

After a moment of consideration, Marco agreed. With a final nod, he imparted instructions for reaching the train station, his gaze lingering on me for a moment longer, a silent wish for my safety.

The pavement resonated beneath my feet, a steady drumbeat marking the rhythm of my escape. With each assured stride, I could feel the identity of Rose Solinas dissolving into thin air, her existence shrinking with the distance from that alleyway.

I wove through the crowds, just another face among many, but inside, I was shedding a history marred by fear and restraint. The clamor of the city engulfed me, blocking out the whispering fears of capture. Here, among the bustle, I became anonymous. It was a freedom like I had never known.

My fingers brushed against the contours of the envelope, the papers within crackling softly, a sound as sweet as any melody. The air shifted as I approached the grand facade of the train terminal, its clock tower standing sentinel over my fledgling journey. Rose Solinas was now a mere echo, lost in the din around me. Kensi Morrow's heart thrummed in my chest, eager to beat free from the cage it had known too long.

A swell of gratitude rose within me, warm like the sun's first rays after the darkest night. Marco had done more than craft an alias; he had unlocked the shackles that had bound me to a life not of my choosing. His gift was not merely one of paperwork and planning; it was the key to reclaiming a soul that had been held captive.

At the threshold of the station, I paused, taking in the enormity of the moment. As I stepped under the archway and into the glow of the interior lights, Kensi Morrow took her first true breath of freedom. I was reborn, not just in name, but in spirit, and for that, my silent thanks to Marco would stretch into this new life I was stepping into.

4

KENSI

The sound of the train wheels against the tracks was a relentless rhythm, like the pounding of my heart as I slouched in the cushioned seat, trying to blend with the throng of travelers around me. From Newark to Atlanta, each mile unfurled in an array of landscapes, but the scenic views were nothing more than a blur to my adrenaline-fueled gaze.

My fingers curled around the strap of the backpack that rested on the duffel bag nestled between my feet, my only companions on this journey. No one paid me any mind. No curious glances lingered, no eyebrows raised in suspicion. It was as if I had become just another face in the crowd—insignificant, unremarkable, safe.

For a fleeting moment, as the cityscape gave way to rolling hills and open skies, I let the tension ebb away from my shoulders. I allowed myself the luxury of a deep breath, tasting the air of liberation that seeped through the gaps in the crowded space. Despite the paranoia clawing at the edges of my consciousness, no one appeared to care that I existed.

The moment I stepped off the train in Atlanta, the bus station swallowed me whole. The air was thick with diesel and sweat, voices clamoring over one another drowning out my own racing thoughts. A screen flickered above with arrivals and departures, but it might as well have been flashing my own fears back at me—each name of a place where Luka's reach could extend.

I shuffled through the crowd, my grip on my bags like a lifeline, weaving between bodies propelled by their own urgent agendas. It was as though I had stepped into a stream of human current, everyone rushing past in a blur that mirrored my desperate need for flight.

Finding my bus, I heaved myself aboard, taking a seat near the back where I could watch the new passengers as they boarded. Each time the door hissed open and someone climbed inside, my heart lurched, fearing the face of an ally—or worse, an enforcer—of Luka's would appear.

The bus was cramped, the air stale and thick with the scent of too many people packed too closely together. I found myself constantly vigilant, flinching at every new passenger who boarded, at every stop the bus made, terrified that Luka's reach might somehow extend even here. My companions on the bus were a motley crew, each absorbed in their own world, yet I couldn't shake the feeling of being watched, of being vulnerable.

Sleep was elusive, the hard, uncomfortable seats making it impossible to find a position that didn't leave me aching. I spent the hours staring out the window, watching the landscape shift from urban sprawl to endless fields and back again, lost in thoughts of what awaited me in Texas. Would I find the sanctuary I so desperately sought, or would it be just another place to run from?

The physical discomfort of the journey was nothing compared to the mental toll it took. With each passing hour, the pressure of knowing the potential consequences of my decision grew. The fear of being caught, of facing Luka's wrath, warred with the fear of the unknown.

As the bus shuddered to a halt with a loud hiss from the engine, a collective groan echoed from the passengers, a chorus of frustration and disbelief. A knot formed in my stomach, the initial stirrings of panic that I quickly tried to quash.

Around me, snippets of conversation began to rise above the murmurs of discontent.

The bus shuddered to a stop, a loud hiss from the engine breaking the uneasy silence. Disgruntled murmurs rose from the passengers around me. I gripped my backpack tighter, dread snaking up my spine.

"What do you mean, 'broken down'?" an irate man a few seats ahead of me demanded, his voice loud enough to draw attention. "My son is getting married this weekend and I have to be there by tomorrow morning!"

A woman across the aisle clutched her child closer, whispering reassurances that did little to soothe either of them. "It'll be okay, honey. They'll fix this, you'll see."

The bus driver's voice, barely audible above the noise, promised replacement buses. But the idea of waiting—of being exposed in transit—made my skin crawl.

I sank farther into my seat, pulling my backpack into my lap as if it could offer some protection, some semblance of control in a situation where I had none. This wasn't the plan. Not even close, I thought, a bitter laugh threatening to escape at the absurdity of my predicament. But when has anything gone according to plan the first time lately?

After what felt like an eternity, the driver hung up his phone, clearing his throat as he turned to face us. "Folks, I'm sorry for the inconvenience. The company's arranged for replacement buses to pick us up. They'll be here within the hour. We'll be splitting up based on final destinations."

A murmur of relief and renewed frustration rippled through the bus. The idea of further delays was met with resigned sighs and hurried checks of watches and phones.

I remained silent, observing, my mind racing. Splitting up? That could work in my favor, or it could be a disaster. Too many variables, too many unknowns. The thought of being even further delayed, of spending more time in transit, was suffocating. Yet, the alternative, staying put, was not an option.

When the replacement buses finally arrived, chaos ensued as everyone scrambled to gather their belongings and find out which bus they were supposed to board. I hung back, waiting for the crowd to thin before making my own exit.

As I boarded the new bus, the seriousness of my situation settled heavily on my shoulders. The other passengers were engrossed in their own concerns, their own dialogues of frustration of their own trips being derailed.

The bus driver's announcement was a jolt back to reality, a reminder of the precariousness of my journey. "Folks, due to the delay, we've arranged for these buses to continue along the route. However, we'll need to drop any additional passengers at the next available bus stop to make their own arrangements. We apologize for the inconvenience."

My heart sank. Make their own arrangements. The phrase echoed ominously in my mind as I took a seat near the back of the replacement bus, trying to blend into the fabric of its worn seats. The buzz of conversation around me grew distant, as though I were observing the scene from afar.

My plan had been to make it to Houston. But, there hadn't been room on the bus headed straight for Houston. And because I had bought my ticket the same day, I wasn't given priority.

The bus finally pulled to a stop, the driver's voice ringing out, "Liberty, Texas—this is where we drop any additional passengers." A sinking feeling settled in my stomach as I stood, gripping my bag like a lifeline. Liberty was never part of the plan, yet as I stepped out, the stillness of Main Street was almost startling. The town was quiet, untouched, as if it existed outside the chaos I'd left behind.

Gathering my bags, I stood, my legs stiff from the journey and my heart pounding in my ears. The other passengers barely glanced up as I made my way down the aisle.

Liberty, Texas, was not my intended destination. Yet, as fate would have it, I was the only "additional passenger" to disembark at the quaint station that looked as though it had sprung up from the very heart of Texan folklore. The bus pulled away, leaving me alone on the curb, all of my belongings clutched tightly to my chest.

The quiet streets stretched out before me, lined with shops frozen in time. A clock tower stood at the center, ticking away with steady purpose. This place—Liberty—was almost mocking me with its name. I was supposed to hide in a city where I could disappear, yet here I was, in a town where everyone would likely notice a newcomer. But as I watched an elderly couple pass by with gentle smiles, something within me loosened.

Maybe this was a sign. Maybe the broken-down bus and the chaotic detour were leading me to a different kind of sanctuary. Peace saturated the air, a sensation as rare as hope in my life lately. A sense of calm settled over me. Maybe this was what normal felt like. Or hope. Either way, I couldn't help but almost smile as I walked with no destination in mind. For the first time in a very long time, I let myself believe everything was going to be OK.

5

KENSI

The heat of Texas was more oppressive than I had anticipated, and despite my need to keep moving, the promise of air conditioning and a moment to collect my thoughts was too enticing to pass up. I spotted a sign for a store called The Liberty Dollar General Store. I immediately headed in its direction hoping for a respite from the heat. Pushing the door open, I was greeted by the welcome blast of cool air and the familiar sight of aisles stocked with everything from snacks to essentials.

I wandered through the store, picking up a bottle of water and a pack of granola bars, my mind racing with thoughts of what to do next. My attempt at appearing casual and unfazed was not entirely successful. The ever-present fear of being found wrapped around me like a second skin, making my movements jittery and uncertain.

As I wandered through the aisles of The Liberty Dollar, the cool air provided a brief escape from the heat outside. I noticed the shelves were stocked with a combination of everyday items and unique local finds. My eyes were drawn to a display of Liberty-themed souvenirs, including postcards featuring the town's historic landmarks and mugs with witty sayings about community pride. There was a quiet ease in the unassuming simplicity of the store.

Taking a steadying breath, I maneuvered towards the checkout, my grip tightening around the handle of the basket. It was just a simple transaction—nothing more. No one here knew who I was, what I was running from, or why every new town spelled danger. Yet the fear clung to me, a second skin I couldn't shed, no matter how many miles I put between myself and my past.

At the register, a woman with a warm smile and an air of kindness waited for me. Her name tag read "Sarah".

"Is that all for you today?" she asked as she scanned my items.

I hesitated for a moment, the question I needed to ask sitting heavily on my tongue. "Actually, I was wondering," I lowered my voice. "Is there a place to stay around here? A hotel or something?" My voice betrayed the nervousness running over every nerve fiber of my being, but Sarah's smile didn't waver.

"Oh, we don't have any hotels in Liberty, but there's a lovely bed and breakfast not too far from here. The Yellow Rose Inn. It's owned by Evelyn Mitchell, a dear friend of mine. She keeps a beautiful place, and I'm sure she'll have a room for you," Sarah explained, her tone both reassuring and friendly.

A wave of relief washed over me, accompanied by gratitude for the kindness of a stranger. "Thank you so much. Could you tell me how to get there?" I asked, feeling a small flicker of confidence.

"Of course, dear. It's just up the way, about three blocks on your right. You can't miss it. Tell Evelyn that Sarah Thompson sent you," she said, handing me a small map she had drawn on the back of the receipt.

"Thank you, Sarah. I really appreciate your help," I said, feeling slightly more grounded with a destination in mind.

Sarah waved off my thanks with a smile. "It's no trouble at all. We look out for each other here in Liberty. I hope you enjoy your stay."

As I left the store, the air hit me like a wall of heat, making me sweat instantly. My brief interaction with Sarah had lifted my spirits somewhat, easing the intensity of the moment. I made my way along the quiet streets of Liberty, each step taking me closer to The Yellow

Rose Inn, and hopefully, a haven where I could regroup and plan my next move.

DRAGGING my feet up the steps to The Yellow Rose Inn, I was more than a little out of sorts. The place looked like something out of a storybook with its white facade and those vibrant yellow roses out front, smelling like summer. Honestly, it was a welcome change from the jumbled mess of worry and exhaustion that had taken hold of me.

Stepping inside, I found myself blinking in surprise at the cozy setup. It was like walking into someone's living room rather than a business. The woman at the desk greeted me with a warmth too genuine to be mere politeness.

"Welcome to The Yellow Rose Inn. How can I help you?" Her voice was like a soft, reassuring hug and full of what I could only identify as Texas twang.

I hesitated, my new identity sitting awkwardly on my tongue. "I, uh, need a room for the night," I managed to get out.

"Of course," she replied, her demeanor unchanging. She introduced herself as Evelyn Mitchell, the innkeeper.

She made signing in and getting the key feel like no big deal, even though my heart was racing the whole time. The interior of the inn was a patchwork quilt of home like I'd never seen before. Soft lighting, worn books on mahogany shelves, and the faint scent of lavender hung in the air. It was as if the building itself exuded tranquility, urging me to lower my guard.

As she busied herself with the keys, Evelyn chatted amiably about the inn and the town, suggesting places I might like to visit. "If you're looking for a bite to eat or just to unwind, my son owns The Anchor down on Main Street. Tell him I sent you," she suggested, her eyes twinkling.

"I might check it out, thanks," I said, more to fill the silence than anything. Her smile in response was cryptic, leaving me wondering if I'd missed something as I headed for the room she'd assigned me.

Pushing open the door, the room greeted me with a stillness that bordered on reverence. I stood for a moment at the threshold, taking in the soft cream walls and the quilted bedspread in hues of sage and lavender. Through the sheer curtains, sunlight filtered gently, casting lacy shadows across the wooden floorboards. Outside the window, the rose bushes swayed slightly, their blooms a vivid yellow against the backdrop of emerald leaves.

I let my backpack slip from my shoulder, its weight thudding softly against the floor. My legs, wobbly from the stress of travel, carried me to the edge of the bed where I sat, feeling the pliability of the mattress beneath me. The bed beckoned me to surrender, to let down my defenses and drift off to sleep. With a heavy sigh, I laid back, feeling the cool caress of the pillowcase against my cheek.

My eyelids fluttered shut, heavy with exhaustion. I allowed myself to sink into the embrace of the bed, the tension ebbing from my body bit by bit. It was a peace I hadn't experienced in far too long, a gentle reprieve that cradled me into slumber.

But this peace, it seemed, was not meant to last.

The darkness surrounded me like a thick fog, my feet pounding against the cold pavement as I darted through narrow alleys, my breath ragged. The sound of my pursuers was a constant echo in my ears, their footsteps a relentless reminder that I couldn't stop, couldn't rest. My heart was racing, panic clawing at my throat with each turn I took, desperately trying to put distance between me and them.

I could almost feel their fingers grazing the back of my shirt, hear their breaths mingling with mine in the chill air. Every shadow concealed a threat, and every noise made me jump. I was running blind, the fear of being caught overshadowing everything else. "Kensi, run!" my mind screamed. My feet were cemented to the spot when an all-too familiar voice rumbled behind me. "Hello, Rose."

And then, with a start that ripped me from the clutches of the nightmare, I awoke. My breath came in ragged sobs, my shirt clinging to my skin, damp with sweat. I groped blindly in the dark, heart slamming against my ribcage—a stark reminder that while I might have fled my old life, it was never too far behind.

In the dim glow of the bedside lamp, I caught my reflection in the mirror. My eyes, wide with the remnants of fear, stared back at me. The terror of the dream lingered, a ghostly afterimage that blurred the lines between reality and the haunted realm of sleep. With each pounding beat of my heart, I knew that true sanctuary remained just out of reach.

As the water cascaded over me in the shower, each droplet echoed the chilling touch of my dream's pursuers. The steam filled the bathroom, creating a veil that momentarily separated me from the harsh realities waiting beyond the inn's protective walls. Yet, as much as I wished the hot stream could wash away my fears, the imprint of my nightmare clung to me, a stubborn shadow that no amount of soap could erase.

Wrapped in a towel, the silence of the early morning weighed heavily, amplifying the echo of my own thoughts. The room was still dark, the curtains drawn tight against the promise of dawn. Hunger gnawed at me as I realized I'd slept long past dinner.

I reached for a granola bar, the act mundane but soothing in its normalcy. As I chewed, I couldn't shake the feeling of being watched, the paranoia from my dream seeping into reality. It was just a dream, I told myself, trying to shake the sense of dread. You're safe here. Luka doesn't know where you are.

As I sat on the edge of the bed, the crinkling of the plastic wrapper was the only sound in the room. The stillness pressed in around me. In this moment, alone with the remnants of my terror, the enormity of my situation sat heavily on my shoulders.

The dream, though a figment of my sleep-addled mind, was a mirror to my reality.

"Hello, Rose," the voice had said, a cruel reminder of the identity I was fleeing, of the life I was desperate to leave behind.

Kensi Morrow. The name was alien on my tongue, an ill-fitting costume that did little to disguise the truth beneath. With each bite of the granola bar, I could taste the bitter edge of a reality I'd tried to leave behind. Rose Solinas—a name synonymous with secrets and flight—was who stared back at me from the vanity mirror.

Kensi was just a veneer, a flimsy barrier between me and the world that I knew would be hunting me soon, if it wasn't already. In the vulnerable solitude of this room, wrapped in nothing but terrycloth and trepidation, the distance between who I was and who I needed to be stretched too wide. The threat of discovery loomed over me, overshadowing the false sense of security that came with my new identity.

I knew then, with a clarity that cut through the fog of my fear, that Liberty, for all its charm and the temporary sanctuary it offered, was not a place I could afford to grow too fond of. The dream had underscored a truth I had been trying to outrun: safety was a luxury I might never fully possess.

I crawled back into bed, the light of dawn slowly filling the room. The second attempt at sleep was easier. When I awoke again, the room was bathed in soft morning light, a stark contrast to the shadows of my nightmare. The beauty of the inn in daylight was undeniable, the yellow roses outside my window a silent promise of new beginnings. I dressed quietly, the events of the night still weighing heavily on me.

Descending the stairs to the dining room, the scent of freshly brewed coffee and the low hum of hushed conversations greeted me. The room itself held its breath, offering a peace that gently soothed my frayed nerves. I chose a table near the corner, my back to the wall.

No sooner had I settled into the chair, trying to appear as if I belonged to this serene morning tableau, then the calm was shattered. The sound of ceramic clashing against hardwood caused my heart to leap into my throat, causing a loud gasp to escape from me. Heads turned, eyes peering at me over coffee cups and newspapers, and a flush of heat spread across my cheeks.

"Sorry," I stammered, my voice barely above a whisper. "Just... startled me." My hands were trembling, so I tucked them under my thighs, pressing down until the shaking subsided. The innkeeper swept up the broken shards with a practiced smile, her movements smooth as she reassured the other guests.

I mumbled another quick apology, my cheeks burning with embarrassment, feeling every bit the skittish, cornered animal I never wanted to become in my efforts to flee my past.

I pushed my empty plate away, the remnants of scrambled eggs and toast crumbs a testament to an appetite I hadn't realized I still possessed. My gaze drifted out to the small garden visible through the open window, where the yellow roses were basking in the sun's morning embrace. The soft clinking of cutlery against plates was the only sound that filled the dining room now.

My mind wandered, tracing the potential roads ahead of me. Liberty had already been kind—a gentle pause in a relentless pursuit. But staying was not an option; the shadows of my past were too dark to bring to this tranquil town. And I was convinced that it wasn't a question of if they would find me, but when.

For just a moment longer, though, I let myself sink into the chair, the solid oak beneath me offering a sturdy reality against the fluid uncertainty of my life. I closed my eyes, inhaling deeply, trying to imprint this fleeting sense of freedom into my memory. The earthy scent of coffee grounds mingled with the sweet fragrance of the roses on every table, creating a moment so ordinary but perfect it was almost painful. With each breath, I attempted to etch the quiet hum of Liberty into the corners of my mind, a sanctuary to retreat to when the nights elsewhere grew too silent or the alleys too dark.

But soon, I stood, the chair scraping softly against the wooden floor as I pushed back from the table. I couldn't afford to get too comfortable. Today, the sun was on my side, and the breeze was a companion rather than a harbinger. Today, I could pretend, if just for a second, that I was simply Kensi Morrow, a traveler passing through without a storm cloud in sight.

6

WYATT

The clink of glasses and hum of conversations filled The Anchor—my bar and, in a lot of ways, my refuge. Friday nights always brought the usual crowd looking to unwind, and I stuck to my routine behind the bar, pouring drinks and keeping things running smooth. It was predictable, steady, and I liked it that way.

Bits of conversation drifted my way as I worked. Regulars shared pieces of their lives without realizing it, and I picked up on more than they probably meant to share. That's something I've always liked about running this place—it keeps me connected, even when I'm fine being on my own.

"Turner, what's the special tonight?" Hank called out from his usual stool.

"The same as always, Hank," I said, sliding a pint his way. "Good beer and good company."

Hank grunted his approval and raised his glass. I moved on to a pair of new faces, smiling as they studied the menu.

"First time at The Anchor?" I asked.

"Yeah," the woman said, smiling back. "Just moved here and heard this was the place to be."

"Well, you heard right. Let me know if you need a suggestion."

They ended up going with my recommendation—citrus IPA— and their smiles told me they'd be back. It was moments like that, seeing people feel at home here, that reminded me why The Anchor mattered.

It wasn't just a bar. It was a place my dad built with his own hands, his dream. When he passed, I shut the doors, overwhelmed by grief I didn't know how to handle. Joining the Navy had been my escape. Becoming a SEAL gave me purpose, discipline, and a sense of brotherhood. But when an injury ended my career, I found myself back at a crossroads.

That's when Stephen, my best friend and a tech genius, came up with the idea for StealthWave Security. It was a second chance for both of us, a way to use what we knew. Stephen suggested running the firm out of The Anchor's basement—practical, discreet, and the perfect excuse to reopen the bar.

Balancing the two was a challenge, but it worked. Then Missy Ryan walked into the picture, and everything shifted. Stephen had been pining for her since we were kids. Watching her walk in that first day, soaking wet from the rain and determined as hell, I could see why.

Stephen tripped over himself trying to talk to her, which was hilarious considering how smooth he usually was. Missy, though, was focused. She'd just ended things with her ex—Tim Rollins, local quarterback turned used car salesman—and wasn't interested in anything more than a drink and some quiet.

Over time, she became a regular. She'd take her usual seat at the bar, scanning the classifieds for a fresh start. One day, Stephen finally worked up the nerve to offer her a job as manager. I backed him up, mostly because it made sense. She had a way with people, and we needed the help.

"Why me?" she'd asked, her expression cautious.

"Because you're smart, you're good with people, and honestly, you already know this place better than most," Stephen had said, trying to sound casual and failing miserably.

Missy considered it, then nodded. "Okay. I'll give it a shot."

She was a natural. The Anchor ran smoother with her around, and Stephen spent every shift pretending not to be completely in awe of her. He tried to play it cool, but anyone could see how he felt.

As for me, I stayed in my lane—running the bar, keeping the peace, and watching it all unfold. It was a good life, a busy one, and I didn't mind being the quiet observer in the middle of it all.

7

WYATT

Saturday nights at The Anchor always had a different energy. Louder, livelier, and tonight was no exception. The bar was packed, the air buzzing with laughter and the clink of glasses. This was my zone—pouring drinks, keeping an eye on things, and making sure the night didn't spin out of control.

Midway through the night, Sarah Jensen snapped a guitar string mid-song, cutting through the buzz of conversation. She was one of our regulars, her voice smooth as aged whiskey, and her bad luck drew a collective groan from the crowd.

Without thinking, I grabbed the old six-string I kept in the back. It wasn't anything fancy, just something I used to mess around with, but it would do. "Here, take mine," I offered.

Sarah shook her head, smiling. "Thanks, but I could use a break. Unless you're about to give us a show?"

The crowd picked up on her challenge immediately. "Come on, Turner! Give us a song!"

They weren't letting it go, and honestly, neither was I. "Alright, alright," I said, shaking my head but grinning.

Music had always been an outlet for me, a way to blow off steam or say the things I couldn't otherwise. I kept it simple—two country classics I knew like the back of my hand. The crowd whooped and hollered when I finished, their energy catching me off guard. For a second, I let myself feel it—the spark of performing, of giving people something to celebrate.

After that, the guitar came out more often on Saturday nights. Word spread, and before long, folks started showing up as much for the music as the drinks. It wasn't something I'd planned, but I couldn't deny the way it brought people together.

"Turner, when are you ditching this bar and hitting the big stage?" Harold called from his stool, teasing as usual.

"Can't leave you, Harry," I shot back. "You'd miss me too much."

The crowd laughed, and even Missy smirked from behind the bar, managing the chaos like the pro she was.

Later, as the night wound down, Missy leaned over. "You ever think about recording some of those songs?"

I shrugged. "Nah. I'm good right here."

She gave me a look like she knew better but didn't press. "By the way," she added, her tone shifting, "you thought any more about hiring some help? Business is booming, and we could really use another set of hands."

"I've been thinking about it," I admitted, wiping down the counter. "I'll start looking."

"Good," she said, relief creeping into her voice. "We'll make it work till then."

As closing time hit, the patrons filed out, waving and promising to be back. Cleaning up with Missy and Stephen was as close to a ritual as anything we did here. They were my team, my people, even if Stephen spent half his time trying to win Missy's attention.

"Night, Wyatt," Missy called as they left, Stephen hot on her heels.

"Night, you two," I replied, locking the door behind them. The bar was quiet now, the hum of the jukebox replaced by silence.

I lingered for a moment, taking it in. This place wasn't just a bar. It was a heartbeat, a steady rhythm that kept me grounded. As much as I joked about it, there wasn't anywhere else I'd rather be.

After locking up, I headed to my office, flipping on the small lamp. The stack of invoices and reports on my desk waited like they always did, but tonight, I couldn't focus. The restless feeling in my chest was back, gnawing at me like it had been for weeks.

I rubbed my eyes and leaned back in the chair, giving up for the night. Tomorrow, there'd be more work, more questions, more decisions to make. But for now, The Anchor was quiet, steady, and mine.

8

WYATT

I flexed my fingers, feeling the familiar ache of old wounds as I surveyed the blueprints laid out across the table. Stephen leaned in beside me, his keen gaze darting over the schematics, a spark of excitement lighting up his features. He was a literal genius, the kind whose brainpower had drawn the CIA's eyes during his M.I.T. days. To them, he was an asset to be acquired, but to me, he was the partner I needed for a vision that was slowly taking shape between us.

"Right here," Stephen pointed at an intersection of corridors on the blueprint, "this is where traditional security measures would fall short." His finger tapped the paper as if to punctuate the gaps in existing protocols that we were determined to bridge.

"Exactly," I agreed, my voice tinged with the gravel of experience.

StealthWave Security didn't come from some eureka moment. It was born out of necessity—a drive that went bone-deep, every time my old service injuries flared up, reminding me why I started this.

After coming back from the SEALs, the adrenaline from missions was gone, leaving behind a restless energy I didn't know how to channel. I tried. I drafted business plans for the bar until the early hours, as if pouring myself into spreadsheets and projections might settle my mind. At one point, I even thought about throwing myself into thrill-seeking—skydiving, racing, anything to feel that rush again. But somewhere along the way, I realized that wasn't the answer. I needed something real, something with purpose, to get my feet back on solid ground.

That's when the concept of StealthWave began to crystallize—a firm that could operate in the shadows where law enforcement and military hands were tied.

"Think about it, Wyatt," Stephen had said with his analytical prowess I'd come to admire. "We have the expertise to anticipate the unexpected, to offer protection where others can't even see the threats." He'd been right; we were perfectly poised to fill a void in private security, two pieces of a puzzle coming together to create a new picture of safety and defense.

We'd brainstormed over countless cups of coffee and probably too many beers, mapping out the structure and services of our future company. The name StealthWave Security emerged from those sessions, symbolizing the silent but powerful impact we aimed to have in the private security sector. Drawing from my military contacts and Stephen's extensive network, we assembled a team of former military personnel and specialists with the skills and dedication necessary to fulfill our mission.

With our mission clearly defined and our team in place, Stealth-Wave Security quickly gained a reputation for excellence and reliability in the field. It was a far cry from my days in the military, yet it allowed me to channel the same commitment to protection and service into a new battlefield.

Over time we built our reputation on a foundation that was as varied as it was detailed. Our personal protection work brought us face-to-face with people constantly looking over their shoulders, each with a story as unique as the threats they faced. We didn't just stand guard; we integrated security into their daily lives with a subtlety that belied the strength of the protection we offered. Every assignment was a new puzzle, demanding not just physical presence but a strategy that was two steps ahead of any potential danger. And we prided ourselves on being anything but your average security firm. We're a mixed team of muscle, brains, and a whole lot of guts, tackling everything from the front lines to the fine print. And whether we were training up our team or tracking down a threat, we're putting everything we have into keeping our clients safe.

Stephen and I were gearing up for something a bit different this weekend. Instead of diving headfirst into another high-stakes assignment, we'd decided to focus on honing our skills and tightening our team cohesion. Even with several of our team out on assignment, the rest of us, including Stephen and me, were meeting up to participate in a tactical training weekend. It was a chance to step back, assess, and improve — essential for a team that often found itself in unpredictable situations.

The sprawling basement beneath The Anchor, our usual command center, was abuzz with a different kind of energy as we prepped. Stephen was particularly animated, hardly able to contain his excitement about the new tech he planned to introduce. "You're going to love this," he kept saying, his eyes sparkling with the thrill of innovation. "It's going to change the game for recon missions."

I couldn't help but share in his enthusiasm. Stephen's knack for blending cutting-edge technology with field operations had given us an edge more than once, and I was eager to see what he had up his sleeve this time.

As we packed up the gear, the rest of the team started trickling in. There was a strong bond of familiarity among us, a band of brothers in arms brought together by a shared commitment to protect and serve. The training weekend wasn't just about drills and technology; it was about reinforcing the trust and reliance we placed in each other.

"We're heading out in an hour," I announced, glancing over the checklist of equipment and supplies. "Make sure you've got everything you need."

We piled into the SUVs, the engines growling to life in anticipation. Gravel crunched beneath tires as we left the familiar streets behind, heading toward the training grounds that promised a weekend of growth and grit. We were a private security firm, yes, but at our core, we were protectors, each of us drawn to this work by a desire to make a difference.

The clank and zip of gear being secured underscored the steady hum of conversation as the last of us arrived. I checked the action on my sidearm, a rhythmic motion that came as natural as breathing. Around me, Velcro straps adjusted, magazines clicked into place, and boots thudded against the concrete floor. We moved with a shared rhythm, the dance of warriors prepping for the day.

"Hey Wyatt, think you'll keep up today?" Martinez tossed a smirk over his shoulder, his hands deftly checking his rifle's sights.

"If you're setting the pace, I'll have trouble hanging back," I shot back, grinning despite the challenge. The jabs were part of our language, a way to say 'I've got your back' without the sappiness.

Stephen's laugh cut through the banter, light and infectious. "Just make sure all that gear's on tight. Wouldn't want anyone to lose their pants in the field again."

"Once was enough for a lifetime, thanks," Jackson called out, the memory igniting a round of laughter that echoed through the room.

The training ground was an isolated piece of land we'd secured for just this purpose, complete with a mock urban environment for scenario training. The mock urban site came into view, a labyrinth of lean-to buildings casting long shadows in the early morning light.

"Alright, let's see what Stephen's been cooking up in his lab," I said as we disembarked, the scent of earth and anticipation thick in the air.

Stephen took center stage, his hands unveiling the compact drone with a magician's flair. It was a sleek piece of machinery, its dark body absorbing the light around it as if to vanish before our eyes.

"Meet the NightWing," he announced, a proud father introducing his child. "Thermal imaging for those fun night games, and silent enough to sneak up on a ghost."

Thompson whistled, his gaze fixed on the drone like a kid at Christmas. "You've outdone yourself, Parker."

The team circled the device, questions and comments flying. How far could it fly? How much weight could it carry? Could it withstand a hit?

"Enough to get the job done, and then some," Stephen assured them, his confidence as solid as the tech in his hands.

"Let's put it to the test," I suggested, the prospect of incorporating this new asset lighting a fire in my chest. It wasn't just about playing with new toys; it was about harnessing innovation to protect lives.

"First scenario in fifteen," I added, nodding to the group. They dispersed to their starting points, the air charged with a renewed sense of purpose.

As the quiet hum of the NightWing's rotors lifted it into the sky, we stepped into the roles we had each embraced when we joined StealthWave. Bound by trust, driven by duty.

Over the next two days, we put ourselves through a rigorous series of exercises, from close-quarters combat to emergency medical response. Stephen's drone proved invaluable, offering us a bird's-eye view of our mock engagements and allowing us to critique and improve our tactics in real time.

But it wasn't all work; the evenings were spent on the back deck of the cabin I'd rented for the crew. It was during these moments that I was reminded of why I started StealthWave Security. It wasn't just about the thrill of the job or the satisfaction of a challenge met; it was about the people beside me, each with their own reasons for choosing this path, yet united in our mission.

The last night of our training weekend found us gathered on the back deck of the cabin, the sound of the crackling fire the only sound against the quiet as we unwound from the day's rigor. It was one of those rare moments when the burden of responsibility lifted, and was replaced by the simple pleasure of good company. The conversation easily came and went, interspersed with silence. There was talk of past missions and plans for the future. The topic unexpectedly shifted to music—a passion of mine that my team had come to know through occasional performances back at The Anchor. Justin "Ollie" Oliver, one of the team members whose knack for disarming tension with humor had earned him a special place in the group, turned to me with a proposition that caught me off guard.

"Hey, Wyatt, you know how you're always strumming away at the bar? Well, there's this benefit coming up for the wife of one of my Marine buddies who was KIA. They're looking for folks to perform, and I immediately thought of you. Would you be up for it?" His tone was sincere, not like his usual jesting.

The idea of performing outside the familiar confines of The Anchor, in front of a crowd gathered for such an important cause, made me hesitate. My music had always been a personal outlet. Yet, the thought of lending my voice to support a fallen comrade's family stirred something within me.

"Sure, man. I'd love to," I responded, the words out before I could second-guess them. Ollie's face lit up with a grin.

"Awesome! I'll pass your name along to the organizer then."

I nodded, a mixture of apprehension and resolve settling in. This was uncharted territory for me, a step outside my comfort zone.

The next morning, as we packed up and prepared to head back to Liberty, I had a renewed sense of connection to my team and to the purpose we served. And as we drove back to The Anchor, I realized that this benefit concert was another part of that story, a chance to give back in a way I hadn't expected. The thought of contributing to something so simple but went beyond the day-to-day that touched the lives of those who had sacrificed so much gave me a different sense of purpose that was hard to ignore.

9

KENSI

Having been in Liberty for a few days now, as much as I love the quaint charm and warmth of The Yellow Rose Inn, the practical side of me couldn't ignore the cost of staying here. My escape from Luka had been carefully planned over the course of a year, but without direct access to my own financial resources, I had to get creative with the little money I had been able to squirrel away.

Luka never explicitly restricted my spending, but he always kept a detailed account of every penny spent and where I spent it. Occasionally, I managed to navigate around his scrutiny, shopping for items only to return them later in hopes of cash back, but most stores had policies that thwarted that plan. My wallet housed a few gift cards, remnants of my old life, but in a town like Liberty, they were as good as useless; the local businesses didn't accept them, and there were no large box stores or chains in sight.

Each morning for the past four days, as I had woken up in the cozy room Evelyn had provided me, I told myself it was time to move on, to put more distance between myself and the life I fled. Yet, something about Liberty held me back. There was a sense of peace I found in the simple routines of the Inn.

Before I knew it, I was with Evelyn, kneeling down and caring for her flowers like a real gardener. My hands, unaccustomed to soil and stems, fumbled at first, but the rhythmic nature of the work calmed my scattered thoughts. Each pluck of a weed or pruning of a dead blossom was a meditation, grounding me in the present and allowing me to forget, if only momentarily, the shadow of my former life.

"Have I told you about the time Ed and I got lost in the souks of Marrakech?" Evelyn's voice broke through the morning stillness, rich with a nostalgia that painted her words with the spice-scented air of far-off exotic markets.

I shook my head, brushing a stray lock of hair from my face with a dirt-smudged hand. "No, you haven't." My curiosity piqued, eager for the distraction that her stories provided.

She chuckled, her eyes twinkled with the joy of shared memories. "Oh, it was quite the adventure. We turned one corner after another, each alleyway identical to the one before. But the people were so friendly, guiding us back to the main square. There's something about getting lost in a new place... it's freeing, isn't it?"

"Freeing," I echoed, the word taking on a meaning I'd never known. Freedom was what I sought, yet it remained just out of reach.

"Where else have you been?" I asked, the longing to experience such wanderlust.

"Let's see..." she pondered, trowel in hand as she surveyed her garden kingdom. "We've wandered through the cobbled streets of Prague, sailed down the Nile, and once, we even danced under the stars in the Australian Outback."

"Sounds incredible," I murmured, my heart aching with the desire to lose myself in such stories—worlds away from the prison I had left behind. The only exception had been that honeymoon in Italy, a sweet beginning marred by the bitterness of what followed. Luka's villa, while beautiful, had been a prelude to a life of surveillance, not exploration.

"Kensi, dear, life is meant for living, for making memories that warm you on cold nights," Evelyn said, her gaze meeting mine with an earnest intensity that spoke of lessons learned and wisdom earned.

I nodded silently, grateful for her kindness, for the escape of her garden, and for the stories that allowed me to travel vicariously through her experiences. In those moments, surrounded by blossoms and bathed in the light of new beginnings, I could almost believe that Liberty was more than just a brief respite.

I'd formed a tentative bond with Evelyn, one that was unexpectedly easy, as if we were old friends rather than recent acquaintances. It was this budding relationship that gave me the courage to approach her with my predicament.

"Evelyn," I began, hesitantly interrupting our work, "I've run into a bit of an issue with my travel plans... they've changed, and I find myself needing to look for a more permanent place to stay." I paused, unsure how to continue. "And, well, I was wondering if you might know of anyone hiring? I have a degree in hospitality and event management, but I'm willing to do anything really."

Evelyn straightened up, wiping her hands on her apron. She regarded me with kind eyes that cut straight to the heart of things.

"I was hoping you'd stay a bit longer," she said, her voice soft yet carrying an undercurrent of joy. Her eyes sparkled as she gestured towards the back of the Yellow Rose Inn. "There's a groundskeeper's cottage behind here. It's currently being used as storage, but I've always thought it could be a lovely living area again with some work. You could stay there and help out around the Inn. With your background, I'm sure there's much you could contribute."

The sense of relief that came over me was like the first rainfall following a drought. Here was an opportunity, a glimmer of hope in the form of an old storage building and a chance to put down roots, however temporary. The generosity of her offer was unexpected, yet it fit perfectly with the woman who had welcomed me without question, shared her stories, and offered solace without even knowing she was doing so.

"Thank you, Evelyn," I said, my voice thick with gratitude. "That means more to me than I can say."

"It's settled then," she declared, her tone leaving no room for argument. "We can start figuring out the details tomorrow. For now, why don't you join me for a glass of tea? There's something quite soothing about planning the future over iced tea."

As we sat together later, sipping tea and discussing plans for the space behind the inn, I found myself feeling a sense of belonging I hadn't realized I was missing. Evelyn was sweet and supportive and her genuine concern for my well-being was so vastly different from the isolation and fear that had characterized my life with Luka.

Evelyn's kindness enveloping me like a soft blanket, my mind wandered to thoughts of my mother. She passed away when I was just a child, leaving behind a void that never quite filled. Growing up, I clung to stories about her, tales that painted her as strong, independent, and unafraid to voice her opinions on any matter. She was described as a force of nature. Her presence alone was said to alter the atmosphere of any room she entered.

I remembered her not just through the stories shared by others, but through my own fragmented memories, where she was always my favorite person. There was a kindness in her smile, a gentleness in her touch that made me feel like the most important person in the world. She had a way of making everything feel alright, even when the world was shrouded in darkness and uncertainty.

Sitting with Evelyn, I couldn't help but feel a renewed connection to those memories of my mother. There was a similar trait in Evelyn, a kindness that didn't demand anything in return. It was a rare quality, one that made me feel seen and understood without having to say much.

Evelyn's offer to stay and work at the Inn, to find a new purpose within the safety of its walls, had been a gift. In my former life, I had learned that gifts often came with strings attached, hidden hooks waiting to pull me back under someone else's control. But standing here, surrounded by Evelyn's kindness, I wanted to believe this gift was different—simple, genuine, and freely given.

The thought of settling, even temporarily, in Liberty, brought with it a rush of emotions. There was a steadiness in the routines I'd started to establish, in the time spent with Evelyn in the garden or sipping tea on the porch, discussing plans for the future. These simple moments held the promise of healing and growth. They offered so much more than the life I'd left behind where my voice and my choices were suppressed by the unyielding demands of expectation and control.

Yet, beneath the calm, uncertainty lingered. The knowledge that my stay here was a strategic pause rather than a final destination colored my days with a sense of impermanence.

My decision to stay, to work and save, was rooted in practicality, but I also decided it was a chance for time and space. I needed to give myself a chance to at least begin to heal. Liberty, with its gentle pace and the unexpected sanctuary of The Yellow Rose Inn, was where I would gather my strength and start working towards the next chapter of my life.

10

WYATT

The morning sun was already high in the sky by the time I made my way over to the cottage behind The Inn. Mom had called early, her voice laced with a mix of excitement and urgency, asking for my help to clear out an old storage space for someone new. Walking closer, I could hear the murmur of voices from inside the building, a sign that I wasn't the first to arrive at the scene of today's project.

As I approached, the distinct sound of laughter mixed with the shuffling of objects being moved echoed softly through the air, piquing my curiosity further. The door groaned on its hinges, a grating sound that tore through the stillness of the morning. As I pushed it open, the sunlight flooded the darkened space within, and she emerged into the brilliance—a silhouette at first, then quickly morphing into a figure that demanded my full attention.

Her dark hair was pulled up on top of her head in a messy knot, revealing the graceful curve of her neck. The strands that had escaped shimmered in the light, while her flawless, sun-kissed skin appeared to radiate an inner glow. Her features were striking, a beauty that made her impossible to ignore. Her dark eyes held a quiet intensity that drew you in, making you feel as though they could see more than what was visible, as though they carried untold stories waiting to be shared.

With her eyes locked on mine, something shifted in her expression—a flicker of calculation, like two soldiers sizing each other up to decide if the other was friend or foe. She moved with the kind of precision you pick up when trust can mean life or death, and it was clear she wasn't one to let her guard down easily.

I found myself staring longer than I should've, drawn in by more than just her looks. There was a strength in the way she held herself, in the set of her jaw and the slight square of her shoulders as she faced this unfamiliar place. She didn't belong here, surrounded by the cluttered remnants of other people's lives, yet she stood her ground with a resolve that anchored her, even as every tense line in her body suggested she was ready to bolt at a moment's notice.

Years of experience in identifying and managing threats made my protective instinct kick in forcefully. It wasn't that she appeared weak—far from it. It was the sense of someone standing firm against a storm, one that most people couldn't even see. But I saw it, the storm raging beneath the surface, the quiet battle she fought within herself.

Who was this woman who carried such a careful balance of grace and grit? What had forged that vigilance in her?

My mother's voice cut through my thoughts, pulling me back to the present.

"Wyatt, this is Kensi Morrow. She'll be working with us at the Inn and staying here once we get this place cleaned up. Kensi, this is my son Wyatt," Mom introduced us, her gaze flitting between us with a knowing smile that suggested she had noticed my reaction.

"Nice to meet you," I said, my voice steady despite the awkwardness of the moment. I closed the distance between us with purpose, extending my hand to the woman standing before me. Kensi hesitated, her eyes flickering with something unreadable before she accepted the gesture. Her grip was firm but fleeting.

"Thank you," she murmured, her voice almost too soft to catch, like she was afraid of being heard. There was a tension in her posture, a wariness that spoke of someone always ready to retreat if things went south. It triggered something in me—an instinct to protect, to figure out what had put that edge in her. The brief handshake was anything but a simple formality; it was a silent exchange, a tell that trust, for her, was a hard-won commodity.

"Over here we've got some old linens that can be washed or tossed," my mother's voice interrupted my thoughts, guiding us back to the task at hand. She was pointing towards a stack of boxes marked with years of neglect.

"Sure, I'll take care of that," Kensi replied, her voice steadier than before. As she spoke, her gaze lingered on the cobwebbed corners of the room as if she was piecing together a puzzle only she could see.

"Let me show you around," my mother continued, her tone maternal and inviting. They moved together, my mother leading with the ease of one who had spent decades within these walls, Kensi trailing behind with measured steps.

"Here will be your kitchenette," my mother gestured, "and through that door is the bathroom..."

With each new feature introduced, Kensi's eyes darted about, absorbing the details: the peeling paint begging for a fresh coat, the windows that looked out to the tranquil garden, the sturdy shelves that would soon hold her belongings. Her expression softened when she glanced through the window, the sunlight catching on her rogue wisps of hair, casting a halo around her face.

As Mom continued detailing the work that needed to be done, I watched Kensi, noting the way her eyes scanned the room, taking in the details of what would soon be her new living quarters. There was a curiosity there, mixed with a touch of apprehension, as if she was mentally preparing herself, though I wasn't sure for what.

Mom and Kensi's words bounced off the walls, filling the room with a warm, familiar energy that hadn't been there before. And yet, for all the details she shared, I could sense that Kensi was holding back. It only strengthened my resolve to get to know her, to uncover the stories behind those guarded eyes.

The conversation shifted when Mom mentioned getting the air conditioning up and running in Kensi's soon-to-be living space. "It's going to be a scorcher this summer, and we can't have you melting away in here," she said with a chuckle, glancing at me with a look that clearly added a new task to my list.

Kensi quickly jumped in, "Oh, that's not necessary. I'm sure I'll manage without it." Her voice was light, but there was a hint of insistence, like she didn't want to be a burden.

I shook my head, already imagining the relentless summer heat. "That's not an option," I said, keeping my tone gentle but firm. "Around here, air conditioning isn't just a luxury; it's a necessity. Trust me, you don't want to go through summer without it. Have you ever experienced one of our summers?"

She hesitated, then gave a small smile. "No, I guess not. I'm from up north, so I'm used to dealing with more cold than heat."

"Up north, huh?" I noted the vagueness of her answer but decided not to press. "Well, the heat here is a whole different challenge. But don't worry, we'll make sure you're comfortable."

The brief exchange opened a small window into Kensi's past, her mention of being from "up north" piquing my curiosity. Still, I sensed it wasn't the time to push for more. Instead, I focused on what mattered most right now—getting her new space ready and making sure she felt at home.

"Let's start by clearing out these boxes," I suggested, pointing towards a stack near the window. "We'll sort through what needs to stay and what can go."

She nodded, a determined look settling across her brow. Together, we began the methodical process of sifting through the remnants of the past, each item we handled lifting, ever so slightly, the veil that time had drawn over this place. In the simple act of cleaning, we found a rhythm, a shared purpose.

The last of the heavy boxes landed with a thud, sending dust swirling in the air like tiny golden dancers in the shafts of light streaming through the window. I wiped my hands on my jeans and surveyed our progress. The room was starting to resemble something that might actually be called livable.

"Good work," I said, nodding at Kensi. She offered a tight smile in return that didn't reach her eyes.

My mother popped her head in through the doorway, her gaze sweeping over the room before landing on us. "It's looking much better in here," she remarked with satisfaction.

Then, turning to Kensi with an encouraging grin, she added, "Kensi, why don't you join Wyatt for lunch at The Anchor? It's just down the road, and they serve some of the best food in town."

I saw a flicker of hesitation in Kensi's eyes. Maybe it had been fear as her first instinct appeared to be retreating into herself.

Wiping the dust from my hands onto my jeans, I leaned against the doorframe, watching her wrestle with the decision. Her fingers traced the scarred wooden table we had just cleared, her touch lingering as if searching for something steady to hold onto. It wasn't the table itself she needed, but the act seemed to keep her grounded, keeping her thoughts from spiraling too far away.

I didn't know her whole story—didn't know what made her hesitate, what had taught her to rely on herself over anyone else. But watching her now, something deep inside me stirred, a quiet pull to be someone she didn't have to second-guess.

"You're welcome to come by if you feel like it," I said, keeping my tone light to ease the tension. "No pressure. The food's great, but I get it if you need some time to settle in or have other plans."

Kensi bit her lip, clearly weighing the offer. After a moment, she responded with a cautious, "Maybe. I'll see how I feel once we've finished up here." Her voice was polite, but carried that same uncertainty I'd noticed earlier.

Mom gave Kensi an encouraging smile, then turned to me with a look that was soft yet full of meaning, the kind of look that mothers reserve for moments they recognize as important.

As we parted ways, I was struck by an undeniable protectiveness toward Kensi. It was a little disconcerting, considering I'd only met her a few hours ago.

11

KENSI

The building was set a little ways behind The Yellow Rose Inn. It was a modest structure with a history as rich as the main house itself. Once serving as worker's quarters, it had been repurposed for storage after Evelyn took ownership of the property. Its exterior, though weathered by time, still held a certain charm, with its weathered wood siding and a roof that had seen better days but somehow added to its rustic appeal.

Inside, the space was surprisingly spacious. The main room, which would serve as the living area, was filled with an assortment of boxes and old furniture, remnants of its years as a catch-all storage space. Despite this, the potential was undeniable. Large, dusty windows allowed sunlight to filter through, casting patterns across the wooden floorboards. The high ceilings added a sense of openness, making the room feel larger than it was.

Adjacent to the main room was a small kitchenette, its fixtures outdated but functional, hinting at the building's past life as a self-contained living space. The cabinets, though worn, were sturdy, and with a bit of work, I imagined they could be restored to their former glory.

The bedroom, separated from the living area by a simple door, was compact but cozy. A small, frosted window provided privacy while still letting in light. The room was a sanctuary, a quiet, personal space that could be transformed into a homey retreat.

At the back of the building, a narrow door led to a tiny bathroom. It was clear it would need the most work, with its cramped shower stall and an ancient sink that had seen better days. Yet, even here, there was potential for transformation into a functional living space. Throughout the building, the floors were a patchwork of old linoleum and exposed wood, suggesting a history of repairs and makeshift solutions. The walls, covered in layers of peeling wallpaper and paint, told stories of the many lives and purposes this building had served.

As Evelyn showed me around and I assessed the space, envisioning its transformation, I smiled thinking about having the opportunity to do something for myself even as temporary as it would be. Then he stepped through the door. For a moment, it was as though someone had pressed pause on a movie.

His presence was unexpected, a sudden intrusion into the quiet, yet he fit there seamlessly, filling the space effortlessly. He was tall, towering well over six feet, with broad shoulders that hinted at strength beneath his relaxed posture. Muscles stretched taut beneath his shirt, the fabric barely containing the powerful build of a man accustomed to physical work. His dark hair was slightly unruly, framing a face that balanced ruggedness with an understated handsomeness. But it was his eyes so dark but warm that drew me in. The way they locked onto mine with such intensity made me feel seen in a way I hadn't experienced in a long time. His gaze was steady, carrying a quiet confidence that, for a brief moment, stole the breath right out of me.

But it was his smile that truly disarmed me, a genuine expression that lit up his entire face. There was a kindness there, a gentleness that I found myself drawn to despite the walls I had built around myself. He made me feel safe, a feeling I hadn't experienced maybe ever.

Evelyn introduced us, explaining that I would be working at the inn and staying in the building we were clearing out. I tried to focus on her words but the gaze of the steel gray eyes fixed on me were unnerving.

"It's a pleasure to meet you," he said, his voice calming me instantly despite my racing heart and a strange feeling I couldn't quite name. His handshake was firm, reassuring, and for a moment, I allowed myself to feel a sense of connection, fleeting as it might have been.

When the conversation turned to the practicalities of making the space livable, including the need for air conditioning, I tried to insist that it wasn't necessary. But Wyatt was adamant, explaining with a light but firm tone that surviving the Texas heat without AC was not an option. His concern was touching, and his effort to make me feel comfortable was evident in the way he spoke, the way he tried to reassure me.

"I'm from up north," I admitted when he asked if I'd experienced a Texas summer. My answer was vague, a reflex born of caution, of guarding my past and my secrets, and yet I couldn't help but think I'd given away too much. His curiosity was clear, but he didn't press, for which I was grateful. There was an understanding in his acceptance of my brief explanation, a silent acknowledgment of the boundaries I wasn't ready to cross.

We turned our attention to the task at hand, and I rolled up my proverbial sleeves, determined to make myself useful. Together, we dove into the cluttered chaos of the building, hoisting boxes marked with years of dust and moving them to the attic in the main house. My muscles protested under the strain, but I persisted, finding a rhythm in the labor. Wyatt led the way, easily maneuvering the heavier cartons as if they were filled with nothing more than feathers.

"Watch your step here," he cautioned, pointing to a loose floorboard, his voice steady with concern. He moved with an ease that spoke of a man accustomed to hard work, his body attuned to the demands of physical exertion. I followed, lifting what I could, pushing through the discomfort that knotted in my shoulders.

Each box transported was a small victory, each swipe of dust off my clothes a mark of progress. The heat built within the confines of the room, and beads of sweat made their way down my back. Glancing over, I caught sight of Wyatt's own sweat-drenched shirt, a testament to the effort he was putting in alongside me.

"Doing okay?" he checked in after setting down a particularly large box, his forehead glistening.

"Better than okay," I lied, forcing a smile I hoped would pass as convincing. I wanted him to see me as strong, someone worthy of this fresh start, not just another person who needed looking after.

"Good," he said, and there was a note of approval in his voice that made something inside me stand a little taller.

As we continued, the space slowly transformed, not just in appearance but in feel. What had once been a forgotten repository for the discarded was becoming a canvas for a new beginning.

When we reached a point that would require more muscle than I could contribute, Evelyn suggested I join Wyatt for lunch at The Anchor. My initial reaction was to immediately decline, the thought of stepping into a new, unfamiliar situation filling me with apprehension. But Wyatt's friendly, inviting demeanor made it hard to resist. "You're welcome to come by if you want. No pressure, though," he said, his tone gentle and understanding.

I hesitated, torn between the safety of solitude and the draw of his kind offer. "Maybe. I'll see how I go once we've finished up here," I finally said, my voice betraying my certainty.

Wyatt nodded, his response a perfect balance of respect for my hesitance and openness to the possibility. He assured me the invitation stood, a smile tugging at the corners of his mouth.

As they left, I stood alone in the soon-to-be my space, basking in the silence of a job well done but also in my own thoughts. The brief encounter with Wyatt had left me unsettled, not because he did anything wrong, but because he didn't.

His demeanor was open and friendly, a stark contrast to the men I'd known, especially Luka. His kindness, while reassuring on some level, also triggered a wariness within me. I've learned the hard way that trust is a luxury I can't really afford, especially when it comes to men. Their intentions, no matter how benign they seem, often hide ulterior motives. And while Wyatt showed none of the red flags I've come to look for, my instinct was to keep my guard up, to protect the fragile sense of security I've only started to feel.

THE LAYER of dust and sweat on my skin was a tangible reminder of the progress made and the effort exerted. Retreating to my room at the inn, the tranquility of the space welcomed me like an old friend after the flurry of activity and introspection that had occupied my morning.

The urge for a shower was immediate, almost a craving, as if the hot water could wash away more than just the physical remnants of the day. As I stood under the spray of hot water, my thoughts inevitably drifted back to the wheels I'd set in motion before my escape. The meticulous planning, the covert exchanges with Marco, and the heavy reliance on hope were all like chapters from another life, yet they were the very foundation of my newfound freedom.

The quiet nights at The Yellow Rose Inn gave me no escape from the haunting memories of those final days. The tension of living under Luka's scrutinizing gaze, the constant surveillance—it had been a life marked by fear, each day an exercise in caution. Yet, amidst that stifling control, I had managed to carve a path to freedom, a sliver of light in an otherwise oppressive existence, with help from an unexpected ally.

But it was the documents I'd left behind, the ones intended for the FBI, that pushed their way into the forefront of my thoughts. There was no way to know if they had reached the right hands, if the evidence of Luka's crimes I'd risked so much to gather would bring about his downfall. It was a gamble, one whose outcome remained shrouded in uncertainty. I didn't know if he'd been able to make contact with the agent, but I sincerely hoped Marco had stayed under the radar—that my actions wouldn't bring harm to him for standing by me when escape had merely been a dream.

The fear of being followed, of Luka's reach extending even to this small Texas town, was a constant shadow, a reminder of the life I had fled. Yet, with each passing day, Liberty offered a sense of peace, a respite from the chaos of my former existence. The kindness of strangers, of Evelyn and the tentative bond we had formed, provided a semblance of normalcy, a whisper of the life I yearned for.

Still, the knowledge that my stay in Liberty was a pause, not a permanent solution, lingered in my mind. The need to remain vigilant, to anticipate the moment when I might have to flee once more, colored my days with a sense of impermanence.

The soft cotton of the shirt slid over my head, a fabric choice made without coercion. In my old life, Luka would have had opinions, directives on how I should present myself to the world. But here in Liberty, enclosed by the walls of my temporary shelter, I relished the freedom of selecting an outfit that spoke to me, not him. The jeans hugged my legs, an armor against the unknowns outside. Slipping into a pair of sneakers, I allowed myself a small smile—no stilettos to navigate today.

I stood before the mirror, studying the reflection that stared back at me. Kensi Morrow—that was who I saw now, a name I chose, a woman I was determined to become. This face, though familiar, no longer bore the same resignation, the same quiet compliance that had once defined it. There was a new resilience in my eyes, a strength that came from breaking free, from taking the first steps toward reclaiming myself.

I wanted to be someone who lived on her own terms, someone who didn't fold under another's control. Someone unafraid to speak, to take up space, to embrace life without apology. I wanted to know what it was to be bold, to take risks for my own sake, not just to escape. And while I didn't yet know exactly who Kensi Morrow would become, I was certain of one thing: she would never be defined by anyone else again.

A rumble from my stomach broke the spell of my thoughts, pulling me back to simpler, more immediate concerns. Hunger. A basic human need that now served as a reminder there was a life to be lived beyond these four walls.

In that moment, an unexpected thread of confidence wove itself into my fabric of fears and uncertainties. Perhaps it was the physical exertion of helping clear the space, or the warm shower that washed away not just the grime but a layer of my apprehension. Whatever the source, it emboldened me, whispering that maybe I could venture out, step beyond the familiar yet confining walls of the inn.

The suggestion to visit The Anchor for lunch lingered in my mind. Wyatt's invitation, offered with kindness and clear understanding of my hesitancy, didn't feel like a demand but an open door —a choice freely given, without pressure. It was this sense of freedom, so rare in my recent life, that nudged me toward a decision.

I found myself frozen in front of the mirror trying to steady the flutter of nerves at the idea of going out, of potentially exposing myself to unknown dangers. Yet, alongside that fear was a flicker of curiosity, a desire to see more of this town that had become my temporary haven, to experience something as normal as having lunch in a bar.

After getting directions from Evelyn, who was clearly pleased with my decision, I began my trek. The walk to The Anchor was a journey of its own, every step defying fear, fighting for freedom and life. There was an almost magnetic pull toward the place, an invisible force guiding my steps and reassuring me with each stride that this was the right path to take.

Anticipation and anxiety warred within me as The Anchor came into view. The sound of laughter and conversation could be heard just outside the door, an echo of normalcy in a world that had been anything but normal for far too long. Standing at the threshold, I paused, taking a moment to gather my courage, to remind myself that I was Kensi Morrow now. She was real and I no longer had to hide in the shadow of the woman I had been.

12

KENSI

Standing at the entrance of The Anchor, a wave of nervousness washed over me. My hand hovered over the door handle, hesitating as a barrage of thoughts raced through my mind. The fear of being recognized, despite the improbability, clung to me like a second skin. As much as I wanted it to be true, I wasn't just Kensi Morrow here; I was a fugitive from a past that haunted every step I took, every decision I made.

The paranoia that had become my constant companion whispered warnings of dangers lurking in public spaces, of eyes that might see beyond the facade I had carefully constructed. My heart pounded in my chest, the hard rhythm a reminder of the reality I lived in—a world where being seen could mean being found.

I found myself calculating the risks, weighing the desire for a semblance of normalcy against the potential threat of exposure. The streets of Liberty, as welcoming and serene as they had appeared, was now a minefield of what-ifs. What if someone from my old life was somehow here? What if Luka had set people to look for me even in the most unlikely of places? The thought was ludicrous, yet fear rarely bowed to logic.

Leaving the safety of The Inn to enjoy a meal elsewhere had once marked progress toward reclaiming my life. Now, it was too much of a risk. Every scenario I imagined painted me as a target, easy prey for the hunter that was my past.

I reminded myself this was Texas, not New York. The chances of being recognized were slim to none. Yet the fear persisted, a testament to the scars Luka had left on my psyche.

I was trapped, unable to move, caught between wanting to be free and the burdens of my past. The simplicity of walking into a bar, of being just another patron, was a luxury I couldn't afford. Yet, as I stood there, wrestling with my fears, a spark of defiance ignited within me. I was tired of hiding, of letting the mere shadow of Luka dictate my every move.

With a shaky exhale, I pushed the door open, stepping into the unknown. The buzz of The Anchor welcomed me, gently loosening the cold grip of fear. It was a small victory, a moment of courage in the face of the invisible ties that bound me.

As I made my way inside, the paranoia remained, a silent observer to my act of defiance. But for the first time in a long while, it didn't dictate my actions. The ghosts of my past haunted me, but I was here, in public, choosing to live.

Walking through the door, a woman around my age greeted me with a friendly smile, her presence a reassuring touch of normalcy in my otherwise chaotic life. "Sit wherever you'd like," she said, her voice carrying a strong Texas accent that sounded both kind and welcoming.

Tables dotted the room, clusters of locals lost in their own worlds. Scanning the space, I tried to gauge which seat would afford me the most privacy, a spot where I could blend into the background and observe without drawing attention to myself. My internal debate was interrupted when Wyatt emerged from behind the bar, his face lighting up in recognition.

The sight of him, his face lighting up as though he was pleased to see me, sent a wave of emotions crashing through me—surprise, apprehension, and beneath it all, an unexpected sense of relief. Despite myself, despite everything, a part of me couldn't help but sense the quiet reassurance in that simple, genuine happiness in his eyes.

"You came," he said, a note of genuine happiness in his voice that made me momentarily forget my fears. His approach was unhurried, yet there was an eagerness in his steps. For a fleeting second, the smile that touched his lips and reached all the way to his eyes made the world feel less threatening, as if my fears had no place in the light of his genuine happiness.

At the same time, the woman approached with a menu in hand, her friendly demeanor momentarily shifting to one of curiosity at Wyatt's evident recognition and excitement. It was clear from her glance between us that my presence held more significance than that of a regular patron.

Wyatt, ever the gracious host, introduced us. "Kensi, this is Missy, the manager here at The Anchor," he said, his pride in his establishment and its people evident in his tone. Turning to Missy, he added, "Missy, this is Kensi.

Missy's initial curiosity faded as she extended her hand to me, her smile genuine "It's so nice to meet you, Kensi," she said with a thick country twang, her eyes twinkling with humor and a hint of suspicion.

"Thank you," I managed, my voice steadier than I'd expected.

Missy's friendly demeanor was infectious, and despite my initial reservations, I found myself drawn to her. She handed me the menu with a smile. "If you need any recommendations, just let me know. We're all about good food and good company here," she said, her tone easygoing yet genuinely sincere.

Wyatt nodded in agreement, his gaze lingering on me for a moment longer than necessary. It was clear he wanted to ensure I knew I was welcome, but sensing my unease with too much attention, he took a step back. "I'll leave you in Missy's capable hands," he said, his voice carrying a reassurance that was both soothing and sweet.

As Wyatt excused himself, disappearing behind the bar, I caught myself wanting to call him back. The thought startled me—I didn't know him well enough to want that, but something about his presence made the darkness feel less oppressive, like he could chase it away just by being nearby.

I shook the thought off and looked up at Missy. Her warmth, her grounding presence, reminded me why I was here. This was what I needed—a chance to feel normal, to just be another person sitting in a bar, even if it was only for the length of a meal.

I'd chosen a table near the window, a spot that offered a view of the street. Missy promised to check in on me shortly and left me with the menu, her departure marking the beginning of a new, albeit small, chapter in my journey towards finding peace.

Missy returned with a glass of water and asked, "Anything catch your eye?" I smiled, feeling a sliver of confidence weaving through my nervousness.

"I'll have the side salad, please," I said, handing the menu back to her. My voice was steady, but the underlying tension of conserving my limited resources was impossible to completely hide.

Missy nodded, her eyes meeting mine with what looked like understanding that went beyond my simple order. "Great choice," she responded, her tone devoid of any prying or judgment.

As she wrote down my order, she asked, "So is it just you in town or are you here visiting family?"

The muscle in my jaw tightened, a reflex against the intrusion. The question hung in the air, innocent on its surface, yet to me, it resonated with the echo of threats from a past that refused to stay silent. In the span of a heartbeat, my mind raced through a thousand lies, each a potential shield against further inquiry.

"I..." The word lingered, betraying the onset of a vulnerability I couldn't afford. "It's complicated," I admitted, the words hiding the truth of my reality.

Missy's expression didn't shift to pity or suspicion, and for that, I was silently grateful. Her pen resumed its dance across the paper, as if our exchange was nothing more than a ripple on the surface of an otherwise calm lake.

Her subtle nod acknowledged the unspoken truth hidden beneath my words.

She placed her pen behind her ear, offering me a genuine smile. "I get it," she said, her voice a whisper of shared secrets. "Life's too short to be stuck in situations that don't make you happy." There was no judgment in her tone, only an echo of understanding that bridged the expanse of my fears.

Missy retrieved the menu and left to place my order. I found myself looking around The Anchor, feeling a sense of belonging I hadn't anticipated. The fear and paranoia were still there, lurking in the background, but for the first time in a long while, they didn't dominate my thoughts.

The clink of dishes signaled Missy's return, and she set down a plate in front of me with a flourish. To my surprise, the "side salad" I had ordered appeared to be a much larger meal, generously topped with grilled chicken, vibrant greens, and an assortment of colorful vegetables. My eyes widened at the sight, both at the generosity of the portion and the immediate worry about the cost.

Missy caught the look on my face and winked. "I hope you're hungry. Enjoy!" she said cheerfully, placing the bill facedown next to the plate.

As she turned to leave, I quickly picked up the bill, my heart racing as I braced myself for the total. To my astonishment, the charge was only for the side salad I had initially ordered, significantly less than what this meal would surely cost. Confused and concerned about the mistake, I called Missy back.

"I'm sorry, there seems to be a mistake," I began, holding out the bill towards her. "This is much more than a side salad."

Missy glanced at the bill and then back at the salad with a playful shrug. "Oh, would you look at that? Innocent error on our part," she said, her tone light and dismissive of my concern. "Consider it a little welcome to Liberty. We're all about making sure folks feel at home here."

I opened my mouth, ready to marshal a response that would insist on paying my way—after all, I wasn't one to take charity lightly. But as I looked up into Missy's face, saw the firm set of her jaw that belied her easygoing demeanor, I found my resolve waning.

"I really can't—" The protest died on my lips as she raised a hand, palm outstretched as if she could physically push away my objections.

"Just enjoy your meal," she insisted, her tone brooking no argument but still soft, like a benediction rather than a command. There was an authority in her casual dismissal, a reminder that here in The Anchor, her word was as solid as the aged wooden beams that held up the ceiling.

I hesitated, caught between the instinct to argue and the desire to accept this unexpected act of grace. Finally, with a reluctant nod, I conceded, capitulating to the kindness I hadn't known I needed.

A quiet voice in the back of my mind urged caution, reminding me of the fleeting nature of my current refuge. The kindness and sense of belonging I was finding in Liberty, as inviting as they were, couldn't become ties that bound me in a new way. I was here on borrowed time, each day bringing me closer to an inevitable departure—a truth I couldn't allow myself to forget.

But even as the flavors melded in my mouth, the quiet whisper of caution began to rustle through my thoughts, like leaves warning of an approaching storm. Liberty, this small town with its big-hearted inhabitants, was nothing more than a temporary harbor in the tempest of my life. Missy's kindness, Wyatt's recognition, the serenity of The Inn; they were ports in the storm, not destinations.

Getting too attached, letting down the walls I'd painstakingly erected around my heart and my history, posed a risk I wasn't sure I was ready to take. The pull of connection, of something resembling a normal life, was strong, but the reality of my situation was stronger.

I took another bite, the salad a mixture of bitterness and sweetness that somehow mirrored my own internal conflict. Enjoy the moment, yes, but never forget the ultimate goal: freedom, not just from Luka, but from the fear and uncertainty that had become my constant companions.

Missy's act of kindness was a great example of the potential for good in the world, a reminder of the humanity that still existed outside the shadows of my past. But it was also a reminder to tread carefully, to protect the fragile semblance of safety I'd found here.

As I finished my meal, the internal promise to remain guarded, to not get too attached, solidified. Liberty was a chapter in my story, perhaps one of the most pivotal, but it was not the conclusion. My journey was far from over, and while the kindness of those around me was a balm to my weary soul, it was not a cure. The path ahead remained uncertain, and my resolve to face it, unencumbered by attachments that could hold me back, was as crucial as ever.

13

WYATT

The storeroom door groaned as I pushed it open, arms loaded with a shipment for the shelves behind the bar. The midday hum of The Anchor rolled over me—steady, familiar, a rhythm I didn't have to think about.

I maneuvered through the narrow hallway, stepping into the filtered daylight of the main floor. That's when I saw her.

Kensi sat by the window, sunlight catching in her hair and throwing soft shadows across her face. She was so still, so focused on something beyond the glass, that for a second, it felt like the rest of the room fell away.

It hit me that she'd actually shown up.

The noise of the bar surrounded her, all the usual jokes and easy laughter, but she stayed apart from it, calm and quiet. She didn't fit the scene, but somehow she didn't feel out of place either. It was like she existed on a different frequency—still steady, just...different.

I crossed the worn wooden floor, my boots tapping a familiar rhythm against the boards. My steps slowed as I neared her, surprise still settling in.

"You came," I said, surprise slipping into my voice before I could catch it. I kept my pace steady, doing my best to hide the spark of eagerness running through me. When her eyes met mine, there was something there—a flicker of relief, perhaps, or a glimmer of recognition. Whatever it was, it settled something in me I hadn't realized needed settling.

At that moment, Missy sidled up beside us with the grace of a woman who had navigated crowded rooms for years. In her hand, she held a menu, the corners slightly bent from use.

I made introductions, knowing that if anyone knew anything about making a fresh start, it was Missy. And I somehow knew Kensi needed someone like Missy in her corner.

Missy's gaze, previously narrowed with a manager's scrutiny, noticeably softened as she extended a hand towards Kensi. Her initial suspicion, ingrained after years of running a bar frequented by all walks of life, dissolved into genuine interest.

"It's so nice to meet you, Kensi," Missy greeted her with a smile that could disarm the most guarded of customers. Laugh lines crinkled around her eyes as they sparkled with an intriguing blend of humor and curiosity, suggesting that she had instantly taken a liking to Kensi.

"Thank you," Kensi managed, her voice steadier than she looked. Though poised, there was a tightness around her eyes that betrayed an inner tension, like a sail pulled to its limits against a brewing storm.

Missy's cheerful demeanor practically lit up the space as she handed Kensi the menu, her easy manner making the interaction feel effortless. "If you need any recommendations, just let me know. We're all about good food and good company here," she said with a casual sincerity that was hard to resist.

I nodded in agreement, Missy's hospitality mirroring my own desire for Kensi to feel welcomed here. Yet as I watched, my eyes refused to part from her too quickly, lingering on the delicate way she tucked a strand of hair behind her ear.

"I'll leave you in good hands," I said, keeping my tone light even as part of me wanted to stay rooted right there.

Behind the bar, I kept an eye on her without making it obvious.

She studied the menu like it held the answers to something bigger, her movements deliberate but tense. It wasn't just shyness; it was something deeper. I could see it in the way she sat, shoulders tight like she was braced for something. Whatever her story was, it hadn't been an easy one.

As I wiped down the counter with a practiced motion, my attention remained tethered to her. Every tentative smile she offered Missy, every cautious glance she cast around the room added another layer to the mystery she presented. I found myself drawn to that enigma, an inexplicable pull that was more than mere attraction. It was as if she were a puzzle, and I had stumbled upon the first piece, my mind already reaching for the next.

Her hesitance wasn't just shyness; it was a kind of armor, built from things I could only guess at. It hung around her, weighing down her shoulders and keeping her eyes guarded. Watching her, I could tell there was a story there, a past or maybe a secret big enough to cast a shadow over who she was now. If Kensi was in trouble, just standing by wouldn't be enough.

After passing on my instructions to upgrade Kensi's order, Missy joined me behind the bar, her curiosity piqued. The clink of glasses punctuated the steady hum of conversation as she set herself to the task of straightening up behind the bar. Her eyes flitted back to Kensi before settling on my face.

"She didn't say much," she started, her voice just above a whisper, almost lost amid the chatter and laughter that filled The Anchor. "But it's obvious she's running from something." The towel in her hand moved in slow circles on the glass, mimicking the wariness I saw in Kensi's every move. Missy had always had a sense for reading people, a skill honed from her time managing The Anchor and her own personal history with a cheating fiancé.

I leaned against the polished wood of the bar, my arms crossed as I watched Kensi peruse the menu, her fingers tracing the edges with a delicate touch that was hardly seen in the rugged coziness of our establishment.

"Yeah, I got that feeling too," I murmured. She reminded me of a bird ready to take off at the slightest noise—poised and beautiful, but with a tension that never fully left her. It was there in the set of her shoulders, in the way she held herself, like she was braced for something.

Missy leaned in closer, lowering her voice despite the din of the bar. "Wyatt, just be careful. You have a big heart, and she looks like someone who needs a friend right now. But we don't know what she's running from." Her words were tinged with the wisdom of someone who had learned the hard way that not every story had a happy ending.

"I know," I replied, my concern for Kensi mingling with a resolve to help however I could. "I won't push her. But if she needs help, I want her to know she's not alone here."

Missy gave me a knowing look, one that said she understood my need to protect and support those around me. "Sometimes the best help you can offer is just being there, giving someone the space to heal on their own terms."

Maybe she was right, but my instincts didn't leave much room for patience. Even if Missy was right, I'd already made up my mind to be there, however it played out.

The conversation shifted as we returned to the rhythm of serving customers, but nothing seemed to keep me from getting distracted by thoughts of Kensi. The brief interaction we'd had was enough to tell me she was someone worth getting to know, worth extending a hand to, even if she wasn't ready to take it yet. And more than that, I really wanted to know her.

As I set down a pint for Mr. Joe, who tipped his hat in thanks, the door swung open, letting in a rush of warm summer air. Stephen walked in with Mrs. June, her arm hooked through his, both of them laughing like co-conspirators. As Stephen started to lead her toward a table, she quickly shooed him away with a gentle swat, glancing over to make sure Mr. Harold wouldn't think she was "running around with the young folks." With a grin, Stephen headed straight for the bar, catching my eye as he approached Missy and me.

Stephen, ever the charmer, made a beeline for her, flirting with an openness that made even the most stoic of patrons smile. Their dance was a familiar one, full of unspoken emotions and missed opportunities.

"Late again, are we?" she teased, tucking a loose strand of hair behind her ear—a subconscious tell I'd come to recognize.

"Busy day?" he asked after a moment, nudging an empty abandoned beer bottle side-to-side, though his gaze wasn't on the bar but rather on Missy, who simply nodded, her lips curving in a smile she tried to contain.

"Same as any other," she replied, her attempt at nonchalance undermined by the light in her eyes.

Their banter tapered off as Stephen's attention shifted toward me, his demeanor changing like the tide. The easy grin faded, replaced by a sharper, more probing look. Stephen was always the type to notice things others missed, and he didn't waste time on small talk when something caught his eye. Sidling up next to me, he cast a quick, discreet glance toward Kensi, who sat by the window, absorbed in her own world.

"So, who's the new girl?" he asked quietly, tilting his head just enough to gesture in her direction without drawing attention. His tone was casual, but I knew him well enough to see it was more than idle curiosity—he was already sizing up the situation, taking it all in.

I sighed, the complexity of the situation not easily explained.

"Kensi Morrow," I found myself saying, and a hush fell over the room's other sounds—though I think that was only in my head. "She's new in town, staying at The Inn, working there, even." My tone held a note of protectiveness.

Stephen, who could read a room better than most, picked up on it instantly. His eyes, always sharp, took on the focused intensity of a hawk. They narrowed slightly, and the lines around them creased in thought. "Do you think we should run a background check? Just to be safe?" The way he said it made it sound as inconsequential as asking if I wanted another coffee, but his question lingered between us, heavy with implication.

In our business—where secrets were currency and safety was

paramount—the suggestion wasn't out of order. But as I glanced back at Kensi, her silhouette framed by the window, an unease settled in my gut.

I hesitated, conflicted. On one hand, ensuring Kensi's story checked out was a logical step, especially given her proximity to my family. On the other, it felt like a breach of trust, even though we hadn't built much of it yet.

My instincts as a former SEAL, always to protect and assess threats, stood in sharp contrast to the personal connection I had formed with her. It was a delicate balance, protecting without overstepping, trying to offer safety without imposing too much.

"Maybe," I finally said, weighing the need for security against the desire to respect her privacy, "but let's keep it discreet.

Stephen nodded, understanding the delicacy of the situation. "Consider it done," he assured me, his loyalty never in question.

Our conversation shifted back to lighter topics, but I was fixated on Kensi, on the mystery she represented, and the undeniable pull she had on me.

As the day wore on, the brief interaction with Kensi and the conversation with Stephen lingered in my mind. The decision to run a background check on Kensi wasn't one I took lightly. It was a precaution, a means to ensure not just my mother's safety but Kensi's as well. If she was running, as we suspected, then understanding the threat she faced was crucial. Yet, part of me hoped we'd find nothing, that Kensi's secrets were her own and not a danger to her or those around her.

Kensi Morrow, with her quiet strength and guarded eyes, had unwittingly become a puzzle I was determined to solve, and not just for my mother's sake, but for my own as well.

14

KENSI

As I sipped my Diet Coke, my gaze drifted over The Anchor, each corner and beam now familiar, carrying traces of evenings I hadn't expected to mean so much. In the weeks since I'd arrived, Wyatt, Missy, Stephen, and I had spent a few evenings here together after hours, sharing easy conversations and laughter that sometimes surprised even me. Those late-night gatherings had become small moments of peace—of normalcy, even. We'd gather around the bar or out on the small back patio, swapping stories and sparking jokes. Wyatt would tell tales of life in Liberty, Stephen and Missy chiming in with their own local color, while I mostly listened, feeling a quiet contentment in their presence.

It had taken some convincing from Missy to get me to join them in the first place. She'd been gently persistent, brushing aside my reluctance with a bright, "Come on, Kensi, you don't want to miss out on Liberty's finest company! People literally pay to hang out with us."

Her quick wit and genuine kindness left me with little choice but to accept, if only to avoid the blend of amusement and sympathy in her eyes whenever I tried to refuse. Eventually, her persistence chipped away at my defenses, and I found myself sharing quiet laughter and clinking glasses with these people who were slowly beginning to feel like friends.

But even so, I kept a careful distance. Wyatt would joke or reach out with an open smile, but I'd still hang back, listening more than I shared, keeping parts of myself hidden because they were too tangled to explain. And yet, each time we gathered, those walls I'd built began to slip, just a little, as if some part of me was remembering what it was like to simply be me again, free from the shadows of the past.

There were nights when Wyatt would catch my eye and hold my gaze a fraction longer than necessary, and something inside me would stir. I couldn't deny the attraction I had to him—the quiet sincerity in his expression, the unspoken kindness that reached parts of me I'd nearly forgotten were there.

Still, there were limits—hard limits—and Wyatt didn't know them. He didn't know the truths I kept hidden. A truth that had my thumb unconsciously reaching for the empty spot on my left hand— a habit I hadn't been able to break, even though I'd long since left the ring behind. The thought of explaining it was daunting, impossible even. And yet, I never doubted that he'd respect it, respect me, once he knew.

For now, though, our small circle was just what I needed: a place of refuge and the security of people who didn't push for what I wasn't ready to give, and Wyatt. Wyatt's presence, his steady calm, was fast becoming one of the few places where I could truly breathe.

"Quiet morning," Missy remarked, as she wiped down the bar with practiced ease.

"The best kind," I replied, the corners of my mouth lifting into a half-smile.

I shifted on the worn stool, my fingers idly tracing the condensation on my cup. Wyatt and Stephen's laughter mixed with the clink of tools as they worked, filling the quiet with a familiar cadence.

But the tranquility was short-lived. The sudden blare of the breaking news alert sliced through the ambiance, yanking my attention towards the TV. The screen filled with the bold reds and yellows of urgency, and then there he was—Luka Solinas. His face, once so familiar and now a symbol of my deepest fears, peered out from behind the lower-third banner that screamed his crimes to the world. My heart lurched, a cocktail of terror and disbelief coursing through my veins as the anchor's voice droned on about racketeering, extortion, and a litany of offenses that barely scratched the surface of Luka's darkness.

For a moment, time stood still, the anchor's words muffled by the sudden rush of blood in my ears. With an involuntary spasm of dread, my hand jerked, sending the can tumbling. Diet Coke cascaded over the edge, a waterfall of fizz and syrup that spread across the polished wood, the dark liquid pooling at the base of Missy's hands.

"Kensi!" Her voice cut through the fog of my shock, clear and tinged with worry. "You okay?"

I could feel her eyes on me, but mine were locked on the screen, on the image of Luka being led away in handcuffs. The reality of it all was too much to take in, each word from the anchor's lips unraveling the fragile peace I had woven around myself. Missy's concern hovered at the edges of my consciousness, but it was the sight of Luka's downfall that held me captive, a spectacle both horrifying and mesmerizing in its finality.

I nodded, unable to tear my gaze away from the screen, from the finality of seeing Luka's empire begin to crumble. It was over, or at least, it was the beginning of an end I had hardly dared to hope for. The relief that washed over me was tinged with disbelief, with the remnants of fear that had dictated every moment of my existence since I'd left New York.

Wyatt's and Stephen's voices quieted as they paused their work, their attention drawn to the television and the unfolding story.

I could feel Wyatt's gaze settle on me.

"An anonymous source," the news anchor intoned, "provided documents that spearheaded this landmark investigation." My throat constricted as if those words wrapped around it with an icy grip. The room spun momentarily, the ramifications of what I had done—what

I had unleashed—crystallizing within me with a chilling clarity. The documents I'd painstakingly gathered, the ones I'd sent off shrouded in the anonymity I thought would be my safeguard, were now the keystones of Luka's undoing.

A shiver ran down my spine, even as I held myself rigidly upright. The warmth of Missy's hand on my arm had faded, replaced by the cold realization of my vulnerability. I stared at the screen, feeling exposed, no longer hidden behind the same veil of obscurity that had once been my armor. In the quiet of The Anchor, among the few who had come to symbolize a semblance of normalcy, I stood at the precipice of my past and future, both now inextricably linked by a trail of paper I'd left behind.

For a moment, the world around me slowed, the voices and sounds blending into a distant hum as I processed the magnitude of what was happening. The documents I had risked everything to send to the FBI had done their job, and triggered the domino effect that led to this moment. The overwhelming thought combined vindication with a fear of the future.

Wyatt stepped closer, his presence carrying a calm that eased the edge of my unease. His nearness anchored me, steadying the rapid beat of worry in my chest. His voice was soft, meant only for me, laced with genuine concern. "Hey, are you alright?"

He didn't touch me, but his hand hovered just behind my back, close enough that I could sense its reassuring presence, as if he were ready to steady me if I faltered. That silent promise, coupled with his calm, steady presence beside me, soothed a part of me that had been frayed for far too long.

He was standing just a breath away, but didn't press for answers. Instead, his presence offered silent solidarity, a promise that I wasn't alone in whatever was coming next. It was a reassurance, knowing that despite the turmoil, I had allies here, even if they didn't fully understand the scope of my past.

Stephen, meanwhile, leaned against the end of the bar, his casual posture belied by the keen interest in his eyes. Ever observant, he glanced from me to the screen and back to Wyatt, a silent understanding passing between him and Wyatt. Without needing to exchange words, they clearly both knew something significant was unfolding, something directly connected to me.

The murmurings of the newscaster sounded distant, as if I were hearing them through a long tunnel. They were discussing legal repercussions, potential trials, but their words fell flat, muffled by the pounding of my heart in my ears.

Inhaling slowly, the cool air of The Anchor filled my lungs and steadied the tremor of nerves that threatened to overtake me. My fingers clasped the edge of the bar, finding solace in the solid wood grain beneath them. I could feel Wyatt's gaze, the quiet intensity of his concern reaching out to me like a lifeline.

"I need to tell you something," I said, meeting Wyatt's eyes with a resolve I hadn't known I possessed. The words were heavy on my tongue, laden with the gravity of secrets held too long in the dark.

The story of Rose Solinas, of my escape from a life of fear and control, was about to unfold.

15

WYATT

When Kensi said, "I need to tell you something," the whole room seemed to shift. Her voice wasn't loud, but it carried a weight that made everything else fall away.

The bar wasn't open for another hour, but I found myself locking the door anyway, cutting off the outside world. Missy muted the TV without a word. We didn't need distractions. Whatever Kensi was about to tell us, it was big.

I turned to face her. There was something in her eyes—fire, determination—but underneath it, fear. Not the kind you could run from, but the kind you had to face head-on.

Missy, Stephen, and I instinctively closed the space between us, forming a loose circle around her. None of us spoke, but we were all there, ready. My mind raced, flipping between wanting to protect her and wanting to steady her, to take on whatever she was carrying.

Stephen's usual smirk was gone, replaced with a sharp focus I rarely saw outside of work. Missy, always the first to lend comfort, gave Kensi a small nod. It wasn't just encouragement; it was a promise.

And me? I kept still, my fists curling at my sides as I fought the urge to pull her into my arms. Whatever she was about to say, I wasn't sure if I wanted to stop it or hear every word.

Kensi's voice broke the silence. Each word was deliberate, laced with a courage that was equal parts inspiring and heartbreaking. She told us about Luka Solinas, a man whose name had just been all over the news, tied to everything from money laundering to murder. Her story painted a picture of survival—a fight to escape, to find freedom in a world that didn't make it easy for someone like her.

Missy's hand shot to her mouth as Kensi spoke, her shock impossible to hide. She didn't interrupt, but her whole face reflected the pain she felt for Kensi.

Stephen leaned forward, elbows on his knees, his brows pulled tight. I could practically hear the gears turning in his head as he pieced together the threat Kensi had been running from—and how close it might still be.

My pulse hammered. Anger simmered just below the surface, not directed at her but at the world that had put her through this. At Luka. At anyone who thought they could take from her again.

But more than that, it was her strength that hit me. Sitting here, laying out a story like this—it wasn't just brave. It was extraordinary. Most people would've folded a long time ago, but Kensi didn't. She was still standing.

After what felt like forever, Missy reached out, her hand finding Kensi's. "We're here for you," she said softly, her voice steady in a way that left no room for doubt. "No matter what comes next."

Stephen nodded, shooting me a look that said we'd be taking action. He didn't have to say it out loud; I already knew what needed to happen.

I swallowed hard, trying to push down the fire threatening to boil over. Missy stayed close to Kensi, her words quiet but sure, while my mind jumped back to the day Stephen and I had dug into Kensi's past. Or tried to.

We'd found nothing. No history, no trace of Kensi Morrow before a certain point. It had raised a flag at the time, but now, it all made sense. She'd erased herself, built a new life brick by brick, to stay one step ahead of the man she'd just told us about.

She hadn't lied to us. She'd survived.

In our line of work, spotting the gaps—unknowns, risks, threats—was the job. But as Kensi... no, as Rose Solinas laid everything bare, the meaning behind what we'd uncovered changed. This wasn't about exposing her; it was about understanding how far she'd gone to claw her way to safety.

Every decision she'd made, every step she'd taken to cover her tracks, wasn't just about running. It was about surviving a world where the odds were stacked against her.

But by taking Luka's empire apart, by pulling that pin, she might've put herself in even more danger. Standing up to someone like Luka Solinas was gutsy, but it was also like painting a target on your back. It wasn't just about running from a husband who wanted to control her. It was about staying ahead of a whole criminal network that might want revenge.

I let out a slow breath, the weight of it all settling heavy on my chest.

Stephen's voice broke through my thoughts. "We need to act fast. If Luka's people are looking for her, we've got to be ahead of them."

He was right. This wasn't just Kensi's fight anymore. It was ours.

I glanced back at her, catching the way her shoulders sagged with the weight of the truth she'd just shared. Her vulnerability, her bravery—it left no room for hesitation in me.

"Kensi," I began, trying to keep my tone even, "you've done something incredibly brave, but it's important to consider all possible outcomes. Luka's arrest could stir things up. Do you know if he had any associates that might see you as a loose end?"

The question was deliberate, aimed at gauging any immediate threats we needed to be aware of. Every piece of information Kensi provided could help us build a more effective safety net around her.

With a hesitant gaze, both determination and fear were evident in her eyes. "Luka's connections run deep, and not just within his so-called legitimate businesses. There's a network, people who might not take kindly to what I've done."

Her admission was a confirmation of my worst fears, but also a vital piece of intelligence. Stephen caught my eye, a silent exchange that said we'd be discussing this further, mapping out contingency plans and security measures to ensure her safety.

Kensi's confusion was palpable, mirrored in her furrowed brow and the slight tilt of her head as she regarded Stephen and me. It was Stephen who broke the silence, his voice carrying a reassuring confidence.

"We have some contacts in law enforcement, friends who can help keep an eye on things. It's about making sure you have an extra layer of protection."

Her guarded expression softened slightly, a glimmer of understanding in her eyes. It was a lot to process, the sudden shift from feeling isolated in her fight to having a small, albeit formidable, team rallying around her.

"I...I appreciate that," Kensi said, her voice a mixture of gratitude and lingering apprehension. "But why go through all this trouble for me?"

Stephen smirked. "Let's just say we're not fans of bullies, especially the kind that think they can control others through fear and intimidation. Helping people like you, it's part of what we do. Plus, Wyatt's mom would have our heads if we didn't do everything we could to keep you safe."

The tension in the room eased, a shared moment of levity that was a welcome break from the seriousness of the situation.

Kensi offered a small, tentative smile. "Thank you," she said. Then as though a curtain had been lifted, she remembered the drink that had been spilled and began reaching for napkins to mop up the mess. Missy waved her off and grabbed a couple of towels from under the bar and a spray bottle of cleaner.

As Missy cleaned, I couldn't help but watch Kensi. The gratitude in her voice, the way she moved to help despite the emotional upheaval she'd just experienced, revealed a resilience and a strength that was admirable. It was clear that Kensi Morrow, or Rose Solinas, was no damsel in distress; she was a survivor, fighting her way to a new beginning.

16

WYATT

It had been a few days since Kensi had shared her truth, and although the initial shock lingered, life at The Yellow Rose Inn had begun to find a new rhythm. With her past out in the open, our protective efforts had only tightened, evolving into a quiet but constant vigilance. Even so, I found myself more captivated by her presence than I realized, my focus so intensely fixed on keeping her safe that the rest of the world blurred into a haze.

I had just ended a video call with our security team, discussing contingency plans and protocols down to every last detail. Each new precaution became another line in the mental checklist I found myself reciting at night.

Interrupting the stillness, my phone buzzed. Glancing at the screen, I recognized the name: Tammy Green, the coordinator from the benefit committee—the benefit to support the family of a local Marine who'd fallen in the line of duty. A pang of guilt rose up as I remembered the benefit concert—a cause I'd committed to weeks ago but hadn't given a second thought to in days.

Putting the call on speaker, I answered.

"Hey, Tammy," I greeted her, keeping my tone neutral even as I braced for whatever reminder or last-minute request she might need.

"Hi, Wyatt! I hate to call so close to the event, but we've hit a bit of a snag," she said, her cheerful tone betraying an edge of nervous hope. "One of our musicians just canceled, and we're hoping you could cover some extra songs—maybe five instead of two?"

The thought of nearly forgetting about it in the midst of everything with Kensi sent another rush of guilt through me.

"Of course, Tammy," I replied quickly, resolving to set aside whatever hesitation was rising up. "I'll handle it."

Her relief came through the line like a warm breeze. "Thank you, Wyatt. Really, you're saving the day. The family appreciates it more than you know."

"Happy to help," I said, meaning every word as I hung up, the echo of her gratitude lingering in the room.

Sighing, I turned to Stephen, who was preoccupied with his laptop, but I felt a renewed sense of purpose. "I can't believe I let the benefit concert slip my mind," I confessed, feeling a bit sheepish.

Stephen looked up, his teasing smirk softening into a more understanding smile. "That's understandable, man. You've had a lot on your plate, especially with Kensi's situation," he reassured me, closing his laptop to give me his full attention. "But it sounds like you're stepping up just when they need you most. Five songs, huh?"

"Yeah, five songs," I repeated, the reality of the commitment settling in. "I need to pull together a setlist. It's in three days."

Stephen leaned back in his chair, his expression thoughtful. "You know, this could be good, not just for the benefit, but for you too. A chance to take a break from all the heavy work and do something you love. Plus, it's for a great cause."

I nodded, the initial panic giving way to a sense of resolve.

"Speaking of heavy work," Stephen segued with a half-grin, "how's the Fort Knox setup going for Kensi's quarters?"

I frowned slightly at his reference. "It's not Fort Knox. It's necessary," I countered, not finding the humor in the situation. "We're just installing a few security cameras and making sure the locks are upgraded. My mom thinks it's overkill, though."

Stephen chuckled, shaking his head. "I'm with your mom on this one. But I get it. Better safe than sorry, right?"

I didn't share his light-hearted take on the matter. "It's not about being overcautious. It's about ensuring Kensi feels safe and actually is safe. You know the stakes."

His smile faded, replaced by a look of understanding. "Yeah, I know. Just didn't expect you to go all out like this."

He paused, eyeing me with a speculative gaze. "You really like her, don't you?"

The inquiry struck like a rogue wave, unexpected and forceful, threatening to capsize the boat of composure I'd been meticulously navigating since Kensi's arrival. I stiffened, feeling the protective walls around my thoughts crack under pressure.

"She's married," I replied curtly, my voice a shield raised swiftly to ward off any further incursions into forbidden territory. The words were terse, a line drawn in the sand that I dared not cross, even in the privacy of my own mind.

Stephen's hands lifted in surrender, his fingers splayed wide against the backdrop of the cluttered room. "Hey, no judgment here. Just an observation," he said, his voice a gentle nudge rather than a push. I could tell by the way he tilted his head slightly to the left and offered a half-smile that he recognized the boundaries of this conversation. He wouldn't venture any further down that path, but the air remained charged, his unsaid thoughts swirling silently between us.

I cleared my throat and shifted my gaze to my desk. Picking up a notepad and pen I started scratching out ideas for a set list. The mundane task was a welcome distraction, though Stephen's question about Kensi had burrowed itself into my thoughts, stubborn as a splinter.

Every time I was around her, I was certain my heart would abandon my chest just to be closer to her. The day I went over to install the air conditioner, Mom had roped Kensi into planting some flowers, and Kensi, ever the sport, had dived in with enthusiasm. Her laughter, real and unguarded, had cut through the air, reaching me where I worked nearby. It was infectious and had me wishing I could bottle the sound to replay it again and again.

One afternoon I had stopped by the inn to help my stepdad, Ed, haul some furniture out. Kensi was in one of the rocking chairs on the porch, her eyes lost in the pages of a book. She was completely engrossed, a soft smile playing on her lips as she read. I was taken aback by the emotions that welled up inside me as I watched her enjoy the quiet moment of the day.

But it wasn't just these moments of connection that drew me to her; it was her resilience, the strength she carried like a mantle. Despite everything she'd been through, Kensi possessed a kind of grace under pressure, a determination to move forward. It was admirable and only gave me a stronger desire to protect her, to offer support, and maybe, in another world, something more.

Yet, the reality of her situation, of the invisible barriers between us, was never far from my thoughts. Kensi was married, entangled in a past that threatened to overshadow her present and future. My feelings, as real as they were, had no place in the complicated situation that was her life. Acknowledging this didn't stop the what-ifs from swirling in my mind. I rubbed at my temple, the turmoil of unspoken emotions colliding with my sense of duty. No matter how deep the feelings ran within me, I knew where lines were drawn. My role was protector and friend... nothing more.

17

KENSI

I'd finished my shift and dashed to my new home to shower and change. Wrapped in a towel, I stood before the small, fogged mirror, fingers combing through stubborn curls. They resisted at first, tangling around my fingertips.

With a sigh, I admitted defeat, deciding it was still far too warm to wear it down, anyway. I twisted it into a knot on top of my head when there was a knock on the door.

"Just a minute!" I yelled, certain the person knocking hadn't heard me. I threw on a pair of cut off denim shorts and the t-shirt Missy had gifted me that read "Hey, Y'all!"

She'd thought it was funny when I used "y'all" in my less than southern accent. So when she saw the shirt she said she bought it immediately with me in mind. She'd given it to me that night when I stopped by The Anchor. When the tears sprang up, it had sent Missy into a frenzy apologizing.

I'd been embarrassed that I had to explain my reaction was simply because it had been so long since anyone had given me a gift just because they thought of me. We were both blubbering messes and she'd had to call a very confused Stephen over so we could take five and pull ourselves together.

Pulling open the door I was greeted by three faces I'd come to relate to a feeling akin to happiness and security.

"Ready for tonight?" Her voice danced with notes of excitement, each syllable lifting the corners of my lips into an almost smile. She was dressed in a light summer dress that fluttered with the breeze, her demeanor radiating the kind of joy I found both infectious and, in moments like these, slightly overwhelming.

"Almost," I replied, the word feeling like a pebble in a stream—smoothed by constant touch but still solid and grounded. My eyes shifted past her effervescence to the two men trailing behind.

Wyatt's entrance was less of a flourish and more of a deliberate stride, his frame filling the doorway as if to shield us from anything beyond it. His eyes met mine, and in their depths, I read the silent conversations we'd had about the risks of stepping out into the world tonight. Conversations very similar to the one he was starting now.

"Are you sure you want to do this, Kensi? Crowds, public places... it's not exactly laying low," he murmured, the bass of his voice vibrating through the room, as if voicing the thoughts I'd been wrestling with myself.

I couldn't help but feel a wave of gratitude for his concern; it was more care than I'd received in a long time. Yet, part of me rebelled against the idea of being cocooned away from the world indefinitely.

"Wyatt, I appreciate your concern and everything you've done for me, I do. But, Missy and Stephen will be there the whole time," I reasoned, trying to assuage his fears without dismissing them entirely. "I'll be fine. I need this... a chance to just be Kensi for a night, not someone running from her past," I found myself saying, more to convince myself than them.

Stephen, leaning casually against the doorframe, offered me a reassuring smile. "We've got your back. Plus, Wyatt's only on stage for five songs. It's not like we're venturing into the belly of the beast."

Missy looped her arm through mine, her determination clear. "Exactly! It's going to be fun. And besides, it's not every day we get to see Wyatt play on a big stage. We wouldn't miss it for the world."

Wyatt's jaw tensed, the subtle shift speaking volumes of the battle he fought between overprotection and support. Yet, despite the concern etched in the creases of his forehead, there was a relenting— a softening in the way he finally nodded back at me, acknowledging my need for this night of reprieve.

As I looked at the faces before me, I realized that despite my nerves and the underlying fear that was a constant companion, I was genuinely looking forward to the evening. It was a step towards reclaiming a part of myself I thought I'd lost, a step towards normalcy, however fleeting it might be.

I allowed myself a small smile, feeling it stretch muscles that had forgotten the feel of true joy. The evening ahead shimmered with potential, with the promise of laughter and fun, of music that could drown out the whispers of my past.

Stephen's lighthearted interjection cut through the tension. "Besides, if anyone even looks at Kensi the wrong way, they'll have to answer to me," he joked, though the underlying promise of protection wasn't lost on any of us.

Wyatt's gaze lingered on me, searching, as if trying to read the myriad of thoughts racing through my mind. The intensity of his look sent a jolt through me, sharp and unexpected. It was a reminder of how easily he could unsettle me, how much being near him affected me in ways I couldn't name yet.

Finally, he sighed, the lines of his face softening in reluctant agreement. "Alright, but we're staying together, and we leave if anything feels off," he conceded, his gaze lingering on me with an intensity that sent an unfamiliar shiver down my spine.

"Thank you," I murmured, the words barely more than a whisper, but they were enough to break our locked gaze.

With Wyatt joining Stephen by the doorway, the tension in the room disappeared. Anticipation hummed through me. The nerves and apprehension about attending the event lingered, a natural reaction given everything I'd been through.

The brightness of the room seemed to grow, the walls less confining as I let myself imagine joy unshadowed by fear.

"Let's do this," I said, a smile tugging at my lips. My voice carried a new note of determination, one that sprang from choosing to embrace life rather than cower from it. Tonight, under the protective wing of friends and the veil of dusk, I would reclaim a piece of myself lost to the darkness. Tonight, I would laugh, dance, and for a few precious hours, live.

18

KENSI

The road to Ashfield stretched out ahead, a gray ribbon winding through endless green fields and clusters of wildflowers swaying in the breeze. To me, it might as well have been a foreign country. Even in New York, where I'd spent most of my life, my world had been small—compressed by fear, controlled. Open spaces like this, where the horizon seemed to go on forever, were almost unreal, too vast to belong to the same planet as the narrow streets and shadowed alleys I once called home.

I leaned back in my seat, the worn fabric of Stephen's truck rough against my skin but not grating. My gaze drifted between Missy, her face glowing with excitement, and the landscape rushing by. Awe filled me, but beneath it a subtle unease pulsed, a slight tremor in the otherwise steady rhythm of my heart. It was beautiful, yes—but also overwhelming, as if the sheer openness might swallow me whole.

"Did you see that old barn we just passed?" Missy pointed out, her voice bubbling with enthusiasm. "It's been there since my grandpa was a boy."

"Planning to restore it?" Stephen teased, his eyes catching hers in the rearview mirror, a playful smile tugging at his lips.

"Maybe," she replied, her laughter light. "That is, if you're volunteering to help."

Stephen chuckled, a low, melodic sound. "You know I'm always up for a challenge, especially if it means spending more time with you."

Missy rolled her eyes, but the blush that crept up her cheeks betrayed her amusement. "Keep dreaming, cowboy."

Watching their exchange, I was flooded with longing for my own chance at happiness coupled with anxiety at the idea I could ever trust someone enough to connect with them like that. It was foreign, yet fascinating—this game of flirtation where the stakes were affection, not duty. I was an interloper in their moment, but I couldn't stop watching. Their connection was unlike anything I'd ever known but desperately wanted to.

As we pulled into the bustling venue, the reality of the event hit me. The sprawling grounds were alive with the energy of thousands, a communal heartbeat thumping to the rhythm of a common cause. The air was a cocktail of grilled foods, earth after a day in the sun, and the undercurrent of excitement for the music that promised to fill the night. It was overwhelming, yet exhilarating, a stark contrast to the solitude and tension that had defined my life lately.

We made our way through the sea of people, and I couldn't help but notice the American flags and different military flags that danced in the gentle evening breeze. They were not just decorations but emblems of honor, each one telling a story of valor and loss. Symbols of respect and remembrance were worn like badges over hearts and woven into the fabric of clothing, turning every attendee into a testament to those who had given everything for the common good.

The camaraderie and collective reverence were so beautiful. Each fluttering flag, each solemn nod exchanged between strangers, every embrace was a reminder of the sacrifices that had built and bolstered this community. There was a lump forming in my throat, grateful and sad for these strangers who acted like family with one another.

"Kensi, are you alright?" Stephen's voice cut through my reverie, laced with concern.

"Yes," I managed, swallowing hard. "It's just... I didn't expect..."

"I know. It's a lot to take in," he said softly, understanding dawning in his eyes.

And it was. It was a story of lives coming together, with each person's tale adding to a bigger story of strength and togetherness.

Stephen and Wyatt casually weaved through the festival crowd, their arms full of our camping chairs and their expressions serious but calm. They claimed a small empty space not too far from the stage. Around us, families had staked their claims like colorful settlers; blankets were unfurled across the grass, chairs popped open with satisfying clicks, and pop-up tents twinkled with strings of light powered by humming generators.

"Here should be good," Stephen declared, his voice carrying over the murmur of the crowd as he set down the chairs in a neat row.

"It's perfect," I murmured, taking my seat and feeling the solid ground beneath me. From here, I could see the stage clearly, the musicians already coaxing melodies from their instruments that made the air thrum with anticipation.

Wyatt stood at the edge of our claimed territory, his profile sharp against the backdrop of fading daylight. He and Stephen exchanged hushed words, their heads bowed together in a strategic huddle. The seriousness etched on their faces was unmistakable, a sense of duty overshadowing even the lightheartedness of the concert.

Though I couldn't hear their conversation, I didn't need to. Their protective nature was as much a part of them as breathing—a trait that stitched them seamlessly into the fabric of my newfound safety. Wyatt's keen eyes scanned the masses, always watchful, always ready. His initial reluctance to come had given way to steadfast duty; he stood sentinel, close enough to act, yet distant enough to survey our surroundings with meticulous care.

Because of that vigilance, I felt safe and could fully appreciate the music and the people around me. With every bass note that vibrated through the ground, with every swell of cheer from the crowd, the tension that had been my constant companion began to loosen its grip, replaced by a lively energy that was infectious.

Wyatt took his seat next to mine, and for a moment, we just sat together in companionable silence, letting the sounds of the festival wash over us. I could feel the hum of the crowd's energy, the anticipation for the music that was about to start. Wyatt's presence was calming, grounding me in the moment.

He leaned back in his chair, his eyes scanning the stage, then the crowd. He was always vigilant, always alert. It was one of the things I loved about him—his quiet strength, his unwavering focus. He turned his head slightly, catching me watching him. A small smile played on his lips. "What?" he asked.

"Nothing," I said, shaking my head. "Just thinking about how different this is from my life six months ago."

Wyatt's eyes softened. "Good different?" he asked, his voice low, so only I could hear.

I nodded. "Very good different," I said. "But still... a lot to take in."

He nodded, understanding. We both had our pasts, our ghosts that sometimes hovered closer than they should. But right now, those ghosts were distant, retreating in the face of the evening's warmth, the music, and the presence of the people I was starting to consider family.

"Music was always a refuge for me," Wyatt said suddenly, his voice thoughtful, almost introspective. "Even in the worst of times, it was always there. A constant."

I turned to him, curious. Wyatt didn't often talk about his time in the military, about what he'd gone through. It was something we both understood—some wounds were too deep to expose to the light. But when he did share, I listened, knowing these glimpses into his soul were precious.

"How so?" I asked, keeping my voice gentle, inviting him to continue if he wanted.

He glanced at me, then back at the stage where a band was setting up. "When I was deployed, music was one of the few things that could take me out of the moment, you know? When everything was... too much, I could put on my headphones, listen to a song, and it was like I was back home, even if just for a few minutes."

I nodded, trying to imagine what it must have been like, to be so far from everything familiar, everything safe. "Did you have a favorite song?" I asked, sensing this was important to him, this connection to music.

Wyatt chuckled softly, a sound that vibrated through the warm night air. "We had this running joke in our unit. Every time someone started feeling down, we'd play *Don't Stop Believin'* by Journey. It was corny, but it worked. It made us laugh, made us remember that there was more waiting for us beyond the desert."

I laughed with him, picturing a group of tough, battle-hardened soldiers singing along to a classic rock anthem. "I can see that," I said, my heart swelling with affection for this man who had been through so much, yet still found joy in the simple things.

"It wasn't just for fun, though," Wyatt continued, his tone growing more serious. "Music was a way to keep in touch with my humanity, with my emotions. It gave me something to hold on to when everything else was falling apart."

He paused, his gaze meeting mine, and I could see the depth of his feelings in his eyes. "Music was always there for me when nothing else was. It's how I stay grounded. Even now.

It's why this concert means so much. It's not about recognition. It's about the connection, the way a song can reach out and touch someone, make them feel less alone."

A lump formed in my throat, moved by the sincerity in his voice, the openness in his words. I reached over, placing my hand on his, feeling the warmth of his skin, the strength of his grip. "I understand," I said softly. "And I think it's amazing. That you have this gift, this ability to connect with people through your music. It's something special, Wyatt."

He smiled, a small, genuine smile that made my heart skip a beat. "Thank you," he said, his voice filled with a quiet gratitude. "For listening. For being here."

As the first notes of the concert filled the air, Wyatt's thumb brushed the side of my hand several times before he pulled it away and tapped his fingers to the beat of the music.

The opening act took the stage, setting the tone for the night with their upbeat rhythms and soulful chords. I found myself caught up in the simple joy of the moment, grateful for the presence of those who'd made this reprieve possible.

Missy's voice drew me back, her hand lightly tapping mine to catch my attention. "I'm so glad you're here with us, Kensi," she said, her words rising above the music. "Liberty… it's been good to you, hasn't it?"

A wave of emotion rose up, mostly gratitude for this life I was only just starting to figure out. I nodded, the gesture small, almost too simple to express the complexity of what was in my heart at that moment.

"It has," I found my voice, stronger than I expected, rising above the symphony of sound surrounding us. The sun dipped lower, its warmth slowly fading. "I never thought I'd find a place like this, or people like you all."

The gentle hum of conversation ebbed around us as the horizon blushed with the final strokes of sunset. I shifted in my chair, stealing a glance at Stephen's profile against the dimming sky; his laughter mingled with the music and chatter, grounding yet somehow distant. Missy's hand fluttered to her heart, her eyes following the melody of our dialogue.

The conversation drifted naturally, as conversations between friends do, until curiosity overtook me. I hesitated, then ventured, "So, you and Stephen… there's obviously something there. Are you planning to keep him in the friend zone forever?" It was a bold question, perhaps, but one inspired by the genuine affection and respect I'd observed between them.

Her laughter was sudden and bright, cutting through any tension my query might have caused. It was the kind of laugh that carried stories and secrets all its own, unencumbered and sincere. Missy's gaze found Stephen, who was now tossing a friendly jest at Wyatt, oblivious to our scrutiny.

"Stephen," she began, her tone fond yet marked by a hint of caution, "he's been through a lot with me. More than most would have bothered to. And I... I do care for him, more than I've admitted to anyone, even myself." She paused, glancing in the direction the guys had gone, a softness in her eyes that hadn't been there before. "But after everything, it's hard to let someone in, you know? Even someone as persistently wonderful as Stephen."

I swallowed hard, the lump in my throat a stark reminder of past sorrows. "I do know," I murmured, my voice barely rising above the hum of conversation and music around us.

My thoughts began to wander down a trail of my own fears and the walls I'd built around my heart after being forced into a marriage that was more transaction than partnership. Missy's eyes met mine, a silent acknowledgment of our shared vulnerabilities.

My father had brokered my marriage to Luka as if it were just another business deal, a strategic alliance between two powerful families. I'd clung to the naive hope that maybe one day love could grow from such an arrangement. But instead of blossoming into something beautiful, it had spiraled into a nightmare, one where control and fear replaced any chance of affection or understanding.

Reflecting on those days, the contrast between my forced union with Luka and the genuine affection I saw between Missy and Stephen was stark. They had something real, something that looked like mutual respect, admiration, and shared experiences. It was the kind of connection I'd longed for but had been denied, first by the circumstances of my marriage and then by the sheer necessity of survival.

The idea of love had become a distant concept, something I watched from afar but never truly experienced. The shiny façade of our marriage couldn't mask the truth: it was a prison, no matter how lavish it was. It was a relationship built on the sands of obligation and power, not the solid ground of mutual affection or choice.

Sitting there with Missy, witnessing her cautious dance around the possibility of something more with Stephen, I couldn't help but wonder about the paths not taken, about what life could have been like if choices had been mine to make. The thought was a bittersweet pill, one that brought both longing and a sense of relief. Relief that, despite everything, I was now in a place where new beginnings were possible, even if the scars of the past remained.

Here, surrounded by people united in support of a cause, I found a sense of belonging I hadn't known I was missing. And as I listened to Missy talk about Stephen, about the fears and hopes that tangled between them, I recognized the echo of my own desire for connection, for a love that was chosen, not forced.

The notion of being truly seen and known, outside the constraints of a title or a surname, was as distant as the stars beginning to prick the darkening sky above us. The love promised to me had been nothing more than a cage, its ornate bars glistening to distract from the imprisonment within. Luka had held the key, his grip as tight on it as his hold was on me, ensuring compliance through fear, not the tender touch of devotion.

"Kensi? You okay?" Missy's voice pulled me from the shadows of reflection, her brow creased with concern.

"More than okay," I lied, offering her a smile that I hoped reached my eyes. "Just enjoying the night."

As the band on stage hit a crescendo, I let the music wash over me, trying to believe in the possibility that somewhere amidst these notes and chords, there might be a melody for me—one that spoke of freedom and choice, not the echoes of a loveless legacy.

Missy's hand fluttered to her necklace, a delicate heart pendant, as she watched Stephen joke with a group of volunteers. Her fingers traced the silver contours, a telltale sign of her inner turmoil. I studied her, this woman who had become a friend, and saw the hesitant steps of someone poised on the edge of something profound, something that could elevate or shatter her heart.

"Scary, isn't it?" I murmured, breaking the silence that had settled between us. "Considering what might be if we let go of our fears."

She turned to me, an uncertain smile tugging at her lips. "Terrifying," she confessed, her eyes darting back to Stephen. "But maybe worth it."

I nodded, knowing all too well holding on to the what-ifs and might-have-beens and letting them dictate your every move. My life, once dictated by the heavy hand of expectation, now held a fragile hope within this community. It was as if Liberty had opened its arms to me, offering refuge and a hint of redemption from the shackles of my past.

A sudden movement snapped me back to the present. Wyatt squared his shoulders, the lines of his frame etched against the backdrop of revelry. For a moment, he paused, looking back at us, and his eyes found Stephen's across the distance. A silent understanding, like an electric current, flowed between them. The world around me paused and even the hum of the festival quieted around their exchange. I watched, feeling the strength of their silent promise to keep me safe.

With a final nod, Wyatt turned, his guitar case gripped firmly in hand. He wove through the sea of bodies with an ease that belied the watchful tension in his stride. His path was unerring, a steadfast line drawn toward the stage where he would soon bare his soul in song. The setting sun cast a golden hue over the scene, igniting the sky with fiery streaks that mirrored the intensity of the moment. The crowd's energy surged, a wave of expectation building as the night prepared to embrace its next performer.

Missy's gaze lingered on Wyatt's retreating figure before she pivoted to face me. Her eyes danced with flecks of twilight, mirroring the scattered festival lights that began to pierce the encroaching dusk. There was a vibrancy to her, an eagerness mixed with a quiet pride that swelled from within. Her lips curved into a smile, one that reached all the way to her eyes.

"Have you ever heard Wyatt sing?" she asked, leaning in closer to ensure her voice carried over the surrounding noise of the festival.

The question caught me off guard. My mind, still shadowed by the imprint of Wyatt's resolute gaze, struggled to align this new image of him with the protector I knew.

"No, I haven't. Is he good?"

Missy laughed, the sound bright and full of genuine amusement. "He's incredible. It's like his voice was meant to be heard by the world, but he's so humble about it. You'd never know how talented he is just by talking to him."

The idea of Wyatt, always so composed and protective, revealing a different side of himself through music piqued my interest. "Really? I wouldn't have guessed. He seems... more reserved."

"That's just it," Missy continued, her gaze drifting towards the stage where Wyatt had vanished moments earlier. "When he sings, it's like he's sharing a part of his soul. It's powerful and raw. But off stage, he just shrugs it off like it's nothing special. I swear, he doesn't see his own brilliance."

I found myself smiling, captivated by this new dimension to Wyatt's character. "Then I'm looking forward to hearing him."

"You won't be disappointed," Missy assured me, her confidence infectious.

Before I could respond, Stephen leaned in, a playful gleam in his eye. "Let me tell you about one of Wyatt's early forays into music. He's been singing since he was a kid," Stephen's voice carried a tinge of nostalgia. "There was this donkey on one of the farms we'd pass on our way to our favorite fishing hole." His grin broadened as if the memory itself amused him. "Every time Wyatt sang, that donkey would start braying back, louder and prouder, as if she was challenging him to a sing off."

Missy's laughter bubbled up, her imagination tickled by the image. "Are you saying the donkey thought she was a better singer than Wyatt?"

Stephen nodded, his eyes twinkling with the joy of the memory. "Exactly. Wyatt used to say she was the most honest critic he ever had. He'd sing a line, and she'd bray back, each time a bit louder, as though she was saying, 'That all you got?'" His laughter joined Missy's.

"It was hilarious," Stephen concluded his story wiping away tears of laughter from his eyes.

"I think, in a way, those silly duets with the donkey taught Wyatt to embrace his voice, no matter the audience," Stephen added, his voice tinged with respect. It was clear how much he admired and cared for Wyatt, a sentiment echoed whenever anyone spoke of him.

"Wow," I whispered, touched by the glimpse into Wyatt's past.

Stephen nodded, a soft smile gracing his lips. "Yeah, Wyatt's full of surprises."

The conversation shifted as my curiosity peaked. "Speaking of surprises," I began, my thoughts turning to the meticulous security setup at my new home. "How were you and Wyatt able to get my place set up so quickly? And so thoroughly?"

He paused, choosing his words with care. "Wyatt's background in the Navy SEALs gave him a unique set of skills–not just in defense tactics, but in strategic planning and surveillance. Combine that with my tech know-how, and we were able to put in a security system that's both thorough and discreet."

Missy chuckled, nudging Stephen playfully. "I swear, between the two of them, they could probably wire a toaster to become a surveillance device."

Stephen laughed, the sound light and genuine, easing the tension that had momentarily gathered. "Don't give us too many ideas, Missy. But seriously, ensuring you were safe was our top priority, Kensi. After all, everyone deserves a sanctuary, right?"

I nodded, trying to prevent the sudden burn of tears from becoming more than a feeling. "It's more than I could have asked for, really. I just didn't realize I was moving into the Bat-Cave."

"That's us," Stephen quipped, winking. "Just a couple of regular Bruce Waynes at your service. Minus the capes. Though, I can't speak for Wyatt; he might have one stashed away somewhere."

Missy and I found ourselves in a fit of giggles, Stephen looking at Missy with what could only be described as pure enjoyment knowing he put the smile on her face.

Before my thoughts could be reclaimed by the pinprick of jealousy their connection brought me, a voice from the stage interrupted, a familiar timbre that commanded immediate attention. It was Wyatt's turn, and as the spotlight found him, the crowd hushed, a collective breath held in anticipation.

Wyatt, with guitar in hand, transformed under those lights. Who knew that the same guy, who I've seen be all business, could hold the stage with such ease? His first song hit the air, and his voice was something else—deep and rich, every note packed with emotion. It wasn't just his singing; it was the way he owned the stage, chatting up the crowd between songs like he was born to it. The man was a natural, sharing laughs and stories that made you feel like you were just hanging out with him, not watching from a sea of faces.

Each song he played pulled the crowd in closer, his set moving from toe-tapping beats to the kind of ballads that tug at your heart-strings. The benefit concert, meant to honor a fallen Marine, was already charged with emotion, and Wyatt's set only added to it. His understanding of the significance of the occasion was evident, his song choices mirroring both the solemnity of why we were gathered and the celebration of life and shared support.

By the time he got to his last song, a hush had fallen over the crowd. Wyatt belted the lyrics of *God Bless the U.S.A.*, while clearly paying homage to family, friends, and the sacrifices made by those who serve. I couldn't help but get teary-eyed watching Wyatt pour his heart out. It was powerful, seeing someone lay their soul bare like that, especially in service of a cause bigger than any one of us.

When the final note lingered in the air before fading out, the silence was deafening. And then, as if on cue, the place erupted. Cheers, applause, whistles—you name it. Looking around, I saw faces wet with tears, smiles wide with gratitude. Missy squeezed my hand, her eyes sparkling, "Told you he was amazing," she whispered, pride evident in her voice.

"Yeah," I managed to get out, completely in awe. "He's something special, alright."

A few minutes later Wyatt made his way back through the crowd, people patted him on the back, offering words of thanks and admiration. Watching him, you'd think he was just another guy, not the one who'd just held the entire crowd in the palm of his hand. When his gaze locked onto mine, there was a brief but intense moment where nothing else around us mattered. It was as if, in that exchange, something unspoken passed between us—a recognition of the emotional journey he'd just taken us on, and perhaps, an acknowledgment of the growing connection between us, complicated as it was.

He walked over, his stride easy yet deliberate. Missy, ever perceptive, noticed the subtle shift in the air and gave a kind smile before excusing herself, her hand resting briefly on my shoulder in a gesture of quiet support as she left Wyatt and me the space to talk.

"Hey," Wyatt said, his voice carrying a softness reserved for moments of genuine interaction. "Did you enjoy the show?"

I nodded, struggling for a moment to find words that could encapsulate the depth of what I'd experienced during his performance. "You were incredible. You really have a gift."

He shrugged modestly, a faint blush coloring his cheeks under the stage lights' afterglow. "Thank you. It's for a good cause, you know? Just doing my part."

His humility, so at odds with the commanding presence he'd just displayed on stage, only added layers to my understanding of him. This man possessed the power to captivate an audience with his voice, his words resonating with their souls. Yet, he wielded this gift with humility, using it to uplift others rather than seeking accolades for himself.

"I think what you did tonight was more than just 'doing your part,'" I said, my voice earnest. "You touched a lot of people, Wyatt. Including me."

There was a beat of silence, charged with an energy that had nothing to do with the music or the event itself. It was a moment that defied the boundaries of our current realities.

His eyes, the ones that had captivated the crowd, were now staring at me so intensely it was as strong as a physical touch. We stood there as though we were completely alone.

For a few heartbeats, the silence between us was alive, charged with things neither of us dared to say. The moment stretched, vast and significant, as though the air itself carried the gravity of everything we couldn't express.

Our separate realities, the worlds we each carried, seemed to blur in that pause. The boundaries between us were fragile, tested by something unspoken but undeniable, something growing in the space we shared.

Wyatt started to speak but I raised my hand pressing fingers gently against his lips to forestall his words. Even as I did so, my pulse raced at the contact, an electric charge buzzing through me at the brush of my skin against his.

"I know," I whispered, drawing back just enough to meet his gaze squarely. The dim light from the stage cast shadows across his features, but they couldn't hide the intensity in his eyes, nor the concern etched into his brow. "And thank you. For tonight, for the music... for everything."

There was a pause, heavy with unspoken understanding, as he absorbed my interruption. He nodded slowly, his deliberate movement acknowledging the boundaries we both knew were there. As I lowered my hand, I saw the recognition in his eyes—the line my past had drawn, and the sense of duty he carried because of it.

The air went electric as a silent understanding settled between us —a mutual respect for the struggles we bore and the secrets we kept. For a moment, we stood together, two souls drawn close by what divided us, connected and yet held apart by the reality of it all.

My gaze drifted past Wyatt, scanning the crowd as it broke into smaller groups, people laughing and chatting like it was any other night. And then I saw him—Jimmy Golden, my father's right-hand man. My stomach dropped. He wasn't supposed to be here. He was supposed to be a thousand miles away, not in Texas, not anywhere near me. He was a ghost from the life I'd run from. In an instant, my entire world shifted on its axis.

My chest tightened, my heart pounding so hard I thought it might burst. How? Why? The questions hit me all at once, a tangle of panic and dread that made it hard to breathe. Jimmy being here couldn't be a coincidence. It wasn't just bad luck. My past, the one I'd fought so hard to escape, had found me. The peace I'd started to believe in was gone, shattered.

All the blood drained from my head, leaving me lightheaded and unsteady. My breaths turned shallow and rapid as panic tightened its hold on my chest like a vise. Wyatt must have noticed the change, because his expression shifted in an instant—from calm and affectionate to sharp with concern, his focus fully on me.

"Kensi? What's wrong?" His voice was sharp with worry, his eyes scanning mine for clues, then following my gaze into the crowd.

But I couldn't speak, couldn't form the words to explain the danger, the fear that Jimmy's presence heralded. To speak it out loud was to make it real, to acknowledge that the fragile sanctuary I had found here might be shattered by forces I had no power to stop.

My throat constricted, the words I needed to say caught somewhere between dread and disbelief. Jimmy's appearance spun a web of fear around me, pulling everything else out of focus. The crowd's laughter and cheers became a distant hum, like they belonged to some other world. All I could hear was the pounding of my pulse, all I could feel was the cold sweat slicking my palms. Danger had found its way in, shattering the sense of safety I'd started to believe in.

Wyatt's eyes stayed locked on mine, his expression shifting to something sharp and protective. He stepped closer, his body instinctively positioning itself between me and the crowd. His nearness was the only thing keeping the panic from swallowing me whole, a lifeline I wasn't sure I deserved to grab.

But even with him so close, I couldn't say it. I couldn't shatter the fragile peace of the evening with the truth clawing at my throat, desperate to be let out.

"Kensi." His voice was a lifeline thrown into the turbulent waters of my panic.

I tried to respond, but the specter of Jimmy loomed larger than any words I might summon. The ghost of my old life was here, its shadow falling over the bright lights and jubilant faces.

Wyatt, sensing the urgency, the silent plea in my eyes, subtly shifted his stance, a protector once more. "Tell me what you need," he said, his voice low, a promise of support and action woven through the words.

I could only shake my head, the terror gripping me rendering me mute. How could I explain? How could I drag Wyatt, Missy, and Stephen into the tangled web of my past? I'd already put too much on them. They had their own lives, their own burdens.

Yet, as I stood there, caught in the storm of my own fears, I realized that whether I wanted it or not, my past had found me. And with it, the realization that I would have to face it, to confront the demons I had run from, if I ever hoped to truly be free.

A shift in the crowd drew my eye, and for a single, gut-wrenching heartbeat, I saw Jimmy again—his gaze skimming over heads, searching. My breath caught, but his eyes moved past me, unaware. In that fleeting reprieve, a thread of resolve took root, weaving itself through the fear engulfing me.

This man—this link to the life I'd fought so hard to escape—couldn't be allowed to destroy what I'd started to build here. My friends, these unwitting guardians of hope, didn't deserve to be dragged into the shadows I carried.

I clung to that spark of strength, forcing it to grow, to push back against the rising tide of panic. The refuge of real friendships, the joy in shared laughter, the silent steadiness I found in Wyatt's eyes and this life I was beginning to believe in was worth fighting for. Jimmy, a harbinger of everything I'd left behind, wouldn't take it from me. Not if I could help it.

Swallowing hard against the knot in my throat, I turned toward Wyatt. My fingers brushed his arm, light but insistent, and his gaze snapped to mine. His eyes, full of unspoken questions, searched my face, but I couldn't explain. I could only hope he understood the silent urgency in my touch—that we needed to act before it was too late.

"We have to go. Now," I murmured, the words squeezing out through the tightness in my chest. My voice was barely a whisper, yet it bore the urgency of my unspoken plea.

19

WYATT

From the moment Kensi's expression shifted, a knot formed in my gut. Fear wasn't new to me—I'd faced it in places where every shadow could hide an enemy. But this wasn't the fear I knew. This was different. This was Kensi. She wasn't just a fighter—she was someone who'd walked through fire and come out the other side. Seeing her now, frozen and braced against something I couldn't see, twisted something deep inside me.

"Kensi?" I kept my voice low, calm. She didn't respond, her focus locked on something distant, unseen, but entirely too real to her. That knot tightened.

I took a step closer, deliberate and measured, careful not to startle her. Kensi had walls, layers built by things she hadn't yet shared. Seeing those walls shake like this lit every instinct I had. I scanned the area, searching for whatever had her on edge, my body already in defense mode.

"Kensi," I tried again, this time placing my hand on her arm. Her head snapped toward me, and the look in her eyes nearly knocked me off my feet. Wide, haunted—they weren't the eyes of someone present. They were the eyes of someone who'd just seen their past resurface, dragging every demon back with it.

"We need to go," she said, her voice a thin thread of steel barely holding together. "Now."

I nodded. No questions—not yet. Whatever had her ready to bolt could wait until we were somewhere safe. I caught Stephen's eye, and his subtle nod told me he was already on it, gathering our things with quiet efficiency. He shifted slightly, moving Missy behind him, his stance protective but controlled, just like we'd always trained.

I moved closer to Kensi, resting a steady hand on the small of her back. The warmth of my palm felt like the only barrier between her and whatever storm was threatening to break. "Let's move," I said, my voice calm but firm.

As we weaved through the crowd, every movement felt sharper, every face a potential threat. My senses were dialed to a razor's edge, the years of training clicking into place. My job had always been to protect, to keep danger at bay. But this was different. This was personal.

When we reached the truck, I opened the door and ushered Kensi inside before taking one last look at the crowd. The faces blurred together—laughing, oblivious, or focused on their own lives. None of them gave away what had set Kensi off, but that didn't ease the tension coiling tighter in my chest.

Sliding into the driver's seat, I glanced back at her. Kensi was half in shadow, her face unreadable but her shoulders rigid.

"Kensi," I said, keeping my voice low, steady. "Whatever this is, I'm here. You're not facing it alone."

Her eyes flicked toward me, and for a moment, the fear gave way to something else—trust, maybe, or the beginnings of it. She nodded, the movement small but deliberate, as if leaning into that truth one step at a time.

The drive back to The Anchor was silent. Stephen stayed focused on the road, Missy close to him in the backseat, her confusion clear but unspoken. Kensi didn't say another word, her arms wrapped tightly around herself like she could hold her own pieces together.

When we reached The Anchor, we didn't waste time. The parking lot was dark and quiet, but the unease hadn't left me. I guided Kensi inside, keeping her close. We moved straight to the back, where the door to StealthWave's office waited.

Stephen punched in the code, and the door clicked open. The cool air of the room hit us, its stark functionality a sharp contrast to the warmth of the bar above. Monitors cast their glow over the walls, showing every angle of The Anchor and its surroundings.

"Get them settled," I told Stephen quietly, nodding toward Kensi and Missy. He didn't hesitate, leading Missy to a chair and murmuring reassurances I didn't catch. His hand lingered at her back for a moment longer than necessary.

I turned my attention to the monitors, scanning the feeds for anything out of place. My fingers itched for action, but this wasn't a battlefield—it was a chessboard. Every move needed to count.

Stephen joined me, his voice cutting through the quiet. "We need to lock this down," he said, already tapping at the keyboard. "If something's coming, we can't afford to be unprepared."

He didn't need to say it twice. My focus zeroed in, adrenaline sharpening every movement. "Agreed. First, we figure out what we're dealing with."

The weight of Kensi's fear was still heavy in the air, but now it was mixed with a resolve that settled in my chest. I glanced back at her, sitting stiff and silent beside Missy, her eyes darting to the screens like they might hold the answer.

"Kensi," I said, my tone gentler this time. "Whatever this is, we'll handle it. But I need to know what we're up against."

Her gaze met mine, and for a long moment, she didn't speak. Then, slowly, she nodded. It wasn't much, but it was enough.

This wasn't just a job anymore. It wasn't even just about keeping her safe. It was about being the person she could trust, the one who wouldn't let her down.

And I wasn't about to fail.

20

KENSI

The ride back to Liberty was heavy—the kind of quiet that presses on you, thick with everything unsaid. My thoughts were a mess: wild, loud, refusing to settle. I didn't question it when Wyatt steered us toward The Anchor instead of my cottage. I was too distracted to care, following him and Stephen through the back door without a word.

It wasn't until we headed down a staircase I'd never noticed before that my brain kicked into gear. The air was colder here, sterile. And when we stepped into the room at the bottom, I stopped dead in my tracks. It wasn't just unexpected—it was unreal.

The place looked like something out of a spy movie: walls lined with monitors streaming security footage, sleek desks loaded with computers humming softly. The Anchor had always been welcoming and warm. This? This was something else entirely.

Missy's voice broke the spell, sharp and clear. "What is this? How long has this been here?"

Wyatt turned to face us, his expression calm but guarded, like he'd been waiting for this moment. "This is StealthWave Security," he said, his voice steady, reassuring. "Stephen and I built it before we reopened The Anchor. It's...our private security company."

I blinked, trying to process what he'd just said. Private security? Wyatt and Stephen? The pieces started falling into place—the security at my house, their unshakable calm when things got dicey. It all made sense now. Too much sense.

And that's when the panic hit. My past wasn't just a ghost trailing behind me anymore; it was here, alive, and dangerous. And now, I'd pulled these people—Missy, Wyatt, Stephen—right into its path.

Missy seemed to take it in stride, nodding as she glanced around the room, her gaze eventually landing on Stephen, who was typing something on one of the computers. But me? My heart was pounding, my chest tightening as the reality of it all came crashing down.

Wyatt stepped closer, his movements slow, careful, like he didn't want to spook me. He gestured to a chair, and Missy's gentle nudge was all it took for me to sit, my legs too shaky to argue.

When I was finally seated, Wyatt knelt in front of me, his eyes locking onto mine with a warmth that was out of place in this cold, high-tech room. "Kensi," he said softly, his voice low and steady, "we want to help you. But we need to know what's going on. Can you tell us what you saw?"

His words cut through the chaos in my head, grounding me. I could feel the tension radiating from him—not anger, but focus. Determination. Like he was trying to will me into trusting him.

I opened my mouth, but the words caught in my throat. The image of Jimmy Golden flashed in my mind: his smirk, his presence, the weight of everything he represented.

Finally, I forced the words out, each one feeling heavier than the last. "I saw Jimmy G." My voice was barely audible, trembling. "Jimmy Golden. He's...he's my father's right-hand man."

Wyatt didn't flinch, didn't interrupt. He just listened, his gaze steady.

"If he's here, my father knows where I am. Which means Luka does too."

The silence that followed was deafening, my words hanging in the air. When I finally dared to look up, Wyatt's jaw was set, his fists clenched at his sides. But his eyes? They were soft, steady—a promise written in their depths.

"We'll keep you safe," he said firmly, every word hitting like a hammer. "You have my word."

Something inside me cracked at his tone—not fear, but something I didn't want to name for fear of losing it. Hope.

But it wasn't enough to drown out the fear. "I can't stay here," I said, my voice rising with panic. "I can't drag you all into this. You don't understand—these people don't stop. They don't care who gets hurt."

Wyatt rose as I stood, his calm demeanor never wavering. "Kensi," he said, his tone firm but kind, "running isn't going to solve this. It'll only put you in more danger."

He gestured toward the monitors, the computers, the entire room. "We've built this for situations like this. You're not dragging us into anything. We're choosing to be here, to stand with you. You're not alone."

His words stopped me in my tracks. I wanted to argue, to run, to shove the responsibility back onto my own shoulders where it belonged. But Wyatt wasn't budging.

"You don't have to face this by yourself," he continued, his voice softening. "Let us help you. Let me protect you."

My resolve faltered, the weight of his words sinking in. My gaze shifted to Missy, who was watching me with the same quiet determination, her fingers knotted together in her lap. Then to Stephen, who'd stopped typing, his calm presence like a silent agreement with everything Wyatt had said.

For the first time in a long time, I didn't feel like I was standing alone on the edge of a cliff.

"Okay," I whispered, the word shaky but real. "Okay, I'll stay. But I don't want anyone getting hurt because of me."

Wyatt nodded, his expression softening just slightly. "We'll take precautions. We've faced danger before, and we'll face this too. Together."

Something in his voice broke through the walls I'd spent years building around myself. For the first time, I let myself believe it. Just a little.

Hope. It was small, it was fragile, but it was there.

21

KENSI

The past month in Liberty had been like living in a bubble—one of those perfect, shiny ones you don't want to pop. Waking up each morning, excited to immerse myself in the inn's buzz, the smell of brewing coffee, and listening to guests' stories, had quickly become my new normal. It was strange how easily I slipped into the rhythm there, handling everything from making beds and pulling weeds to sorting out the paperwork chaos. It was busy work, but in a good way, making me feel part of something bigger than myself for the first time in a long time.

The inn's gardens had become my personal retreat. There was something about digging in the dirt and watching things grow that was incredibly satisfying. It was a place where my mind could wander, where I dared to think about a future without looking over my shoulder. The people in Liberty had been amazing, too, welcoming me with open arms and making me feel like I belonged—which was both wonderful and a bit scary.

That feeling of safety had become normal. Bit by bit, I found myself dropping my guard, letting the New York nightmares and the constant edge I used to live on fade into the background. It was a sneaky sort of peace, one I was all too happy to sink into.

Hanging out with Missy, Wyatt, and Stephen had become the highlight of my days. We fell into an easy friendship, sharing dinners, late-night heart-to-hearts, and random trips around town. Laughing had become my new favorite hobby, something I hadn't realized I missed until now. Missy was the sister I'd never had.

Even Wyatt and Stephen appeared to have mellowed, their ever-alert tendencies easing a bit more each day. Seeing them genuinely smile and throw their heads back in laughter made me believe we'd somehow managed to slip under the radar. Wyatt had been a rock, offering a kind of silent support that was healing in ways I hadn't known I needed.

One quiet evening, they explained their process in detail, showing me maps on their computers, lists of contacts they'd reached out to, and surveillance footage they monitored daily. The depth of their commitment to ensuring my safety was both humbling and overwhelming. "We've got a network of eyes and ears, Kensi. Nothing gets past us without a check and double-check," Wyatt had said, his voice steady and sure. Stephen, ever the tech wizard, nodded in agreement, his fingers dancing across a keyboard as he pulled up encrypted files that tracked any potential threats. Their profession-alism and dedication alleviated my anxiety.

Then, four weeks to the day after the concert, the call came. A music producer in Nashville, who had attended the concert as a friend of the family who had lost their husband and father, reached out to offer Wyatt an opportunity to compete on a new reality television show called *Real American Country*.

When he told Stephen, Missy, and me about it after closing down The Anchor one evening, the news was a shock. It was also a reminder of the world beyond Liberty's borders. The decision wasn't easy for Wyatt; I could see the conflict in his eyes, and I knew it hinged on me.

"You have a chance to make a difference, Wyatt. Not just for you, but for others who have given so much," I told him, my voice steady despite the turmoil inside me.

His gratitude was unmistakable, but he remained hesitant. "I'm doing this because I believe in it, Kensi. But I don't feel right about leaving you," he admitted.

"I'll be okay here. You've taught me that much."

Wyatt's eyes met mine, searching for reassurance. "I'm serious, Kensi. This is a big opportunity, but I won't go if it means leaving you unprotected."

"You won't be leaving me unprotected," I assured him, my voice steady even as there was a slight ache in my chest. "Stephen and Missy are here. And besides, you've set up everything to make sure I'm safe. I'll be fine."

He sighed, his gaze still conflicted, softening in a way that made my resolve falter. "It's just, I've gotten used to being around, making sure you're okay."

His words made me feel things. There was always a current of gratitude, but there was also an unnamed emotion I wasn't ready to face. Wyatt had become my closest ally, someone who had shown me unwavering kindness without expecting anything in return.

I had promised myself not to blur any lines—not while I was still tied to a life I was trying to escape. And yet, I'd be lying if I said I wouldn't miss him. His presence had been my lifeline, making me feel things in ways I couldn't fully explain.

"And I appreciate that more than you know," I said, stepping closer. "You've done so much for me already. It's time you did something for yourself. And what an amazing opportunity."

Wyatt nodded slowly, a small smile tugging at his lips. "Alright, I'll do it. But you have to promise to call me if anything happens. I don't care what time it is, just call."

"I promise," I said, feeling a mix of relief and sadness at the prospect of him leaving.

Stephen clapped Wyatt on the back, breaking the tension. "Looks like we've got ourselves a future country star. Better start practicing those autographs."

Missy grinned, her excitement for Wyatt evident. "We'll be rooting for you every step of the way."

As the night wore on, we celebrated Wyatt's upcoming adventure. He was an amazing man who had given so much for so many. Sure, I'd miss him. But this was something I could tell he wanted, even if he'd been too afraid to reach for it. He'd been here for me, so I knew I had to be there for him.

22

WYATT

Did I ever imagine performing on a real stage? No. It had been just for me—a way to cope with the pain life had thrown my way. Music had gotten me through my dad's death when I was in high school and, later, when I came home from the SEALs. I'd turned to it as an outlet, a distraction, a lifeline.

Four weeks to the day after the benefit concert, I was back at The Anchor, lost in the rhythm of strumming my guitar, when my phone buzzed on the table beside me. I glanced over and saw an unfamiliar number flash across the screen. Squinting in confusion, I picked up the call.

"Hey, Wyatt, it's Jim Lucas," he said, his tone cordial. "I was at that benefit concert you played a few weeks back."

"Yeah, I remember," I replied hesitantly, wondering what this call was about.

I'd met Jim after my set at the concert. He was a music producer from Nashville, Tennessee, who happened to be a friend of the family the concert had been honoring. He'd inquired whether I'd be open to other opportunities like the one I'd just been a part of. After telling him I'd be open to discussing it if it came up, he insisted on exchanging numbers. Now I was wondering if I'd made a mistake, because I was not expecting a call this soon after.

"Listen, I have an opportunity for you," he continued. "There's a new reality television show called *Real American Country* starting up, and I think you'd be perfect for it. It's a twelve-week competition in Nashville for country music artists."

My heart skipped a beat as I tried to process his words. "That's... Wow, that's a lot."

"Think of it as a chance to make a difference, Wyatt," Jim urged. "As a veteran myself, I see great potential in you using this platform to draw attention to the needs of veterans and their families. I saw what you did in just one night. Imagine if you had weeks."

His words struck a chord within me, but I still hesitated. I didn't want to go to Nashville. I had two businesses in Liberty to take care of. Not to mention, there was a real threat out there against Kensi.

"Can I think about it?" I asked, knowing that if I answered immediately, I would say no.

There was a moment of silence before Jim shifted in his seat. "I think that would be a good idea, son. If you could let me know in a day or two, that would be great."

I thanked him and hung up the call.

Sitting in StealthWave's bunker-like office, I listened as Stephen told me for the fourth time that Kensi could not be the reason I passed up Jim's offer.

"Look, Wyatt," he began, "I know you're worried about leaving her, but we've got this. You trust me and the team, right?"

"Of course I do," I replied, shoving my hands into my pockets. "It's just hard to let go."

Stephen's gaze softened, and he clapped a hand onto my shoulder. "I get it. But if you don't go to Nashville and take this opportunity, I'll personally put you on a plane and make sure your ticket is one-way with no option for return."

I chuckled, knowing he was partly joking, but also recognizing the truth in his words. This was a huge opportunity. It was one I'd probably never get again.

Kensi could be nothing more than a friend, yet that didn't stop my heart from wanting what it couldn't have. Maybe putting some space between us by going to Nashville would do me some good. I trusted Stephen and my team to keep her safe, and Missy was more than capable of running The Anchor in my absence. There really wasn't a reason not to go.

Telling Missy and Kensi had been the hardest part. I opted to do it after closing down The Anchor one evening. We were only open for lunch on Sundays, so it was still early in the evening. We'd all crowded around one of the tables.

I cleared my throat and started to tell them about Jim's call. Missy and Kensi both looked far more excited about the opportunity than I'd yet to feel.

"You understand that means you and Stephen will have to run The Anchor—together?" I asked Missy.

With an affronted look, she retorted, "And?"

Glancing at Stephen, who was biting back the smile he always wore when he looked at Missy, I turned back to her and said, "I would like this place to be standing when I get back."

Kensi and Stephen both laughed while Missy rolled her eyes and said, "Wyatt, I practically run this place every single day whether the two of you are here or not. How will this be any different?"

She wasn't wrong. I held her stare and watched for any indicator that she was just telling me what she thought I needed to hear. But I knew better. She wouldn't have said it if she didn't mean it.

Turning to look at Kensi, I asked, "Do you have any thoughts on it?"

What I was really asking was, "Do you feel safe enough for me to leave? Because if you don't, I'll stay." And somewhere in the recesses of my mind, I was begging her to tell me to stay. Instead, she studied me for several beats before reaching out and putting a hand on my arm.

"You have a chance to make a difference, Wyatt. Not just for you, but for others who have given so much," she said. "I'll be okay here. You've taught me that much."

With that, I apparently no longer had a reason not to go.

* * *

With Kensi's encouragement still echoing in my mind, I left Liberty behind and stepped into the unknown. As the sedan wound its way through Nashville, I couldn't help but reflect on how I got here —and where things could potentially go. This wasn't just a change of scenery; it felt like crossing into a whole new life.

The house they'd put us in was massive, the kind of place you see on TV and think can't possibly be real. A colonial-style farmhouse sitting on six acres, with every inch polished and sprawling. I couldn't help but pause as I stepped inside, taking in the towering ceilings and pristine details. It was a far cry from the simple comfort of The Anchor, and for a moment, I felt like a fish out of water.

The house was alive with energy—contestants chatting, production crews buzzing around like clockwork. Everyone seemed at ease, laughing and introducing themselves like they were old friends. I found myself hanging back, observing. It wasn't nerves exactly, but this world wasn't mine. I wasn't here chasing a record deal. This wasn't my dream.

Even so, I couldn't ignore the camaraderie forming around me. Names and faces blurred together at first—Austin Blake's easy grin, Nash Montgomery's back-slap welcome, and Willow Gracin's bright eyes and infectious laugh. The patio came alive as Austin broke out his guitar, and before long, the night was filled with music. The way these folks slipped into harmonies, letting the songs carry them, was something special. I stayed off to the side, taking it all in, my mind drifting to Liberty—and to Kensi.

Kensi. She'd been in my thoughts since the moment I left, her image as steady as a heartbeat. I thought about calling her but held back. Instead, I sent a quick text to the group chat with Kensi, Missy, and Stephen. Their replies came back fast—Missy's humor, Stephen's dry wit, and Kensi's simple encouragement anchoring me more than they probably realized.

This wasn't my dream, but it was a chance to do something for the people I cared about, to make them proud. The Anchor, the team at

StealthWave, and the life I'd been carving out back home—those were my dreams. And yeah, if I let myself admit it, maybe Kensi was part of that picture too.

I wasn't here for fame or fortune, but I'd give this my all because it mattered to them. And because, if nothing else, Liberty and the people there deserved to know I wouldn't let them down.

23

KENSI

My feet ached with every step I took away from the inn's front desk, the last guest's words of gratitude lingering in the air behind me. It had been one of those long, drawn-out days where the sun's retreat doesn't promise rest, just the end of daylight. The sky, a canvas of blues and purples, had already kissed the day goodbye, leaving only the melancholy echo of twilight.

I tugged off my gold-embossed name tag that simply read Kensi and slipped it into my purse. Each step toward my house was slug-gish, as if I were wading through molasses, my body protesting the extended hours on my feet. As I dug through my purse for my keys, my phone began to buzz rather insistently. Missy's name flashed across the screen.

"Hey, girl," I answered, trying to inject a semblance of energy into my voice.

"We're really slow tonight, and if I have to hear one more of Stephen's jokes, I might throw something at him. Please come save me or at least keep me company," Missy's persuasive tone came through the line, tinged with desperation and the ambient noise of clinking glasses in the background.

"Miss, I can't," I said, pinching the bridge of my nose. "I'm beat.

Evelyn needed me to cover her shift today, and now I'm running on fumes."

"Aw, I'm sorry," she said, her voice full of understanding.

"Raincheck?" I offered, guilt mixing with relief as I unlocked my front door.

"Raincheck. Get some rest—you deserve it," she conceded. "See you soon?"

"Promise." With that, I ended the call, my thumb lingering over Wyatt's last message before I tucked the phone away. The idea of socializing was not at the top of the list of things I wanted to do after an exhausting marathon at work that spanned the last fourteen hours. Evelyn had been apologetic when she asked me to cover for her unexpected leave mid-day, but duty called, and I answered.

As I slipped off my shoes, the tension in my shoulders began to unwind, tendrils of stress unfurling. This little corner of the world was mine. My escape from the suffocating luxury of my past had led me to a life where I was just Kensi, free from the constraints of my former self. And I loved everything about it.

Sinking into the couch cushions, I clicked on the TV, letting the familiar drone fill the space around me. My gaze fell on the clock, its hands inching beyond the half-hour mark. 8:30 PM—the digital numbers were indifferent to my spent state. I draped an afghan across my legs, a patchwork of blues and greens. The TV's glow bathed the room in a wash of shifting light and shadows, but the murmurs of a sitcom I'd seen a dozen times before became white noise to my weary mind.

My eyelids grew heavy, and I surrendered to the quiet embrace of exhaustion, the worries of the day receding like the tide. The last thing I remembered was the laugh track from the television, a distant echo to my fading consciousness. What I hadn't heard, couldn't have heard in my unintended slumber, was the silent intrusion that turned my simple evening into a nightmare.

Waking up was disorienting, my head thick and heavy, every thought slipping through my mind like sand. My limbs were heavy, and a dull ache pulsed at the base of my skull. The soft fabric of my pajamas clung to my skin—a small comfort until I took in my surroundings. Instead of the cozy, familiar living space I'd fallen asleep in, I was back in the extravagant penthouse I'd given up everything to escape six months earlier.

I tried to sit up, but a wave of nausea hit me, forcing me to steady myself against the silk sheets—a cruel reminder of where I was. The silk, once a luxury, was now a traitor's caress against my skin, trapping me in this nightmare with its softness. The gilded frames and ornate furnishings sneered at me from every corner, their presence as cold and unforgiving as the marble floors beneath my feet. This penthouse, a palace to some, was my personal hell—the place I had clawed my way out of with nothing but raw desperation as my strength.

Every nerve in my body buzzed with a sickly unease, my senses dulled even though I was very aware of the faint chemical taste in my mouth and the lingering dizziness that clouded my mind. Whatever I'd been given was wearing off, but not fast enough to quell the surge of panic rising in my chest.

"Please, no," the words slipped from between my lips, a prayer to a god of dreams who turned a deaf ear to my plight. The trembling started at my fingertips, spreading like ripples through my body.

I stood, legs unsteady, as if the floor beneath them was the pitching deck of a storm-tossed ship. My heart hammered a frantic rhythm, a staccato beat urging me to flee, to wake up from this horror. But the towering windows, the cityscape beyond, all screamed the truth with silent vehemence—I was back in the penthouse, back to a life I thought I'd left behind forever.

Panic seeped into my veins like poison, each heartbeat pounding a terrifying rhythm of fear. My memories, once suppressed, now clawed their way to the forefront, replaying those last desperate days in stark relief. The thought gnawed at me, relentless and cruel: they had found me.

How? Why now? The questions spiraled, each more frantic than the last, as the chilling realization settled in: I was not safe. The safety and peace I'd found in Liberty, the friendships and fragile sense of belonging—all of it playing out like a crude joke now.

In that moment, the terror was all-consuming. It was not just the fear of being back in the penthouse but the utter violation of my sanctuary, my new life. They had come into my home, my refuge, and torn me away from it. The thought of Missy, Wyatt, Stephen... they believed I was safe, just as I had started to. The betrayal of that safety, the shattering of that illusion, left me reeling.

As I sat there, trying to steady my breathing, trying to force my mind to work, to plan, to find a way out, the crushing reality of my situation settled over me. I was alone, back in the lion's den, with no immediate escape. But I had to get out, had to find a way back to Liberty, back to safety, back to Wyatt.

That thought hit me like a jolt, sharper than any fear. Wyatt. In the chaos of my thoughts and the terror of my situation, the realization of what he had come to mean to me cut through the darkness.

The idea of being trapped again, of being pulled back into a life I had fought so hard to escape, was an unbearable thought. But now, the fight was different. It wasn't just about escaping a physical place or a legal bond; it was about escaping to a life where my heart had started to plant its roots, however tentatively.

The irony wasn't lost on me. Here I was, kidnapped and brought back to a cage by a man who claimed me, yet all I could think about was another. Wyatt's silent support, his understanding, and the shared moments of laughter and peace had offered me a glimpse into a world I wanted to belong to—a world where I could be free, truly free.

As the reality of my situation pressed in, my resolve hardened. I needed to escape, not just for my own sake but to protect the fragile hope for a different life that had started to take root. I wouldn't let my story end here—not when a new chapter had just begun to unfold, not when I had finally found a reason to fight for something more than just survival.

24

WYATT

I squinted against the glare of studio lights, my guitar cradled in my arms like an old friend. The vocal coach, a lady with an obvious penchant for perfection, gestured emphatically from behind the sound booth's glass. "Wyatt, remember to open up on those high notes. Let it resonate," she called out, her words slicing through the melody I was trying to nail down.

I nodded, adjusting my posture and strumming the opening chords again. Back at The Anchor, my audience barely looked up from their drinks. Here, every note felt dissected. It wasn't just singing —it was performance, something I wasn't sure I wanted to master.

"Again, but this time, think about the emotion behind the song. Your voice has to carry that story," the coach instructed, her patience waning in the face of the ticking clock. I appreciated her guidance, even if part of me longed for the simplicity of pouring drinks rather than pouring my soul into a microphone.

I tried, letting her advice sink in, and found the thread of the melody again. By the time the session wrapped, I could feel the difference—small improvements carving out the rough edges. But as I stepped out of the booth, the controlled chaos of the studio hit me. Crew members buzzed past with clipboards, cameras rolled into position, and producers threw around words like "branding" and "star quality."

None of it felt like me.

They shuffled me from one spot to another, positioning me in front of backdrops as fake as the smiles they were asking me to put on. "Just act natural," they'd say, which only worked to make the whole setup feel even more staged. The cameras, the bright lights—it was all about as far from natural as you could get. I'd stared down enemy combatants with less discomfort. But their words pushed me to try.

"Great energy, Wyatt! Just what we're looking for," one of the producers said after a take, his enthusiasm genuine, even if it didn't make me feel any less like a camel in an ice storm.

When I finally got a break, I leaned against the wall with a water bottle, taking a long drink. My mind wandered back to Texas, to the quiet of home—the one place where I didn't have to perform. Running The Anchor and StealthWave was real, grounding. But I reminded myself why I'd agreed to this. If stepping into the spotlight meant bringing attention to the ones still in the shadows—the brothers and sisters I served with—it'd be worth every awkward moment.

"Ready for the rest of the shoot?" someone called, pulling me back.

"Yeah, let's do it," I said, keeping my tone steady and reminding myself that I'd faced tougher situations than this. I walked over to the set, repeating the words I'd lived by: adapt and overcome.

Standing on the taped X, the lights blazed down like a Texas summer. I squinted, adjusting to the brightness, feeling every set of eyes and cameras zeroed in on me. The scene around me was all props—a guitar, a barn door facade—and I tried to just go with it. Sure, I was definitely an outsider, a guy playing a part. But I stayed open to the experience, willing to see where this road might lead.

"Remember, Wyatt, the women are going to fall in love with you, and the men—they're gonna wanna be you," one of the producers said, his grin wide and overconfident. He winked, like we were sharing some kind of joke. I didn't laugh.

A crew member slipped behind me, threading a microphone wire down my shirt, the chill of the metal a sharp contrast to the heat building under my collar. The producer's words echoed, clashing with everything I believed in.

This wasn't why I was here. It wasn't about being admired or envied, about playing some larger-than-life cowboy. The cameras, the lights—all of it was just a tool, a way to draw attention to something bigger than me. Something that mattered.

"Tell us about why you joined *Real American Country*, Wyatt," another producer prompted, her eyes expectant behind the camera. I took a deep breath, pushing aside the discomfort, and focused on the real reason I'd stepped into this circus ring.

"Truth is, I'm not here for the reasons you might think," I began, finding my voice. "It's about giving voice to those who serve quietly, without expectation of recognition. Their stories aren't heard nearly enough." I kept it brief yet sincere, speaking of service and sacrifice.

I spoke of my time in the military, the brothers and sisters I served with, and the families back home who lived in the constant shadow of sacrifice. My voice found its strength. "I was given a chance to shine a light on those serving and their families. It's a story that needs to be told, and if my being here can help even a little, then it's worth it," I explained, my commitment unwavering.

I wasn't sure if they grasped the depth of my words, but something flickered in their expressions—acknowledgment, maybe even respect.

But that brief connection was gone as fast as it came, replaced by the bright, artificial glare of a staged photoshoot. I stepped onto the set, squinting a little under the harsh lights while photographers directed me. The snap of shutters and the hum of the lighting gear filled the air, creating this strange rhythm I wasn't used to.

"All right, Wyatt, just give us a casual stance," one of the photographers called out, motioning for me to loosen up. Casual? Sure, I'd handled high-stress missions, even kept calm under fire, but "casual" in front of a camera? That was a different story. I shifted, trying to look relaxed, but it was as though my body was fighting me at every turn.

"Chin up, shoulders back," another voice added, and I went through the motions, feeling more like a mannequin than myself. Each flash reminded me that these pictures would be out there, analyzed by strangers who didn't know the first thing about me.

"Let's see that charm, Wyatt. You're a natural," someone called from the sidelines. I tried to let the words sink in, but they rang hollow. There was nothing "natural" about most of this.

"Think of someone who makes you smile," someone suggested from behind the lens.

Her words broke through my guard, slipping right past my defenses to a memory that had nothing to do with this artificial setup. Kensi. I remembered the way she looked at me that day out on the back patio of The Anchor—sunlight catching in her hair, her eyes narrowing as she challenged me, half-serious and half-joking, to name one good reason I didn't belong in Nashville. I'd tried to keep my answer light, to play it off, but the way she'd looked at me—like she saw right through me, straight to everything I tried to hide— made me falter. I'd never felt so exposed and yet somehow understood.

And just like that, my armor fell away. A real smile tugged at the corners of my mouth, genuine and unguarded, like a piece of home I'd almost forgotten.

"Perfect, Wyatt. That's the shot right there," the photographer exclaimed, a note of triumph in her voice as she captured the image.

"Keep that up, cowboy," she said with a grin, sensing the shift in me. "Hold on to that feeling."

I held onto it, alright. Held onto it like a lifeline, because in that moment, it was Kensi's belief and encouragement that saw me through the glare of the lights and the click of the camera.

～

THE HALLS WERE BUZZING, every corner filled with the sound of someone warming up their voice or strumming through their set. We were all in our own little worlds, but together. There were folks everywhere tuning guitars and belting out notes, trying to nail every part of their performance. After spending the week getting grilled by vocal coaches and running through our songs until they were stuck in our heads, the air was thick with focus. Today was different, though. Today, the real deal was breathing down our necks.

The tension backstage was like a Texan pre-storm sky, heavy and charged. Everyone was gearing up, pouring every ounce of their soul into their performances. Being slated to close the show added an extra layer of anticipation to my wait. Watching my fellow contestants take the stage one by one, I could feel the bar being raised with each performance, the energy backstage both supportive and competitive.

When my turn finally came, the reality of the moment sank in. Strapping on my guitar was like arming myself for battle, the familiar strings under my fingers readying me. The plucky opening chords of Joe Diffie's *Pick Up Man* flowed through me like a current, and I surrendered to its rhythm. My fingers danced across the strings, each strum a note in the story I was telling. Humor and lightness filled my voice as the lyrics spilled out—a tribute to simpler times, to joyrides in pickup trucks, and the freedom of a country road. The crowd's energy surged with mine.

I leaned into every chord, the guitar a part of me as much as my own heartbeat. There was no thought, just the music and the movement; it was an act as natural as breathing. The stage was no longer a platform but a wide-open field where I ran unfettered. I let loose, allowing myself to fully inhabit the song, my guitar an extension of my expression. It was like breaking free from a shell, the joy of performing, of sharing this piece of myself, eclipsing any lingering nerves.

By the time the last chord faded, my face ached from the smile that had been permanently plastered there. As I handed off my guitar to one of the crew members, I was vaguely aware of the whispers starting to ripple through the backstage area. A couple of people offered comments like, "That's the way to do it!" and "You'd have my vote if I could." The one I hadn't expected to hear was the murmured, "He's the one to beat."

The energy from the performance still pulsed through my veins as I navigated the maze of backstage corridors, the buzz from the crowd and the echo of my guitar fading into a surreal backdrop. The dressing room was almost oppressively quiet compared to the adrenaline-fueled crowd that had fueled me just moments ago. In the dressing room, I traded the borrowed clothes for my own, then grabbed the lockbox they'd stored my keys, wallet, and cell phone in and unlocked it.

But as the lid swung open, my eyes caught on the persistent glow of notifications blanketing the screen of my phone. Missed calls stacked upon missed calls—all from Stephen. My fingers went cold around the device. It wasn't like him to hammer at the call button; something was wrong, something serious. The kind of serious that used to send me into hot zones with little more than my wits and my team.

The phone vibrated once more, a jarring pulse that cut through the silence of the room.

"Talk to me," I said, my voice steady despite the turmoil churning inside me. Stephen's response was a gut punch I hadn't been braced for.

His voice was laced with the strain of bearing news no one wants to deliver. "It's not good, Wyatt. They got her."

Those words detonated in the quiet of the dressing room, echoing off the walls and inside my skull. My jaw clenched, bracing for the aftershock.

"I don't know how, but Jimmy G and two other guys I'm still working to identify pulled a smash-and-grab a few hours ago. I'm sorry, Wyatt. They took her. They took Kensi."

The words hit me like a physical blow, each one a hammer strike against the foundation we'd built over the past months. The safety net we'd meticulously woven around Kensi, the layers of security— all of it had been torn apart in a matter of moments. The room spun slightly as I forced myself to breathe, to think past the panic that clawed at my throat.

My fist collided with the wall as I cursed loudly, a futile attempt to channel the surge of helplessness tearing through me. Plaster dust settled over my knuckles like an accusation as I watched it mix with the blood already beginning to bead on the surface of my skin.

"Where are you now? What's our next move?" I demanded, pacing the length of the dressing room. My voice was a blade, cutting through the fog of shock, seeking something solid in the chaos.

Stephen was already in motion—I knew he would be—but we had to be smart, calculated.

"Already on the road, heading towards the last known location," Stephen's reply came quick, his words a lifeline thrown into the maelstrom of my thoughts. "I need you to stay put until I can get a handle on this. We play this wrong and—"

"Play this wrong?" I snapped back, the soldier in me rising to the surface, taking command where the man was failing. "This isn't a game, Stephen. This is Kensi."

"Exactly why we need to be smart about it, Wyatt." His tone was steady, a counterbalance to the storm inside me. "Let me do what I do best. Keep your head clear. She needs that from you right now."

"Clear," I muttered, repeating the word like a mantra. I had to compartmentalize, had to shove the terror aside and lock it down tight. There was no room for error, not when her life hung in the balance.

"Keep me updated," I said, finally stilling my restless movements. My gaze fell to the blood my knuckles had left on the wall, a glaring reminder of the stakes. "Every minute, Stephen. I mean it."

"Will do," he assured me before the line went dead, leaving me alone with the task of waiting and the echo of a promise I intended to keep.

I didn't doubt that Stephen was as committed to this as I was, maybe more. He understood the stakes, understood what Kensi meant to me, to all of us.

Hanging up, I leaned against the wall, feeling the cold seep into my back as a relentless wave of dread washed over me. My hands shook, my breaths coming short and shallow, and anger—hot, consuming—rose up, fighting to take over. Kensi's face kept flashing in my mind: her bright, confident eyes, the way her laugh cut through any darkness, her voice steady as she'd encouraged me to go after this new path. She'd believed in me, believed in the security we'd set up to keep her safe. And I'd walked right into Nashville, sure she was protected.

That faith she'd put in us, in me, twisted like a knife in my gut. She was the one who pushed me to take this shot, and I'd left her behind, thinking she'd be fine. Going to Nashville was supposed to be about honoring something bigger than myself. Now, I couldn't be convinced it wasn't the biggest mistake I'd ever made.

The applause, the noise, the pride I'd carried only minutes before —it all burned away, turning to ash. In its place was a single, pulsing need: to find her, to bring her back, to make this right.

25

WYATT

Under the harsh fluorescent lights of the backstage area, my fingers worked the phone with urgency, dialing Jim Lucas, the music producer who'd been instrumental in landing me this contract. The gravity of the situation settled in my stomach like lead as the call connected.

"Jim, this is Wyatt Turner. I need a favor, and it's urgent," I began, without preamble. The calm in my voice was forced, my mind racing with the implications of what I was about to ask.

Jim's response was immediate, a mix of concern and professionalism. "What's going on, Wyatt?"

I cut in, the words tumbling out in a rush. "I need to get out of Nashville, back to Liberty, as soon as possible."

There was a pause on the other end, the kind that filled the space between desperation and reality. "Wyatt, I'm not sure I understand. You signed a contract."

"It's not about the show, Jim," I explained, hesitant to give too many details. But I was at a point where I knew I had to communicate the urgency of the situation if I was going to make any kind of progress. "Someone very important to me is in serious danger. I need to get back to Texas and find her before something worse happens."

There was a long silence on the other end of the call. "I'll make some calls, see what I can do to help, but I can't promise anything right away. In the meantime, you've got to keep up your end. You're a professional, and this show is a big deal."

His words were supposed to make me feel better, but they made me feel trapped. Yet, the gravity of his position wasn't lost on me. "I get it, I do. But please, do whatever you can. She's—" My words faltered. "She's everything, Jim."

Another silence followed before he said, "Give me some time. I'll see what I can do."

Calling Stephen next, I relayed the conversation, my voice steady but the undercurrent of fear palpable. "Keep me in the loop with any updates. I've got to play along here until we figure something out."

I had never felt so completely helpless in my entire life.

Slipping my phone back into my pocket, the conversation with Jim pressed heavily on my mind as I made my way through the labyrinth of backstage corridors. Despite the urgency gnawing at my insides, I forced my steps to be measured and calm—far from how I was feeling.

The shuttle waited outside, ready to ferry us back to the mansion. The air was thick with a cocktail of emotions as I boarded—relief, excitement, and fatigue mingling in the close confines of the vehicle. My fellow contestants were abuzz with post-performance adrenaline, rehashing their moments on stage, their voices a steady hum of shared experiences and lingering nerves.

I was the last one on, the door closing behind me with a soft click. I settled into a seat near the back, my mind a million miles away from the laughter and conversation that filled the space.

As the bus pulled away, the lights of Nashville receding into the night, I found myself caught between the worlds of my fellow contestants and the silent battle raging within. One part of me, tethered to the duty and feelings I'd developed for Kensi, begged to break free and rush to her aid. Yet another part, bound by contracts and the expectations of professional obligations, held me in place. This war of opposing forces left me feeling like a marionette, dancing on strings pulled by fate and circumstance.

THE VIBRATION of my phone broke the silence of the early morning. Stephen's name flashed across the screen.

"Stephen, tell me you have good news," I said, my heart racing in anticipation of his words.

"A private jet took off from Houston around 11:00 p.m. last night and landed in New York a few hours later," Stephen's voice was firm, indicating the urgency and significance of the lead. "Our analysis suggests that Kensi could be on that jet. It's a solid lead—the best we've had so far."

The information sent a jolt through me. A brief wave of fear washed over me, hot anger burned in my throat, and a surge of icy determination filled my veins. "Do we have eyes on the ground there?" I asked, already mentally mapping out the next steps.

"We're on it," Stephen assured me. "I've got one of our guys, Mike. He was on assignment in Charlotte but is already on a flight to New York. He knows the city and has the contacts we need to start our search the moment he lands."

Moving swiftly meant the plan offered a greater chance of success.

"Good. Keep me in the loop every step of the way. If Kensi is in New York, we need to find her before—" I cut myself off, not wanting to think about what could happen to her. Based on what she'd shared about her past, her father, and her husband, there was a reason she'd risked running.

"I will, Wyatt. We're doing everything we can. Just hang tight and focus on what you need to do there."

My mind was already in New York, racing through streets I didn't know, searching for Kensi in places I couldn't see. But I was stuck here in Nashville, forced to face a day that no longer held any significant meaning.

As I climbed onto the shuttle, the noise of the others barely registered. They were excited, energized for whatever was next, while I sat in silence, the knot in my chest tightening with every mile that took me further from where I wanted to be.

The thought of performing—of smiling, playing along for the cameras—made frustration burn hot in my gut. How was I supposed to care about any of this when Kensi was out there, alone, in danger? Every second I stayed here felt like a betrayal of what mattered most.

And yet, I had no choice but to sit, to wait, to hope that Stephen and the team could do what I couldn't right now. The powerlessness gnawed at me.

The news from Stephen, the movement in Kensi's search, sharpened my focus. But it was a double-edged sword, offering a glimmer of hope while underscoring the helplessness of my situation. And here I was, about to face another day in the spotlight, pretending to be someone I hardly recognized. I had to compartmentalize and focus.

The shuttle came to a stop outside the studio, pulling me back to this distraction called my current reality. The task at hand was clear, and despite the chaos swirling within me, I knew I had to maintain the facade. Today, I would be Wyatt the performer, even as Wyatt the soldier schemed silently in the background, waiting for the opportunity to act.

As we filed out of the bus, I steeled myself for the day ahead. Today, we were to be the faces of Nashville for those who dreamed of visiting this city vibrant with music and life. Yet my heart lay elsewhere, caught in a nightmare it could not wake from.

Upon arrival, the producers gathered us together, their excitement palpable in the warm morning air. "Today, you'll be filming commercials and promos for the Nashville Tourism Board," they announced, a statement full of excitement that ran counter to my personal turmoil. I was paired with Savannah, a bright-eyed girl from Tennessee whose enthusiasm for this opportunity was a lot bigger than my own.

Our assignment was clear: bring the spirit of Nashville alive for the Nashville Predators NHL team.

The Ford Ice Center greeted us with its vast, chilly expanse, a stark contrast to the warm Tennessee sun outside. Decked out in our Predators jerseys, we looked the part, even if I didn't quite feel it. The ice—the cold, slippery surface under my boots—mirrored my internal state: unstable and out of my element. Trying to muster a semblance of enthusiasm, I found myself going through the motions, an exterior of positivity that was as thin as the blades on which the players skated.

Savannah, on the other hand, was in her element from the jump. A die-hard fan, she flirted and chatted with the team like old friends, her excitement genuine and infectious. She even donned a pair of skates and took on the assignment with gusto.

The team welcomed us with open arms—maybe a bit too enthusiastically in Savannah's case. They were all about the cameras, showing off, and Savannah ate it up, her laughter echoing across the ice. Me? I was more focused on not falling flat on my face.

The crew buzzed around us, catching every moment. Savannah shone under the spotlight, her banter with the players effortless. I did what I could, sticking to smiles and nods, throwing in a comment here and there.

During a break in practice, one of the Predators approached. A cameraman, never far away, started filming.

"Saw the show's premiere last night," he said, his gaze earnest. "What you said about veterans and their families—it meant a lot. Lost my dad in the Army. He was killed in action when I was in middle school. I'm glad you have the chance to talk about the real impact on families and bring some attention to it."

His words cut through me, reminding me why I had agreed to be here. For a moment, the ice, the cameras, and the lights faded into the background. Here was someone who understood the gravity, someone who knew firsthand the pain and the pride that came with the sacrifice of service to the country.

His acknowledgment was a reminder of the bigger picture, even in the haze of my current predicament. It grounded me, pulling me back from the edge of my personal turmoil with Kensi.

"Thanks, man. And I'm sorry for your loss. It's never easy," I managed to say, my voice thick with emotion. "It's stories like yours that need to be heard. Makes all this"—I gestured around us at the cameras and microphones—"much more meaningful."

As filming wrapped and we headed back to the mansion, the ride home was a quiet affair. Savannah, buried in her phone, was no doubt scrolling through reactions to today's shoot or messaging friends. I, on the other hand, was texting Stephen, seeking updates, clinging to any piece of news about Kensi.

Stephen's response was immediate but sobering:

We think we have a location on Kensi, but it's too precarious to make a move just yet. We're setting up surveillance to confirm.

Reading his message, a sense of frustration washed over me. The helplessness of being miles away, unable to do anything but wait, was agonizing. Yet, I understood the necessity of caution. A wrong move could jeopardize everything.

The first to arrive back at the mansion, we were met by the peaceful quiet of the early evening. The vastness of the house, usually buzzing with activity and noise, was still. It made the thoughts in my head far too loud.

I glanced over at Savannah, still engrossed in her phone, unburdened by the world beyond the screen. How I envied that ignorance, even if just for a moment. Instead, the distraction the day had offered was now behind me, replaced once again by the heavy cloak of reality.

As Savannah disappeared inside, I lingered outside for a moment longer, taking in the quiet of the Tennessee countryside. The tranquility of the setting sun did little to ease the storm inside me. With Kensi's situation unresolved and my role in this reality show charade continuing, I was caught between worlds, each demanding a piece of me I wasn't sure I had to give.

Turning my phone over in my hand, I contemplated calling

Stephen again, hungry for any update, no matter how small. But I knew better. Interrupting him meant interrupting his progress.

With a heavy sigh, I turned and made my way into the mansion, the door closing behind me with a finality that mirrored my resolve. Whatever it took, I was going to find Kensi. The waiting was hard, but losing her was not an option.

26

WYATT

By the time the rest of the contestants started trickling back into the mansion, my mind was already miles away, plotting my course to New York. The buzz of their returns, the sounds of laughter and chatter grew distant as I made my way to my room. Each step was laden with resolve; I was leaving Tennessee, one way or another.

The vibration of my phone cut through my thoughts like a siren call. Jim Lucas's name lit up the screen, and a surge of hope shot through me. I answered the call as I pushed my room's door open, already mentally processing how quickly I could pack.

"Jim," I greeted, my voice betraying the edge of my anticipation.

"Hey, Wyatt. Look, we've been through it with the producers and the judges," Jim started, and I could hear the weariness in his voice—the sound of too many conversations leading up to this call. "Given your situation, we've managed to work something out."

I paused, a shirt in hand, as I waited for him to continue. The quiet of my room had me intensely focused on Jim's next words.

"We can put you in the bottom two for tomorrow's elimination reveal. Took a lot of convincing, given the circumstances, but everyone's agreed to it," he revealed, and for a moment, the relief was so intense it was almost palpable.

"But," he quickly added—and I knew there was more to it— "you're sworn to secrecy about this. There will be a non-disclosure agreement to sign. And there's a stipulation. You have to be on the *Real American Country* tour after the show ends, or it's going to cost you. A lot."

The conditions were a compromise I couldn't reject. It was a way out, but with strings attached, tying me to a future I had already pushed out of my mind. But what choice did I have? Kensi's safety, her well-being—it all hinged on my ability to be where I needed to be. And if that meant securing my exit through the show's orchestrated drama, then so be it.

"Understood, Jim. I'll play along," I said, my decision firm. "Thank you for making this happen."

We ended the call with a few more details about the next day's taping, but my mind was only half there. I resumed packing, the motions mechanical. My thoughts were with Kensi—alone and probably scared—and with the daunting task that awaited me. The promise of action, of being able to do something, was a bittersweet reprieve.

It was the not knowing that gnawed at me—the uncertainty of what I would find when I arrived in New York. That fear, the apprehension of the unknown, mingled with the resolve that had settled deep in my bones.

As I folded clothes and arranged them in my bag, my mind raced through a thousand different scenarios. Each one played out like a movie I couldn't pause—scenarios ranging from the hopeful to the unimaginable. The thought that I might be on the verge of finding Kensi, of bringing her back, was the only light in a tunnel that had appeared endless. But it was the shadows in that tunnel that scared me—the possibilities that whispered of things going wrong, of arriving too late, of not being what Kensi needed me to be.

I zipped my bag shut and tossed it in the closet, the sound echoing in the quiet of my room. The challenge of what lay ahead pressed down on me, a constant reminder that while I was moving forward, the path was fraught with uncertainty.

Sitting on my bed, elbows resting on my knees, I clasped my cell phone, resting my forehead against it in a moment of overwhelmed silence. The room was too small, the walls too close, as if they were pressing in and allowing the thoughts racing through my mind to echo off of them. I blocked out the noise and chaos of the mansion as my focus remained on the device in my hands.

The door swung open, and my roommate Nash walked in, pausing as he noticed my hunched form. "Hey, man, you OK?" His voice was laced with genuine concern, cutting through the fog of my thoughts.

I looked up, meeting his gaze. My expression must have painted a clear picture. I managed a sigh before lying to the guy. "Yeah, all good."

With a nod, Nash grabbed some clothes before heading to the shower without further question.

I pressed Stephen's number and waited for him to answer.

"Jim and the producers are on board. They're setting me up for the elimination tomorrow morning. I'll be in the bottom two," I began, the words coming out in a rush. The plan, with all its conditions and stipulations, spilled out of me.

Stephen was quiet for a moment after I finished, letting it all sink in. "Good," he finally said, the faint clatter of his keyboard in the background.

We ran through the next steps, laying out what needed to happen for me to leave for New York on short notice. When the call ended, the weight of our conversation hit me hard. My thoughts churned, louder than the silence that filled the room.

I was leaving Tennessee, heading straight into the unknown. The road ahead was anything but clear, but at least it was a road. Taking action—finally doing something—was the only thing keeping me steady right now.

I just needed Kensi to hold on and fight until I could get to her.

27

KENSI

I tried to think through my options, each one tinged with the desperation of a trapped animal. The elevator was well-guarded and, without a key, not a straightforward escape route. Perhaps the back stairwell, if I could find a way past the guards who lingered at every corner. Or maybe a window—some way to signal to anyone outside who could help. But from this high up? Highly unlikely.

There were new faces among Luka's entourage, some who might not recognize me, who might be swayed by money or pity. I would need to act fast, to stay vigilant. There had to be a weakness some-where—a door left unlocked, or a route left unguarded even for a moment.

The sound of approaching footsteps froze me in place. Heart pounding, I turned to see one of Luka's men, his expression unreadable.

Without a word, he grasped my arm, his grip firm and unyielding. There was no use resisting; the imbalance of power was obvious. As he led me through the silent corridors, each step was a reminder of the life I had fled—a life of golden bars and velvet chains.

The door opened, and I was unceremoniously ushered inside.

Luka sat behind his desk, the picture of power and control. His eyes met mine, and for a moment, the world stood still. "Rose," he greeted, his voice smooth as silk, a dangerous undercurrent lurking beneath the charm. "Or should I call you Kensi now?"

I remained silent, staring at him with what I hoped was a reflection of the hatred I felt for Luka Solinas and not the fear coursing through my veins alongside it.

Leaning back in his chair, his gaze never left mine. "You've caused quite the stir, disappearing like that. Did you really think you could run away and start a new life? Without consequences?"

The room spun, the air grew heavier with each word he spoke. Yet, despite the fear, a spark of defiance ignited within me. "I didn't run away from you, Luka. I ran toward freedom. Toward a life where I'm not a pawn in someone else's game."

His laughter was cold, devoid of any real amusement. "Freedom? Is that what you call it? You belong here, with me. Your little escapade has been entertaining. But it's time to come back to reality."

"I'm not a possession. I'm a person, with my own will, my own dreams," I found myself saying, each word a declaration of my resolve.

For a moment, he regarded me, his expression unreadable. Then, slowly, he stood, coming around the desk to stand before me. "Dreams," he mused, the word almost a whisper. "Let's see how long those little dreams last, Kensi."

His threat hung in the air, a chilling promise that sent shivers down my spine. Facing Luka was like staring into the void—a man who saw me as nothing more than something to control, to own. Fear gnawed at my courage, my heart pounded, yet I projected a confidence I didn't feel.

Freedom felt distant, like a dream I couldn't let myself abandon no matter how impossible it seemed. But as his eyes bore into mine, I couldn't stop the flicker of doubt. The cost of fighting him—of defying someone who thrived on breaking people—was impossibly high.

Without warning, his hand rose, brushing a strand of hair from my face before trailing a line down my cheek. My skin crawled, the touch so light it might have seemed gentle to anyone else. But I knew better. His presence was a prison, his touch a reminder of every moment he'd stolen from me.

I flinched before I could stop myself, a reaction I hated because I knew he'd notice. Luka always noticed. The slight curve of his lips was cruel, satisfied, and it made nausea twist in my gut. I clenched my fists at my sides, grounding myself in the one truth I could cling to: I was still here. Still breathing. And as long as I was, there was a chance I could escape.

The satisfaction that flickered across his face at my reaction was unmistakable—a smirk of triumph that he could still intimidate me with such simplicity. "You need to be dressed and ready for dinner in one hour. We're having company," he declared, his tone leaving no room for argument.

His words hung heavy in the air, a reminder of the control he wielded with ease. As he withdrew his hand, the physical distance did nothing to alleviate the suffocating hold he had over me. The threat of company, of having to play the part he had crafted for me in this twisted charade, was another link in the chains he delighted in binding me with.

The gravity of my situation was not lost on me. Facing the man who saw me as nothing more than an asset to be manipulated and controlled, I clung to the hope that had bloomed all those months ago within me.

There had to be another way, another plan that could be formed, other allies in shadows yet to be found. It was a path fraught with danger and uncertainty, but it was mine to tread. I'd done it before. I would do it again.

28

KENSI

The relentless ticking of the clock echoed through my room as I stood frozen before the open closet, its darkness mirroring the dread pooling in my gut. The closer Luka's dinner charade came, the more I dreaded the inevitable costume. The idea alone—putting on a dress to play his game—was a marionette dance, and I was the unwilling puppet, strings taut in his unforgiving grip.

I swallowed hard, steeling myself against the memory of cold retribution for far less defiance than what simmered within me now. A shiver crawled up my spine as I contemplated the consequences of rebellion. No, this wasn't the hill to die on; the stakes were simply too high. With reluctant resolve, my hand reached out, brushing against the fabric of my past.

Past dresses hung like ghosts, their silhouettes whispering tales of who I had been molded to be—each fold and stitch a testament to a life not mine but one thrust upon me. My fingers paused, hovering over the hem of one dress in particular. It served as a reminder of my confinement, a relic from a time when I was merely a phantom, forced to conform to others' wishes and control.

With a heavy exhale, I pulled the dress from its hanger. It

wrapped around me, the fit more intimate than I remembered, hugging places I once starved into submission. The garment was a cruel reminder of days fueled by caffeine and hunger, where exercise was punishment instead of pleasure—a tool to whittle away any hint of defiance my body might dare to show.

This dress was once my armor, a shield against a world that demanded flawlessness at the cost of my own well-being. But as I zipped it up, the fabric whispered not of protection but of chains, links forged in self-deprivation binding me to a history I longed to forget.

The silk slid over my skin, a whisper of fabric that clung to newly embraced curves. Shadows and light played across the room, casting ghostly versions of myself against the walls, each one telling a tale of transformation. I stood there flooded by memories so visceral they left echoes on my flesh—memories of a time when the mirror was an enemy, its surface a battlefield where every inch of me lost the war against their ideals.

I turned slowly, the dress hugging every part of me I'd fought to reclaim from their rigid standards. The mirror now reflected a different reality, one that glowed with the truth of who I had become.

My eyes met my own gaze in the mirror, and a small, defiant smile played on my lips. The dress, once a symbol of my imprisonment, now fitted to me like a glove—snug, but not restrictive. It accentuated lines and forms I had grown to love, every contour a rebellion against their oppressive molds.

This body, once policed to adhere to an impossible standard, now stood as a testament to my rebellion. It carried stories of survival and newfound happiness. The dress no longer fit like a shackle but a piece of armor chosen by me, for me.

With the dress now hugging my form, I turned my attention to the floor, where shoes lay scattered like fallen soldiers—none willing allies for the night ahead. Each pair a futile patch for a wound that ran far deeper, their pointed toes and high arches mocking the impossible choice before me. Sighing, I settled on a pair of black pumps, plain but bearable—the least offensive option for feet that longed to run rather than step willingly into the lion's den.

The shoes slipped on more out of obligation than preference, their familiar pinch a minor discomfort compared to the storm brewing in my core. With each step, unease curled through me, creeping like smoke into the quiet corners of my mind, feeding my fears. The mystery of tonight's guests gnawed at me, but one possible face haunted me more than the rest—my father.

The thought alone was enough to send icy tendrils slithering down my spine, a chill that rivaled the dread Luka always inspired. The image of them together, my father's cold look meeting Luka's cunning smirk, created a scene that filled me with dread.

The two of them teaming up was like a horror show I didn't buy tickets for but got front row seats anyway. My father's ability to turn affection into cold indifference paired with Luka's perverse talent for making cruelty look like care? It was the worst of both worlds. And there I was, stuck in the middle, probably their favorite topic of discussion—or, more accurately, negotiation. I was an involuntary target caught in the crosshairs.

Gripping the banister tighter with each step, like it could save me from the growing fear, I made my way down the stairs. The murmur of voices grew louder as I grew closer. I moved forward, propelled by a sense of inevitability that had long since replaced any illusion of choice in these matters.

I reached the bottom of the stairs; the tap of my heels on marble punctuated the silence that followed my entrance. Each click a note in an overture to the night's grim symphony.

As I approached, Luka's conversation ceased abruptly. With a single gesture, he dismissed his lackey, who vanished with a deference that bordered on fear. The exchange was brief but telling of the power Luka wielded without needing to utter a single word. And then, suddenly, I was the sole focus of his hawk-like attention.

His eyes traced the contours of my form, a slow and deliberate sweep that left a trail of unease on my skin. In that moment, reduced to nothing more than an object within his gaze, there was a familiar claw of anxiety scratching at the walls I had built around myself. Luka's scrutiny was oppressive, a silent assertion of the control he enjoyed and the submission he expected.

Taking another step, I steeled my nerves for the encounter. Luka's presence filled the space, a formidable force that demanded attention, and it was clear I had his in full. The distance between us closed, each step measured and deliberate.

"Rose," he growled, his voice a velvet rumble that belied its thorny edges. The name fell from his lips like a brand, searing into my identity, reshaping me into the image he desired. His eyes gleamed with a counterfeit kindness, but the icy knot in my chest warned me not to trust it.

His gaze lingered, an unwelcome guest tracing the lines of my figure. "I must say, I like what I see." The words slithered out, disguised as a compliment, but their undercurrent carried the poison of his true intent.

There it was, the veneer of admiration concealing the barbs beneath. He paused, his eyes a predator's, cold and calculating, taking in every aspect of my defiance. "Those curves..." he mused, his voice a slow pour of honey laced with arsenic, "a delightful departure from your usual appearance."

The way he emphasized 'usual' was a mockery of my past efforts —the times I had twisted myself into knots to meet his impossible standards. His so-called approval churned my insides with revulsion, another reminder that in his eyes, I was little more than a possession to be appraised and judged.

The silence that followed was thick with tension, the extravagant hallway magnifying each moment. His compliment, if it could even be called that, was nothing more than another one of his meticulously crafted manipulations—a reminder that, to him, I was just another asset to be molded and controlled. But this asset had learned a few tricks, and I wasn't about to let him forget that.

Yet, as his scrutiny continued, a simmering anger began to replace the disgust within me. His words were meant to ensnare, to remind me of my place in his world, but they only served to reinforce my resolve. This dress, these curves—they were no longer his to critique. While tonight I would endure his theater, his dinner table machinations, it would not be as his puppet, but as a warrior in disguise, ready to reclaim my narrative from the very man who sought to write it for me.

My fingers curled into fists at my sides, the delicate fabric of the dress bunching slightly as I fought to keep my composure. Luka's eyes still clung to me, his gaze dissecting every inch of my form as if he were a sculptor and I his unwilling clay. "Thank you," I managed through gritted teeth, the words tasting like ash in my mouth.

I squared my shoulders, lifting my chin defiantly. The cool air of the hallway grew colder with every breath I took, and I could almost see my resolve condensing before me, visible and unyielding. "Shall we?" I asked, signaling that I was ready to proceed to the dinner despite the dread that clawed at my insides.

As we navigated the marbled expanse toward the looming dining room doors, I sensed the enormity of the night ahead. With each step, my heels clicked on the floor like a metronome ticking down to an inevitable confrontation. Luka's appraisal, the heavy expectation of meeting the unknown guest, and the veiled threats lingered in the air. This was no mere meal—it was another battle in the ongoing war for my autonomy.

I could feel the fight rising within me, fueled by every condescending word and power play. Tonight, I was not just defending myself; I was fighting for a future where I was free from Luka's oppressive grasp, a future where my worth wasn't measured by the curve of my hips or the compliance in my eyes. This dinner, this twisted display of control, would not define me. Not tonight, not ever. With each step closer to the dining room, I reaffirmed the silent oath I had made to myself: the war for my future was mine, and I would not surrender.

My heart pounded a loud steady rhythm as I trailed behind Luka. The rich scent of polished wood and lingering cologne did little to mask the undercurrent of tension that clung to the air like a second skin. With every step, I drew upon an inner reserve of courage that had been tempered in fires hotter than the one awaiting me beyond those imposing dining room doors.

Luka's back was a rigid line of authority, his suit perfectly tailored to a form unyielded by doubt or weakness. He didn't look back at me, assured in his dominance, certain that I would follow. And I did, not out of submission but calculation. I measured each breath, each heartbeat, syncing them with my stride, turning my body into an instrument of control—my control.

As we stepped into the space where shadows played across the marble floor, cast by the ornate chandelier above, I'm pretty sure the world tilted ever so slightly. There stood my father, an imposing figure carved from years of cold ambition. His eyes, void of any trace of light they might have once held, locked onto me with an intensity that stripped away the layers of my bravado, probing for any weakness in my armor.

"Father," I greeted, my voice steady despite the storm of emotions roiling inside me. It was a simple acknowledgment, stripped of affection or fear, a neutral ground upon which I could stand.

"Rose," he greeted, his voice as icy as his gaze. The use of that name, a blade twisted in my heart, reminded me that in his eyes, I was nothing more than a pawn in his elaborate game of power and deceit. The tenderness of a father's love was foreign to me, replaced by the cold calculation of business transactions. My desperate grasp for freedom had caused him inconvenience, a blemish on his meticulous plans with Luka.

Luka observed the interaction with the faintest trace of a smirk playing at the corner of his mouth—a spectator at a gladiatorial match, eager for blood to be drawn. But what he, nor my father, understood was that within me, a quiet rebellion simmered. They saw my compliance as victory when it was nothing more than a strategic retreat, gathering strength for the moment when I would claim my life as my own.

Dinner unfolded like a theater of war, the table set with crystal and fine china serving as the battleground for our silent conflict. My father's demeanor was frigid, each word and gesture measured to convey his displeasure without overt confrontation. Luka, ever the embodiment of controlled danger, matched my father's coldness with a smooth, menacing grace that belied his potential for violence.

The silverware clattered softly against the fine china, a stark contrast to the tension that suffocated the room. The crystal glasses refracted the light, casting prismatic shadows across the tablecloth, as if they too sensed the approaching storm.

"Your little escapade, Rose, has upset a delicate balance," Luka's voice cut through the silence, low and dangerous, like the rumble of thunder forewarning a tempest. He leaned back in his chair, fingers steepled, eyes fixed on me with predatory focus. "Your actions reflect not just on you, but on your father here. And we wouldn't want his investments to suffer because of a momentary lapse in judgment, would we?"

Across from me, my father's face hardened, his expression an intricate sculpture of controlled anger and calculated restraint. His fingers curled tightly around his fork, knuckles whitening—a bulwark holding back the tide of his frustration. Yet, he said nothing, allowing the silence to fill the space between us.

Luka's attention returned to me, his gaze piercing, as sharp and cold as the knives lined up beside our plates. "Your cooperation is not a request," he continued, every syllable laced with the threat of hidden daggers. "It's a requirement. Should you decide to test my patience again, it won't be just your well-being at stake."

He paused, letting the words hang heavy in the air, a guillotine poised above my head. I met his stare unflinchingly, determined not to show the tremor vibrating within me.

"There are consequences, Rose—consequences that your father here would bear the brunt of." His voice was soft now, yet it carried the unmistakable echo of a verdict delivered by a merciless judge.

The threat hung in the air, a noose tightening around my neck. The implication was clear: my rebellion could cost my father his life. It was a power play designed to cage me with my own fears, to bind me to compliance with the chains of familial obligation.

The crystal chandelier above us cast a cascade of trembling light, each ray reflecting off the polished surfaces of the dining room like a spotlight on the silent drama unfolding below. I could feel Luka's warning settling over me, wrapping around my throat in an invisible stranglehold. My father's life dangled precariously at the end of that metaphorical rope—my rebellion potentially the hand that might unwittingly sever it.

The fine china clinked softly as I set down my fork, the sound disproportionately loud in the tension-filled room. The taste of the rich food turned bitter, and I pushed the plate away, appetite lost to the gnawing anxiety in my stomach. I fisted my hands under the table, nails digging into my palms trying to force myself to stay in the moment.

Across from me, my father remained a frozen pillar of restraint, his eyes fixed on some point just beyond the room, as if he could ignore the peril we faced through sheer force of will. Luka sat at the head of the table, his chair positioned like a throne, his posture relaxed yet commanding, a king surveying his domain and its unruly subjects.

I tried not to choke on the air that thickened with his threats. The silence was a void, waiting to be filled with the next volley in this cold war of wills. Yet, within that void, something unexpected stirred—a flicker of resistance that grew brighter with every beat of my heart.

"Your compliance is essential, Rose," Luka said, his voice a silken thread weaving through the stillness. He folded his hands on the table, fingers laced together in a posture of calm control and authority. "As is your father's."

I lifted my gaze, meeting his eyes with a resolve I hadn't known I possessed. "Using my father's safety as leverage is a new low, even for you." The words spilled from me, quiet but firm, infused with the fire of my newfound defiance.

A muscle twitched in Luka's jaw, the only break in his otherwise impassive expression. Beside him, my father shifted ever so slightly, a crack appearing in his icy exterior. His glance flickered toward me, a brief spark of something unreadable before it was extinguished by the return of his stony facade.

"Consider it motivation, not leverage," Luka corrected smoothly, though the undercurrent of danger in his voice belied the calm exterior. "I trust you understand the importance of aligning our interests."

My chest tightened, the specter of their intertwined ambitions squeezing the breath from my lungs. But beneath the suffocating pressure, the ember of rebellion refused to be snuffed out. My anger burned, fueled by the injustice of their manipulations. I was more than a pawn in their game.

"Is there nothing sacred to you?" I challenged, my voice steady despite the turmoil roiling inside me. "Not even family?"

"Everything has its price," Luka replied, his gaze never wavering from mine. "And everyone has their role to play."

The message was clear: I was to fall in line or face the consequences. Yet, as I sat there ensnared in the conflict between these two men, the steel in my spine hardened. No longer would I allow their ego-driven chess game to dictate my moves. If they sought to bind me with fear, they would find that the chains they imagined holding me were nothing but smoke and mirrors.

For in that moment, amidst the dazzling displays of wealth and machinations of power, I envisioned a new path. It was perilous but it beckoned me toward a freedom I was willing to fight for. And fight I would.

Luka's unflinching eyes held me in my seat, a hard gaze that didn't just see through, but sought to unravel and dissect. In the glacial silence that followed, I watched as a muscle twitched along my father's jawline—a silent scream against the chains of his own making. It was a chilling revelation, seeing him not as the omnipotent patriarch, but as another piece cornered on Luka's chessboard. My chest tightened with a mix of pity and disdain.

Dinner resumed, a charade where every course was served with a side of contempt. I found my thoughts drifting, the scrapes and clinks of dishes around me fading into a distant hum as my mind slipped away to Liberty.

There, life had a rhythm so different from this world of pretense and power plays. I could almost feel the warmth of Liberty's sun on my face, smell the rich earth of Evelyn's garden, and hear the soft murmurs of friendly conversation on the porch. The town had a pulse of its own, steady and simple, filled with people who lived without hidden agendas and tangled loyalties. It was a place where trust wasn't a rarity and where I could finally breathe, even laugh—a freedom I hadn't known in years.

"Pass the salt, Rose," Luka commanded casually, snapping me back to the present—a present where each word exchanged was a dance over a pit of vipers. I handed it to him, our fingers brushing, and I recoiled at the contact as if scorched. My father's critical eye dissected my every move while Luka's sardonic quips sliced through the air, their dual assault a choreography designed to belittle and control.

With every second that passed, my mind raced, trying to plot and plan an escape. Fear and anger were battling it out with fear whispering warnings and conjuring doubts. Yet, anger seared hotter within me, fueling a defiance that simmered beneath my calm exterior. Each attempt he made to control me, with his words and actions, only pushed me further away from his grasp. Luka saw compliance; I clung to the hope of freedom.

As the evening wore on, the shadows cast by the dim light danced menacingly along the walls, mirroring the dark intentions seated around me. But within me, something else stirred—something that matched the intensity of the darkness.

I stood up, pushing my chair back with a quiet scrape that echoed throughout the room. "Excuse me," I said, my voice steady despite the storm raging inside. I didn't wait for their acknowledgement; I didn't need it as I began to walk away.

They had underestimated me, and that was their gravest mistake. For in their quest to control, they had forged the very weapon that would undo them: my resolve to reclaim my power and emerge victorious on my own terms.

29

WYATT

The steady hum of the private plane's engines served as a constant reminder of the distance closing between us and New York. Stephen sat across from me, his laptop open as he poured over the latest intel, but my gaze was fixed on the darkening sky outside, lost in thought.

"I've cross-referenced the latest surveillance with our on-ground contacts," Stephen broke the silence, his voice steady, analytical. "Luka Solinas and Alessio Romano are definitely there. Our window of opportunity is narrowing."

I nodded, barely processing the words. My mind was a whirlwind of scenarios, each more daunting than the last. The penthouse in New York wasn't just any location; it was the lair of a man whose very name evoked fear. And yet, amidst the apprehension, a fiercer emotion clawed at my chest. I was driven not just by the mission, but by something far more personal.

"You've been quiet," Stephen observed, his tone shifting from professional to concerned. "You know we're walking into a hornet's nest, right?"

"I know," I ground out. "It's just—" my words caught in my throat.

"It's Kensi. Everything we're doing, it's risky, but I can't shake this feeling that I'm not going to be there in time."

Stephen eyed me, the unspoken words hanging between us. We both knew the risks, the stakes. Yet, it was the unvoiced thoughts about Kensi that filled the cabin with a palpable tension.

Back in Nashville, the production team from *Real American Country* had been informed of the plan on a need-to-know basis. When I was put in the bottom two contestants, just to be revealed as the first one to be eliminated, there were massive shockwaves.

The audience, both in the studio and watching live from home, sat in stunned silence as the host announced my name. Whispers quickly spread like wildfire. Wyatt Turner, the golden boy of the season, the one everyone whispered would be the last man standing, was out first. Cameras panned across the shocked faces in the audience—fans with wide eyes and slack jaws, some already pulling out their phones to tweet their disbelief. The judges, seasoned veterans of the industry, were no less taken aback. They exchanged glances, their expressions a mixture of confusion and disbelief. This wasn't how the narrative was supposed to go.

In the contestants' area, the remaining singers were just as floored. Some struggled to mask their surprise, while others couldn't help but openly react. I'd been labeled the one to beat, and now, the playing field had shifted dramatically.

Fans apparently took to social media to express their outrage, with theories ranging from rigged voting to backstage politics. Some declared they would no longer watch the show, feeling cheated out of a fair competition. Others speculated about what could have possibly led to my early exit, with a few even suspecting something bigger at play.

Meanwhile, the producers were in full damage control mode. Press statements were hastily drafted, emphasizing the integrity of the show's voting process while trying to steer the narrative toward the unpredictable nature of live television.

Yet, amidst the chaos, there was one group that remained calm— the few who knew the truth. My elimination was not a twist of fate but a carefully orchestrated move to get me out of the public eye and into the heart of a dangerous mission. As the nation buzzed with speculation, I was already en route to New York, my thoughts far from the glitz and glamor of a reality show.

Stephen closed his laptop and looked at me.

"You know as well as I do we can't account for every circumstance. But we're the best at what we do. And I know this isn't just another job." Stephen's words cut through the fog in my mind. "Kensi means a lot to you, more than you let on. She means a lot to all of us. We're going to get your girl back, man. You just have to trust the team."

My girl. The way Stephen acknowledged my feelings for Kensi may as well have been a punch to the gut that left me breathless. It was true; my connection to Kensi went beyond anything professional. It was intense and personal in a way that scared me. But facing that was stepping into an uncharted territory without a map, because, as much as I felt for her, she wasn't mine. She belonged to someone else, whether her heart was in it or not. To be honest, I didn't even know how she felt about her husband. That was never something we discussed—his name only came up in conversations about keeping her safe.

"We'll find her, Wyatt. We'll bring her back, no matter what it takes," Stephen's voice was steady, full of a resolve that had carried us through tight spots before.

The conversation shifted back to logistics, the details of our plan. But beneath the tactical discussion, my heart pounded. The thought of Kensi, trapped in that New York penthouse, her safety in question, set a fire in me. I was scared. Not to take action but of what we might find when we did. But the fear was drowned out by something stronger: an overpowering need to bring her back, whatever it took.

As the plane continued its journey, the lights of New York began to come into view, a sprawling metropolis that held both danger and the slimmest hope of salvation. The reality of what we were about to undertake hit me full force. We were about to confront not just a crime lord, but a network that had eluded law enforcement for years.

Yet, for Kensi, for the chance to bring her to safety, it was a risk I was willing to take.

Stephen and I reviewed our equipment, went over our entry and exit strategies one last time, and prepared for every conceivable scenario. But as much as we planned, I knew that the unpredictable nature of what lay ahead could throw us curveballs we could never anticipate.

The plane touched down, and as we made our way to the rendezvous point, the bustling sounds of the city filled the air, creating a sense of both familiarity and unease. New York, with its pulsing energy and endless possibilities, now held a singular purpose for me—Kensi.

Adrenaline coursed through my veins as we set foot in the city. We were walking into the unknown, but I clung to the belief that somewhere in that city, Kensi was waiting. And I would find her.

The chill of the New York evening was a stark contrast to the warmth of the private jet we had just left. As Stephen and I made our way to an unassuming warehouse in a quieter part of the city, the anticipation was palpable. Inside, Masterson and Reeves were already prepping, their figures illuminated by the sparse overhead lighting, surrounded by an array of tactical gear.

Masterson, a tall, lean figure with a gaze as sharp as his wit, was the first to acknowledge our arrival. "Glad you could make it," he said, his voice tinged with the kind of sarcasm that betrayed the seriousness of our situation.

Reeves, stockier and with a demeanor that spoke of quiet strength, nodded in agreement. "Let's get you geared up. Time's not on our side."

As Stephen and I donned our tactical vests and checked our weapons, Masterson laid out the blueprints of the penthouse on a makeshift table. The detail was meticulous, showcasing the layout of Luka Solinas' stronghold.

"We've been keeping eyes on the building," Masterson began, pointing to the service entrance they planned to use. "Security is tight, as expected. Cameras, armed guards, the works. But we've found a pattern in their movements we can exploit."

Reeves chimed in, his focus on the blueprints. "Once inside, we'll need to move fast. There are two main elevators, but we'll use the service elevator here," he said, indicating a secluded part of the layout. "It's less monitored and will take us straight to the penthouse level without raising alarms."

I leaned in, studying the path we were about to take. "What about internal security? Cameras, motion detectors?"

Masterson nodded, acknowledging the concern. "Reeves and I managed to hack into the building's security system. We'll have a short window where the cameras on our path will be looped footage. As for motion detectors, we've got jammers. They'll give us a small but crucial advantage."

The atmosphere in the room was thick with tension as we continued to gear up. Each of us knew the risks, understood the stakes. Yet, there was a shared resolve, a collective determination that bound us together.

Stephen, ever the strategist, raised another crucial point. "And if we encounter resistance? Luka's men won't just stand down."

"That's where the real fun begins," Masterson said, a grim smile playing on his lips. "We'll have to be quick and decisive."

I jumped in. "Non-lethal force where possible, but we stay alive. Remember, the goal is to get to Kensi and get out. We're not here to start a war." What I didn't say but knew was understood, was that I wanted as little chance as possible for Kensi to be caught in the crossfire.

Reeves handed me a compact tactical headset. "We'll maintain constant communication. Masterson and I know the layout, so follow our lead. Once we hit the penthouse, it's going to be on you and Stephen to navigate the final stretch. We believe Kensi is being secluded away from the main areas."

The finality of our preparations settled over us like a cloak. Checking our gear one last time, we shared a look that needed no words. This was it—the culmination of all our planning, fears, and hopes.

The night air crackled with energy, setting the stage for the mission that awaited. In that moment, bound by a common purpose, we were more than just a team; we were a force united against the darkness, stepping into the fray with a single, unyielding intent: to bring Kensi home.

The city awaited, its shadows and lights a maze we were about to navigate. And as we stepped into the night, our purpose was clear. Whatever we would face, we would face together with every ounce of skill and determination we possessed. The mission was dangerous, the odds daunting, but there was no turning back now.

30

KENSI

I sensed it before I could name it, a tension in the air that crawled over my skin like an omen. The penthouse had been steeped in a deceptive calm, the kind that lulls you into a false sense of security, but I was too familiar with Luka's world to fall for its lies.

There was a barely discernible shift in the air, like the charged quiet before a storm. It wasn't long before the storm broke. The sudden commotion outside the door snapped the facade of civility like a twig. Shouts echoed from the hallway, followed by the unmistakable crack of gunfire.

My heart leapt into my throat.

Within moments, the penthouse turned into a battleground. The doors burst open, splinters of wood flying like shrapnel. Luka's men swarmed in, guns drawn, shouting orders in rapid Italian. But they were met with equal force - figures clad in black tactical gear surged into the room, weapons at the ready.

Among the chaos, two familiar faces stood out. Wyatt and Stephen were here. For me, I thought. Wyatt was here for me.

As though he could sense my thoughts, Wyatt's eyes locked with mine across the room, a silent message passing between us. Despite the danger, relief flooded through me at the sight of him. With Wyatt here, I knew I stood a chance.

As bullets ripped through the air and men grappled in hand-to-hand combat all around us, I knew the final stand had begun. My fate, and the fates of those I loved, would be decided in this luxurious penthouse turned war zone. Whatever happened next, there was no turning back.

My heart raced, each beat a drum of panic urging me to flee. But before I could act, before I could decide whether to run, hide, or fight, my fate was sealed by a familiar touch. Luka was out of his seat, his grip on me iron-clad. The scent of him, a mixture of cologne and danger, filled my senses with dread and caused bile to rise into the back of my throat.

"You're not going anywhere," Luka growled, his breath hot against my ear. He yanked me towards him, using me as a human shield as he faced off against Wyatt and Stephen.

"Let her go, Solinas," Wyatt demanded, his voice steady despite the fury burning in his eyes. "It's over."

Luka laughed, a harsh, grating sound. "You think you can come into my house and take what's mine?" He pressed the barrel of his gun against my temple, the cold metal biting into my skin. "I don't think so."

I met Wyatt's gaze, silently begging him to understand what I couldn't say. I need you. I want you. I'm sorry. His jaw tightened, and for the briefest moment, fear cracked through his determined expression. It was the kind of fear you couldn't mask—the fear of losing someone you'd risk everything for. I knew he'd do anything to save me. But what if the cost was too high?

The room crackled with tension, each passing second amplifying the chaos. Luka's grip on my arm was unrelenting, a physical reminder of just how trapped I was. Around us, the shouts and frantic movement blurred into white noise, the kind of noise that made it hard to think, to breathe.

I had to act. Every instinct screamed at me to fight, to run, to do something, but with Luka's hold like a vice and Wyatt on the other side of the room, any move I made could tip this into disaster. I could see Wyatt calculating too, his eyes flicking between Luka, me, and the gun in Luka's other hand.

Desperation clawed at me, and my thoughts spun as I searched for a way out. Luka's grip tightened, jerking me closer, and I saw the cruel glint in his eyes—the kind that told me he thought he'd already won.

No. I couldn't let it end like this. Wyatt's gaze burned into mine, and I held onto it like a lifeline, grounding myself in the strength I saw there. Somehow, we had to find a way to turn this standoff into an escape.

Stephen, his eyes darting between Luka and me, took a cautious step forward. "You're outnumbered. Don't make this worse for yourself."

Luka's grip tightened, his nails digging into my arm. "Worse?" he scoffed. "You have no idea what I'm capable of."

I swallowed hard, my heart pounding against my ribs. The air crackled with tension, each breath a struggle against the fear that threatened to consume me. I had to do something, anything, to break free from Luka's hold.

"Luka, please," I whispered, my voice trembling. "It doesn't have to be like this."

He leaned in close, his lips brushing against my ear. "Oh, but it does, darling. You're mine, and I'll never let you go."

I shuddered at his touch, revulsion mixing with the fear that coursed through my veins. But beneath it all, a spark of defiance ignited, a burning desire to break free from the chains he had placed on my life.

"I belong to no one," I hissed, my voice trembling with a mixture of fear and fury. "Least of all, you."

Luka's grip tightened, his fingers digging into my skin with bruising force. "You'll learn, bella rosa. One way or another, you'll learn."

Wyatt's eyes narrowed, his jaw clenching as he watched the exchange. I could see the tension in his body, the coiled energy of a predator ready to strike. He was a man of action, a protector to his core, and every fiber of his being was focused on finding a way to end this.

My father's voice cut through the tension, a calm in the eye of the storm. "Let her go, Luka. This is between you and me. Leave my daughter out of it."

Luka laughed, a cruel, mirthless sound that echoed through the room. "But don't you see, old friend? She is the very heart of it. She is my leverage, my insurance. As long as I have her, you'll do exactly as I say."

I could feel the eyes of every person in the room on me, the pawn in a game of power and control.

The room was a tinderbox, every movement fraught with the potential to ignite. My father, Luka, Wyatt, and Stephen, all played their parts in this deadly dance, a dance that could end in tragedy or liberation.

My heart raced as I glanced at Wyatt. There was no need for words; the understanding was implicit. This was a rescue operation, but it was also so much more. The silence that stretched between Wyatt's gaze and my own was a battlefield of unspoken promises and steel resolve. In his eyes, I saw the reflection of every fear and hope I'd harbored since the day I'd fled from Luka's grasp. The standoff, a razor's edge on which our fates teetered, was about to tip.

Wyatt's voice, steady and controlled, broke the silence. "Luka, you're a businessman. Release her, and we can talk about a deal."

Luka's grip on me tightened, his breath hot against my ear. "You're in no position to negotiate, cowboy. One wrong move, and she's dead."

I could feel the rapid beat of Luka's heart against my back, a betrayal of the fear he tried to conceal beneath his bravado. He was cornered, and he knew it.

My father's eyes narrowed, his voice a low growl. "You harm one hair on her head, and I swear, I'll..."

With a sudden burst of motion, my father fired a shot into the ceiling, the deafening crack echoing through the room. The sound stunned everyone for a heartbeat, a split second of confusion that was all Wyatt and Stephen needed.

Stephen lunged at Luka, tackling him from the side as Wyatt kept his aim steady, covering them and scanning for any further threats. The room erupted into chaos, a blur of movement and sound—a desperate fight for control.

The scuffle was a blur, a chaotic dance of desperation and survival. Luka's grip loosened as Stephen managed to wrestle the gun away, but in the struggle, a shot rang out, a sound that would haunt my nightmares. Time slowed as I saw the realization dawn on Luka's face, the understanding that his reign of terror was over. He collapsed, a puppet with its strings cut, his weapon clattering to the floor.

But the victory was short-lived. In the aftermath, as adrenaline coursed through my veins, a stray bullet from one of Luka's men, desperate to avenge their fallen leader, found its mark. The impact was sudden, an intense burst of pain. The world spun wildly, a maelstrom of noise and color that slowly faded to black.

My last conscious thought was of Wyatt's voice, distant and urgent, calling my name as darkness claimed me. The battle had been won, Luka's reign brought to an end, but at what cost? The evening's events weighed heavily on me, leaving me overwhelmed with a multitude of unanswered questions and an uncertain future.

31

WYATT

A third gunshot pierced the air, instantly destroying the illusion of finality I had experienced moments earlier. My ears rang, my breath hitched, but I forced my attention through the disarray. Luka's empire was crumbling, but all I could see, all I cared about, was Kensi.

Amidst the shards of shattered glass and the cries of panic, I locked on her figure—the woman who unwittingly held my future in her hands. Her eyes met mine, wide with shock, and for a split second, we were the only two people in the world. Then she crumpled, like a marionette with its strings cut, her body betraying her strength as it succumbed to gravity's pull.

"Kensi!" Her name ripped from my throat, raw and ragged, cutting through the ensuing silence left by the gunfire. The room spun, time stretched thin, each tick of the clock a lifetime as I stumbled to her side, my legs moving of their own accord.

Luka lay motionless, the threat he posed extinguished, his final chapter written in blood on the floor of his decadent tomb. For a moment, a bitter taste of victory tainted my tongue. But it dissolved quickly.

My body was a machine honed by years of discipline, and it

carried me to Kensi's side with a speed that defied the heavy air of shock that filled the room. My hands, marked by scars of service and survival, now hovered over her, the tremble in them betraying the stoic calm I had always worn like armor. The clarity of combat left no room for the paralysis of fear, even as the scent of blood and gunpowder intertwined in a grim dance.

The red stain spread across her dress, a glaring contrast to the pale silk, growing wider, deeper, like a macabre flower blooming in fast-forward. It saturated the fabric, seeping into the very fibers of our reality, rewriting our story with each passing second.

"Stay with me," I pleaded, though no sound escaped my lips. I pressed down, hard and unyielding against the wound, my training taking over where my emotions threatened to engulf me. The pressure I applied was firm, practiced, but inside, something recoiled at the necessity of causing her more pain to keep her alive.

There was a grim satisfaction in knowing Luka would never harm anyone again, but it was poisoned by the sight of Kensi's pale face, her vitality ebbing away under my hands.

"Help is coming, darlin'" I promised her, though I wasn't sure if she could hear me. But I needed her to fight, to cling to life with the same determination that had defined her every action since the day she arrived in Liberty.

As I worked to save her, my mind rebelled against the thought that these could be our last moments together. The realization of what she meant to me—what she had come to mean—was a searing truth that I had never allowed myself to fully feel until now. In the high stakes game we played, love was a vulnerability I couldn't afford. But there it was, undeniable and raw, pushing me to desperately hold onto her.

Memories flickered through my mind like a reel of moments I'd never let go of. The sound of her laugh—a real one, not the polite kind—ringing out across The Anchor that night she beat Stephen at pool. The way she didn't just smile but threw her whole self into it, lighting up the room like she didn't even realize she was the brightest thing in it.

The steady strength in her voice the day she stood her ground, refusing to let anyone get hurt because of her past.

The heat of her gaze the night she'd looked at me, really looked at me, after I promised to keep her safe. There was no fear in her eyes, no hesitation—just trust. Trust she shouldn't have given so easily but did anyway, like she believed in me more than I've ever believed in myself.

The brush of her hand against mine in moments of passing, her touch lingering like it meant something—like she meant something.

And then there were the quiet moments. The way she curled up on the couch in my office at The Anchor, shoes kicked off, completely at ease, her guard slipping just enough to let me see the girl who lived underneath the armor. The girl I couldn't stop thinking about.

Each memory was a thread, weaving something stronger than I ever thought possible. It wasn't just one moment, one glance, or one laugh—it was her. The way she made me want to be better, stronger. For her.

It had crept up on me, hidden in the grit and grime of our reality. Now, it refused to be ignored, standing defiant against the madness that surrounded us.

Love. I hadn't let myself think about it when it came to Kensi. From the start, our relationship wasn't simple—she was married, and the connection between us had been born out of survival, not dates or quiet moments. Her husband wasn't just a problem; he was the kind of man we both stood against.

But as I worked to save her life, there was no denying the truth anymore. What started as a bond forged by circumstance had grown into something more. Over the last six months, every late-night conversation at The Anchor, every laugh shared in the middle of chaos, every glance that lingered too long—they weren't just moments. They were pieces of something bigger. Something I couldn't ignore anymore.

The gravity of my admission to myself was heavy, a burden and a blessing all at once. There had been no right time, no perfect moment to explore these feelings under the shadow of Luka's tyranny. Yet, in the least desirable of scenarios, my heart had found its answer.

I didn't remember being moved aside but I could feel Kensi's fingers cold in mine, their usual strength ebbed to a fragile tremor. I wrapped my hand around hers, willing warmth back into her skin. I watched the medics work with clinical efficiency. It was then a promise formed within me, unspoken but unbreakable. I would protect her, fight for her, and if given the chance, love her openly, free from the chains of her past.

There was a lot we didn't know about what came next, but one thing was clear—I wasn't going anywhere. Whatever battles we faced, I'd be by her side. Not just as a protector or a friend, but as a man who loved her, plain and simple.

The stretcher unfolded with a snap, its metallic legs locking into place as the medics maneuvered it beside Kensi. Watching them lift her fragile form onto it, The raw edges of my composure began to fray. The stretch of fabric beneath her became a canvas for the red that continued to seep from her wound, a stark contrast to the pale severity of her face. As they secured her, buckling the straps like a grim echo of safety, a rage unlike anything I'd known before surged within me.

Luka's reign was over, his lifeless body was proof. But as the stretcher carried Kensi away from the shattered luxury of the penthouse, the victory tasted bitter. My knuckles whitened as I clenched my fists, the helplessness gnawing at me with vicious teeth. She should've been celebrating freedom, not fighting for her life.

"Easy there, Wyatt." Stephen's voice was soft, but his grip on my shoulder was firm, grounding. He knew the battle within me, the soldier's turmoil when victory came at too high a price. His touch didn't erase the anger, but it reminded me I wasn't alone.

We followed the procession through the chaos left in the aftermath, stepping over debris and shattered remnants of what had been a front line just moments ago. Kensi's father, caught in the peripheral vision of my gaze, was being ushered out by Masterson and Reeves.

Handcuffed and defeated, he was a walking cliche of betrayal and blood ties.

My breathing was loud in my ears, the only steady thing I could focus on as we moved through the wreckage. Each step felt heavier, like the weight of the night was pulling me down. The penthouse was an abandoned battlefield, littered with the pieces of Luka's empire and everything he'd tried to control.

But my focus was solely on Kensi, her fragile form strapped to the stretcher, her life hanging in the balance. The medics moved with practiced efficiency, their faces set in expressions of grim determination as they worked to stabilize her. I followed them, my eyes never leaving her face, silently willing her to hold on.

And as the rage still simmered within, it was now tempered by a new purpose: I would not let this be where our story ends.

We emerged from the penthouse into the cold night air, the sirens of emergency vehicles blaring in the distance. The city was alive with the sounds of chaos and confusion, replacing the deathly quiet that had permeated the penthouse just moments before. The flashing lights of the ambulance illuminated the scene, casting harsh shadows that mirrored the darkness within me.

"Wyatt," Stephen's voice was a low rumble beside me, a tether to reality as I fought to keep my emotions in check. "They need to get her to the hospital. There's no time to waste."

I nodded, my throat too tight to speak. The medics lifted Kensi into the back of the ambulance, and I climbed in after them without hesitation. Stephen moved to follow, but I stopped him with a hand on his arm, shaking my head.

"Stay with her father," I managed to say, my voice rough. "Make sure he doesn't slip away. I'll go with her."

Stephen hesitated, his eyes searching mine, but he eventually nodded. He knew as well as I did that this was the only way. Kensi needed me with her, and I needed to be there, to make sure she survived this.

As the ambulance doors slammed shut, enclosing us in a world of sterile white and the smell of antiseptic, I reached out and took

Kensi's hand in mine. Her skin was cold, her fingers limp, but the faint pulse beneath my fingertips was a lifeline I refused to let go of.

The paramedic worked quickly, assessing the damage, administering fluids and oxygen, his focus entirely on the task at hand. But all I could do was watch Kensi's face, willing her to open her eyes, to give me some sign that she was still fighting.

"She's stable for now," the paramedic said, his voice steady but edged with urgency. "The bullet missed anything vital, but she's lost a lot of blood. We need to move fast."

I nodded, not trusting myself to speak. My hand tightened around Kensi's, grounding me as the ambulance roared to life. The sirens screamed, the city flashing by in a blur of lights, but all I could focus on was her—pale, too still, her hand limp in mine.

Fear clawed at my chest, anger chasing close behind. She was more than someone I'd sworn to protect. Somewhere along the way, she'd become part of me, and losing her wasn't an option I could even let myself consider.

The hospital loomed ahead, its harsh lights cutting through the night like a lifeline. The ambulance jerked to a stop, the doors flying open as the paramedics moved fast, pulling Kensi out and rushing her inside. Their voices blurred, drowned out by the pounding in my ears.

I followed, barely keeping pace as they wheeled her toward the operating room. But just before I could step through the doors, a nurse stopped me, her expression calm but unyielding.

"You can't go any further," she said, her hand on my chest stopping me in my tracks. "The doctors need space to work. You'll have to wait out here."

I wanted to argue, to push past her and stay by Kensi's side, but I knew she was right. My presence wouldn't help Kensi now. All I could do was wait.

The nurse must have seen the anguish on my face, because she softened, giving me a small, understanding smile. "She's in good hands," she said gently. "We'll do everything we can."

I nodded, my throat tight with emotion, and watched as the doors to the operating room swung shut, sealing Kensi away from me.

For a moment, I just stood there, staring at the closed doors, my mind numb. The adrenaline that had been driving me finally started to wane, leaving behind a hollow ache that threatened to consume me.

I turned and walked to the waiting area, each step feeling like I was trudging through quicksand. The sterile smell of the hospital filled my lungs, and I sank into one of the plastic chairs, my hands trembling as I buried my face in them.

Time became meaningless as I sat there, lost in the void of my own thoughts. Every minute that ticked by passed like an eternity, every second a reminder of how fragile life could be.

I didn't know how long I sat there, but eventually, I became aware of a presence beside me. I looked up to see Stephen standing there, his expression a mirror of my own exhaustion and concern.

"He's in custody," Stephen said quietly, taking the seat next to me. "Her father will face justice for his role in this. We've got everything we need to make sure he never hurts anyone again."

I nodded, though the news did little to ease the knot of fear in my chest. "And Kensi?"

Stephen's face softened, his eyes filled with the same uncertainty that had been gnawing at me. "She's strong, Wyatt. She's a fighter. We have to believe she'll pull through."

I swallowed hard, unable to find the words to express the storm of emotions raging inside me. The only thing that mattered now was Kensi's survival. Everything else could wait.

The hours crawled by, each one slower than the last. The waiting room may as well have been a prison, every quiet moment giving way to more worry. I kept trying to focus on the good—Luka was gone, Kensi was free—but it didn't stick. The fear of losing her now, after everything we'd fought through, hung over me like a dark cloud I couldn't shake.

Finally, a doctor approached us, his expression calm but serious.

"Mr. Turner?" he asked, his gaze flitting between me and Stephen.

I stood, my heart in my throat. "That's me. How is she?"

The doctor gave a small, reassuring smile. "She's stable. The surgery went well, and we were able to stop the bleeding. She's in recovery now, but it will be a while before she wakes up. She's going to need time to heal, both physically and emotionally."

Relief crashed over me like a wave, leaving me weak-kneed and dizzy. "Can I see her?"

The doctor nodded. "Of course. But only for a few minutes. She needs rest, and so do you."

I didn't argue. I just nodded and followed him down the hallway to the recovery room. My heart was pounding as he pushed open the door, revealing Kensi lying in the bed, her face pale but peaceful.

I approached her slowly, my breath catching in my throat as I took in the sight of her, alive and safe. The machines beeped softly around her, a reminder that she was still with me.

Gently, I reached out and took her hand, careful not to disturb the IV lines that snaked around her arm. Her skin was warm now, a sign that life was flowing through her veins, and I squeezed her fingers gently, willing her to feel my presence.

"I'm here, Kensi," I whispered, my voice thick with emotion. "I'm not going anywhere."

She didn't respond, but that was okay. She was here, she was alive, and that was all that mattered.

As I stood there, watching her breathe, I made a silent vow to myself and to her. I would be there when she woke up. I would help her heal, help her reclaim her life, free from the shadows of her past. And when the time was right, when she was ready, I would tell her how I felt—how much she meant to me, how much I loved her.

But for now, I would wait. I would be patient, because Kensi was worth it.

32

KENSI

Six weeks had passed since the events that altered my life in ways I'd never thought possible.

Luka was dead, eliminated by his own ambition and cruelty. My father, the man who should have been my protector, was behind bars. Safety and peace of mind should have been mine to embrace, yet there I sat, shrouded in the emptiness of a life interrupted, a life I was hesitant to rebuild. Memories, like relentless waves, crashed against the fragile barriers I'd erected, threatening to pull me under.

Agent Ramirez, the FBI agent who had been the recipient of the documents I'd sent through Marco, had been in touch, following up after Wyatt had reached out to him in the aftermath of the showdown with Luka. I should have been relieved. Instead, there was only this pervasive numbness, an emptiness that echoed with the memories I was trying desperately to leave behind.

I had tried to avoid people as much as possible, a task made difficult by the limitations of my injury. The bullet wound, while not life-threatening, had left me weakened and dependent, a state that grated against every instinct I had to retreat and shield myself. For those first weeks, I'd reluctantly accepted their help—mostly because I had no other choice. Wyatt had been there the most, hovering with a watchful intensity that both reassured and unsettled me. He could tell I needed space but refused to let me disappear entirely, his presence quiet but unwavering.

Missy stayed with me during those first nights, quietly tending to the smallest things—adjusting pillows, bringing water, making sure I was as comfortable as I could be. She was both nurse and therapist, always gentle, never pushing. She seemed to know I wasn't ready to open up and let me keep my silence. Even though I'd let her in more than anyone else, there was still a wall between us—one I wasn't sure I'd ever let anyone cross again. I'd learned the hard way that connections were fragile, dangerous things. Keeping my distance felt safer, easier than risking the pain of loss again.

Stephen dropped by regularly, his visits almost like clockwork to share bits of town gossip or sometimes just sit quietly.

Wyatt, though, was different. His presence wasn't just supportive —it was solid, grounding me even when I tried to push it away. He made sure I had what I needed, handling practical tasks without fanfare, as if he understood that my physical wounds were only part of the fight. Sometimes I'd catch his gaze lingering on me, his eyes steady with a quiet strength that seemed to see right through me. And every time, I'd turn away, shutting down the feelings his presence stirred. His kindness felt like an offering I didn't know how to accept—or if I even deserved to.

As the weeks wore on, Missy continued to stay over, her presence evolving from a practical support into something more essential. She was the only person I could tolerate nearby, and even then, I kept a distance, rarely letting my guard down. She understood without asking that I couldn't be coaxed into trust, that I needed my walls up, thick and strong. When I'd wake from nightmares, drenched in sweat and shaking, Missy would sit beside me without a word, her steady presence a quiet assurance that I wasn't alone, even if I refused to acknowledge it.

Despite their best efforts, my heart remained cautious, locked away behind layers of self-preservation. I feared letting them in, feared the vulnerability that came with human connection. These people, who had gone out of their way to care for me, who had become a lifeline I hadn't asked for, were too precious, too fragile. In a world that could snatch them away at any moment, I didn't know how to let myself need them.

And so, I stayed quiet, distant, keeping them at arm's length even as they pulled me back from the edge.

When I was physically able, I found escape in the gardens of The Inn and the mundane tasks of housekeeping that I was capable of doing, losing myself in the rhythm of the work, increasing my workload each day.

A soft sigh escaped me and with it a release of the tension I'd been holding. Perhaps it was time to acknowledge that while the physical wound on my shoulder would fade, the unseen scars were the ones that needed tending. It was time to face that healing would require more than just time and distance; it would demand confronting the ghosts that haunted my every step in this small Texas town that had once promised hope.

My hands delved into the rich, earthy soil of the garden, the cool dampness seeping into my skin as I worked to bury the roots of a young camellia. Sunlight filtered through the leaves of the tall oaks surrounding the Inn's grounds, casting dappled shadows that danced over the beds of budding greenery. With each seedling planted, with every weed pulled, the sharp edges of my thoughts dulled, giving way to the simple clarity of the task at hand.

"Hand me the trowel, will you?" Evelyn's voice was soft, not wanting to break the quietude that had settled over us like a gentle shawl. I passed it to her without a word, our fingers brushing in the exchange—a momentary connection that grounded me.

She moved with an assured grace from years spent nurturing these gardens, coaxing life from the soil with maternal patience There was wisdom etched into the lines of her face, and strength in her hands that made light work of the planting. Yet, she never imposed her presence, allowing the silence to stand between us as a quiet companion rather than an awkward stranger.

I watched as she pressed the earth around a freshly planted sapling, her movements deliberate and caring. The garden was her realm, and within it, I found a modicum of the peace I'd been desperately hoping for. The repetitive motions of digging and planting acted as a meditation, each breath coming easier than the last, each thought less insistent on being heard.

Our work continued in unison, the rhythm we'd established acting as a language unto itself. It was a ballet of sorts, performed with spades and watering cans instead of pirouettes and leaps. The cadence of our labor was punctuated only by the occasional chirp of a bird or the rustle of leaves in the wind.

At times, I stole glances at Evelyn, noting the way the afternoon sun caught the silver strands in her hair, creating a halo effect which was fitting for someone who was practically an angel on earth. She carried a quiet strength, the kind that came from weathering life's storms and offering solace to others without needing to say a word.

"Looks good," she finally said, stepping back to survey our work with a nod of approval. "It'll be beautiful come spring."

"Thanks to you," I replied, feeling a small smile tug at the corner of my mouth.

"Thanks to us," she corrected gently, meeting my gaze with eyes that held no pity, only understanding. In that look, I found acknowledgment—not just of the garden before us, but of the effort it took for me to simply be here, among the living, trying to heal.

THE DOOR CLICKED SOFTLY behind me, the familiar sound of Missy's entrance filling the small living quarters. Her presence had become as regular as the setting sun, yet it did little to dispel the chill that permeated even the warmest corners of the room. I glanced over my shoulder, watching her drop a canvas bag onto the kitchenette counter with a weary sigh.

"Hey," she greeted, her voice a soft lullaby in the quiet space. She kicked off her shoes and padded across the room in socks adorned with whimsical cats—a contrast to the gravity that often hung between us.

"Hey," I echoed back, forcing my muscles to relax as I shifted on the sofa, making room for her to join me. The simple act was a nightly ritual now; Missy, claiming her makeshift bed as if it were the most natural thing in the world.

She sank down beside me, tucking her feet beneath her. "Bad day?" she asked, her gaze searching mine with a gentle probing that I both welcomed and dreaded.

"Same as usual," I replied, trying to keep my voice even, but the tremble betrayed me. Sleep eluded me like a scorned lover, each night a battle waged against the darkness and the horrors it brought forth from the depths of my memories.

"I'm here, you know." Her hand found mine, holding tightly as if she could physically hold the nightmares at bay. And perhaps in some ways, she could. Her presence was what I clung to when the past threatened to pull me under.

I nodded, swallowing hard against the lump forming in my throat. "I know."

In our shared silence, the hum of the fridge and the steady tick of the clock filled the space—simple sounds that somehow made the chaos inside me feel even louder. It was a strange mix, having Missy so close. Her presence was comforting, but it also made me acutely aware of how fragile I'd become. The independence I thought I had gained was a distant echo, fading in the wake of this new need.

Later, as the darkness pressed against the windows, we settled in for the night. Missy curled up on the couch, a quilt pulled up under her chin, and I was in the narrow bed, feeling like it was far too big for just one person. I stared at the ceiling, hoping it might have the answers to the questions that kept turning over in my mind.

Safety. The word was a mirage, taunting me with its promise but always just out of reach. The shadows of my past stretched out across the room, creeping into every corner, every thought. I tried to close my eyes and push them away, but they lingered, thick and heavy, like cobwebs I couldn't shake off.

A husband I never loved, now gone. A life narrowly escaped, yet still clinging to me with cold, ghostly fingers. How do you mourn a monster?

My thoughts kept drifting, caught between the life I'd left and the future I wasn't sure I could face. The battles I'd fought had left their marks—some visible, some not—and even though the physical scars were healing, the emotional ones were different. It was as if the ground had shifted beneath me, and I wasn't sure how to stand on it alone.

"Missy," I whispered, my voice barely there in the dark.

"Still here," she answered, her voice soft and reassuring.

"Thank you," I said, the words catching in my throat.

"Always," she murmured before sleep claimed her once more.

As I lay there, the weight of memories, grief, and the unknowns of what was to come hit me all at once. In the middle of it all, my mind kept drifting to Wyatt—the man who had risked everything to pull me out of the dark. The man who kept showing up, quietly reminding me who he was. He'd been my hope when everything else was lost. Now, after all that had happened, my feelings for him were a mess of confusion and longing, a mess I wasn't sure I could untangle.

Before that night, I'd let myself dream of a life where Luka wasn't in charge anymore, a life where maybe Wyatt and I could see where things between us might go. But those dreams might as well have belonged to someone else now, so far out of reach. How could I even think about what I carried for Wyatt when our bond was born out of violence and loss? That question stuck with me, lingering in the silence, adding to the ghosts that never seemed to leave.

I dozed on and off, the October sun slowly slipping through the blinds, casting long, slanted shadows on the floor. Another night had gone by without peace, but as morning crept in, I knew I'd face it. I'd get up, like I had before. Because healing, I was starting to understand, wasn't about forgetting or running away—it was about finding the strength to keep going, one step at a time.

33

WYATT

Shutting down The Anchor each night was a routine we could probably do blindfolded. The soft chime of last call, the clinking of glasses going back on shelves, flipping chairs onto tables—it was the rhythm of familiarity. But tonight, something was off. Stephen, Missy, and I moved through the motions, but Kensi's absence was a shroud that hung over us. The tension in the air was a reminder of just how much had changed since her life had been torn apart.

Stephen turned the key in the lock, securing the front door, and then glanced at Missy with his usual offer. "Need me to walk you home?" he asked casually, though we all knew it was more than just routine concern.

Missy gave him a faint smile, though it didn't quite reach her eyes. "Drove myself tonight," she replied, her voice carrying a weariness that went beyond simple exhaustion. "Gonna crash with Kensi again."

Stephen's expression hardened briefly before he asked. "Again?"

Missy exhaled a heavy sigh, as if weighed down by the nights she'd spent by Kensi's side, watching her struggle against something none of us could see. "I know. It's like she's there but not there, if that makes sense. It's like she's here physically, but somewhere else, lost in her mind."

Her words sliced through the quiet, exposing the fears we'd all been holding back. I couldn't shake the feeling that Kensi was slipping away from us, from herself, getting lost in a pain she didn't know how to share.

The silence stretched, and I finally broke it. "We've gotta do something. We can't just watch her fade away."

Stephen nodded, his face set, though worry flashed in his eyes. "But we have to be careful. She's been through hell. The last thing she needs is to feel any more pressure from us."

Missy spoke up, her voice thoughtful. "What if we keep it simple? Something familiar, like dinner here after hours. Just us, no pressure."

The idea struck a chord with all of us. The Anchor wasn't just a bar—it was home, a place where we'd built memories, shared laughs, and leaned on each other. It could be the kind of low-key night that might help Kensi feel grounded again.

"Dinner here sounds perfect," I chimed in, picturing her at the table with us. Maybe she'll see how much she matters to all of us, I thought, though I felt a familiar pang as I realized how much more she meant to me.

In truth, I wanted more than anything to be the one who could pull her out of the shadows, but I also knew it wasn't about what I wanted. Kensi wasn't mine to save, no matter how much I wished she could be. She was fighting battles I could only guess at, and all I could do was be there, to help her find her own way out—if that's what she wanted.

Missy nodded, already thinking through the details. "And if she needs to leave, no questions asked. The last thing we want is for her to feel trapped or overwhelmed."

Standing there in the dim bar, our little plan became a flicker of hope in the darkness we'd all been caught in. It wasn't much—just a dinner among friends—but maybe it was a start. I couldn't make Kensi feel what I felt, but I could be there for her. I'd be whatever she needed me to be, even if it meant always wanting something I'd never have.

34

KENSI

The soft morning sunlight streamed through the window, warming the little two-person dining table where Missy and I sat, each nursing a mug of coffee. The coziness of my cottage made moments like this feel easy, like the world outside didn't exist for a while. Missy had become this steady, grounding force in my life—showing up when I needed her most, keeping me tethered when everything else was coming apart at the seams.

I stared into my coffee, trying to stay in the moment. I focused on the heat of the mug in my hands, on the way Missy's quiet presence filled the space beside me. But no matter how hard I tried, that nagging guilt crept in. She had her own life, her own responsibilities, and here she was—again—sitting with me, giving me more than I deserved.

Missy was always busy. She had her job, her friends, her...everything. And yet, she still showed up for me, day after day. I knew I couldn't ever repay her for that. The more she gave, the more I felt like I was taking something I had no right to take. Like I was dragging her away from a life she should be living.

The guilt bubbled up and spilled over before I could stop it. "I don't want you to feel like you have to babysit me," I blurted, my voice shaky. "You've got your own life, and I—I just feel like I'm keeping you from it."

Missy didn't even blink. She leaned forward, her voice steady, like she'd been waiting for this. "Kensi, I'm here because I want to be. This isn't something I have to do. It's my choice. You're not a burden, okay? You're my friend. And I know if it were the other way around, you'd do the same for me without even thinking about it."

Her words hit me straight in the chest. She said exactly what I needed to hear, but it didn't make it any easier to believe. I glanced at her, but couldn't hold her gaze for long. That little voice inside me still wouldn't let up—the one that told me needing her made me weak. That leaning on her meant I wasn't the person I was supposed to be.

The room went quiet, the kind of quiet that's full of everything you can't say out loud. Missy didn't push, though. She just sat there, calm and steady, like she always did.

Then, she broke the silence, her tone gentle but firm. "You know, the guys and I were talking last night. We really miss seeing you at The Anchor. It's not the same without you there, lighting up the place."

Her words hit me hard. The Anchor wasn't just a bar to me—it was home. Or, it used to be. It was the place where I laughed, where I thought I belonged. But now? Now, the thought of going back was...wrong. Like I didn't fit there anymore. Like I didn't fit anywhere anymore.

"I don't know, Missy," I said, my voice barely above a whisper. "I'm not sure I can handle that. It feels like...like I'd be stepping into a life that doesn't feel like mine anymore."

Missy reached across the table, her hand finding mine. Her grip was warm, solid, like she was trying to anchor me to the moment. "What if it's just a small dinner?" she said softly. "Just the four of us. No pressure. No expectations. Just...us."

It wasn't a big ask, but it felt monumental. Admitting I needed them, that I needed anything, felt terrifying. But buried under all the fear was a flicker of something else—a tiny spark of hope. The idea of sitting with friends, in a place that used to mean so much to me...it wasn't just scary. It was tempting, too.

I took a shaky breath, letting the idea settle in. "Maybe," I said finally. "Maybe it could be nice. Just the four of us?"

Missy smiled, squeezing my hand. "Just the four of us," she promised. "And if you want to leave, we'll leave. No questions. No pressure. We just want to be there for you, Kensi. You don't have to do this alone. We miss you."

Her words wrapped around me like a blanket, and for the first time in a long time, the walls I'd built around myself started to crack. I wasn't just hearing her; I was letting it sink in. The dinner wasn't the point—it was the message behind it. That I wasn't alone. That it was okay to need people.

"Okay," I whispered, the word feeling heavy and light all at once. It wasn't much, but it was a step. A tiny step toward letting people back in, toward finding the pieces of myself I thought were gone for good.

35

WYATT

I couldn't understand why my nerves were frayed; this wasn't a date. Stephen and Missy would be there, just a casual gathering of friends. Yet, I found myself overthinking every detail—what to wear, the playlist for the drive. It wasn't just about making things perfect for Kensi; I needed it to be right, not just for her, but for me, too.

Volunteering to pick her up had seemed trivial at first, but now it carried greater significance. Missy and Stephen were back at The Anchor, finishing up with the last of the lunch crowd, leaving me with the task of bringing Kensi. It wasn't just about the ride; it was about offering her a sense of safety and care, something reliable, something I wanted her to feel.

The drive to her place passed in a blur. My mind kept running through possible conversations, trying to find the right balance between offering reassurance and giving her space. By the time I pulled up outside her house, my palms were sweating, and my heart pounded with uncertainty.

When Kensi opened the door, it knocked the breath right out of me. She wasn't dressed to impress—just jeans and a sweater—but there was something in her eyes. Vulnerability, maybe, but layered with a quiet strength that made it impossible to look away.

"Hey," I said, keeping my tone easy. "Ready to go?" I didn't want her to feel rushed. The last thing I wanted was to push too hard, too soon.

She nodded, her gaze flicking up to meet mine for half a second before shifting away. "Yeah. Ready," she said, though her voice carried just enough hesitation to make me wonder if she was trying to convince herself.

As we started driving, the radio filled the car with soft music. I glanced over, wondering if she'd ask me to change the station, but she was already lost in the song, her forehead creasing slightly as she listened.

"Who sings this?" she asked, curiosity in her voice.

"Rascal Flatts," I replied. "The song's called *Every Day*." She nodded after a moment, a small smile breaking through. "I like it," she said, almost to herself.

"Do you like music?" I asked, seizing the chance to learn more about her.

She shrugged. "I don't mind it, but I don't know much about country," she admitted, with a touch of curiosity in her tone.

I smiled. "Well, I could help change that if you'd like." It was a small offer, a way to share something I loved with her.

She studied me for a moment, then smiled softly. "I would like that," she said.

That small hint of a smile may as well have been a firework exploding inside my chest.

As the earlier tension eased, the rest of the drive took on a lighter mood. As we arrived at The Anchor, I glanced at Kensi, hoping this evening would be the start of something new for her—a chance to find joy in small moments and feel supported by those who cared about her.

Inside The Anchor, Stephen greeted us first, giving Kensi a gentle side hug. Missy followed with a full embrace, as if they'd been apart for longer than a day. What I wouldn't give to pull her close, to hold her and never let go. To be the person she could turn to when everything got to be too much. But wanting that and understanding what she truly needed were worlds apart. Right now, what mattered most was making sure she knew she was safe, that we were here for her—without asking more than she was ready to give.

As we settled in, I noticed Kensi's laughter coming more easily, her smiles reaching her eyes. It wasn't just about making the night perfect; it was about showing her that she was surrounded by people who cared, who were there for her no matter what.

Stephen couldn't resist adding his humor to the mix. "Hope you're ready for a gourmet feast. I personally oversaw the pizza ordering. Very technical stuff," he joked, earning a laugh from Kensi and an eye roll from Missy.

Missy played along, "Yes, watching you debate between pepperoni and sausage was truly awe-inspiring."

Their banter was light and easy, and I noticed Kensi's smile growing more genuine with each exchange. Stephen winked at me, as if to say, "See? Everything's going to be just fine."

As the evening wore on, Missy started to yawn, and Stephen took the cue. "Time for me to play chauffeur," he announced, but then Missy hesitated, glancing at Kensi, a question in her eyes.

Kensi noticed and spoke up. "Missy, it's okay. I'll help Wyatt clean up, and if he doesn't mind, he can take me home."

I didn't hesitate. "Of course, I'd be happy to."

Missy looked relieved, though her eyes lingered on Kensi a moment longer. As Stephen and Missy left, there was a tension between them, something unspoken.

Kensi and I began to clean up, the silence between us more comfortable now. After a while, she broke the silence. "Was it just me, or was their goodbye...weird?"

I paused, then decided to be honest. "There's something going on with them, but they haven't said much yet. I'm sure they'll talk when they're ready."

She went quiet. The weight of her guilt was evident in her downcast eyes, the slow dawning of realization visible in the subtle tightening of her jaw.

"Hey," I waited for Kensi to look at me. "Missy's been exactly where she's wanted to be. You're important to her, to all of us."

Kensi nodded, a small smile forming. "I know. It's just hard not to feel like I'm keeping her from living her life."

"Missy makes her own choices, just like we all do. Right now, she chooses to be there for you. We all need help sometimes. Doesn't make us any less strong."

As we continued to clean, the conversation shifted to lighter topics, the tension easing. And as I caught another one of Kensi's slight but genuine smiles, I knew tonight had been a success. I also knew that I would do anything in my power to get her to smile as often as possible for the rest of my life.

36

KENSI

As we drove in silence, the hum of country music filling the space between us, my thoughts lingered on Missy and everything she'd given me these past few weeks. Missy had set aside so much of her time, rearranging her life to be there for me. And yet, even with all her support, there was someone who'd given up even more—the man sitting quietly beside me.

Wyatt had sacrificed something far bigger, something that had the power to shape his future. He'd walked away from Nashville and a dream that could have changed his life. The chance to compete in that prestigious country music competition wasn't just an opportunity; it was a rare shot at recognition, the kind of break people spent their lives chasing. Yet he'd let it go because of me.

Knowing everything he'd sacrificed for me settled heavily on my heart, mingling with an ache of guilt. I couldn't ignore the unfairness of it: Wyatt had a clear path laid before him, and I'd pulled him from it without meaning to. I couldn't even begin to repay what he'd done for me, couldn't fathom how someone could set aside so much just because I needed them. That kind of loyalty, that kind of care, it was a gift so precious I didn't know how to accept it.

By the time we pulled up to my house, I knew I needed to say something. The silence was thick, loaded with words I hadn't dared speak.

My voice was barely above a whisper when I finally spoke. "You know, every time I think about what you gave up for me, it overwhelms me. I know how much that opportunity in Nashville meant to you, and I can't help but feel guilty that you had to make that choice."

Wyatt's gaze held mine, steady and intense, a kind of softness underneath that made my chest tighten. "Kensi, I need you to know something," he said, his voice low but clear. "Going to Nashville wasn't some big dream for me. It was just an opportunity—one I'd leave behind in a heartbeat if it meant keeping you safe. There's nothing I wouldn't do for you, nothing I wouldn't risk. I need you to know that."

He paused, his eyes searching mine, as if making sure I understood. "You mean more to me than anything. I don't want to scare you, but I don't want there to be any doubt, either. I'm here, Kensi. For you."

I couldn't breathe for a moment, the tension pulsing between us like a live wire. Wyatt's steady gaze grounded me, even as his words rippled through me, rooting me in place.

I hadn't dared to consider the depth of his feelings, hadn't let myself imagine that anyone could care for me like that. But here he was, looking at me like I was something precious, something he'd protect without hesitation. My insides were a mess.

That intensity terrified me. It was unlike anything I'd ever known, and yet some part of me had been waiting, aching, to hear those words. But this wasn't just about safety or friendship. His words carried a deeper meaning, one that scared me almost as much as Luka ever had.

Because connections like this—connections that mattered—were fragile, dangerous. They could be torn away without warning, leaving nothing but wreckage behind. And I wasn't sure I was ready to trust, to risk opening my heart to someone who could so easily be taken from me.

I swallowed, his confession burrowing itself into my heart. My voice barely surfaced, a murmur caught somewhere between hope and fear. "Wyatt... I don't know what to say."

He simply nodded, his hand reaching over, lightly brushing mine as if to reassure me without demanding more. "You don't have to say anything," he said, his voice soft. "Just know that I'm here, whenever you're ready."

The silence returned, but this time, it wasn't hollow. It carried a quiet understanding, a presence that both settled and unsettled me.

I stared out the windshield as memories surfaced. "The night I was taken, it was the first night of the competition. I was watching it. I saw your performance before... everything happened." I paused, the memory of that night still vivid. "You were amazing. The judges said you were the one to beat. You could have won it all."

It was important for him to know that I understood what he had given up for me.

Wyatt looked surprised by my words. After a moment of silence, he reached out and took my hand. "My decision to come for you was the only one I could have made. It's the same decision I would make again and again."

I nodded, unsure if there were even words capable of expressing what I was currently feeling.

As we sat there in the quiet, the reality of going inside alone hit me all at once. For the first time in weeks, I would be alone at night, and the thought of it was suddenly overwhelming.

Sensing my hesitation, Wyatt asked, "Kensi, do you want me to come in and check the place? Make sure everything's okay?"

Relief washed over me. "Yes, please. I would really appreciate that," I whispered.

We got out of the truck, and I led the way to the door, feeling more confident with Wyatt by my side. He stepped in first, turning on lights and checking each room, making sure everything was safe.

As he moved through my home, I stood quietly in the entry, the sound of his footsteps reassuring. His presence made the house feel less like a place of fear and more like a safe haven.

When he was done, Wyatt turned to me with a soft smile. "All clear, Kensi. Everything looks good."

"Thank you," I said, overwhelmed with gratitude.

"If you need anything, anything at all, call me," Wyatt added, his tone serious. "It doesn't matter what time it is."

A sudden wave of anxiety gripped me as I watched him move toward the door, each step tightening the knot in my chest. The thought of him leaving, of the silence that would take over this place after he was gone, was agonizing. I had the urge to ask him to stay, but the fear of seeming weak—of needing him too much—held me back.

But then, as his hand brushed the doorknob, the words spilled out before I could stop them. "Wyatt," I started, my voice barely audible. "Would you... maybe want to stay and watch TV or something? I know it's late, but—"

Wyatt didn't let me finish. He turned back, releasing the doorknob, and said, "Of course. I'd like that." His tone was calm, steady, effortlessly giving me exactly what I needed without me having to explain.

Relief coursed through me as we settled on opposite ends of the couch. The distance was just enough to feel safe, but his presence anchored me in a way that softened the edges of my lingering anxiety. Wyatt leaned into his corner, his arm draped casually along the back of the couch, his steady calm filling the room in a way that silence never could.

I reached for the remote, hesitating for a second before handing it to him. "Guest's choice," I said, adding a small smile to keep the moment light, like this was just any other evening.

Wyatt took the remote, his eyes meeting mine briefly. There was something in his gaze—understanding, patience—that made the room feel smaller and the emotional distance between us lesser. I realized I'd missed his closeness more than I wanted to admit. But what could I do about that now?

A thought stirred uneasily in the back of my mind: maybe I was too broken to ever let someone all the way in. Sure, he was here now, filling the space with a quiet steadiness I craved, but what would happen when he got too close? Would he see the fractures, the jagged edges I worked so hard to hide? Was it fair to bring someone into the wreckage of my life?

He began scrolling through the options slowly, unhurried, as if this simple choice was something we had all the time in the world to decide.

I stole a glance at him, watching as he flipped through channels, so effortlessly calm. I envied that calm, that sense of balance. It was everything I lacked, everything I wasn't sure I could ever offer someone in return.

The thought settled like a stone in my chest. Maybe it was better this way—keeping the distance, staying safely on opposite ends of the couch, of my life. But when he glanced at me again, a small, easy smile breaking through his focus on the screen, something inside me shifted. It wasn't that he didn't see my brokenness; it was that he didn't seem afraid of it.

I settled back, letting myself sink into the cushions, the tension in my shoulders gradually easing. The silence between us wasn't heavy or awkward; it was peaceful, each of us content in our own space, connected by the shared moment. The quiet din of the television was a welcome background, filling the silence without demanding anything from us.

A noise stirred me awake—a faint clinking of dishes, the low hum of the coffee maker sputtering to life. My heart leaped in my chest, a rush of alarm flooding my senses as I lay there, frozen, straining to make sense of the sounds coming from the kitchen. For a few tense seconds, I was caught in the disorienting fog between sleep and waking, unsure if I was truly safe or if danger had found its way back to me.

But then I remembered—Wyatt was here. I took a shaky breath, the tension slowly melting away as reality settled in. Wyatt was here, moving quietly in the kitchen, and I was safe.

The initial fear gave way to a quiet gratitude knowing that I wasn't alone. I let myself relax, taking in the sounds of someone else being there, looking out for me. Not just someone. Him.

I rubbed the sleep from my eyes and sat up, noticing a blanket carefully draped over me. Morning light seeped through the curtains, and the faint sounds from the kitchen carried a calm that eased through me.

Gathering the blanket around me, I walked to the kitchen.

Lingering in the doorway, I watched Wyatt move through my kitchen with effortless ease, quietly owning the space. A sense of calm settled over me, easing the ache that had lodged in my chest. This glimpse of normalcy was unfamiliar after everything that had happened, yet him being here was more—something I knew I would come to crave in the stillness of my home when he wasn't here.

He looked up as I entered, a smile spreading across his face.

"Good morning," his voice, carrying a soft cheerfulness, greeted me. The simplicity of the gesture, him handing me a mug of freshly brewed coffee, felt natural. Taking the mug, my hands brushed against his, sending a flutter through me that was equal parts pleasant and unsettling.

37

WYATT

When Kensi asked me to stay, my decision was instant. Shadows of fear clung to her voice, but even if they hadn't, I would have stayed. We settled on the couch, the only light from the TV. I watched her slowly unwind, the tension easing from her shoulders, bit by bit. Seeing her finally relax gave me a sense of purpose, a quiet relief. Before long, her breathing softened, slowing into the steady rhythm of sleep. Watching over her was second nature to me.

As dawn edged in, I woke from a light doze. I stretched out the stiffness in my muscles, already thinking of small ways to ease her into the day. Moving quietly, I made my way around her kitchen, familiarizing myself with where things were, careful not to wake her. The soft hum of the coffee maker filled the silence, the sound grounding me.

I poured coffee into two mugs, as I thought back to last night— her asking me to stay. It wasn't just a night on her couch. It was more than that. A quiet promise that I'd be here for her, for as long as she needed. I just hoped she felt it the way I meant it.

Hearing the soft pad of her footsteps, I turned, finding Kensi standing in the doorway, a sleepy, vulnerable figure that tugged at something inside me.

"Morning," I said, lifting my mug in a casual greeting. She looked soft in the way only mornings could make someone—hair a little loose, sleep still clinging to her edges. The sunlight caught her face just right, and for a second, I forgot the coffee in my hand. There was something about this—sharing a quiet morning—that felt like more than it should. Like a glimpse of a life I didn't know I wanted until now.

Watching her take that first sip of coffee, seeing the small smile that played on her lips, I knew that this was where I was meant to be.

Kensi's gaze lifted from the mug to meet mine, a flush of embarrassment coloring her cheeks. "I'm so sorry. I can't believe I just crashed like that," she began, her voice tinged with a hint of sheepishness. The blanket she had wrapped around herself acting as a shield, a soft barrier between her and the world.

"It's okay," I reassured her, taking a sip from my own mug to give her a moment. "You needed the rest. Besides, it gave me a chance to play knight in shining armor, minus the armor."

A soft laugh escaped her, dispelling the brief tension. "More like my guardian angel, then," she countered, the gentleness in her gaze softening the words. "Honestly, I can't remember the last time I slept so well. It's been a while."

The admission hung between us. It took a lot of restraint not to reach for her. "I'm glad," I replied. "You deserve that kind of rest, Kensi. You deserve peace."

She took another sip of her coffee, a thoughtful look crossing her face. "Having you here made a difference," Kensi confessed, the morning light casting a soft glow around her.

The simplicity of her words struck a chord.

"I'll always be here, Kensi. Whenever you need me," I promised.

A smile touched her lips, genuine and filled with a quiet gratitude. "Thank you," she whispered.

As we finished our coffee, the morning stretched before us, filled with the promise of a new day.

38

KENSI

As Wyatt left, his reluctance was hard to miss. A whirlpool of emotions began to churn within me. The door clicked shut behind him, and with it, the energy in the room shifted. In the quiet house, alone again, I found both solace and the familiar embrace of solitude. But this morning, that solitude felt different—less somber and more peaceful.

Each step of my morning routine was heavy with my thoughts. The space around me still held traces of Wyatt's presence.

I paused in front of the mirror, the brush in my hand stilled midstroke. I barely recognized the person staring back at me in the reflection. There was a hint of color in my cheeks, a brightness to my eyes that had been absent for a long time. Who was this woman, who now bore traces of hope where there had once been only fear and weariness? The night's rest, the most peaceful sleep I'd had in weeks, had left its mark.

As I headed to work, the lightness in my step surprised me. It was like putting on an oversized sweater. At first it appears bulky or ill-fitting, but once you sink into its warmth and softness, it feels like a wearable hug.

When I arrived at the Inn, Evelyn's sharp eyes caught the change immediately. She had a way of seeing beneath the surface, of understanding more than she let on.

"You're different today, Kensi," Evelyn remarked, her tone gentle but curious, as she handed me a vase of fresh-cut flowers to place on the table. Her sharp eyes, always kind but unrelenting, studied me in that way of hers, as if she could read the thoughts I hadn't yet spoken aloud.

I paused, the vase cool against my hands, and offered her a small smile. "I got some actual rest for a change," I replied, my voice light, though even I could hear the trace of surprise in it. The peaceful night had been unexpected, a gift I hadn't dared to hope for.

Evelyn's lips curved into a knowing smile. "I'm glad to hear it," she said. "Sometimes all it takes is the right company to remind us how to live again."

Her words hung in the air, and I felt my cheeks heat as I looked away, busying myself with the flowers. Evelyn's intuition was uncanny and I knew she'd catch the shift in my mood without having to say anything.

As I arranged the flowers on the table, my thoughts drifted back to Wyatt. There was a gentleness to him, a quiet strength that never demanded but always offered. He had a way of making space for me without pressuring me to fill it, an unspoken understanding that I was still finding my way.

"That boy has a heart as big as Texas," Evelyn said suddenly, breaking into my thoughts. "He has a way of seeing people, of knowing what they needed before they could ask."

I glanced up, startled by how perfectly her words echoed my own thoughts.

The link between them became so clear in that moment, and I realized how much of her must have shaped the man he'd become.

"Yeah," I murmured softly, my hands stilling on the vase. "I can see that."

Evelyn's gaze lingered on me, her expression thoughtful but kind. "It's a rare thing, you know. Someone who carries their goodness so openly, without letting the ugliness of the world chip away at it."

I nodded, unable to find the words to respond. Her insight left me feeling both exposed and unsettled, as though she'd uncovered something I wasn't ready to confront, even within myself. Wyatt's presence in my life was something I hadn't anticipated, and while it frightened me to admit how much it mattered, it also brought a quiet sense of solace I couldn't deny.

Evelyn's smile was knowing and without judgment.

"How would you feel about joining me at the town hall meeting tonight?" she asked.

I paused, the suggestion catching me off guard. "The town hall meeting?" I echoed, trying to mask my surprise. "I've never been to one of those before. Is it like a business meeting?"

Evelyn chuckled, her eyes twinkling with amusement. "Oh, it's much more than that. It's a Liberty tradition. The whole town comes together—there's always food, laughter, and some good-natured arguments. But more than anything, it's a chance for everyone to connect, to feel like part of something bigger. I think you'd enjoy it."

Her invitation was casual, though I knew it was more than that. She was offering me a glimpse into the heart of Liberty, a place I had cautiously navigated and kept at arm's length until now. Despite the anxiety I had at the thought of being around so many people, knowing I'd be with Evelyn calmed my nerves.

"I'd love to," I agreed, trying to keep my tone light.

Throughout the day, my thoughts often drifted back to the quiet morning shared with Wyatt. I replayed the moments in my mind— the easy silence between us, the way he seemed to know exactly what I needed without me having to ask. There were mixed feelings that came alongside the realization of how much his presence had come to mean to me.

I was so thankful for Wyatt, but everything was complicated and I wasn't ready to try and unpack it. The fear and trauma were still present, but underneath, a growing awareness of something more was taking root. Something that had the potential to be life-changing if I allowed myself to explore it. But for now, I held onto the lighter feeling, the sense of safety and belonging that came from simply being around Wyatt.

Later that evening, as we made our way to the town hall, I couldn't help but feel a flutter of nerves. The building, a charming mix of old-world architecture and modern touches, stood proudly at the center of downtown Liberty. Its doors were wide open, inviting anyone who passed by to join in.

Carrying a casserole dish wrapped in a quilted carrier, Evelyn explained that the meeting was a "potluck affair". I'd never even heard of a potluck before, much less attended one. It was clearly not something that happened in New York—at least not in the circles I'd once moved in. The concept itself was foreign to me: a communal meal where everyone contributed, a patchwork of foods and effort coming together into something shared. The whole thing was almost too wholesome to be real.

Inside, the atmosphere was a lively hum of voices, laughter, and the clinking of dishes. The scent of freshly baked pies mingled with the savory aroma of roasted meats, making my stomach growl in anticipation. Long tables stretched across the hall, each one adorned with simple, homey decorations—mason jars holding flickering candles, scattered autumn leaves adding a rustic charm. It was welcoming, lively, and filled with an energy that was both weird and wonderful.

Evelyn led me to a group of people gathered near a table laden with food. "Kensi, this is Mrs. Harper from the bakery and her husband, Bob, from the barbershop," Evelyn introduced. "And this is Maria, she owns the art store down the street."

Each person greeted me with a smile, their friendliness easing the tension in my shoulders. "It's so nice to finally meet you, Kensi," Mrs. Harper said, her voice kind. "I've heard so much about the wonderful work you're doing at The Inn."

"Thank you," I replied, feeling a blush creep up my cheeks.

Maria handed me a plate and guided me toward the buffet. "You'll want to try my tamales," she insisted, her voice rich with pride. "They're a hit every year."

As I approached the tables, I was struck by the sheer variety of dishes. There were casseroles in glass Pyrex dishes, salads heaped in large wooden bowls, and pies presented on intricately patterned ceramic plates. Someone had brought fried chicken piled high on a silver platter, while a steaming crockpot sat in the corner, its lid slightly askew to reveal bubbling chili. Platters of cookies, loaves of fresh bread wrapped in cloth napkins, and even a cake delicately balanced on a tiered stand completed the spread.

The sight left me feeling oddly moved. In New York, meals were often about convenience or pretense—takeout in cartons, restaurant plates designed more for aesthetics than for sustenance. Here, food was personal, an extension of the people who made it. The thought was both humbling and intimidating.

Tentatively, I filled my plate, wondering if it was obvious to everyone else that this was my first potluck. The tamales Maria had mentioned were warm and fragrant, their golden corn husks folded with care. I added a slice of pie to my plate, then a small scoop of chili, each choice feeling like an experiment in trust.

As I navigated the room to sit next to Evelyn, I noticed the ease with which everyone interacted. People moved from one group to another, sharing stories, offering food, and laughing as if they had known each other all their lives. It occurred to me most of them probably had. There was a sense of unity, a shared understanding that transcended differences. It was as if the town itself was one large family, each member playing a vital role.

Evelyn's plate was piled just as high with food as mine was. "This," she said, gesturing to the room, "is what makes Liberty special. We come together, no matter what, to celebrate, to support each other, and even talk about business and the town. We do it as a town but also as a family."

For so long, I'd believed that attachments were dangerous, that depending on others was a risk I couldn't afford. Connections had always been fragile, like anything could be ripped away at any moment, leaving behind only pain. But watching the way the townspeople came together, supported one another, and genuinely appeared to like each other, made me wonder if I'd been wrong. Maybe connections weren't inherently fragile; maybe they were only as strong as the care and intention behind them.

I glanced at Evelyn, who was happily munching on her tamale and chatting with someone across the table. She made it sound so simple, so obvious—that life was better when it was shared, when people came together instead of drifting apart.The thought stirred something in me, equal parts hope and fear. Could I ever belong to something like this? Did I even have the right to?

The conversation flowed around me, drawing me in. People were genuinely interested in my thoughts, my ideas. They asked about the Inn, my plans for the holidays, and how I was settling in. I found myself sharing more than I had expected.

The door swung open, and I spotted Wyatt, Stephen, and Missy entering. Their eyes scanned the room, and when they saw me sitting with Evelyn, their expressions turned from surprise to delight.

"What are you doing here?" Wyatt asked, a smile spreading across his face as he approached with his own plate of food.

"Evelyn invited me," I explained, glancing at Evelyn, who simply shrugged, her eyes sparkling with mischief.

"I thought it was about time Kensi saw what Liberty's all about," Evelyn said, winking at me. "Besides, I figured you wouldn't mind."

Stephen and Missy exchanged amused glances before taking seats beside us. "Welcome to the inner circle," Stephen joked, reaching for a dinner roll from the basket in the center of the table.

Just as we were getting settled, a loud voice rose above the din. "I'm telling you, Margaret, the turkey needs to wear the cowboy hat this year!" Mr. Thompson was gesturing wildly, his face flushed with enthusiasm.

"No, no, no!" Margaret, a tall woman with an air of authority, crossed her arms, her brows knitting together. "The turkey should wear the pilgrim hat, like tradition. We're not changing it just because you think it's funny."

I turned to Wyatt, raising an eyebrow. "What's that all about?"

Wyatt grinned, clearly entertained by the argument. "Every year, they have a big debate about how to dress up the lead turkey for the Turkey Trot. It's a Thanksgiving tradition. The whole town comes out to see the turkey dressed up, and then it leads the parade down Main Street. Last year, they put it in a tutu. It was quite the spectacle."

"A tutu?" I echoed, unable to hide my laughter. "Is this a real turkey we're talking about?"

"Oh, it's real alright," Missy said, joining in with a chuckle. "Poor thing, every year it's a different outfit. Some folks even take bets on what it'll be. And trust me, the Turkey Trot is a big deal around here. It's like our version of Macy's Thanksgiving Day Parade, but with a lot more feathers and a lot less marching bands."

The lively debate over the turkey's wardrobe showed no signs of slowing down. Margaret's voice rose above the chatter. "I'm not letting the turkey trot down Main Street looking like a joke like it did last year, Harold. Pilgrim hat. Back to tradition. End of story."

Harold Thompson, clearly not one to back down, pointed an indignant finger at her. "Tradition is boring! We need to spice things up, get some laughs! That cowboy hat has personality!"

Before Margaret could fire back, another voice piped up from across the room. "Can we give the turkey BOTH hats? Let people vote on which one it wears halfway through the parade!" This suggestion from Mrs. Betty Harper, sent a ripple of gasps and murmurs through the crowd, as if she'd just proposed a revolution.

Wyatt leaned closer, his grin widening. "This is about to get good."

Sure enough, the town clerk, a wiry man named Frank, stood and tapped a spoon loudly against a ceramic coffee cup. "Alright, alright, that's enough squawking for one night!" he called out, drawing all eyes to him. "If we're gonna settle this, it needs to be done properly— on the record! I hereby call this meeting to order."

A hush fell over the room, save for a few stifled giggles. Margaret and Harold exchanged glances, clearly gearing up for an official showdown.

Frank, who took a moment to relish his moment of authority,

adjusted his glasses and pulled out a small notebook. "Now, I'll enter-tain a motion. Margaret, you're proposing the pilgrim hat, correct?"

"Yes," Margaret said firmly, smoothing her blouse as if preparing for battle. "It's traditional. The turkey deserves dignity."

"Harold, you're advocating for the cowboy hat?"

"Darn right, I am! That turkey deserves flair!"

Mrs. Betty waved her hand in the air, her bracelets jingling. "And don't forget my compromise—both hats!"

Frank sighed dramatically. "Alright, folks, we'll open the floor for discussion. Three minutes per speaker. Let's keep it civil, remember?"

As the debate over the turkey's attire continued, I found myself laughing along with the others, swept up in the absurdity of it all.

The meeting continued, the discussions and light-hearted debates were entertaining. The more I listened, the more I realized how much these people cared about each other, how invested they were in their town and its traditions.

Before long, the evening concluded with promises of pies and pumpkin carving for the upcoming fall festival, and everyone began to drift toward the doors, still chatting and laughing. The argument over the turkey's costume had ended in a reluctant compromise thanks to Maria, who suggested they let the turkey decide.

As we left the town hall, the cool night air filled my lungs, refreshing and invigorating. I felt a new sense of belonging stronger than I had known before, a fulfillment that came not just from the food or the laugh-ter, but from the realization that I was no longer an outsider looking in. I was part of this community, part of something larger than myself.

Evelyn linked her arm through mine as we walked back to the Inn. "You did great tonight, Kensi," she said, her voice filled with pride. "You're one of us now."

Her words were a sweet reassurance that eased the tension I didn't realize I'd been holding. As I looked around at the familiar streets, now quiet under the starlit sky, I knew she was right. Liberty wasn't just a place where I lived—it was home.

Wyatt stayed close by my side as we stepped out into the cool night air. The stars glittered above us, and the streetlights cast long, golden pools along the sidewalk. The energy from the meeting still hummed around me, making the quiet feel less like solitude and more like contentment.

"Can I walk you home?" Wyatt asked, his voice low.

I glanced up at him, a shiver dancing through me at his nearness. "I'd like that," I said, smiling softly.

We walked in companionable silence for a few moments, the sounds of our footsteps the only noise against the backdrop of the quiet town. My mind drifted back to the meeting, to the affability of the people, the laughter, and the sense of belonging that had settled in my chest.

"That was something," I said, breaking the silence. "I've never been to a town hall meeting before. I didn't expect so much enthusiasm."

Wyatt chuckled, his eyes shining in the dim light. "Yeah, Liberty folks take their traditions seriously. Especially the Turkey Trot. It's one of those things that's been around forever, and no one's really sure how it started, but everyone looks forward to it."

"It's nice," I admitted. "To see people care so much about their community, about each other. It's not something I'm used to."

Wyatt glanced at me, a thoughtful expression on his face. "You fit right in, you know. You've got a way about you, Kensi. People can tell you care. It's why they've welcomed you so easily. And they'd care about you, too, if you'd let them."

His words reached a part of me I'd thought was beyond repair. "I wasn't sure I'd find a place like this," I confessed. "After everything, I didn't think I could feel anything again. But tonight, it was the first time in a long time I've felt genuinely happy."

Wyatt's hand brushed against mine, a brief touch that sent a spark of electricity through me. "I'm glad to hear that," he said quietly. "You deserve to be happy, Kensi. To feel safe. And you've got a whole town here that's got your back, not to mention me."

We reached my door where I paused, turning to face Wyatt. The night was cool, the air crisp and clean, and the world went still, as if it were holding its breath just for us.

"Thank you for walking me home," I said, my voice soft. "And for everything else. I don't think I could have made it through these past months without you."

Wyatt smiled, causing my heart to flutter at the sight. "Anytime. You know that."

There was a beat of silence, a pause where the only sound was the rustling of leaves in the breeze. Wyatt's eyes searched mine. Clearing his throat, he said, "So, are you still up for that country music education?"

A huge grin spread across my face."I'm ready when you are," I replied, feeling a sense of anticipation stirring inside of me.

Wyatt's smile widened, his eyes twinkling with mischief. "Alright then. Be prepared, because once we start, there's no going back. I'm talking about the classics, the legends, and the new stuff too. We're going to cover it all."

Unable to control my smile I nodded. "I'm looking forward to it. It's about time I learned what all the fuss is about."

We stood there for a moment longer just staring at each other, smiling like idiots. Finally, Wyatt took a step back, his hand lingering on the porch railing. "Goodnight, Kensi," he said, his voice soft.

"Goodnight, Wyatt," I replied, watching as he turned and walked away, his figure blending into the shadows.

As I climbed the steps and slipped inside, a sense of peace settled over me. The weight of the past few weeks lifted, replaced by a gentle optimism that filled my heart. I was finding my place, my home, and with my people by my side, I was ready to face whatever came next.

39

WYATT

When I told Kensi I'd gladly educate her on country music, I hadn't thought much about it until it was all I could think about. Creating a playlist for her was an act of revealing parts of myself I had been saving just for her. The idea to show up armed with said playlist and dinner from The Anchor was a spur-of-the-moment decision, one that had my stomach in knots the whole drive over to her place.

I sat in my truck debating my next move but I knew that she had to have seen me on the security camera. When I finally mustered the courage to step out of the truck, the cool evening breeze did little to ease the heat creeping up my neck.

The playlist, a mix of classic country and newer hits, was more than just songs. Every track was chosen with Kensi in mind. I wanted her to hear songs that reminded her of her strength through her struggles, and the peace I knew she could find in Liberty.

I knocked on her door, mostly excited, definitely nervous. My heart was drumming faster than any country two-step. The door swung open, revealing Kensi standing there, a shadow of surprise crossing her features before a smile took its place. She was wearing a simple t-shirt and jeans, but to me, she looked more beautiful than anyone I'd ever seen.

"Wyatt, hi," she said, her voice a melody that played right into my heart.

I managed a smile, holding up the bag of food from The Anchor. "I thought, if you were free, we could do some Country Music 101 tonight," I said, hoping my attempt at casual didn't betray the racing of my heart.

Her smile widened. "I love that idea," she said, stepping aside to let me in.

Her place always had an inviting atmosphere. I couldn't resist glancing at the couch where we had spent that night, not touching but sharing something as real as the cushions we'd sat on. It reminded me of the distance we'd both come since then, physically and emotionally.

Kensi led me to the kitchen, where I set the food on the counter. "It's the special of the day—smoked brisket, crispy fried green tomatoes, and coleslaw that will knock your socks off. I probably should have called first. Sorry about that."

She was already reaching for plates when she said, "I'm not sorry. I was just trying to decide how much effort I wanted to put into dinner. This is way better than the box of Mac and cheese I've been eyeing for the last ten minutes."

We filled our plates, moving around each other in the small kitchen with an ease that was completely natural. She handed me a plate without looking, already focused on dividing up the brisket with a grin. "You're lucky you brought enough food for two," she teased, "or you'd have been stuck with mac and cheese."

"I wouldn't complain," I replied, grabbing the fried green tomatoes. "Boxed mac and cheese beats a lot of things I had in the service."

Kensi smirked. "I'll keep that in mind next time I'm feeling generous." She slid a piece of brisket onto her plate and leaned back against the counter, glancing at me.

"So, how's work been? Things getting busy with Thanksgiving around the corner?" I asked.

She smiled, the genuine one that had been rare not long ago. "It's really busy but I love it. Everyone's got that holiday energy, even if it's chaotic. I helped your mom decorate the dining room this morning, and the regulars wouldn't stop giving us tips on where to put the lights. Evelyn said it's the busiest we've ever been."

I couldn't help but notice the lightness in her demeanor, her voice bubbling with excitement. It was a far cry from the fog she'd been stuck in weeks ago. Seeing her like this, talking about things she loved, made me realize just how much she'd changed. It was as though she was finally growing into herself. It was beautiful.

We sat down at the table, the smell of smoked brisket and fried tomatoes filling the room. I watched her as she took a bite, her eyes lighting up. Seeing her like this, so at ease, brought me a kind of peace I hadn't realized I'd been searching for.

"You okay?" she asked suddenly, catching me looking.

"Better than okay," I replied, covering the moment with a playful smirk. "I mean, how could I not be? I've got brisket, fried green tomatoes, country music, and the best company a guy could ask for. It sounds like a country song in the making, actually."

Kensi laughed, shaking her head as she reached for her drink.

As we ate, the first chords of a classic country tune filled the room, a look of curiosity crossed Kensi's face, illuminated by the glow of the overhead light.

"This one's a staple in any country music collection," I explained, as the twang of guitars blended with heartfelt lyrics. "It's about holding on through the tough times. Kind of reminds me of something I've seen in you."

Kensi smiled, a touch of surprise in her eyes. "I've never really listened to country music except when you've played."

"You'll find there's a story in these songs that feels universal," I said as we ate and listened to Gary Allan sing about every storm running out of rain.

"This one," I gestured towards the speaker as a new song started, "talks about finding home wherever your heart is. Made me think of how you've found a new beginning here in Liberty."

She leaned back, her expression open yet guarded, like she was testing the waters. "I guess I never thought music could capture something like that. It's been a long road to feeling like I belong somewhere. And there are still days I feel like a tiny rabbit, always looking over her shoulder."

The corner of my mouth twitched, but I didn't interrupt. I could tell there was more.

She hesitated, her fingers brushing her glass, then finally asked, "You're going back to Nashville for the finale and then the tour, aren't you?" Her voice was even, but there was something in her eyes—a flicker of worry she wasn't trying hard enough to hide.

I exhaled slowly. "Yeah, I have to. It's part of the contract. But leaving, especially now..." I stopped, letting the unfinished thought linger. "It doesn't sit right with me."

Kensi looked down at her lap, her fingers picking at the corner of her napkin. When she spoke, her voice was quiet, almost like she was trying to convince herself more than me. "I know it's important. And after everything that happened, I can't help but feel like I've... like I've invaded your world. Taken up too much of your time and energy."

Her words were quiet and full of sadness and regret. "You've done so much for me, Wyatt. More than I deserve."

I leaned forward, catching her eyes. "Kensi, stop. You've got this backwards. You didn't invade my world—I brought you into it because I wanted to. And I don't regret a second of it."

She shook her head slightly, a faint, bitter laugh slipping out. "You say that now, but... what if I've been holding you back? What if I've just made things harder for you?"

"You haven't." My voice was firm, but I softened it when I saw the doubt in her face. "If anything, you've reminded me why all of this matters in the first place. You're not a complication, Kensi. You're the reason I want to figure all this out."

Her shoulders slumped, as if the guilt she carried was finally weighing her down. "I don't want to need anyone," she whispered, almost to herself. "It feels weak. And after everything... I just don't want to take more from you than I already have."

I reached across the table, my hand hovering just above hers before resting lightly. "You're not taking anything. I'm giving it because I want to. And needing someone doesn't make you weak—it makes you human. You've carried so much on your own, Kensi. You don't have to anymore."

For a moment, the tension in her softened, her gaze flicking to our hands and back to me. "I don't know if I can be that person. Not yet."

"That's okay," I said gently. "I'm not going anywhere. Well, except to Nashville and then a lot of other places for the tour," I said, trying to lighten the moment.

She chuckled. Her hand turned under mine, and she gently squeezed my fingers. "I know. And it's such a big opportunity for you, Wyatt. I'd feel awful if you missed it because of me."

I shook my head. "The show was never about fame for me. I didn't go on that show to chase some dream of stardom. I had made it a mission, but I was clearly needed on a much more important one. And if I didn't have to go back, I wouldn't. But I'm under contract, and I have to finish what I started. That said, I'm not happy about leaving, especially now."

Kensi offered a tentative smile that was a mix of understanding and something more I couldn't quite place. "Thank you for saying that. But I still want you to go and make the most of it, for yourself and for the cause you care about. Just promise me one thing—don't worry about me while you're gone. I'll be okay."

A smile slowly worked its way over my lips. "I will always worry about you so I can't make that promise. But, I can promise I'll make every moment count when I'm back in Nashville. And I want you to promise me something, too. No more looking over your shoulder. You're not alone in this, okay? And you are safer and stronger than you've ever been."

Kensi's smile was tentative but genuine. "Okay," she agreed softly, her eyes meeting mine with a newfound strength. "The show is lucky they get to have you back, even if it's just for a little while."

Releasing her hand, we continued our meal with the playlist serenading us. Our conversation meandered with the playlist, each song a prompt for new revelations. Kensi shared stories of her childhood and dreams of travel and adventure. I found myself hanging on every word, the stories she shared painting a picture of a woman far stronger and more resilient than she realized.

"And what about you, Wyatt? What dreams do you chase when you're not rescuing damsels and running bars?" Kensi's question was light, but the interest in her eyes was genuine.

I paused, a song about chasing dreams under a wide-open sky playing softly in the background. "I guess I'm living part of it—helping people, making a difference where I can. But another part..." I hesitated, her gaze encouraging me to continue, "is finding someone to share it all with. Someone who understands the value of a simple life, filled with good music, good friends, and maybe a little adventure."

Kensi's response was a soft smile, her eyes reflecting the kitchen lights like distant stars. "Sounds like a beautiful dream."

The last song played—a gentle ballad about finding home in someone else's heart. When it ended, there was silence, like the world had stopped spinning.

Watching me with an open vulnerability in her eyes, Kensi whispered "Thank you, Wyatt. For tonight, for the music, for being here. It means more to me than you know."

I couldn't help but hope that maybe this was the beginning of something more between us. The possibility filled me with hope and a sense of rightness.

40

KENSI

The air inside The Yellow Rose Inn was filled with the aroma of pumpkin spice and freshly brewed coffee, lingering from the morning's breakfast. I stood on a stepladder, carefully hanging a garland of twinkling lights and autumn leaves around the mantel, adding to the already festive décor. Thanksgiving was only a week away, and the inn was a welcoming haven, its halls and rooms filled with the vibrant hues of fall.

"Those look perfect," Evelyn called out from the kitchen, her voice carrying over the cheerful sound of Classical music playing softly in the background. She bustled in a moment later, her hands full of cinnamon-scented pine cones that she arranged in a basket on the coffee table. "I love what you've done with the place, Kensi. You really have an eye for this."

I climbed down from the ladder, a smile tugging at my lips as I looked around at the transformation. The inn was cozy and inviting, its corners filled with pumpkins, gourds, and leaves in shades of orange, red, and gold. The banisters were wrapped in garlands, and the front door boasted a large, welcoming wreath made of twigs and autumn leaves. It was a far cry from the sterile, ultra-modern penthouse I'd lived in back in New York.

"It's beautiful," I said, my voice filled with a mix of pride and disbelief. This was the first time I'd ever decorated for a holiday. Growing up, Thanksgiving and Christmas had been more about power moves and business dinners for my father than about family and joy. The festive cheer that filled The Yellow Rose Inn was new to me, but it was everything I could imagine wanting to experience this time of year.

Evelyn offered up a smile, her eyes sparkling. "I'm so glad you're here to help, Kensi. The fall festival is one of my favorite times of the year. Tell me you're going to the festival. You have to make sure to swing by the pie-baking contest. You haven't lived until you've seen two old ladies argue over whose pie is the best."

I laughed. "Oh, I'm definitely going and I can't wait," I said, feeling a fizzing sensation spread through me. I'd never been part of anything like this before—a community coming together, celebrating the season with laughter and hopefully friendly competition. It was simple, yet it felt like everything I'd ever wanted.

Later that morning, I met up with Wyatt, Stephen, and Missy to head to the fall festival. We walked together down Main Street, the autumn air finally overtaking the heat of the summer. The streets were bustling with people, stalls lined up selling everything from handmade crafts to hot apple cider. Children ran around, their laughter filling the air as they chased each other through the crowds.

Missy linked her arm through mine, her eyes sparkling with excitement. "You're going to love the Turkey Trot, Kensi," she said. "It's the best part of the festival."

"I can't wait to see it," I replied, genuinely excited. "I have no idea what to expect."

Wyatt chuckled from beside me. "You'll see soon enough. It's a sight to behold."

As we made our way through the festival, I spotted Evelyn and her husband Ed standing by a stall selling homemade candles. They waved us over, their faces lighting up with smiles.

"Kensi! Wyatt! So good to see you!" Evelyn hugged each of us as though she hadn't seen me a few hours earlier. "Are you ready for the parade?"

"Absolutely," Wyatt replied, gently bumping his shoulder into mine. "We wouldn't miss it."

Evelyn beamed at me. "Kensi, you're in for a treat."

We found a spot along the street to watch the parade, the sound of a marching band warming up in the distance.

As the parade began, a hush of anticipation fell over the crowd. Suddenly, a massive turkey strutted down the street, proudly wearing an elaborate Pilgrim costume with a cowboy hat. The crowd erupted into cheers, and I couldn't help but laugh, the sight so absurdly charming that it was impossible not to be caught up in the joy of it.

Behind the lead turkey came a flock of other turkeys, each one dressed in a different costume. There was an Uncle Sam turkey, a superhero turkey with a cape trailing behind it, and even a turkey dressed as a ballerina, its tutu bouncing with each step. The crowd cheered and laughed, clapping as the turkeys waddled past.

"That's the Turkey Trot," Evelyn explained, her eyes sparkling with amusement. "Every year, people dress up their turkeys for the parade. It's a competition, of course. Best-dressed turkey wins a prize."

I shook my head, grinning, my heart full. This town was full of surprises, each one more delightful than the last. I glanced at Wyatt, his eyes crinkling with laughter as he watched me watching the parade.

Out of all the surprises Liberty had offered, he was the biggest and best of all. My feelings for him had grown steadily, though I still wasn't sure what to make of all of it.

The band was a group of high school students in bright uniforms, their instruments gleaming in the morning sun. They marched down the street, playing a lively tune that had everyone tapping their feet while trying not to step in anything the turkeys left in their wake.

Behind them came the floats—homemade contraptions decked out with hay bales, pumpkins, and scarecrows. Kids waved from the backs of pickup trucks, throwing candy to the crowds.

As the parade ended, the festival continued with typical carnival games and booths set up by local businesses. There were booths offering everything from handmade jewelry to jars of honey, and the delicious smell of kettle corn filled the air. We made our way through the crowd, stopping at different booths to sample treats and admire the crafts on display.

Bob, the barber, was up on a small stage with his garage band, playing a mix of country tunes and oldies. His guitar strummed out a cheerful tune, and he winked at me as he sang. The music added to the festive atmosphere, making the day feel like a celebration of everything good in life.

"Want to try your hand at the ring toss?" Wyatt asked, nodding toward a booth where people were aiming rings at bottles.

"Why not?" I said, feeling light and carefree. It was a feeling I hadn't experienced in a long time, and I wanted to hold onto it.

We spent the next hour playing games, laughing as we won and lost with equal enthusiasm. Stephen managed to win a giant stuffed turkey, which he promptly handed to Missy, who beamed with delight. It was such a simple joy, but it was real, and it filled me with a sense of belonging.

As the sun began to set, casting a golden glow over the town, Wyatt turned to me, his expression thoughtful. "Hey, can I walk you home?"

I nodded, my heart skipping a beat. "Of course."

We walked side-by-side, the sound of the festival fading behind us. The streets were quieter now, the shops closed for the day, the town settling into the peaceful rhythm of the evening.

When we reached the inn where I still had a few things to wrap up in the office, we stopped at the bottom of the steps of the front porch. Turning to face me, Wyatt asked, "Did you have a good time today?"

"I did," I said, my voice soft. "Thank you for hanging out with me. I've never experienced anything like this before. It..." Were there even words to describe it? "It was wonderful."

"You're still joining us for Thanksgiving?"

The hint of a plea in his words made my heart swell. "Yes, I'll be there," I said, smiling. "I wouldn't miss it for the world."

"Good," he replied, his shoulders relaxing and his smile broadening. "My mom's already planning to make extra pecan pie just for you."

I chuckled, knowing that he probably wasn't exaggerating. "I'm looking forward to it. That pie is to die for."

Time stretched between us, every second heavy with meaning as we held each other's gaze. It was one of those fleeting moments when the world faded into the background, leaving only us. In Wyatt's eyes, I saw something steady and unshakable—the same look that had quietly become my refuge, a place I never thought I'd find again.

There was so much I wanted to say, feelings that had taken root, growing quietly and quickly. For now, though, it was enough to simply be here, to share this quiet moment and feel the steady presence of someone who made me believe I didn't have to face it all alone.

Wyatt's hand brushed mine, sending the familiar flutter through my heart. "I'll see you soon," he said, his voice low and rough-edged.

I nodded, my smile matching his. "You will. Goodnight, Wyatt."

"Goodnight, Kensi," he replied, his eyes lingering on mine for a moment longer before he turned and made his way down the street.

As Wyatt turned and walked down the street, I watched him go, my heart light and my mind filled with the promise of the days to come. For the first time, the future wasn't so daunting. The future stretched out before me, a series of tomorrows waiting to be filled with laughter, love, and the joy of having a connection to something real.

41

WYATT

Even though it had been a couple of months, I still had flashbacks of the night when we rescued Kensi. Some nights the images played like a film on loop in my mind, dark and relentless. Yet, amidst the chaos, there was a silver lining. The ordeal had brought Kensi and me closer, and in the weeks that followed, I found myself in a delicate dance of emotions with her. She was healing, slowly, like dawn breaking after a long night, and I wanted to be part of the light that would guide her into a new day.

The thought of leaving for Nashville churned my stomach. Not because of the show—but because it meant leaving Kensi. I couldn't shake the sense that I was neglecting my duty to safeguard her, even though I knew it was irrational. I had two days to work it out in my mind and get focused.

It was Thanksgiving Day, and it was a scene right out of a heartwarming holiday movie. My mom had enlisted Kensi's help in the kitchen early in the morning, and despite the initial hesitance, Kensi had donned an apron with a determination that matched any seasoned chef.

I watched from the doorway, unnoticed for a moment, as she followed my mom's instructions, peeling potatoes with a concentration that was both endearing and slightly amusing. The tension that she usually held in her shoulders melted away and was replaced by an ease that was rare and beautiful to witness.

"Wyatt, stop lurking and come help," my mom called out without turning around, her sixth sense never failing. I stepped in, greeted by the rich scents of cooking that filled the air—turkey, herbs, and the sweetness of pie.

Missy and Stephen arrived mid-morning, their entrance marked by the clatter of wine bottles and the unmistakable sound of their laughter. Stephen carried a box laden with various bottles, claiming he couldn't decide on just one, so he brought a selection. Missy, on the other hand, brought a variation of her award-winning green bean casserole, swearing up and down that this year's version would convert even the most stubborn of skeptics. She was referring to me.

The dynamic between Missy and Stephen was like a finely tuned dance. They moved around each other with an ease after years of friendship, their banter light and teasing. "Did you leave any wine at the bar?" Missy teased, nudging Stephen with her elbow as she passed by to set her casserole on the counter.

"Like I'd bring the cheap stuff to Thanksgiving," Stephen retorted, winking at her. The affectionate eye rolls and shared smiles between them did little to hide their true feelings from anyone paying attention.

As the day wore on, the house was filled with the sounds of laughter, the clinking of glasses, and the soft sounds of country music from the radio in the living room. Kensi, who had been quietly observing from the sidelines, gradually found herself drawn into the fold. Missy, with her infectious enthusiasm, pulled her into a discussion about holiday traditions, and even got her to share a few memories of her own. Stephen, ever the storyteller, regaled us with exaggerated tales from his and my childhood escapades, drawing genuine laughter from Kensi, the sound of which set my heart on fire.

The dinner itself was a testament to the collective efforts of everyone. The table was a masterpiece of holiday fare, with the turkey taking center stage, surrounded by an array of side dishes. We took our seats, the flickering candlelight casting dancing shadows and illuminating the simple beauty of being surrounded by people who, though not bound by blood, were family in every meaningful way.

As we ate, the conversation flowed as freely as the wine. Kensi, who had been mostly quiet, started to open up, her comments punctuated by Missy's encouraging nods and Stephen's thoughtful responses. There was an easiness to the evening that had me pushing away the thought that in a few days, I would have to leave this behind.

After dinner, as we sat around the living room, bellies full and hearts lighter, I caught Kensi's eye. Her smile was the most powerful force I'd ever encountered.

"Okay, so hear me out," Missy started, her enthusiasm cutting through the post-dinner haze. "Black Friday shopping in Beaumont. It's only a 45-minute drive, and the deals are going to be insane. We have to go!"

Stephen, already half-asleep on the couch, groaned audibly, his sentiments clear. "Missy, that's a hard pass. Shopping? No thanks. Shopping on a day with hungover crazy women looking for the best deal on a cheap toaster? Hard pass."

But Missy was undeterred, her gaze sweeping over to Kensi, sparking an immediate interest. "Kensi, do you like going Black Friday shopping?"

Kensi's eyes lit up, a mix of curiosity and excitement playing across her features. "I've never been. I've seen the commercials and news clips of it. It always looks like this weird mix of terrifying and fun."

"Yes! That's exactly what it is! See, we have to take Kensi. It's practically a cultural experience!" Missy exclaimed, turning her persuasive powers to full blast.

I couldn't help but chuckle at Stephen's resigned sigh, knowing all too well the futility of arguing against Missy's plans when she had that look in her eye. "And you expect us to wake up at what, the crack of dawn, to stand in line and fight crowds for a discount on a robot margarita maker?" He asked, already knowing the answer.

Missy waved away his complaints with a flick of her wrist. "Oh, come on, it'll be fun! Plus, it's not just about the deals; it's about the experience. And if you really don't want to go, Kensi and I will go alone."

I smothered a laugh as Stephen groaned and closed his eyes. Missy knew exactly what to say to push his buttons.

The room fell silent as everyone considered Missy's proposal. Kensi's enthusiasm was obvious, her usual reserve washed away by the prospect of a new adventure, something so normal, yet entirely foreign to her. I glanced at Stephen, seeing the battle in his eyes as his protective instincts weighed against his disdain for early morning shopping frenzies.

"Fine," Stephen finally conceded, rolling his eyes but with a half-smile that betrayed his good nature. "But if I get trampled over a flat-screen TV, I'm holding you personally responsible."

Missy clapped her hands in victory, her smile infectious. "Deal! It's going to be epic. You'll see."

I shook my head, amused and admittedly curious about the whole ordeal. "Alright, count me in too. Can't let you guys have all the fun without me. Plus, someone's got to bail you out of jail when this 'cultural experience' turns into a shopping cart derby."

The smile that had settled on Kensi's face solidified the decision I'd made, even if the idea of being awake at 4:00 A.M. sounded like a terrible idea.

THE ADVENTURE STARTED BEFORE DAWN, the chill in the air reminding us that winter was here. Staying overnight at my parents' house had turned into a kind of impromptu slumber party. It reminded me of all those nights Stephen and I used to camp out in the living room as kids, surrounded by video games and snacks. Only this time, Kensi and Missy were there too, which gave it a completely different feel— one I hadn't realized I'd been missing. The idea of all of us under the same roof, gearing up for a Black Friday trip, somehow tied together pieces of the past and present in a way that was both strange and perfect.

Morning came all too quickly, the alarm jarring us awake while the rest of the world was still lost in slumber. Bleary-eyed but fueled by the promise of adventure (and copious amounts of coffee), we shuffled around, getting ready in a flurry of whispered conversations and soft laughter.

Stephen volunteered to drive, which had been a decision met with no objections, considering his uncanny ability to navigate through chaos with ease. The exchange of looks between him and Missy as she called "shotgun" to claim the seat beside him didn't escape my notice. You could tell there was something more going on between them, like their relationship went well beyond just being friends. It made me curious and maybe a little concerned. What were they not saying?

Kensi and I settled in the backseat. She was wrapped in a blanket against the early morning cold. As Stephen started the car, the quiet hum of the engine sounded like the opening note to an unwritten song, a prelude to memories yet to be made.

The drive to Beaumont was a blur of half-lit highways and sleepy towns, the world around us slowly awakening as we ventured further from Liberty. Missy, ever the organizer, had mapped out our plan of attack, her enthusiasm infectious as she detailed each store and the deals they offered. Kensi's excitement was palpable, her eyes wide as she listened, absorbing every detail.

"We'll hit the electronics store first," Missy declared, her finger tracing a route on the store's app on her phone. "They're offering the biggest discounts right at opening, and I'm not missing out on that."

Stephen groaned from the front, his sentiments about early morning shopping adventures unchanged despite his agreement to come along. "Just remember, I'm here under duress," he muttered, though the smile tugging at his lips belied his grumbled protests.

The back-and-forth between Missy and Stephen was steady and familiar, their easy exchanges peppered with laughter and the occasional playful jab. Kensi and I joined in, the camaraderie the tether between us all, making the early wake-up call and the chill in the air more than worth it.

As we pulled into the parking lot of our first destination, the scene that greeted us was straight out of a retail war zone. Crowds of people huddled in the cold, their breaths visible in the crisp morning air, all waiting for the doors to open.

Amongst all the craziness, Kensi's hand found mine, gripping it tightly with a mix of excitement and nerves. The touch was unexpected, sending a spark through me that I hadn't anticipated. Her fingers intertwined with mine, and for a moment, the noise and the crowd faded into the background.

"This is it," Missy announced, her voice a mix of command and excitement as she led our little group towards the growing queue. "Ready for your first Black Friday, Kensi?"

Kensi nodded, her smile determined. "Let's do this."

As we approached the crowd of eager shoppers, I noticed Kensi's excitement starting to fade, replaced by a hint of nervousness. The crowd was thick, a mass of strangers packed closely together in the chilly early morning, so different from the quiet, familiar scenes she was used to in Liberty. Her hand, clasped tightly in mine, trembled a little. When she looked up at me, her eyes asked for reassurance without her having to say a word.

In that moment, I understood. The busy crowd, the noise, the unpredictability of it all—it had to be overwhelming for her, maybe even reminding her of times when being in a crowd wasn't a good thing. I squeezed her hand gently and leaned down to whisper in her ear, trying to cut through the chatter and laughter around us.

"I've got you," I promised, my voice steady and sure. "I won't let go. Just stay close to me, and we'll navigate this together."

She looked at me, searching for whatever it was she needed to calm her nerves. When she found it, she nodded, a small smile breaking through her worry. She took a deep breath, ready to step out of her comfort zone, trusting me to be her safeguard in the chaos.

As the doors opened and the crowd surged forward, Kensi's grip on my hand tightened, but she moved forward without hesitation.

The first few steps were the hardest, the crush of energy at its peak as everyone scrambled for position. But once we got inside, I saw her start to relax. Her apprehension gave way to something lighter, her excitement growing with each aisle we explored. The thrill of the hunt and the joy of snagging a deal sparked something in her, pulling her into the moment and into the fun of the day.

Through it all, I kept my promise, our hands locked together as we navigated the crowded store. When space commanded it, I'd pull her close, offering a buffer between her and the pressing crowd, ensuring she knew she was safe and protected amidst the frenzy.

By the time we emerged into the crisp morning air, our mission accomplished, Kensi was aglow with the triumph of her first Black Friday experience. The anxiety that had shadowed her at the outset was gone, replaced by a lively spark in her eyes. And I had quickly formed an addiction to being close to her and touching her.

The drive back to Liberty was filled with stories of our conquests and plans for a next time, the promise of future adventures hanging in the air like a promise.

We'd promised my mom that we'd all come back by the house for leftovers and to say goodbye since I'd be flying out the next day for a week.

As we pulled up to my parents' house, the familiar sight of home was a welcome end to our whirlwind morning. We unloaded our treasures and made our way inside, where the smell of reheated Thanksgiving leftovers promised a feast of its own.

My mom greeted us with a cheerful smile, her eyes lighting up at the sight of our laden bags. "I see the early bird did catch the worm," she teased, ushering us into the kitchen where Ed was already laying out plates and silverware.

Missy was the first to dive into the recounting of our shopping triumphs, animatedly describing each purchase with a flourish that had everyone hanging on her words. Kensi, more reserved but equally excited, chimed in with her own finds.

It was during this exchange that Kensi's demeanor shifted from excited to something more tender, more thoughtful. She reached into one of her bags and pulled out a beautifully wrapped package, her gaze finding my mom. "Evelyn, I saw this and I didn't want to wait until Christmas. I thought of you immediately."

The room went quiet, all eyes on Kensi as she handed the package to my mom. The unwrapping revealed a delicate porcelain teapot.

Mom's reaction was immediate, a soft gasp escaping her as she carefully lifted the teapot from its wrappings. "Oh, Kensi," she murmured, her voice full of emotion. "This... this matches the tea settings we use at the inn. We lost the matching teapot years ago. I never thought we'd find another."

The significance of the gift was not lost on any of us. At The Yellow Rose Inn, with its always welcoming atmosphere, mom had always prided herself on the personal touches that made it feel like a home away from home for its guests. The tea settings, with their delicate porcelain and intricate designs, were a part of that charm.

Kensi smiled, a look of relief and happiness crossing her features at Evelyn's reaction. "I remembered you mentioned it once, how you wished you could find a replacement. I know it's not identical but when I saw this, I just knew..."

Mom, moved by the thoughtful gesture, enveloped Kensi in a hug, her gratitude shining through her tears. It was a moment where the bonds of a family chosen was clearly just as strong as blood ties. And I knew Mom had definitely chosen Kensi, whether Kensi knew it yet, or not.

As Kensi shared her reasons behind the gift, something shifted inside me. Watching her with my mom, seeing the easy embrace and the genuine affection that passed between them, I realized how seamlessly Kensi fit into the fabric of our family. It was as if she had always been a part of it, her presence filling spaces we didn't even know were empty. When I looked at her, I saw a future filled with more of these moments of connection, of laughter and shared stories around the dinner table, of quiet evenings and noisy holidays.

The evening carried on with laughter and the clinking of dishes, I found myself stealing glances at Kensi. Each one only reinforced what I'd already known in my gut: I wanted to be there for her. Not just for a moment, not just until she found her footing again, but for the long haul. I wanted to create a future where she knew, without a doubt, that she was loved, safe, and cherished. The way she made everyone else feel.

I wanted her to be mine.

The thought was as thrilling as it was terrifying. Kensi wasn't just any woman. She'd been through hell—more than she'd ever let on, I was sure—and the last thing I wanted was to pile my feelings on top of whatever she was carrying. She deserved time to heal, space to figure out her own path, but that didn't stop the hope growing in my chest. Hope that someday, I might be part of the life she rebuilt.

In the quiet of my thoughts, as laughter ebbed and flowed around me, I let the truth sink in: I was falling for Kensi. Not just for the way she could brave a Black Friday crowd or pick out a gift that'd make my mom beam for days. I was falling for the woman who, despite everything she'd been through, could still look at the world with courage.

I was falling for the way she fought to keep moving forward, even on the days when it was hard. For the moments when her laugh, so rare and precious, broke through her guarded exterior. And for the way she made me want to be better—not just for her, but for myself.

But I knew I couldn't rush this. Kensi had built walls around her heart, walls that were there for a reason. I didn't want to tear them down. I wanted her to know that if she ever decided to let someone in, I'd be there, ready to stand beside her, no matter what. For now, I'd settle for being the person she could rely on, the one who reminded her that she didn't have to face everything alone.

And as the night went on, filled with the beauty of shared moments, I realized I wasn't just falling for her—I was already in love with her.

* * *

Time had slipped by, and suddenly the pressing reality of my departure loomed over the pleasant haze of the day. I glanced at the clock, the numbers reminding me that my flight to Nashville wouldn't wait.

I stood, clearing my throat slightly to catch everyone's attention. "I hate to say it, but I should probably start heading home to pack. My flight's early tomorrow, and I've still got a lot to sort out before then."

A collective groan of disappointment rose around the table, but it was softened by understanding—sympathetic nods and smiles all around. My mom, ever the perfect hostess, was already packaging up leftovers for me to take. "You'll need a snack while you pack," she insisted, piling containers into a bag. I hated to admit that most of it would probably end up in the fridge uneaten, but I didn't have the heart to tell her.

Kensi caught my eye from across the room, and the flicker of disappointment I saw there mirrored my own. I didn't want to step away from this bubble of contentment any more than she did, but my commitments weren't going to wait.

"You ready to head out?" I asked her, keeping my tone casual.

Her smile was grateful and it hit me square in the chest. "Thank you, Wyatt. I am."

That thought—the idea that maybe she didn't want me to leave, or that she'd been hesitant to say so—buzzed through me, lighting me up in a way I couldn't quite shake.

Saying our goodbyes felt like closing the book on a particularly good chapter, one with the promise of more pages waiting to be read. As we stepped out into the cool evening air, the gentle breeze was a quiet reminder of the changing seasons—and the changes yet to come.

The drive to Kensi's place was quiet. The streets of Liberty were peaceful, the earlier bustle of holiday shoppers now settled into the calm of evening.

"I had a really good day today," Kensi said softly as we neared her cottage. "Thank you for making me a part of it."

Her words blazed through me faster than any fire could. "I'm glad you were there. Today wouldn't have been the same without you."

We pulled up outside her building, the truck's engine idling softly in the quiet. Turning to her, I had a surge of something that made me want to be bold, something that nudged me toward honesty.

"Kensi, I..." I paused, searching for the right words. "Today made me realize how much I—how much we all—value having you in our lives. You fit right in, like you've always been a part of it."

She looked at me, a depth of emotion in her eyes that I hadn't seen before. "I feel the same. I never expected to find a place that felt like home, or people who felt like family. But I have, and it means everything to me."

There was this feeling in me that said this goodbye deserved more, a proper farewell. "Let me walk you to your door," I offered, not ready to let the night end with us sitting in the car.

She nodded, and we made our way up the path to her door, the soft glow from the porch lights casting long shadows. Standing at her doorstep, there was a pause, a moment of hesitation.

"I know you have to go," she started, her back still turned to me as she fumbled with her keys. Still talking to the door she said, "But I'm scared. Not of being alone or of something happening. I'm scared of how much I've come to rely on you, how much I..." Her voice trailed off, laden with unspoken words, heavy with emotion.

Reaching out, I gently turned her to face me. I saw the struggle in her eyes, the battle between her fears and her feelings. Running my hand down her arm, I took her hands in mine, needing to touch her, hoping she would grasp the full meaning of my words.

"Kensi," I said, my voice firm with conviction, trying to break through the wall her fears had built. "I'm not leaving you. Not really. I'll be back before you know it, and Stephen, Missy, and everyone else will be here for you. And," I paused, gathering my courage, "when I come back, maybe we can talk about what everything we're both feeling might mean."

Her eyes searched mine, and in them, I hoped she could see the truth and the depth of my words. For a moment, we stood in silence, communicating without words. She gave a small nod, one I took as a promise.

The trip to Nashville suddenly became inconvenient as opposed to stressful. Yes, I was leaving, but I was also coming back—not just to a place, but to a person. To Kensi. With that realization, my determination surged forward. I would go to Nashville, do what I needed to do, and return. For her, for us.

With the promise of a conversation yet to come and possibilities waiting to unfold, I gently drew her closer. She leaned in without hesitation. We shared a quiet, lingering hug, one that said everything neither of us was quite ready to put into words.

It was a promise of hope, of a future that was slowly piecing itself together from the shattered remnants of the past.

As I boarded the plane the next day, I knew this trip was not a departure but the first stop on a journey towards something beautiful.

42

KENSI

Evelyn's laughter brought me back to reality with a gentle nudge. "You seem miles away, Kensi. Everything alright?" She asked, her eyes sparkling with a mix of concern and amusement as she arranged a vase of flowers behind the counter.

I managed a smile, feeling a blush creep up my neck and into my cheeks. "Oh, yeah, sorry. I got lost in my thoughts for a minute," I admitted. It was strange how often thoughts of Wyatt filled my mind, how I'd repeatedly read the messages we'd exchanged or the sound of his voice on the phone.

Evelyn nodded, pausing as she regarded me, a knowing smile tugging at the corners of her mouth. "I can guess what—or rather, who—those thoughts were about. You miss him, don't you?"

The question wasn't unexpected, but it still made my heart flutter. "I do," I confessed, my voice barely above a whisper. "It's silly, isn't it?"

He'd only been gone a few days, but it feels like an eternity. How was it possible I could remotely feel this way?

"It's not silly at all, Kensi," Evelyn said simply, her words sincere.

Her understanding and acceptance meant the world to me, especially considering everything that had led me here.

Changing the subject, Evelyn's tone brightened. "Speaking of Wyatt, I had an idea. Why don't you, Missy, and Stephen come over to our place for the *Real American Country* finale? Ed and I would love to have you, and it would be a nice way for us all to support Wyatt together."

The invitation caught me off guard but in the best possible way. "That sounds wonderful, Evelyn. I'd love to, and I'm sure Missy and Stephen would too. "

"Excellent! I'll make sure we have plenty of snacks," she declared, her enthusiasm infectious.

As though saying her name had conjured her, the door of the inn opened and Missy appeared. Her bright eyes scanned the lobby until they found me. She wore a smile, but there was a tension in her shoulders that hadn't been there before. As she approached, I slid off the stool, meeting her halfway.

Missy's smile widened as she drew closer, but the tightness in it didn't escape my notice. "Hey, Kenz," she greeted, though she sounded hesitant.

"Hey, Missy. Everything okay?" I asked, concerned, as I noted the subtle shadows beneath her eyes. It wasn't like Missy to look so weighted down.

She hesitated for a moment, glancing over my shoulder at Evelyn, who had discreetly paused her work and moved to the check-in desk to give us privacy.

"Can we talk?" Missy finally asked.

"Of course," I replied, sensing the seriousness of her tone. Turning to Evelyn, I said, "Missy and I are just going to step into the office for a bit."

Evelyn nodded with understanding, her gaze softening. "Take your time, dear. I'll be out here if you need anything."

Missy and I made our way to the small office tucked away behind the main desk. The room was small and cozy.

As soon as we were alone and I had shut the door, Missy's composure faltered. I could see her wrestling with her thoughts, trying to find the right words.

"Kensi, I need to tell you something, and I don't know how to say it," she began, her voice trembling.

My heart went out to her, and instinctively, I reached out, taking her hands in mine. "Missy, whatever it is, you can tell me. We're friends, and I'm here for you."

She squeezed my hands, a grateful glimmer in her eyes before she launched into her confession. "I'm pregnant."

The news hit me with a mixture of shock and joy. "Oh, Missy, that's—"

"It's Stephen's," she continued. "I haven't told him yet," she interjected quickly, her eyes searching mine for understanding. "I'm scared, Kensi. We've never really defined what we are, and now, this," she said, placing a hand on her abdomen.

Her words trailed off, but her fear and uncertainty were evident. The small office seemed to be growing even smaller as I took in her revelation.

"Missy," I started, my voice steady, hoping to imbue her with a bit of the strength she needed. "Stephen cares about you. He's been all-in for you for as long as I've known you and longer than that according to Wyatt. I'm sure it's scary, but I believe he'll stand by you, through this and anything else that comes your way."

Missy nodded, her expression a mix of hope and trepidation. "I want to believe that too. I just don't know how to tell him."

"We can figure it out together," I assured her, squeezing her hands. "Stephen needs to know, and if you need me there when you tell him I'll be there. If you want me to sing a dramatic rendition of 'Baby Got Back' to lighten the mood before you break the news, I'm your girl," I offered, a playful glint in my eye.

The tension in Missy's shoulders lessened as she burst into laughter, shaking her head at me. "Oh my gosh, Kensi, I can't even imagine. Stephen's face would be priceless," she managed to say between giggles.

"See? There's always a way to make things less scary. All of you have taught me that," I said, my voice softer now, but still carrying the thread of humor. "But in all seriousness, whatever you decide, I've got your back. Stephen loves you, Missy. He's been waiting for a sign from you. This," I gestured between us, symbolizing her news, "might be the biggest sign of all."

Missy's smile softened, her eyes reflecting a mix of gratitude and newfound courage. "Thanks, Kensi. I really needed to hear that."

Exiting the office, we met Evelyn at the desk.

"Well, I'm glad to see smiles around here. Missy, has Kensi mentioned the *Real American Country* finale? Ed and I want you and Stephen to join us at the house to watch it together."

Missy's smile broadened, and any remaining tension ceased to exist. "I think it's a fantastic idea."

Evelyn nodded, pleased. "It's settled then. Our place, Friday night." With plans firmly in place, Evelyn excused herself.

"Come here," I said softly, opening my arms for a hug. Missy stepped into the embrace without hesitation, her own arms wrapping tightly around me. The idea of friendship had been foreign to me not that long ago. Now, I couldn't imagine my life without Missy or even Stephen and especially not Wyatt.

Pulling back, I held her arms and while trying not to let the building tears fall, I whispered, "I'm thrilled for you, Missy. Truly, I am. This baby, it's going to bring so much joy to your life, to Stephen's life. You're going to make an incredible mom."

Missy's eyes shimmered, a mix of emotions swirling within them. "Thank you, Kensi. That means the world to me."

My cheeks hurt from smiling.

"I should let you get back to work," Missy said, stepping back, wiping under her eyes. "But thank you, for everything. For listening, for being here, for making me laugh when I felt like I couldn't."

"Always," I affirmed, nodding. As Missy turned to leave, a quiet reflection settled over me. My heart was full for my friend, bursting with happiness at her news and the new path unfolding before her. Yet, beneath that joy, a shadow of jealousy lingered. It was an emotion I couldn't quite grasp or understand. It wasn't envy of Missy's pregnancy specifically, but maybe of the future it represented, something real and new beginning in her life.

I shook off the feeling, chiding myself for even entertaining such thoughts. My life had taken its own dramatic turns, and I was just beginning to navigate the mere idea of a relationship with Wyatt. The future was uncertain, yes, but also filled with potential. For now, that would have to be enough.

43

WYATT

Being back in the bustle of the show environment was a shock to the system. I hadn't been present the first time around for very long—two weeks total before I'd made every effort to get myself released from the show. While I hadn't told a single person why I'd left, as per the agreement I signed, there were suspicious looks coming my way soon after I entered the studio. The air was thick with unasked questions and thinly veiled curiosity, but I kept my reasons close to my chest, offering nothing more than a tight-lipped smile to anyone who dared to broach the subject.

The intense atmosphere and vibrant lights in the studio made it feel confining. Every corner echoed with the whispers and speculation of my hurried departure, the looks from the crew and contestants making it clear I was the center of attention—for all the wrong reasons. Yet, as I navigated through the maze of cables and cameras, there was a singular focus that anchored me: Kensi. I pictured her smile, the way her eyes lit up when she laughed. I knew she was safe. Those thoughts were the only thing keeping me steady.

Nash, my former roommate, was the first to cut through the cloud of scrutiny surrounding me. His easygoing nature was a welcome distraction from the stares and whispers.

"Wyatt! It's good to see you back," he greeted, clapping me on the shoulder with a grin that provided a sense of normalcy in this orchestrated chaos. Nash was genuine, a rarity in this place, and I found myself grateful for his presence.

He introduced me to Cassidy, his arm casually draped around her shoulders. "Not sure if you remember Cassidy. She may have been voted off last week, but she's still the star in my eyes," Nash beamed, and Cassidy rolled her eyes playfully at his comment. I congratulated her on her run in the competition, marveling internally at how drastically the dynamics shifted and formed in my absence.

The rehearsal for the finale was intense. All twelve of us, those who had been voted off and the final contenders, were thrown together for one last performance. The energy was a mix of excitement and nostalgia, a collective effort to put on a show that would be remembered. But as the last note faded and we dispersed, one of the show's producers found me, pulling me aside with a purpose that immediately set me on edge.

There, in the quieter wings of the studio, the air between us thickened with unspoken questions. He didn't dive straight into the heart of his curiosity, but it hung there, palpable, as he glanced everywhere but directly at me. I knew what this was about—I was the anomaly, the variable that hadn't quite fit their carefully plotted course.

"I want to thank you again for letting me leave when I did," I ventured, breaking the ice with gratitude, hoping to soften the ground for whatever confrontation lay ahead. My voice carried a mixture of sincerity and an unspoken plea for understanding, seeking to navigate this conversation with as much grace as I could muster.

He acknowledged my thanks with a nod, his expression tightening just a bit as he did so. It was clear he was wrestling with his professional discretion and personal curiosity, the balance tipping ever so slightly as he finally met my gaze.

"Of course, Wyatt. But you must understand, your departure raised questions. Not just for me, but for the audience, the other contestants." His words trailed off, a clear invitation for me to fill in the blanks, to offer him a sliver of the truth he was so obviously seeking.

My response was measured. I was fully aware of the thin ice beneath our conversation. "I assure you, it was necessary," I said, hoping my earnestness would suffice. "And I'm committed to the tour, to making up for any disruption my absence may have caused."

He considered my words carefully, the tension in his shoulders lessening a bit. Despite my explanation, his curiosity wasn't fully satisfied, the puzzle of my departure was still incomplete.

Then the conversation took an unexpected turn. He mentioned, almost offhandedly, that my leaving was nothing compared to the tour manager's sudden elopement to Vegas.

"Is she coming back?" I asked, my mind beginning to spin in a dangerous direction.

Rolling his eyes along with his entire head he sighed and threw both hands up, "Who even knows?"

His response, laden with a mix of frustration and resignation. An idea quickly began forming in my mind. This unexpected vacancy suddenly presented an unforeseen opportunity—an opportunity that might just align with my own selfish desires.

"So you're in need of what, a new tour manager?" I asked, trying to sound as though I was making casual conversation.

He caught the hint of interest in my voice, his eyes narrowing slightly as he assessed my question.

"Why? You know of a tour manager just waiting around for a job?" His tone was a blend of skepticism and curiosity, clearly invested in the direction of our conversation.

The question hung in the air, charged with possibility. This was the opening I hadn't known I was waiting for, a chance to bring Kensi into a part of my life that had, until now, forced us apart. The thought of having her close and not having to leave her for three months, was more appealing than I could express. I had to play this right, to present the idea as the solution to his problem, not my own.

Seizing the moment, I ventured, "Actually, I might know someone who'd be perfect for the job." The words tumbled out almost before I could weigh them, driven by a spontaneous impulse.

His eyebrows lifted, curiosity clearly piqued. "Oh?"

"Yeah. She's got a degree in event and hospitality management. Unmatched organizational skills," I explained, my mind racing with the possibilities.

I paused, choosing my next words carefully to ensure I painted the most compelling picture of Kensi without revealing too much of my personal stake in this suggestion. "She's managed events from small gatherings to large-scale operations, impeccable at logistics and has a knack for keeping things running smoothly, even under pressure." I kept Kensi's identity under wraps, aware that her qualifications should stand on their own merit.

The producer's demeanor shifted from skeptical to intrigued as he mulled over my words. "That sounds exactly like what we need, especially with the chaos of this tour." His gaze sharpened, focusing on me with renewed interest. "Can you get her to send over her resume? We're on a tight schedule, and if she's as good as you say, I'd like to move quickly."

The agreement was easier than I anticipated, a mutual understanding reached with minimal resistance. The prospect of bringing Kensi on board was suddenly real, tangible, and I could hardly contain my excitement at the thought of no longer facing the impending tour with a heavy heart.

"I'll talk to her when I get back home," I assured him, my voice steady despite the internal whirlwind of emotions. "I'm sure she'll be thrilled at the opportunity."

As we parted ways, the looming stress of the upcoming tour lightened, the edges of my anxiety blunted by this unexpected turn of events. The opportunity to have Kensi by my side, merging our professional and personal journeys in such a meaningful way, was more than I could have hoped for when I boarded the plane back to Liberty.

44

KENSI

The week dragged on even though the inn had been booked to capacity since before Thanksgiving and I'd barely had any downtime. It was finally Friday, however, and Missy was swinging by to pick me up so we could drive over to Ed and Evelyn's together to watch the *Real American Country* finale. Wyatt would only be singing with the full group during the broadcast, but we wanted to see his time on the show come to an end on a high note.

Missy's car pulled up just as I was locking the front door, her timing impeccable as always. She rolled down the window, a playful grin on her face. "Ready to see our boy light up the stage?" she asked, her eyes twinkling with the kind of mischief that usually preceded our most memorable nights out.

I couldn't help but smile back. "Absolutely. Let's not keep the party waiting."

The drive to Ed and Evelyn's was filled with the kind of easy conversation that had defined my friendship with Missy. We talked about everything and nothing, from the inn's upcoming holiday decorations to the latest gossip from The Anchor. Yet, beneath the surface of our chatter, there was a tension that neither of us addressed.

Unable to keep up my disinterest I turned to face her and finally asked, "Have you told him?"

Missy's playful demeanor faltered for a moment, the question hanging in the air like a cloud threatening to burst. She kept her eyes on the road, a sigh escaping her as she navigated a particularly sharp turn. "No, I haven't," she admitted, her voice lower than before. "And I don't know how to. Stephen and I... we're in this weird limbo, and dropping this bombshell feels like it might just blow everything up."

I reached over, placing my hand on hers briefly, offering a silent show of support. "Stephen loves you, Missy. He's been by your side through thick and thin. This might even bring you closer," unsure if I was even qualified to be saying these things. Though I understood her fear. The dynamics of their relationship, so long undefined and now teetering on the edge of a life-changing revelation? I'd be terrified, too.

Missy glanced at me, a wry smile playing at the corners of her mouth. "You sound like one of those relationship gurus on the Internet," she teased, but I could tell she appreciated the effort. "I just need to find the right moment. And the courage."

The rest of the drive passed in a contemplative silence, each of us lost in our thoughts. As we pulled into Ed and Evelyn's driveway, the festive lights that adorned the exterior of the house offered a stark contrast to the turmoil inside the car. It was a reminder of the season's promise of new beginnings and the hope that, somehow, everything would turn out okay.

We were greeted with warmth and laughter as we stepped inside, the cozy living room a welcoming haven from the chill of the evening. Evelyn wrapped us both in hugs, her excitement for the night's event infectious. Ed offered us drinks, and Stephen, who had been fussing with the television settings, looked up and smiled, his gaze lingering on Missy in a way that spoke volumes of his feelings for her.

The tension from our conversation in the car lingered, but soon it began to ebb away, replaced by a sense of contentment. These people had become my family, their struggles and joys entwined with my own in ways I could never have imagined when I first arrived in Liberty.

The table was laden with an assortment of finger foods that Evelyn had spent the better part of the day preparing. There were plates of jalapeño poppers wrapped in crispy bacon, bowls of creamy guacamole paired with tortilla chips, and trays of mini sliders, their patties cooked to juicy perfection. It was a feast designed to be eaten without too much fuss, allowing everyone to focus on the TV screen where Wyatt was about to make his appearance.

As the excitement built, Ed couldn't help but share his enthusiasm for seeing his stepson on TV. "You know," he began, his voice filled with pride, "when Wyatt first told us about going on *Real American Country*, I wasn't sure what to think. But seeing him up there is something else." His eyes gleamed with unshed tears, the emotion palpable in his voice. "I couldn't be prouder of him. He deserves this."

As the show began and Wyatt appeared on screen, the room erupted into cheers. As I watched him perform, his confidence and talent were impossible to ignore, and it filled me with a sense of pride.

When they started to sing *Life is a Highway*, I couldn't contain my excitement. "That's Rascal Flatts!" I exclaimed. Knowing that tidbit of trivia was another point of connection to Wyatt I could claim. We'd spent hours listening to music and sharing songs we'd heard that triggered a new thought or memory. It was like we had a secret language of our own.

Missy squeezed my hand, her earlier apprehension momentarily forgotten as we joined in the celebration of Wyatt's performance. The final notes of the song fading into applause and cheers from the audience on screen and in the living room. The show moved into video montages of the final two contestants before they sang for the final times on the show.

Suddenly, in the midst of our collective jubilation, Missy jumped up from her seat, a hand over her mouth, and darted towards the bathroom. The room fell into an awkward silence, her abrupt departure hanging in the air like a question no one dared to voice. After a few tense moments, I caught Stephen's eye, silently urging him to follow her. He looked puzzled at first, silently asking why with a look, but I nodded firmly, insistent. Understanding passed between us, and he quietly excused himself, disappearing in the direction Missy had gone.

With the focus now shifted, the rest of us tried to recapture the spirit of celebration, our attention returning to the TV screen. The finalists were giving their all, their voices echoing with the desperation and hope of being named the winner of *Real American Country*. As I watched, I couldn't help but think about Wyatt and how, if not for the dire circumstances that had pulled him away, he might have been the one standing on that stage, basking in the glory of the final moment, possibly even taking home the title.

Wyatt had been a strong contender, his talent undeniable. His absence from the competition wasn't just a loss for him, but for the audience who had been captivated by his initial performance. I remembered the judges' reactions, their praise hinting at a bright future in the competition, possibly culminating in a win. It was a thought that weighed heavily on me, the what-ifs and might-have-beens swirling in my mind.

Just as my thoughts began pulling me further into a sea of contemplation, Evelyn approached with a gentle, understanding smile. In her hand, she held out a glass filled with her signature sangria, the rich red liquid catching the light, promising a momentary escape from my spiraling thoughts. "What's got you so tied up in your thoughts?" she asked softly, her voice cutting through the noise and pulling me back to the present.

Taking the glass from her, I allowed the question to linger for a moment, appreciating the genuine care that Evelyn always embodied. I didn't know if Evelyn was aware that Wyatt had left the show because of me and my situation. If she knew anything, she didn't let on. But I considered my words before speaking, anyway.

"I was just thinking about Wyatt," I confessed with a sigh. "About how different things could have been for him if..." My words trailed off.

Evelyn nodded, understanding immediately, as she often did. She had a way of listening that made you feel heard, truly heard.

"Wyatt is stronger than you think, dear," she said with full confidence. "And he's not one to dwell on what might have been. He's always looking forward, finding ways to make the best of what life hands him. That's one of the many reasons we're all so proud of him."

Her words, infused with wisdom and a deep-seated knowledge of her son, offered a new perspective. It was a reminder of Wyatt's resilience, his ability to rise above challenges with a strength and grace that had initially drawn me to him. "You're right," I admitted, a small smile tugging at my lips. "Wyatt has this incredible way of seeing the silver lining, even in the toughest situations. It's just hard not to wonder, you know?"

Evelyn placed a hand on my shoulder, her touch light but filled with empathy. "It's natural to wonder, to worry," she acknowledged. "But remember, it's not the missed opportunities that define us, but how we move forward with the ones we choose to embrace. Wyatt knows that, and so do you."

Taking a sip of the sangria, I let her words wash over me.

As I pondered these thoughts, the bathroom door opened, and Stephen and Missy returned to the living room, their expressions a mix of apprehension and overwhelm. It was clear a conversation had taken place, one that would change the course of their lives together.

Trying to stifle a giggle, I took another sip of my drink.

Missy approached me after a few moments, her expression slightly pale but wearing a brave smile. The room was still filled with the residual warmth of the evening's festivities, but I could see the toll the night had taken on her. "Evelyn, Ed," she began, her voice steady but softer than usual, "thank you both so much for tonight. It was wonderful." She then turned to me, her smile faltering just a bit. "Kensi, I'm sorry, but I'm not feeling great. Do you mind if we head back home?"

Of course, my immediate concern was for her well-being. Standing up, I placed my glass on a nearby table. "Absolutely, let's get you home," I replied, my tone laced with concern. Turning to Evelyn,

I added, "Is there anything I can do to help clean up before we leave?"

Evelyn, ever the gracious hostess, waved off my offer with a gentle smile. "Don't you worry about a thing, dear. You've done more than enough just by being here. Go take care of Missy," she insisted, her kindness as comforting as ever.

Stephen, who had been quietly observing the exchange, chimed in, "I'll stay and help out here. Don't worry about it." His gaze then shifted to Missy, filled with a silent question, but he quickly masked it with a nod towards us. "Let me walk you out," he offered, his actions speaking volumes about his concern and care for us both.

We said our goodbyes to Ed and Evelyn, their warm hugs and well-wishes following us as we made our way to the door. Stephen escorted us out.

Once on the porch, Stephen's demeanor shifted subtly, the concern for Missy evident in his posture. Without a moment's hesitation, he wrapped her in his arms, and sweetly kissed her forehead. "I'll come by after I'm done here," he said quietly.

Missy, her eyes glistening with unshed tears, simply nodded, her smile radiant even in the soft porch light. It was a moment of quiet understanding, a silent acknowledgment of the new path they were about to embark on together. "Thank you," she murmured, her gratitude for his acceptance and support clear in her voice.

Stephen then turned to me, offering a nod that was both a farewell and a thank you. "Goodnight, Kensi," he said, his gaze flicking back to Missy for a moment before he retreated inside, closing the door softly behind him.

The drive back to my place was quiet, only broken occasionally by Missy's recounting of random events of the evening. She shared how the smell of bacon on her plate had been the unexpected catalyst for her nausea that had driven her to the bathroom, and, finally, how she had told Stephen in the midst of her discomfort. His response, she explained with a mix of relief and wonder, had been nothing short of perfect—supportive, loving, and excited.

As Missy parked in front of my cottage, the night's events still fresh in our minds, I couldn't contain the bubbling excitement that surged within me for my friends. Turning to Missy, my voice laced with genuine enthusiasm, I exclaimed, "I am just so happy for you both! I can't wait to see Wyatt's reaction. He's going to be over the moon!"

Missy's laughter filled the space, a sound of pure joy and anticipation. "Oh my stars, he's gonna flip," she said, her southern twang more pronounced. Her eyes bright with amusement. "You know how he gets—all emotional and brotherly. He might even shed a tear or two."

The thought of Wyatt's reaction brought a smile to my face, and I had a sudden rush of affection for the man who had become an integral part of my life. With his big heart and unwavering support, Wyatt would undoubtedly be extremely happy to hear this news.

When our conversation drew to a close, I opened the door and began to step out. "Goodnight, Missy. And remember, I expect a call from you later with updates," I said, my tone playfully stern yet full of the affection I held for her.

Missy nodded, her smile beaming in the dim light of the car's interior. "You got it. I'll fill you in on everything. Thanks for tonight," she replied, gratitude and excitement mingling in her voice. With a wave, she drove off into the night.

Turning towards my apartment, I walked up the path, my mind replaying the evening's events and the promise of what was to come. I approached the door, my fingers expertly disabling the security system, a routine action I'd performed countless times. I stepped into the quiet of the cottage where the silence welcomed me, offering a moment to reflect and unwind.

As I moved through the familiar spaces, turning on a lamp here, draping my jacket there, the reality of the evening began to settle in. Missy's news, Stephen's support, and the anticipation of Wyatt's reaction—all of it was like pieces of a larger puzzle falling into place. I was home.

I had never had a home like this. Growing up in a high-rise luxury apartment where my father managed his "business matters", I was too young to grasp the true nature of his work. The housekeepers were closer to me than he ever was. When my mom, who was everything to our family, passed away, it left this huge void that all the fancy things in our house couldn't make up for. College years came and went, but my residence remained within the walls of my father's domain. Later, after marrying Luka and moving into his penthouse, I found myself wandering from one empty room to another, seeking a place where I belonged. We shared a bedroom in theory, but in reality, I spent my nights alone in one of the guest bedrooms or lost in books within the library. It was never home.

Liberty, however, was different. Here, working for Evelyn, my friendship with Missy, whatever was happening between Wyatt and me, I'd found a sense of belonging I never knew existed. This quaint town, with its simple joys, had embedded itself into my being in ways I hadn't imagined possible. I had what felt a lot like a family.

45

KENSI

I'd been home from The Inn for ten minutes when there was a knock on the door of my place. I hadn't been expecting anyone, so I checked the security camera feed. My heart rate quickly increased when I saw the familiar face with its familiar deep-set eyes and strong jawline visible beneath his perfectly groomed beard. There was a look of contented excitement on his face that I hadn't seen before. I wondered if he'd talked to Stephen or Missy and learned their exciting news.

As though he knew I was studying him through the screen, he looked directly into the camera he had placed months ago and smiled broadly while tilting his head as though waiting for me to answer.

I opened the door, the cool evening air brushing against my skin. Wyatt stood there, the light from the porch softening the sharp lines of his features. I wish I had more time to stand here and take it all in —the way he looked at me, like he was seeing something I didn't even see in myself.

But even if I did, it wouldn't be enough. Because no matter how long I had to study him, I still wouldn't know what to do with the way he made me feel, like I was both found and completely unmoored at the same time.

"Hey," he greeted, his voice warm with a note of excitement that mirrored the expression on his face.

"Hi," I returned, feeling a flutter of curiosity.

Caught up in the moment, I realized I had been staring a bit too long, lost in the depth of those eyes I had come to know so well. Wyatt's smile turned amused, and he gently asked, "Mind if I come in?"

Flustered, I stepped aside, mentally chiding myself for getting lost in my thoughts at the door. "Of course, sorry. Come in," I said, waving him inside. His presence filled my small living room instantly, chasing away the evening chill that had begun to creep in around me.

He walked in, his gaze taking in the familiar yet always slightly chaotic state of my living room. Books and a couple of magazines were scattered on the coffee table, a nod to my attempts at unwinding after long days at work.

Wyatt turned back to me, his expression softening. "You okay?"

I laughed, a little embarrassed by my earlier distraction. "Yeah. I just wasn't expecting anyone tonight. Your visit's a nice surprise."

He nodded, understanding flashing in his eyes as he moved to sit down in the center of the couch, making himself at home as he had countless times before. "I've got news," he started, the excitement barely contained in his voice. "News that I hope will brighten your evening just as much as this visit."

I joined him on the couch, intrigued by the excitement in his tone. He positioned himself to face me.

Before Wyatt could dive into his news, I found myself cutting in, my curiosity about his week in Nashville getting the better of me. "Wait, tell me about Nashville first. How was the finale? It must've been incredible being back there, especially after everything. We watched it and you looked amazing – you all did," I rushed to say, feeling the heat in my cheeks.

Wyatt's eyes lit up at the mention of Nashville, and he was more than happy to share. "It was surreal," he began, his enthusiasm infectious. "The finale was everything you could imagine. The energy, the music, it was all so intense but in the best way. Being back there was like closing a chapter, you know? And," he paused, a smile playing on his lips, "I've got some news related to that, but first—"

I interrupted him again. "Have you talked to Stephen?"

Wyatt's brow furrowed in confusion at the sudden shift. "No, I haven't. Your place was my first stop after getting back to town," he said, a hint of concern in his voice. "Why?"

I scrambled for an explanation. "Oh, I was just wondering if you two had caught up. You know, about the bar, StealthWave, that sort of thing."

He seemed to accept that explanation, nodding thoughtfully. "No, not yet. But I'll see him tomorrow. There's a lot to catch up on."

Satisfied that my clumsy diversion hadn't aroused too much suspicion, I gestured for him to continue. "Sorry for the detour. I'm just excited that you're here. You were saying about Nashville?"

Wyatt's smile returned, and the spark in his eyes hinted at the importance of what he was about to share. "Right, the news. So, about that finale and everything that's coming up next..."

He took my hands in his, an action that sent a pleasant shiver through me. Wyatt had this way of making even the smallest touch feel meaningful.

"The tour manager for *Real American Country* quit. So now the position is open. And I immediately thought of you," he said, watching my reaction closely.

A mix of surprise and apprehension swirled inside me. "Me? But why? I've never managed anything like a music tour."

"Because you're perfect for it," he insisted, his confidence in me both flattering and a bit daunting. "You've got the skills, the drive, and you have a way of making sense of chaos. Plus, it'd mean we could spend these next months together—traveling and seeing new places."

My heart melted on the spot. The thought of being with Wyatt, experiencing the adventure of the tour, was incredibly appealing. Yet, the fear of stepping into such a big role, of possibly failing, gnawed at me. "Wyatt, I would love that and I'm honored you'd think of me, but aren't there people with more experience?"

Wyatt's grip on my hands tightened gently. "Kensi, I've seen you handle more in the past six months than most do in a lifetime. You're strong, capable, and you make things happen. The producer already thinks it's a great idea. I might have accidentally pitched you for the job."

A laugh escaped me, despite the whirlwind of emotions. "You 'accidentally' pitched me?"

"Yeah," he admitted with a sheepish grin. "I might've been a bit more enthusiastic about your qualifications than I initially planned. But Kensi, this could be a fresh start. A way to create something new for yourself, a chance for us to get to know each other outside of normal life. And even if there's not an us to consider, I'd back you every step of the way."

His earnestness, his unwavering belief in me, it was overwhelming in the best possible way. And in that moment, his faith in me was a gift.

"Okay," I said, the word barely a whisper as the magnitude of the decision settled in. "Okay, I'll apply."

The smile that spread across Wyatt's face was like sunrise, bright and full of promise.

46

WYATT

I couldn't remember the last time I'd felt this out of my depth. I could stand on stage and in front of cameras, no problem—sweating more from the lights than nerves. But asking the girl of my dreams out on a date? That had my heart beating so hard, I half-expected it to jump right out of my chest.

I stared at my phone, hesitating for a moment before dialing Kensi's number. The phone rang once, twice, then:

"Hey," Kensi's voice was a gentle embrace, instantly calming my racing heart.

"Hey, Kensi. You busy tomorrow night?" I asked, aiming for casual, even though my heart was doing its best impression of a jackhammer. I already knew she was off—I'd checked with Mom earlier—but I wasn't about to assume.

She paused, and I could almost see her tilting her head, that little curious smile I'd come to look for. "No plans. Why?"

I took a breath, steadying myself before the words rushed out too fast. "I was thinking... maybe we could grab dinner. Just the two of us. And if you're up for it, there's an indoor ice-skating rink in Houston we could check out after."

Her pause stretched longer this time, and I felt every second of it.

My chest tightened as I waited, hoping I hadn't pushed too far, too fast.

"That sounds really nice. I'd love to," Kensi finally said, her voice soft but clear.

Relief hit me first, followed by a rush of something sharper— excitement. My grin broke loose before I could stop it. "Great. I was thinking we could head out around 5:00?"

"It's a date," she replied, her words landing like a direct hit to my chest, in the best way possible.

We said our goodbyes, and as I pocketed my phone, I let out a breath I hadn't realized I was holding. I'd done it. I'd asked her out, for real this time. And she'd said yes.

The next day couldn't come fast enough. I dove into work at StealthWave, reviewing files and juggling assignments, but my focus wasn't worth much. Every spare second, my mind circled back to Kensi—her smile, her voice, the way she'd said, "It's a date."

When quitting time finally rolled around, I bolted home to get ready. By 5:00, I was standing outside Kensi's apartment with a bouquet of wildflowers in hand. They weren't flashy, but they reminded me of her—resilient, thriving in places most wouldn't expect, and beautiful without even trying.

I took a steadying breath and knocked. It had been years since my last real date, and even then, nothing had felt like this. Kensi wasn't just someone I wanted to spend time with—she was someone I wanted to know in every way. The thought of messing this up made my pulse kick harder than I cared to admit.

When the door opened, the sight of her stopped me in my tracks.

She wore a simple sweater and jeans, but somehow, she managed to look more stunning than I'd imagined. Her hair fell loose around her shoulders, and the way her smile tugged at the corners of her mouth just about floored me.

"Wow," I said, the word slipping out before I could reel it in. I held out the flowers, managing to add, "These are for you."

Her eyes softened as she took the bouquet, her fingers brushing mine for a brief, electrifying second. "Thank you. They're beautiful."

She stepped back, putting them in water, then turned to me with an easy smile. "You clean up pretty well yourself."

"Ready to go?" I asked, offering her my arm.

She looped hers through mine, her touch light but grounding. "Ready as I'll ever be," she said, and the way she looked at me right then made me feel like the luckiest guy alive.

As we drove into the night, the conversation flowed easily between us, weaving through topics like favorite Christmas traditions and hopes for the new year. Being with Kensi felt natural—no pretense, no forcing anything.

Dinner passed in a blur of laughter and stolen glances. Every word she spoke, every time her lips curved into a smile, I found myself more captivated by the woman sitting across from me. And then there was the skating rink. I hadn't set foot on ice in years, but I was willing to risk humiliation just to see her happy.

We stepped onto the ice and Kensi's confidence was evident. She moved with a grace and ease that left me in awe while I hung on to the wall and flailed similarly to a baby giraffe learning to walk.

"Where'd you learn to do that?" I asked, trying to sound more confident than I felt as I tried to control my movements beside her.

She turned, that playful spark in her eyes making my embarrassment worth it. "I grew up in New York, remember? Ice skating at Christmas is one of the only memories I can look back on and it not be tarnished."

Her voice softened at the end as though her thoughts were pleasant to recall.

When she reached for my hand, I hesitated—not because I didn't want to take it, but because I wasn't sure I could keep my balance. Still, I let her pull me away from the wall, her laughter ringing out as I stumbled forward. She steadied me, her grip strong and sure, leading me with surprising ease.

The rink echoed with laughter and the scrape of skates on ice, but none of it registered. All I could focus on was Kensi—her joy, her energy, the way she kept glancing back to make sure I was keeping up. She made me forget the world outside this moment.

After a while, we took a break, settling on a bench at the edge of the rink. Kensi's cheeks were flushed from the cold, her breath visible in the chilly air. She looked... happy. Content in a way that made my chest tighten.

"You're not half bad once you got the hang of it," she teased, nudging me gently with her shoulder.

I smirked. "I had a great teacher," I replied, holding her gaze.

The noise of the rink faded until it was just the two of us. She didn't look away, and for a second, I couldn't either.

I reached for her hand, letting my fingers curl around hers. Her skin was cold, but the warmth that sparked between us was undeniable. "Kensi, I—" The words caught in my throat. There was so much I wanted to say, so much I needed her to know.

"Yes?" she prompted, her voice soft, encouraging.

I drew a deep breath, steadying myself. "I'm glad you're here tonight. I can't imagine being anywhere else... or being here with anyone else."

Her lips parted slightly, and I saw something in her eyes that mirrored the ache in my chest.

Kensi's eyes not only softened but glowed under the rink's twinkling lights, reflecting her vulnerability and strength that drew me in deeper. She squeezed my hand, and all I could think was how much I wanted her to trust me with her heart.

"These last few months..." she began, her voice catching. "They've been hard. But this? Being here with you? It's been the best part of my life in a long time. And I want more of it. I'm scared of what the future holds because history hasn't been the kindest to me. But I want this. I trust you."

She wasn't just saying the words; she was giving me a piece of herself, trusting me to hold it.

"Kensi," I murmured, leaning closer.

Our eyes met, and in that moment, there was nothing else. The first brush of her lips against mine was hesitant, testing, but it quickly deepened. The kiss wasn't just about attraction—it was something bigger, an unspoken promise.

When we finally pulled back, the world seemed brighter, sharper. Her smile, soft and genuine, sent my pulse racing.

"This is... something else," I said, my voice barely above a whisper.

She laughed softly, her cheeks dimpling. "It is," she agreed, her hand still in mine.

"This is just the beginning, isn't it?" It was a rhetorical question, one that both of us already knew the answer to, but I felt the need to ask.

Her nod was all the confirmation I needed.

"You want to skate a little longer?" I asked.

Beaming Kensi asked, "Think you can manage?"

"Only if you promise to hold my hand," I replied, half-joking but fully intending to hold onto her for as long as possible.

Kensi's laughter rang out, clear and bright against the backdrop of softly playing Christmas music and the sounds of other skaters around us. "I think I can do that," she said, her voice laced with a hint of playfulness. She tightened her grip on my hand.

As the evening wore on, the crowd around us began to thin, the families and couples gradually peeling away until we practically had the rink to ourselves.

Eventually, we came to a stop. Kensi leaned against the railing, her cheeks flushed, her smile as bright as the lights that illuminated the rink.

"I can't remember the last time I felt this free," she said, her voice rich with contentment. "This was perfect."

"It was," I agreed, standing close beside her.

"We should probably get going though," Kensi said reluctantly, gesturing towards the exit. "It's getting late."

"Yeah, you're right," I agreed, though every part of me wanted to stay in this moment forever. We collected our things, returned our skates, and made our way back to the car, hand in hand.

On the drive back, we were both quite lost in our thoughts. It didn't stop me from grabbing her hand and reveling in the smile she sent my way. Her grip had me convinced she would never let go and I was okay with that.

When we arrived at Kensi's apartment, I walked her to her door, not ready to say goodbye. I reached out and tucked a strand of hair behind her ear, a small, quiet gesture.

"Thank you for tonight. It was perfect," she said, standing on her doorstep.

"Thank you for saying yes," I replied, smiling. Her smile widened, and before I could think twice, she leaned up, kissing me again—a soft, lingering goodbye that I didn't want to end.

"Tomorrow?" I asked, my voice rough with emotion.

"Tomorrow," she confirmed, stepping inside and leaving me standing there, grinning like a fool.

On the drive home, the entire evening replayed in my mind like a favorite song. I was in love with Kensi and nothing about that scared me.

47

KENSI

The sound of my cell phone buzzing on the table next to my bed had me cracking my eyes open to a room full of morning light. Groaning softly, I reached out, my hand clumsily searching for the device. The screen lit up with an unfamiliar number, but something deep inside told me to answer it. "Hello?" My voice was thick with sleep, barely more than a whisper.

"Good morning, is this Kensington Solinas?" A cheerful, female voice echoed through the line, instantly making me more alert.

"Yes, speaking." I sat up, pushing back the tangled sheets and swinging my legs over the side of the bed. Hearing my legal last name sent a jolt through me, a ripple of panic surging before I could rein it in.

I'd debated for days over how to apply for the job, agonizing over whether to use the name I'd assumed when I went on the run or the one I'd left behind. It wasn't just a name; it was a tether to a life I'd fought so hard to escape. But after talking it through with Wyatt, who had assured me it was safe, I'd finally decided to use my legal name. "You don't have to hide anymore," he'd said, his voice steady with quiet confidence.

His words had been exactly what I needed at the time, but now, hearing Kensington Solinas spoken aloud, I felt exposed, as if the name itself could unravel all the walls I'd built. I took a deep breath, reminding myself of Wyatt's reassurance, and focused on the voice on the other end of the line.

"This is Denise from *Real American Country*. I'm calling to offer you the position of tour manager for our upcoming national tour. We were impressed with your qualifications and your phone interview. Not to mention Mr. Turner's recommendation. It was very persuasive." Her tone held a hint of amusement.

A wave of emotions crashed over me—relief, excitement, fear, disbelief. This was the opportunity of a lifetime, a chance to step into a world so different from anything I had known. And yet, it was also a leap into the unknown. But I'd have Wyatt on my side. "I... thank you, Denise. I'd love to accept the offer. And please call me Kensi."

"Fantastic! We're thrilled to have you on board. We'll send over the paperwork today. Welcome to the team, Kensi!"

After hanging up, I let the phone fall into my lap, staring at it in stunned silence. Just months ago, I never could have imagined my life taking such a dramatic turn.

But as the excitement settled, reality quickly set in. I had commitments here, people who had become more than friends—they were family. And there was Evelyn, who had given me a job at The Yellow Rose Inn when I needed it most. Telling her about this new job weighed heavily on my mind.

I got ready for work early, my thoughts racing. The lobby was quiet as I stepped inside, the smell of fresh coffee guiding me to the dining room where I found Evelyn chatting with an unfamiliar guest who must have checked in after my shift the day before.

Noticing my arrival, she excused herself with a kind, "Please, enjoy your breakfast. Let me know if you need anything else." Turning toward me, her smile brightened the room even more.

"Good morning, Kensi!" Evelyn greeted me.

"Morning, Evelyn. How's everything going this morning?" I asked, trying to sound casual despite the mix of emotions swirling inside me.

"Everything's lovely, as usual. But enough about me—how was your evening?" Her question was supposed to sound unassuming, but I could tell she was curious about my date with Wyatt.

A blush crept over my cheeks, and I couldn't help but smile at the memory of the night before. "It was really nice. Wyatt... he's just—" I stumbled, unsure of how much to reveal.

Evelyn's eyes sparkled with delight, but she didn't push. "I'm glad to hear that. Wyatt's a good man."

Her kind words touched me, but they also made me realize I had a difficult conversation I needed to have.

"Evelyn, there's something I need to tell you. Can we talk in the office?"

Evelyn's smile faded into a confused expression, and she nodded, leading the way to her office—a cozy space filled with family photos and mementos from guests over the years. Once we were seated, I jumped right in.

"I got a call this morning from *Real American Country*. They've offered me the tour manager position for the national tour."

Evelyn's face lit up. "Oh, Kensi, that's fantastic! But, goodness, we'll miss you around here."

"Have you told Wyatt?" she asked, her excitement clear.

I shook my head slightly, nerves fluttering in my stomach. "Not yet. I wanted to talk to you first, to sort things out here and let you know I'll help find my replacement."

Evelyn's smile widened, her eyes filled with joy. "Kensi, I appreciate that you came to me first, but I think Wyatt will be over the moon when he hears about this."

"Thank you, Evelyn. Telling Wyatt is my next step. I plan to head to The Anchor after work and let him know."

Evelyn nodded, understanding and supportive. "Well, I won't keep you from your work any longer. We both have busy days ahead."

"You're right," I agreed, suddenly aware of all the tasks waiting for me. "Thank you, Evelyn, for everything." With a shared smile, I stepped out of her office and back into the rhythm of the day.

The hours dragged by as my mind kept wandering to the conversation I'd have with Wyatt. My usual tasks blurred together as I thought about the future, about how this new opportunity would change everything.

Later in the day, my phone buzzed with an email from Denise. It detailed the initial steps of my new role, including a trip to Nashville in early January for a meeting with the producers. The realization that I'd be leaving so soon added urgency to the excitement and nerves already building inside me.

Christmas was only two days away. That meant there wasn't much time to plan for the trip. As I mentally listed what I needed to pack and the arrangements I needed to make, the immensity of this opportunity settled on my shoulders. Despite the busyness around the inn, I found quiet moments where the enormity of what was ahead truly sank in.

Not only was I starting a new job, which would be huge on its own, but I was going to have to travel to Nashville by myself. The thought stirred memories of the dangers that had followed me the last time I'd set out alone, of when I first arrived in Liberty—uncertain and afraid. Those memories were dark, but this time, the nervousness was different. It wasn't about escaping; it was about stepping forward. It was about growth, about proving to myself that I was capable.

As the day unfolded, a quiet realization settled over me: I wasn't the same person who had fled to Liberty. This was my moment to embrace the future, to take the next step toward the life I wanted—on my own terms.

48

KENSI

I walked into The Anchor, greeted by the sounds of country Christmas classics floating through the air from the vintage jukebox in the corner mingled with the voices of several locals who had not yet made it home from work or had no reason to be home just yet. I related to that in a lot of ways because it had been a long time since I'd been excited for Christmas. But now it was just two days away and the more I thought about it, the more excited I got.

That excitement, however, did not compensate for the nervous excitement humming through me as I sought out Wyatt to tell him about *Real American Country*. Missy caught my eye and waved excitedly. I made my way to where she was on the other side of the bar.

"Hey!" she exclaimed with a brightness I hadn't seen much of since our Black Friday excursion.

"Hi!" I beamed back, leaning over the bar for the best half hug we could manage.

Both laughing, I leaned against the bar on both arms. "Is Wyatt here?"

With a nod toward the back she said, "He's in the office with Stephen."

About that time, both men came striding out from a room I knew led to their basement office for StealthWave. As soon as Wyatt's eyes landed on me his face transformed with a smile that set my heart rate skyrocketing.

He made his way over, the casual confidence in his step reminding me of every reason I'd fallen for him. "Kensi," he murmured, his smile curious and his voice a soft caress. "What's got you smiling like that?"

I hadn't realized just how hard I was smiling until he asked. Taking a deep breath, I shared the news that had been bubbling inside me since I accepted the position. "I got the job, Wyatt. I'm going to be the tour manager for *Real American Country*. I know it's probably because they were desperate on such short notice, but I don't even care!"

The reaction was immediate and electric. His eyes lit up, mirroring my own excitement, and without a second's hesitation, he swept me into his arms. The world spun as he lifted me off my feet, a laugh escaping me, a sound I hadn't known I could make with such genuine happiness until now. Around us, the bar's ambient noise faded into a backdrop, our moment the sole focus.

He set me down, his hands resting on my waist as he looked at me with an intensity that sent shivers down my spine. "That's incredible, Kensi! And you got the job because you deserve it." His enthusiasm was infectious, and for a moment, we were the only two people in the world.

The clamor of celebration broke through our bubble as Stephen and Missy approached, their faces alight with shared excitement.

"What's all this about?" Missy asked loudly. "Because we want in on the action!"

I had barely gotten the words out when Missy squealed and hugged me tightly.

"This is amazing, Kensi!" Missy beamed, pulling back but keeping her hands on my shoulders. "We knew you would get it!"

Stephen clapped Wyatt on the back, a wide grin on his face. "Looks like the tour just got a whole lot more interesting. Congratulations to both of you!"

Wyatt's smile lingered on me for a moment longer before he glanced at his watch.

Grabbing my hand, he said, "I've got to make some rounds, but don't go anywhere. Are you free this evening?"

The question caught me off guard, not because it was unexpected but because of the hopeful note in his voice. "Yeah, I'm free," I responded, feeling a flutter in my stomach.

"Great. Make yourself comfortable, and I'll be back before you know it." He squeezed my hand gently and then, in a move that came as natural as the sunrise, kissed me on the forehead. The warmth of his lips lingered long after he had turned away, leaving me with a mix of emotions swirling inside.

As he walked off, I noticed Missy's wide-eyed expression. "I'm going to take five," she told Stephen as she tugged me by the arm and began to walk away.

"Seriously?" Stephen started.

She shot Stephen a look, her hand subtly resting on her abdomen. Stephen's initial protest faded and he nodded, his expression softening.

Missy wasted no time. She led me to a secluded back booth and the moment we sat down, she bombarded me with questions.

"So, tell me everything! What was that forehead kiss about? Is it finally happening?"

I couldn't help but blush, a giggle escaping me at her enthusiasm. It was strange, discussing something so personal, yet it happened so naturally.

Stephen appeared briefly, setting down waters and a basket of fries before us with a tender look exchanged between him and Missy. They didn't need words; their connection was evident in their shared glance.

As he returned to the bar, Missy leaned in closer. "You know, that kiss... It almost looked like he was marking his territory, but in the sweetest way possible."

I sipped my water, the cold liquid failing to cool the flush of emotion rising within me. "I like him so much. It's all happening so fast, but it feels right, you know?"

Missy nodded, her eyes sparkling with excitement. "I do. And with the tour coming up, you guys will have so much time together. It's perfect!"

We spent the next thirty minutes talking about everything under the sun - the tour, our relationships, the baby, and the future. I had never had a girl friend like Missy before and it was nice to have someone to share these moments with.

Just as our conversation began to drift towards plans for the holidays, the ambiance of The Anchor shifted. The chatter quieted, and the previously lively energy of the bar mellowed into an anticipatory hush. Our attention, along with everyone else's, was drawn to the back of the room.

There, under a soft spotlight of the makeshift stage, stood Wyatt. Guitar in hand, he stepped up with the ease of someone who belonged there. His gaze found and held mine as if we were the only two people in the room.

"I want to thank everyone for coming out this evening," Wyatt's voice carried through the bar, filled with genuine appreciation. "I thought I'd share a few songs with y'all to say Merry Christmas and thank you for being part of this community here at The Anchor."

His introduction was met with enthusiastic cheers and claps from the patrons, a mixture of locals and regulars. But as the applause faded and Wyatt began to strum the opening chords to his first song, I was pretty sure the world around me had ceased to exist.

The familiar but now slowed down twangy melody of *All I Want for Christmas is You* began to fill the room, a choice that brought an instant smile to everyone's faces. The song, universally known for its festive cheer and longing, took on a new depth as Wyatt sang. He sang from his heart, each note and lyric infused with an earnestness that captured the essence of the song in a way that was both personal and universal.

As he sang, "I just want you for my own, more than you could ever know," his gaze locked with mine, turning the crowded bar into a backdrop for a moment that was momentarily our own. The glimmer in his eyes, the faint smile tugging at his lips as he navigated the song's highs and lows—it was all for me.

As Wyatt transitioned into the next song, the mood of the bar transformed. The earlier buoyancy returned as the familiar tune of *Winter Wonderland* filled the room, accompanied by the sweetest baritone I'd ever heard. Patrons tapped their feet and even sang along.

After a few more Christmas classics, each infused with Wyatt's signature country style, he wrapped up his set. The applause that followed was enthusiastic, a show of appreciation not just for the music but for the sense of unity he had fostered throughout the evening.

"I want to wish y'all a very Merry Christmas," Wyatt said, his voice carrying over the clatter of glasses and the murmur of conversations. "And remember to tip your servers tonight. They're working hard to make sure we all have a great time." His reminder was met with nods and murmurs of agreement, a gesture of goodwill that reflected the generous spirit of the season.

As Wyatt stepped down, the bar slowly returned to its usual bustling state, the festive mood lingering. Missy took this as her cue to dive back into her duties, a whirlwind of efficiency as she navigated through the tables. Before she was swallowed up by her responsibilities, she made me promise not to leave without saying goodbye. I assured her I wouldn't, and with a smile, she was off, seamlessly blending back into the rhythm of her work.

The space Missy left was soon filled by Wyatt, who slid into the booth opposite me, his eyes still shining with the energy of his performance.

"You were amazing," I replied, my heart still dancing to the rhythm of his songs. "You have a way of making every song feel like it's just for me."

Wyatt's smile grew, his eyes softening. "Because they are," he said simply, his gaze holding mine in a moment of unspoken connection. "I wanted tonight to be special, not just for everyone here, but especially for you."

Wyatt's expression shifted to something more contemplative, a hint of nervous anticipation in his eyes. "Speaking of special," he said, his tone a little lighter but still carrying a nervous edge, "I've been meaning to ask you—what are your plans for Christmas Eve?"

The question was simple, but caught me off guard. "I hadn't really made any plans yet," I admitted, curious about where this was leading.

Wyatt took a deep breath, his gaze never leaving mine. "I was hoping you'd say that. I want you to come stay at my parents' house. Wake up under the same roof with my family for Christmas." His words, spoken with such earnest hope, struck a chord deep within me.

For a moment, I was speechless, emotions swirling in my chest. The offer was more than just a gesture; it was an invitation into his life, his world, in the most intimate way. "Wyatt, I..." My voice trailed off, choked by the sudden surge of happiness and gratitude.

"Only if you're comfortable with it, of course," he quickly added, misinterpreting my silence. "I don't want to pressure you into anything."

Regaining my composure, I smiled, my heart full. "I'd love nothing more," I said, the sincerity in my voice mirroring the emotions in his eyes. "As long as your parents don't mind."

Wyatt's relief was palpable, his smile returning full force. "Mind? Kensi, my mom suggested it before I'd even had the chance to bring it up." His chuckle was infectious, and I found myself laughing along with him, the joy of the moment washing over me.

"What can I bring?" I asked, eager to show my appreciation for their hospitality they were extending to me.

"Just bring yourself," Wyatt replied, his tone soft yet firm. "That's all I want. But if you feel like making something, my parents would love it. My mom's always excited about new recipes or treats."

The idea sparked a flurry of possibilities in my mind, from baked goods to a dish that might complement the Christmas dinner. "I'll think of something special," I promised, already looking forward to the opportunity to be a part of their holiday celebration.

As we studied one another, a yawn unexpectedly crept up on me, reminding me of the late hour and the day's emotional rollercoaster. I covered my mouth, slightly embarrassed, but Wyatt's response was a gentle chuckle, understanding in his eyes.

"If you're ready, I can drive you to your place," he offered, always thinking of ways to make my life easier.

I nodded and let out a sigh. "Yeah, I think that's a good idea. I don't know how Missy does it—everything with so much energy all the time, especially now that she's pregnant."

Wyatt laughed, a soft, affectionate sound. "Missy's always been like that. She cheered at the state high school football championship with the flu and a 101 fever. No one knew until she practically slept through the entire next week."

I chuckled. "That sounds like Missy. Strong and unstoppable."

We stood, and as Wyatt led the way out of The Anchor, the warmth of the evening's conversations and his quiet steadiness making me feel light on my feet. The cold night air wrapped around us, but inside, I was alive with anticipation—of the days ahead, a Christmas filled with new traditions, and the kind of future I'd never let myself imagine until now.

49

WYATT

Christmas was my mom's Super Bowl, and this year, it looked like she was going for a championship ring. While most people might roll their eyes at the over-the-top display, I loved it. Every wreath, every strand of lights, every perfectly placed ornament had a purpose—and this year, that purpose was bigger than just the holidays.

It was for Kensi.

She needed this. After everything she'd been through, she deserved a Christmas that could replace every bad memory with something good. Something that felt like hope.

The house was a masterpiece of holiday cheer. Lights framed every window, garland wrapped the railings like a scene out of a movie, and the air smelled like pine and cinnamon—a combination that somehow always felt like coming home. But the crown jewel was the tree, a towering display in the living room decked out with heirloom ornaments and twinkling lights.

And then there was the kitchen. The smells drifting out of there —cinnamon, roasted meats, fresh-baked pies—could have brought even the most hardened soul to their knees. Mom wasn't just hosting Christmas; she was creating a whole new kind of magic.

When the doorbell rang, my heart rate picked up knowing Kensi would be on the other side.

"I got it!" I yelled to my parents who were singing along to *Frosty the Snowman* loud enough to be heard from the kitchen and definitely hadn't heard me and likely not the doorbell.

The smile hit me before I even opened the door, but when I saw her standing there, it grew into something I couldn't contain. Before me was the most beautiful sight I'd ever seen. Kensi was bundled in a winter coat that hugged her figure, a soft scarf around her neck, and a hesitant smile playing on her lips. Her eyes, always so expressive, revealed her excitement and nervousness, a combination I found endearing and made me want to pull her close and make sure she always felt as safe and happy as she looked right then.

She had multiple gift bags looped over each arm, two packages stacked between her hands and a casserole dish balanced on top.

"Hey, you," I greeted, grabbing the dish before stepping aside to let her in.

"Hi," she replied, her voice soft but filled with awe as she stepped inside. I couldn't help but notice how she took a moment to take in the festive atmosphere, her eyes lighting up as she did. It was clear that the effort my mother had put into decorating was not lost on her.

I took the rest of the packages from her so she could remove her coat. She hung it on the coat rack as though she'd been here numerous times. She removed her boots, revealing cute, festive socks that made me chuckle. "Nice socks," I commented.

"They're Christmas goats," she said, a small laugh escaping her. "I thought they were funny."

Seeing her happy and in my family's home did something to me. It awakened something I hadn't let myself hope for in a long time. It wasn't just that she fit in—it was the way she brought a spark into a place already filled with love, like she belonged here. Like she belonged with me.

I could see us arriving together for future holidays, her hand in mine as we carried gifts and shared laughter. I could imagine her woven into the fabric of this home, into my life, as naturally as if she'd always been there. The thought hit me hard—because it wasn't just a fleeting daydream. It was something I wanted, something that was real, possible.

We walked into the living room, and I watched as Kensi's gaze fell on the Christmas tree. "It's beautiful," she whispered, almost to herself.

"Not as beautiful as you," I murmured, more to myself than to her, but I think she heard because I watched the blush that pinked her cheeks.

The evening was everything I hoped it would be. Kensi fit into the family perfectly. My mom and Ed adored her, and she looked genuinely happy, laughing and engaging in conversations, even helping my mom in the kitchen, which was no small feat.

The rest of the night unfolded like a scene from one of the holiday movies we had all settled in to watch. With a spread of mom's homemade cookies and hot cocoa warming our hands, we lounged in the living room, bathed in the soft glow of Christmas lights. The air was filled with laughter and the occasional sing-along with the movie, making the room feel alive with holiday spirit.

As the evening wore on, Kensi and I shared a blanket on the couch, her head resting on my shoulder as we watched It's a Wonderful Life. Though, if I'm honest, I probably spent more time watching her than the movie. The contentment I had was unlike anything I'd ever known.

* * *

Christmas morning greeted us with the scents of cinnamon and pine as we gathered around the tree, a tradition that was even more meaningful this year with Kensi by my side.

When it came time to exchange gifts, Kensi handed me a beautifully wrapped package, her eyes shining with excitement. Inside, I found a set of high-quality headphones, the kind that promised to drown out the world along with an MP3 player that had to have cost her a pretty penny.

I was floored, but not as much as when she said, "I may have preloaded it with a playlist that I made. I added new ones every time I heard one that made me think about you."

Her thoughtfulness was the real gift. I pulled her into a hug, my heart full, whispering my thanks in her ear.

Sliding the large box to Kensi, I watched her carefully untie the ribbon and unwrap the giant box, her movements deliberate, savoring the anticipation. Inside, the designer luggage set gleamed back at us, its quality evident at a glance.

"I know you've had to run in the past, but this is for the places we can go together, the dreams you'll chase, and the adventures that lie ahead. It's for the life you're building, not escaping." I explained. "Starting with Nashville." I saw the emotions play across her face—surprise, joy, and a hint of apprehension about the upcoming trip.

As Kensi traced her fingers over the luggage, her expression shifted—surprise giving way to something deeper, something unspoken that tugged at my chest.

"But there's one more thing," I said, pulling a small velvet box from my pocket. Her eyes widened slightly as I handed it to her.

She opened the box carefully, her breath catching as she lifted the delicate charm bracelet into the light. The silver links sparkled, each charm glinting with meaning.

"I thought you might like something that tells your new story," I said softly. "Where you've been, and where you're headed. There's room for more, for everything still to come."

Her fingers brushed over the tiny Texas, the yellow rose, the ice skates. She didn't say anything at first, but her eyes told me everything

When she finally looked up, her smile was soft but radiant. "It's perfect," she whispered, her voice unsteady but full of so much gratitude it made me forget everything else.

The rest of the morning passed in a blur of laughter, smiles, and family. My parents, who had watched the exchange of gifts with watery smiles, joined in with their own assortment of presents.

Just as the last of the wrapping paper was being cleared away and the final sips of coffee were being savored, my mother stood up, clapping her hands together in a way that signaled a shift in the day's activities. "Alright, everyone," she began, her voice carrying that sweet but authoritative tone that had orchestrated many a family gathering to perfection, "grab yourselves another cup of coffee and a plate of breakfast before it all disappears. I'm about to clear everything away to start setting up for Christmas dinner."

She shot a meaningful glance at my dad and me, indicating that her directive was especially for us. It was a well-known fact that once my mom started her preparations, the kitchen became her domain, and it was best to stay clear unless called upon for specific tasks.

Kensi shot me an amused smile, and we got up to follow Mom's instructions. The breakfast spread was a mix of muffins, fruit, and savory pastries, everything my mom did best. I loaded up a plate for both of us, making sure to include Kensi's favorites—little things I'd picked up about her in the short time we'd spent together. It wasn't much, but it felt meaningful to know those details.

As we sat back down, Ed launched into stories from Christmases past, his tales full of laughter and just enough exaggeration to keep everyone hooked. The room buzzed with energy, and I caught myself thinking that this—right here—was what I'd remember most about the day.

The doorbell rang, cutting through the chatter. Stephen and Missy walked in, their faces glowing, excitement practically radiating off them. They'd announced their big news to their families the night before, and seeing them now, you could tell they were still riding the high.

"So your parents are all excited to be grandparents?" Kensi asked as she and Missy sprawled out across the couch in the living room.

Missy's laughter was infectious. "Oh, yeah. And Stephen's parents," she continued, still chuckling, "started planning the nursery. They're already talking about painting and themes. It's like they've been waiting for this moment forever."

Stephen, sitting beside them with a proud and somewhat bemused expression, nodded in agreement. "Yeah, they're over the moon. Dad's already talking about teaching the kid to fish and play baseball. It's really been something," he said, his voice thick with emotion.

Kensi smiled at them both, her eyes reflecting the joy of the moment. "That's wonderful," she said genuinely. "It sounds like this baby is going to be surrounded by so much love."

My parents, who had joined us in the living room to share in the excitement, echoed Kensi's sentiments. My mom, ever the planner and organizer, was already asking Missy about baby shower plans.

I watched Kensi, trying to read the emotions that she was clearly trying to keep hidden. The sound of Stephen slapping his thighs before standing pulled me from my observations.

"Speaking of parents," he said, reaching a hand out to Missy. "We better get to yours before they send out a search party. I have a feeling your mom is going to have a very one-track mind for the next several months and I do not want to be the one to derail it."

Missy took Stephen's hand with a laugh, the kind that lights up a room, and stood up, her other hand resting gently on her stomach—a small, subconscious acknowledgement of the life growing inside her. "You're probably right," she agreed, her gaze flitting between Kensi and my parents. "We just wanted to come by and say 'Merry Christmas'."

There was a chorus of Merry Christmas all around. My mom, always the hostess, insisted they take a plate of snacks for the road.

Kensi's gaze followed them, a thoughtful expression crossing her features. I reached for her hand, squeezing it gently. I couldn't begin to imagine what she was thinking. But I knew exactly where my thoughts were. I hoped one day it would be Kensi and me making these kinds of announcements to our family.

Once the door closed behind Stephen and Missy, the room seemed quieter, the absence of their presence noticeable. Yet, the atmosphere remained cheerful.

Kensi and I settled back into the couch. I adjusted our positions, ensuring there was enough space for Kensi to snuggle in closer. She leaned into me, her back resting against my chest, allowing me to drape my arm around her. I was never going to leave this spot.

"They're going to be amazing parents," Kensi mused aloud.

"They really are," I agreed, feeling a surge of pride for my friends. "Is that something you've thought about?"

Kensi smiled, turning to look at me, her eyes shining with a mixture of emotions. "Not until recently," she said. "I'm realizing that new beginnings are everywhere, and I need to be open to all the possibilities they present."

The quiet was punctuated by the sounds of dishes being moved around in the kitchen. It was during this lull that my thoughts turned toward the immediate future—toward Nashville and the impending responsibilities awaiting Kensi. I glanced at her profile, noticing the way the Christmas lights reflected in her eyes.

Breaking the silence, I ventured into the topic that had been looming on the horizon. "Speaking of new beginnings," I started, carefully gauging her reaction. "You've got those meetings in Nashville coming up soon for the tour manager position."

Her body tensed and her expression shifted, apprehension coloring her features. "Yeah," she said, sounding both excited and nervous. "I've been thinking about that. It's a big opportunity, but... I'm not going to lie. I am a little anxious about going alone." Her admission hung in the air, evidence of the fear she still harbored despite the strides she'd made.

I tightened my arm around her. "What if I came with you?" The suggestion was out before I could second-guess it, driven by an instinct and a desire to support and care for her in every way possible.

Kensi turned to face me, her eyes widened slightly, surprise and a hint of guilt mingling in her gaze. "Wyatt. You have your own schedule, and after everything you've done, asking you to come with me feels like too much."

Her reluctance was understandable, yet the thought of her facing any part of this journey alone was something I couldn't entertain.

I wasn't going to argue with her. "Listen to me," I said, my tone gentle yet unwavering. "It's not about imposing or obligations. I want to be there with you. Besides, I'm not asking—I'm telling. I'm going with you."

The firmness in my voice broke through her hesitations, and slowly, a grateful smile spread across her face. "Okay," she gave in. "Okay, if you're sure."

"I'm sure," I affirmed, feeling a sense of rightness about the decision.

Kensi leaned in, her movement slow and deliberate, yet carrying a natural grace that was entirely hers. Her lips met mine softly at first, testing, as if savoring the moment before giving in. Then the kiss deepened, her touch growing more certain, more urgent, until everything else faded away.

The world narrowed to the warmth of her lips on mine, the faint scent of her shampoo, the way her fingertips lightly brushed against my jaw. And just as the moment anchored itself, perfectly balanced between us, it was broken by the sharp sound of someone clearing their throat.

"Well, I was going to ask if you two wanted any more coffee, but I see you're otherwise engaged," Ed announced, his tone laced with amusement and mock indignation.

Kensi pulled back, a deep blush creeping across her cheeks, and I couldn't help but chuckle, feeling a rush of heat that had nothing to do with the fire burning nearby. "Sorry, Ed," I managed, trying to regain some semblance of composure. "We'd love some more coffee."

As Ed retreated, likely still smiling at the interruption he'd caused, I caught Kensi's eye and we shared a laugh.

We all pitched in to get dinner on the table, bumping elbows and sharing jokes that were so bad they circled back to being funny again. Ed, in his element, was orchestrating the transfer of dishes from kitchen to table like a seasoned conductor, while Mom kept shooing his hands away from the food with a playful swat of her tea towel.

After we were seated, Ed cleared his throat to pull our attention to him at the end of the table.

"To family," he said, lifting his glass. "To the ones we're born with and the ones who just walk in through the front door and make themselves at home." With a wink, he glanced at Kensi and said, "Kensi, you've become a part of this family, and we couldn't be happier.

The room filled with the soft clinks of glasses touching, and Kensi's smile in response was a mixture of joy and a touch of surprise.

After dinner, with the table cleared and the last of the pie vanishing, we migrated to the living room. The conversation was easy, filled with laughter and the kind of stories that make your sides ache from laughing so hard. But I could see the fatigue etching its way across Kensi's features the longer we sat there.

Mom caught my eye from across the room and gave me a knowing nod, her silent communication perfected over years of social gatherings. It was time to start winding down, though the company made it hard to break away.

Slipping my hand into Kensi's, I squeezed gently, signaling it was okay if she was ready to call it a night. She returned the squeeze, her grateful glance telling me she was indeed ready, but didn't want to be the reason the night ended. I stood, stretching casually, then reached for Kensi's hand.

Mom and Ed rose as well, the movement prompting a gradual end to the gathering. There were hugs and more laughter, promises to do this again soon.

Stepping out onto the porch to say goodnight, the air was bitingly cold, making our breath fog up in little puffs. The night was clear, stars scattered across the sky like spilled glitter. I turned to Kensi, seeing her wrapped up in her coat, the moonlight catching in her eyes.

I replayed the day, unable to keep from smiling as I thought about how seamlessly Kensi had fit in with my family. It was as if she had always belonged there.

As I walked her to her car, the soft glow of the porch light illuminated her face, and I could see the contentment and weariness in her expression.

"Today was magical. Thank you for including me and for the

luggage, and the bracelet, for well, everything," she started, her voice low and full of emotion. "Today meant a lot to me."

She looked down at her hands for a moment, then back up at me. "It was nice to be part of something like that. I didn't realize how much I needed it."

"You are a part of it, Kensi," I said, my voice gentle but firm. "And you always will be, as long as you want."

Her eyes met mine. It was more than just gratitude that I saw there. It was something deeper, something that had been quietly building over the days and weeks we had spent together. I knew because I felt it, too.

"Thank you," she whispered, her voice thick with emotion. "For everything."

I pulled her close, feeling her shiver slightly against me. Leaning down, I pressed my lips to hers in a kiss that was meant to be a gentle goodnight. But with it, I poured out the depth of my feelings. It was a promise, hope, reassurance, and the future all rolled into one. When we finally parted, the night didn't feel quite so cold anymore.

"Goodnight, Kensi," I murmured.

Kensi's response was a soft whisper, her breath warm in contrast to the chilly air. "Goodnight, Wyatt," she said, her eyes holding mine for a moment longer, reflecting the starlight and something much deeper.

As she drove away, I was left standing in the quiet of the night, feeling a profound sense of peace. The stars above seemed to shine a bit brighter, and the cold didn't bother me as much. I took a deep breath, the air feeling crisper, filled with the promise of tomorrow and all the days after that with Kensi.

50

KENSI

The cool Nashville air was no match for the warmth of Wyatt's hand that I clung to as we made our way down the sidewalk. My future job awaited just a few blocks from the hotel where we'd just finished breakfast. The mix of anticipation and a lingering trace of guilt for having him by my side had me feeling jittery. Wyatt had insisted on accompanying me, his presence a reminder that the days of facing challenges alone were behind me.

Squeezing my hand just a little tighter as if sensing the turmoil inside me, he asked, "You ready for this?"

"More than ever," I replied, hoping to sound convincing. The last time I'd traveled alone, it had been a flight from shadows that clung too closely, from a past that threatened to suffocate me. But now, here I was, stepping into the light of a dream I'd never known was possible.

His attention moved over my shoulder. There was something unsettling in the way he glanced across the street, his gaze lingering on two men who were out of place among the bustle. They were too still, too intent, too put together. He'd noticed them while I had been debating between pancakes and French toast at breakfast, but I'd hoped his instincts were just him being overprotective.

"Kensi, stick close," Wyatt said quietly, giving my hand a gentle tug.

I nodded, trying to mimic his calm, but the unease nesting in my stomach grew heavier with each step towards our rental car parked along the curb. We had only taken a few strides when one of the men Wyatt had been watching broke away from the wall he leaned against, crossing the street with purpose.

"Rose Solinas, is it true you're the widow of the late Luka Solinas, the notorious mob boss?" The voice sliced through the morning hum, a jagged edge that tore at my carefully constructed reality.

I stopped dead, the world tilting as a man with a microphone shouldered his way in front of me. A cameraman hurried to his side, lens zeroing in on my face. My past, a ghost I thought I'd buried deep, clawed its way to the surface.

"Kensi?" Wyatt's voice was a distant rumble, but I couldn't tear my eyes away from the microphone—a black hole threatening to swallow me whole.

"Ms. Solinas, how do you respond to accusations that you were involved in your husband's criminal activities?" another reporter called out, materializing from the growing crowd.

"Did you know about the murders he ordered?" someone else shouted.

The questions came like gunfire, rapid and unending. My heart stuttered, each beat echoing the chaos around us. My breaths turned shallow, sharp as glass shards in my chest. The name—Rose Solinas —it clung to me, a shroud of the life I had fled from, the woman I no longer was.

"Kensi, look at me," Wyatt urged, his voice cutting through the cacophony. His face swam into view, clear bright eyes locked onto mine—a lighthouse in the storm. I blinked, and for a moment, the reporters' voices faded into white noise. There was only Wyatt, his presence a shield against the past that sought to reclaim me.

Without a moment's hesitation, Wyatt stepped in front of me, erecting himself as a protective barrier between me and the onslaught. "That's enough," he declared, his voice cutting through the chaos, commanding silence from those immediately around us. "Ms. Solinas has no comment. Back off."

But the media was insatiable, their questions growing more invasive, their cameras flashing like lightning in a storm. I clung to Wyatt's arm, seeking solace in his strength as the questions continued to fly.

Seeing my distress, Wyatt's protective instincts kicked into overdrive. "We're not answering any questions. You're going to leave us alone," he said, his voice firmer, more forceful. He glanced back at me, offering a nod that was both reassuring and determined before facing the crowd again with a resolve that commanded respect.

When one particularly bold reporter attempted to sidestep Wyatt to reach me, Wyatt physically blocked his path, his stance firm and unyielding. "I said, back off," he repeated, his tone leaving no room for argument. Faced with Wyatt's solid resolve, the reporter stepped back, the crowd finally sensing the seriousness of his command.

Wyatt maintained his protective posture as we made our retreat, using his body as a shield until we reached our car. He helped me inside with care, ensuring my safety before walking around to the driver's side.

Inside the car, the muffled sounds of the outside world couldn't drown out the echo of the confrontation that had just taken place. Shaken, I looked over at Wyatt, my eyes heavy with a mix of fear and an overwhelming sense of gratitude. "Thank you," I managed to whisper, my voice trembling with emotion.

Wyatt's hand found mine, his touch sure and grounding. Our fingers laced together. "Always," he said, his voice a low rumble that resonated within the confines of the vehicle. His thumb brushed over the back of my hand, a gentle pressure that grounded me. "I'll always be here to protect you, Kensi."

As he guided the car onto the main road, the question that had been clawing at the inside of my mind slipped free. "How do they even know who I am?" The words were a whisper, fragile as glass, filled with the ache of old wounds reopened.

Wyatt drove in silence for a moment, his jaw set, his focus on the road ahead, but I could tell his mind was racing, replaying the scene we'd just escaped. Finally, he spoke, his voice filled with self-reproach. "I should've been more vigilant," he confessed.

His hands clenched around the steering wheel, knuckles whitening for an instant before he consciously relaxed his grip. I saw the battle in his eyes, a war between his duty to keep me safe and the reality that some threats slip through the cracks.

"We've had alerts set up for any mentions of Luka's name and yours, just as a precaution." He glanced my way, his eyes dark pools of regret. "Nothing has come up."

My heart ached at the sight of him—the man who had stepped into my dark and twisted world without hesitation, now doubting himself. It wasn't fair. None of this was his fault.

"It's been quiet... too quiet maybe." His voice trailed off, lost in the hum of the engine and the rhythm of the tires rolling across the asphalt. "I've been so caught up in us, in the holidays and just being happy." He shook his head slightly, the internal battle waging on. "I didn't even think to double-check. This must be new, or we would've known sooner."

He sighed, a sound so heavy that it filled the car before pushing against the walls of my heart. "I'm sorry, Kensi. I'm so sorry. This is the last thing you need."

"Wyatt, no, this is not your fault. You couldn't have known," I said, trying to assuage the guilt he carried. "We've been living in this bubble of happiness, and it's been wonderful. We can't let this— whatever this is—taint that." My voice was firmer now, more convincing, not just for his sake but for mine as well.

Wyatt glanced at me briefly, a mix of appreciation and worry in his eyes. "I just hate that this is something you have to deal with. After everything you've been through, you deserve peace, not this circus starting back up."

His words echoed my own fears, but I found strength in him and knowing he was with me. "We'll get through this, like we have every-thing else. Together," I said, squeezing his hand in reassurance.

"I'm going to call Stephen as soon as we get to the studio's office," he assured me, his determination clear. "We'll increase security, keep a closer eye on things. Whatever you need, Kensi, whatever keeps you safe—that's my priority."

The rest of the drive to the studio's office was a quiet one, the earlier events casting a shadow over what should have been an exciting morning. As we navigated through Nashville's busy streets, I replayed the questions and the aggression from the media hounds. At first my anxiety rose. If they knew who I was and where I was, that means someone could have been watching me. We could be in danger. But from who? As far as I knew, the threats had all been dealt with after that terrifying night.

A shudder rolled through me as I remembered, but before the fear could take hold, Wyatt's voice broke through the silence. "Are you okay?" he asked, his eyes flicking toward me, concern etched across his face.

Willing the tension in my shoulders to ease, I replied, "Yeah, I'm okay."

And as the words left my mouth, I began to believe them. Wyatt was here. I wasn't facing this alone—not anymore. The realization settled over me, not heavy, but grounding, like a firm anchor in rough waters. I wasn't the same person who had run in fear, and now, I wasn't running at all. Whatever lay ahead, I had people by my side who wouldn't let me face it alone.

By the time we reached the studio, the panic that had gripped me earlier had loosened, replaced by a calm resolve.

Upon arrival, Wyatt didn't waste a moment. He was on the phone with Stephen before we even stepped out of the car, his tone low but urgent, discussing security measures and the need for discretion. His protectiveness was a shield, his resolve a fortress against the onslaught we'd faced.

The studio's office was a buzz of activity, making it hard to concentrate on where I was supposed to be going. Thankfully, Wyatt took charge of the situation and guided me to the right office. This tour, this job, was not just a professional opportunity; it was a chance to reclaim my life, to stand defiantly against the shadows of my past.

We arrived at the assigned conference room and took a seat just outside awaiting the executives. My thoughts shifted from confident to reeling. There were plenty of reasons I was not qualified to do this job. Yet, somehow, I'd convinced a lot of people otherwise.

"You're going to be amazing," he leaned over and whispered as we awaited my meeting with the tour team. His words chipped away at my anxiety.

The meeting itself was a blur, a whirlwind of introductions, plans, and expectations. Yet, through it all, replaying Wyatt's encouragement in my mind anchored me, rebuilding and fueling my own confidence.

Stepping out of the conference room, I couldn't help the smile that spread across my face. The whirlwind of introductions and discussions had been intense, yet incredibly invigorating. I had finally found a role meant for me.

Wyatt had been seated near the conference room, his posture rigid, the phone pressed tightly to his ear. The sight of him, so contrasted with my own mood, immediately piqued my concern. He looked up as I approached, and stood. His expression shifted from the intense focus of his conversation to a brief flash of relief upon seeing me. However, the relief was quickly overshadowed by the anger and frustration rolling off of him.

He ended his call abruptly and greeted me, his movements tense as he reached for me. His hands settling on my hips, he asked, "How did it go?" The attempt to temper his voice with calm was betrayed by the visible anger still lingering in his eyes.

"It went really well," I started, my excitement momentarily faltering in the face of his mood. "The team seems fantastic, and they're excited about some of the ideas I brought up. I'm really looking forward to this." My smile was genuine, driven by the successful meeting and the thrill of the opportunity ahead.

My enthusiasm waned as I took in his expression, the storm clouds brewing behind his eyes.

"What's wrong?" I asked.

Wyatt sighed, running a hand through his hair, his gaze momentarily drifting away before locking back onto mine.

"It's nothing about you or the meeting," Wyatt quickly assured, his voice attempting to mask his frustration, but the undertone of anger was unmistakable. "It's about how this morning started. Someone at the studio connected the dots between your legal name on your paperwork and Luka Solinas. We don't know who it was yet, but Stephen's working to figure it out."

The revelation hit me like a cold wave, dampening my excitement. "Inside the studio?" I echoed, disbelief and a hint of betrayal coloring my tone. This place, which promised a fresh start, had been infiltrated by the past I'd been running from.

Wyatt nodded grimly. "Yeah. It's too specific to be a coincidence. The timing, right after you submitted your employment paperwork... Someone must have made the connection and leaked it to the press." His gaze never left mine, as if by sheer will he could shield me from the truth of his words. "Stephen's on it, but pinpointing who exactly within the studio was responsible might be tricky."

The gravity of the situation settled between us, pushing out the optimism that had filled me moments before. I suddenly felt exposed, like my carefully constructed walls were falling apart.

Wyatt's shoulders squared, his posture firm with the kind of determination I'd seen in him before. The lines of his face reflected not just resolve but a quiet strength that steadied something in me. His hands, worn but sure, reached out—not with grand gestures, but with the simple, steady reassurance I needed.

"I'm going to have a talk with the show and tour producers," he said, his tone firm, leaving no room for argument. "We need to make sure this doesn't happen again. Your safety and privacy are my top priorities."

"Thank you," I replied, my voice steadier than I felt, bolstered by his unwavering support. "I never expected my past to catch up like this—not now."

"You deserve peace, Kensi. And happiness. I'll do whatever it takes to protect you and our future." His words ignited a spark of hope deep within the parts of me I'd thought were beyond repair.

"Our future," I echoed softly, letting the words settle between us. "I like that."

His features softened. "Good," he said, his voice gentler now, like the words carried their own reassurance. "Because I'm not going anywhere."

After several beats of silence and absorbing the moment that we'd just had, Wyatt continued, his tone shifting back to business. "For now, let's focus on what we can control. We'll increase our vigilance and work closely with the security team. And I'll make sure the producers understand the seriousness of this breach. We're in this together, every step of the way."

Listening to him, the fear and uncertainty that had knotted in my stomach began to ease, replaced by a profound sense of security. His words weren't just promises; they were the proof of his commitment to us, to me. And in that moment, the depth of my feelings for him became crystal clear.

I wanted to say it. The words hovered on the tip of my tongue. I love you. But I hesitated, the weight of those three little words holding me back. Everything would be different once that threshold was crossed. And despite everything within me screaming to let those words free, a part of me was scared—scared of the vulnerability that came with such an admission. I'd never said them before and meant them like this.

Instead, I squeezed his hand, letting the gesture say what my lips couldn't. "Wyatt," I began, my voice steady but laced with something I couldn't quite name. "I don't know what I'd do without you. You've been my rock through all of this, my True North when everything else was uncertain. You make me feel safe, cared for, and so much more."

His eyes softened, and I saw the unspoken emotion there, mirroring my own. It was as if he already knew what I couldn't yet say, the significance of the feelings we hadn't put into words. In that moment, we didn't need to.

"Thank you," I continued, the words coming easier now, even if the most important ones remained locked inside my heart. "I'm so grateful for you. Whatever comes next, I know we'll face it together. And that means everything to me."

Wyatt pulled me closer. In his arms, I found the courage I'd been lacking, the strength to face the unknown. And though the words remained unsaid, everything about us, about this moment, whispered it louder than words ever could.

51

WYATT

Stephen and I agreed to pull Oliver in as an added layer of security but also to keep a watch for lingering media in places we needed to be. The studio had also increased a presence around the offices for the days Kensi would be there. It was inconvenient during that first week in Nashville, but they seemed to pull back when they realized there was no story to be had.

The studio executives had opened an investigation into the Human Resources Department when I dropped the suggestion based on a name that Stephen had shared from his own investigation. Obviously, the details of where we garnered the intel we had were kept between us while the studio scrambled to deal with their talkative employee.

Despite the high stakes, Kensi handled her responsibilities with a grace and professionalism that left no room for doubt. She was in constant motion, coordinating with venue managers, liaising with tour personnel, and ensuring that every detail of the upcoming tour was meticulously planned. Her dedication was an inspiration to anyone in her wake, and I found myself falling even more deeply for the woman who could command a room with her competence and kindness.

In the evenings, when the hustle of the day gave way to the quiet intimacy of night, Kensi and I explored Nashville together. Away from the pressures of work, these moments belonged to just us. And it was during those quiet walks and stolen glances that I came to fully understand the depth of my feelings for her. There was no room for doubt—she wasn't just part of my life now; she was at the center of where I wanted to go from here.

The investigation into the Human Resources Department concluded quietly, with changes implemented to ensure the privacy and safety of all involved. It was a victory, albeit a silent one.

Two weeks after setting foot in Nashville, we made our way back through the bustling Nashville airport, the anticipation of returning to Liberty weighed on both of us. The weeks had been a whirlwind of activity and growth, both professionally for Kensi and personally for us. Now, standing in line for security, with our bags checked and boarding passes in hand, the reality of our return started to sink in.

Our conversation flowed effortlessly as we boarded the plane, settling into our seats. The flight provided a rare moment of stillness, a pause in our busy lives to reflect on the path that had led us here.

With the hum of the engine in the background, I turned to Kensi. "So," I began, trying to keep my voice light, "are you ready to manage the tour?"

Kensi took a deep breath, her eyes alight with a mixture of excitement and apprehension. "I'd be lying if I said I wasn't terrified. But honestly, I'm mostly excited. It's such a huge opportunity, and I can't wait to dive in. I just hope I'm up for the challenge."

I reached for her hand, intertwining our fingers. "Kensi, I've seen you in action. You're more than up for this. You're going to be amazing. I'm incredibly proud of you."

She offered me a shy smile, a blush creeping up her cheeks. "Thank you."

As she spoke, I couldn't help but get lost in my thoughts about her. She had faced so much, yet here she was, stepping into a role that would intimidate anyone. But she was doing it with grace and a smile.

I admired her not just for her professional capabilities, but for her courage to embrace the unknown. Kensi had this remarkable ability to see the best in situations, to push forward with optimism and heart. It was one of the many qualities that drew me to her.

In the quiet of the plane, with the world whizzing by below us, I realized how much Kensi had changed my life. I squeezed her hand gently. Kensi leaned her head against my shoulder, a contented sigh escaping her lips.

Landing in Texas, the familiar winter air greeted us like an old friend. The landscape, the wide-open skies, was a definite contrast to the bustling streets of Nashville. As we collected our luggage, I couldn't help but think about what came next. With rehearsals on the horizon and the tour's kickoff looming, Kensi and I stood on the cusp of an adventure that would take us far outside of our comfort zones. New experiences awaited us. The prospect of what lay ahead was as daunting as it was exhilarating, but there was no one else I'd rather have by my side.

52

WYATT

After "maintenance issues" delayed our take off from Houston, we eventually made it back to Nashville. Thankfully, it was still cool enough outside that we hadn't roasted inside the large metal tube as we waited on the tarmac. Unfortunately, the lack of forward movement had Kensi worked up into a bundle of anxiety which I tried my best to unravel.

As we finally disembarked, I could feel the tension radiating off Kensi like heat waves on asphalt in a Texas summer. She was doing her best to hide it, offering me a tight smile as we made our way through the airport, but her grip on my hand was a dead giveaway. I squeezed back, hoping to lend her some of my calm.

Once our bags were loaded into the rideshare, I slid into the backseat and took Kensi's hand in mine.

"Hey," I began, my voice soft but firm, "You're going to be amazing tomorrow. You've got this."

The ghost of her usual smile flickered across her face. "Thanks. I just... I want to do well. Not just for the job, but for you, too."

I chuckled, shaking my head. "Kensi, you don't have to prove anything to me. I already know how capable you are."

The cab pulled up to our hotel, and as we checked in, the reality of being here, in Nashville, for the *Real American Country* tour began to truly sink in. The lobby buzzed with energy, and I spotted a few familiar faces from the show milling about. I could tell Kensi noticed, too, her posture straightening as she took it all in.

Our room was on the tenth floor, offering a view of the Nashville skyline that sparkled against the night. I dropped our bags by the door and wrapped my arms around Kensi from behind, both of us taking a moment to just look out the window.

"Tomorrow's a big day," I murmured into her hair, "for both of us. But tonight, it's just us, okay?"

She leaned back into me, nodding. "Okay. Just us."

We ordered room service and talked about everything but the tour and the job. It was a conscious effort to just be Kensi and Wyatt, not the tour manager and the country music guy. When sleep finally called, it was with a sense of peace, despite the nerves for what tomorrow would bring.

Morning came all too soon, heralded by an alarm that was as unwelcome as it was necessary. Kensi was up and moving before I fully registered the sound, her previous anxiety replaced with a determined focus. I admired her strength and resilience, knowing that she was stepping into a role far removed from anything she'd done before, yet she faced it head on.

Pride swelled within me as we headed to the rehearsal venue for day one. Kensi was more than just the woman I'd fallen for; she was a force in her own right. And as we stepped through those doors, I knew that no matter what the tour, the press, or anyone else threw our way, we'd face it together, stronger for it.

The studio buzzed with the energy of anticipation, the air charged with the excitement of what was to come. As I made my way through the backstage area, I saw other musicians preparing, focused yet visibly nervous. I was looking forward to catching up with Nash and seeing some of the others I'd met at our last reunion for the finale.

The rehearsal itself was a blur of activity. Kensi was whisked away by the production team to get acquainted with her duties, leaving me to focus on my performances. Despite the constant commotion, my thoughts kept drifting back to her, wondering how she was doing, hoping she felt as supported and loved by me as I did by her.

Nash spotted me first, a wide grin spreading across his face as he made his way over, Cassidy in tow. "Wyatt! Man, it's good to see you back," he said, clapping me on the shoulder. His smile was genuine when he saw me.

Cassidy, ever the radiant presence, smiled and said, "I'm so glad you're going on the tour."

Their warm reception eased the lingering unease I had about reentering this world. "Thanks, guys. It actually feels good to be back."

The conversation shifted easily, Nash and Cassidy catching me up on their lives. It was during this catch-up that I noticed Willow and Austin, standing a little apart from the group, engaged in a quiet discussion. Nash followed my gaze and nodded towards them. "Willow and Austin, they've become quite the duo. We've been hanging out with them this morning and not to gossip," he winked exaggeratedly, "but there might be something there. It's something to keep an eye on."

I chuckled and nodded. "Got it."

Willow and Austin wandered over and I greeted them. Willow's sharp wit and Austin's laid-back charm made them instantly likable and made me glad that I had this chance to get to know them better.

As the day progressed and we dove into the intricacies of rehearsals, I was eager to see the setlist, curious about how my return would be integrated into the show. Finding a moment, I checked the posted schedule and a smile spread across my face. *Let Me Love You* by Lonestar was listed for a solo performance by me, which I was very pleased with. It was a song I had played for Kensi on multiple occasions, and it had quickly become our song. So when we were able to put in our performance requests, even if they weren't guaranteed, this one was at the top of my list.

But it was the "Lead vocalist - God Bless the U.S.A. - (Greenwood)" written plain as day that caught me by surprise. The fact that

I had intended to use the show as a platform to bring attention to the needs of veterans and the families of lost veterans made this song choice feel intentional. I couldn't help but wonder if Kensi had a hand in this. It was too perfectly matched to my reasons for being here to begin with to be mere coincidence. I'd have to remember to ask her later.

As the day wound down, thoughts of Kensi began to occupy my mind more and more. The rehearsal had been all-consuming, but the prospect of seeing her again, of sharing our experiences of the day, brought a new surge of energy. I wondered how she had managed in her new role this morning. Was she feeling the same nerves and excitement that I was?

There was a dinner for the executives and management that Kensi had attended, so I opted for dinner with some of the other performers at a lively restaurant downtown, known for its vibrant atmosphere and live music. As we gathered around the large table, conversations about the day's rehearsals came and went, some shared personal anecdotes, and there was a shared excitement for what the tour promised. Despite the engaging company and the delicious food, my thoughts kept drifting back to Kensi. Paying the check couldn't happen fast enough, because by the time it arrived, I was itching to get back to the room.

When we finally regrouped at the hotel at the end of the evening, I didn't even have to ask how her day had gone because the look on her face as soon as I walked into our room told me everything I needed to know. She was exhilarated, exhausted, and utterly radiant.

"I take it everything went well today?" I asked, pulling her into my arms realizing how much I had missed seeing her today.

"It went so very well," she said, her eyes sparkling with excitement and a hint of relief.

I hugged her tightly against me, her head fitting perfectly under my chin. "I never doubted it for a second."

53

KENSI

The first night as the performers took the stage and made their way through the set, I stood back and watched everything from the sound tech area. I was proud of how well everything had come together and how perfectly executed every song and choreographed movement happened seamlessly. It was what I'd needed to refill the reserves of the confidence I'd practically overspent trying to keep up.

When Wyatt took the stage amid the lights and claimed it as his own, my heart sprouted wings. The opening chords of Lonestar's *Let Me Love You* filled the arena, and a shiver ran down my spine when somehow, through the blinding stage fog and rays of moving lights, his eyes locked with mine. It was a moment suspended in time, the spotlight on him, his voice echoing through the arena.

I watched, my heart in my throat. He sang with such emotion, such raw sincerity, and I knew he was singing directly to me, baring his soul for all to see. The crowd went wild, but for me, it was an intimate confession of love even though we'd both been holding onto the actual words.

The number of moving parts grew exponentially every single day the first few weeks on the road. I stayed so busy that my waking thoughts were focused solely on keeping everyone and everything on schedule and not panicking when things slipped – which they did, but not very often. At night, however, my thoughts and dreams stayed centered on the beautiful soul that I kissed goodbye often as I would leave a concert and head for an airport that funneled me to the next tour location ahead of the crew and cast.

There were many days that I was able to hang back and ride the bus with the female members of the cast which was a new experience in and of itself. It was close and cramped quarters. A few of them viewed me more as a motherly or authority figure when I was practically the same age as a couple of them. Cassidy, however, was a bridge for the most part and made it easier to feel like I fit in more often than not.

As the tour progressed, the rhythm of our days settled into a kind of expected chaos. There was always something to be done, always a fire to put out, but I started to find my footing. I learned the quirks of our crew and cast. I figured out quickly who needed a gentle nudge and who needed a firmer hand. Each city brought new challenges, but also new triumphs. Seeing the joy on the faces of our audience, feeling the energy of the crowd, it was intoxicating. It reminded me we were all here, doing what we loved.

I think the moment that meant the most to me was watching Wyatt cross the finish line at Fenway Park after running the *Run to Home Base 9K*. It was a 9K run through Boston, ending with crossing "home base" at the ballpark. When I was researching promotional opportunities for the performers, as soon as the event popped up on my radar, it was one I immediately forwarded to Wyatt and asked if he wanted me to pitch it to the executives. He didn't hesitate to agree when he read about Home Base, the nonprofit that provided funds that would allow injured warriors and military families to access clinical care and support to help heal visible and invisible wounds they may have.

Seeing Wyatt cross home base, his sweat mixing with the cheers of the crowd, was one of those moments that will stick with me forever. It was more than just a race; it was like he was running for every soldier who couldn't. The crowd was loud, sure, but right then, it was just him and me in that huge space. He was a man with a huge heart and he was always looking out for others. His dedication to his cause shone through in everything he did, whether on stage singing his heart out or doing something like the run. I was bursting with pride, not just because he was supporting a cause close to his heart, but because of who he is—genuine, strong, and always standing up for what and who he believes in.

I'd waited for him to help him navigate to the area designated for our crew but rather than rushing him, I watched as he took pictures alongside families and soldiers who had all served just as he had, some of them coming back a little more broken inside and out. It was beautiful and affirmed every feeling I'd ever had about him.

As he made his way through the crowd, I could see him starting to scan the area and somehow I knew he was looking for me. I pushed through a few sweaty bodies before I could reach him, then placed my hand on his arm that was slick with sweat. If it was possible, I'm pretty sure his smile doubled in size.

Not even caring that I was dressed for work and he was gross from running for the last hour, I let him haul me into his arms and spin me in a tight circle. The crowd ate it up, but I knew this wasn't for show.

While my head was next to his ear, I made sure only he could hear me when I whispered, "I love you."

His entire body seemed to relax for the briefest of moments and he released me, but didn't let me go. With a hard press of his lips to mine he responded in kind, his voice barely a whisper against my lips, "And I love you. Always."

The world around us faded into a blur of noise and movement, insignificant in the moment that held us together. He pulled back slightly, his hands framing my face as his gaze searched mine, the intensity of his eyes conveying emotions too deep for words.

The jostling of people around us reminded me of where we were and why we were there and I snapped back into work mode, even though there was no way the smile I wore would ever leave my face. I dragged him to the *Real American Country* tent and got him situated in a place where fans of the show and of Wyatt could have him sign something or take photos with him.

He slipped effortlessly into his part, greeting every fan with a charisma that made each one feel special. Watching him, I couldn't help but marvel at the way he balanced his public persona with the genuine and humble person I knew. Probably because they weren't all that different from one another. Even amidst the chaos of fan interactions, Wyatt's eyes would occasionally meet mine, a silent communication that spoke volumes.

As the line dwindled and the last fan left with a smile and a story to tell, Wyatt turned to me, the fatigue from the day's events momentarily visible. But it was quickly replaced by that infectious smile of his, the one that could light up a dark room. Checking my watch, it was time to wrap up. I motioned for the other crew members to start packing up.

"Time to head out?" he asked, already moving to help with the teardown.

I nodded, glancing around to ensure everything was accounted for. "Yeah, we've got full cast and crew dinner tonight and thankfully tomorrow is a travel day but you definitely need to shower before you get in close quarters with people."

He laughed as he set down the box of merchandise and draped his arm around my shoulders, pulling me close. "Didn't seem to bother you earlier," he murmured.

I hugged him back, laughing as he kissed the top of my head and released me. "OK, let me rephrase. You need to shower before you get in close quarters with people who don't love you like I do."

His eyes sparkled with humor and affection, a tender look that made my heart skip a beat. "Fair enough," he conceded with a grin.

As we walked towards the exit, the fading voices and the ambient sounds of the venue being dismantled echoed around us, a testament to the day's success. I couldn't shake the sense of contentment that settled over me, knowing that amidst the hectic pace of the tour, moments like these grounded us, reminding us of the simple, beautiful connection we shared.

"Hey," Wyatt said, his tone more serious now as he stopped, turning to face me. His hands found mine, his fingers intertwining with mine as he looked into my eyes. "Just so you know, this... us... it's the real deal, Kensi. I know the tour has us all over the place, but I want you to know, you're my constant. You're my home. Wherever you are is where I want to be."

A swell of emotions, a mixture of love, gratitude, and a deep-seated peace I had never felt before overwhelmed me. "I feel the same. No matter where we are, as long as we're together, I'm home too," I whispered back, the sincerity of my words hanging between us.

He pulled me into a gentle embrace, the kind that said everything words couldn't. We stayed like that for a moment longer than necessary, reluctant to let go, to break the magic of the moment.

Finally, pulling back slightly, Wyatt gave me a quick, promising kiss. "Let's get moving then. A quick shower and I'll be as good as new."

54

WYATT

As the weeks blurred into months, life on tour settled into a rhythm—a steady beat of early mornings, late nights, and everything in between. The pace was relentless, each day a mix of sound checks, performances, and meetings that left little room to breathe. But somehow, Kensi made it look effortless. She wasn't just keeping up; she was thriving. Watching her take charge, smoothing over issues with a calm confidence, I couldn't help but feel proud.

She had a way of transforming the sterile chaos of backstage into something warmer, more human. Laughter followed her, easing the tension in rooms that otherwise felt like pressure cookers. For me, her presence was more than calming—it was steadying, a reminder of what mattered most in all this madness.

Our relationship grew in the quiet spaces between the chaos. A shared look across a crowded stage, her hand slipping into mine as we navigated the wings, or the whispered conversations in the moments before we got pulled in opposite directions—every interaction felt like it deepened what was already undeniable. She wasn't just a part of this journey; she had become the best part.

We never attempted to hide our relationship, but we did try to maintain as much of a professional front as possible for a number of reasons. This became especially true when one of the performers, Lanie Tisdale, got pulled from the tour for speculations surrounding an affair with one of the former judges of *Real American Country*. Everyone knew that Kensi and I had been a thing before the tour began, including the show's executives, and we made sure they were aware even before we had officially become "us". However, now there was little room for doubt that there was an "us".

With the tour drawing to a close and the air tinged with the anticipation of finality, Kensi and I found ourselves wandering Pier 57. It was one of those rare rest days, a momentary pause in the nonstop tour schedule. The Seattle Great Wheel towered above us, a silent observer to the ebb and flow of the crowd.

Nash and Cassidy, having become fixtures in our circle of tour life, suggested an impromptu double date. The unexpected downtime was a gift, a brief escape from the responsibilities that awaited us in Nashville where everything began and where it would soon all wrap up with one final, grand concert and family event.

As we strolled along the pier, sharing stories and laughs, I couldn't help but reflect on the tour's success. It had exceeded expectations in every possible way. We grabbed a table at one of the seafood places overlooking the water.

"This tour," I started, my voice infused with a mix of pride and wonder, "has been a launchpad. I've seen the talent here, which means other people have, too. I really think anyone who really wants it has a chance to go as far as Christopher Jordan, maybe even farther, even though he won the whole thing."

Nash nodded in agreement, his eyes reflecting the same belief. "It's been incredible, man. But you don't sound like music is what's next for you. So what is next for you and Kensi?" His question, genuine and curious, turned the conversation towards the future.

I glanced at Kensi, her hand in mine, and smiled. This was my life. I had to pinch myself a few times a day to make sure it was real.

"Well," I began, squeezing her hand gently, "we're heading back to Texas. I've got my bar, The Anchor, to run and my co-owner is going to need some time off soon when his girlfriend has their baby. It's going to be all hands on deck."

Kensi smiled, the kind that lit up her entire face. "And I'll be working at The Yellow Rose Inn. Evelyn, Wyatt's mom, has been amazing, and who knows, maybe she and her husband, Ed, will take me up on the offer I made to manage the place while they do all the traveling she's talked about doing. If not, it still sounds like a good place to land for a while. What about you two?"

Nash exchanged a glance with Cassidy, a mixture of excitement and apprehension in his eyes. "Well," he started, his voice tinged with a bittersweet tone. "I've signed a contract with a studio in Nashville. I've already started working on my first album there."

Cassidy gave a small, supportive smile, but it didn't quite reach her eyes the way it usually did. "And I'll be heading back to L.A.," she added, her voice softer than before. "I work for EchoStream and I know we've got a lot of projects lined up, and I need to dive back into it."

The mood had shifted slightly, the undercurrent of their separation casting a shadow on the excitement. "It's a huge step for both of us," Nash continued, trying to muster more enthusiasm. "But yeah, it's going to be tough... being on opposite sides of the country."

Cassidy nodded, taking Nash's hand. "We knew this was a possibility when we started, but it doesn't make it any easier. This tour has brought us so close—it's hard to imagine not seeing each other every day."

My heart was sad for them. Kensi and I were fortunate; our paths were leading us to the same place, back to Texas together. "Distance can be challenging," I said, "but it also can make the heart grow fonder, right? Plus, with technology these days, it's easier to stay connected than ever before."

Kensi squeezed my hand under the table, a silent show of support. "And who knows what the future holds?" she chimed in, offering a hopeful smile to Nash and Cassidy. "Maybe there'll be opportunities for collaboration or visits."

Nash and Cassidy shared a look, a silent communication that

seemed to bolster their spirits. "You're right," Cassidy said, finally with a genuine smile. "We'll make it work because it's worth it."

As we finished our meal and walked along the pier, the conversation turned to lighter topics, but the moment of shared vulnerability lingered. It was a reminder that the paths we choose in life often come with their own set of challenges, but it's the people we meet along the way, the connections we nurture, that make the journey worthwhile.

And as the sun dipped below the horizon, painting the sky in shades of pink and orange, I was grateful for the journey, for the music, and most of all, for the people who had become an integral part of our lives during this tour. As I looked at Kensi, her hair catching the last rays of the setting sun through the window, I was grateful. No matter what came next, we had each other, and that was more than enough.

55

KENSI

The final chords of *God Bless the U.S.A.* echoed around us, with Wyatt's voice ringing clear and true above the cheers. As the song ended, the whole place just exploded into claps and whistles. I watched from the side, catching Wyatt's eye as he took his bow. His look sent a little thrill through me, a silent promise just for us. It was the end of the tour, sure, but we were just starting something special, something that was ours.

The festive atmosphere of Fan Appreciation Day was in full swing as the concert wound down, with the smell of barbecue thick in the air. I made my way through the crowd, checking off the last few things I needed to do. The air was buzzing with that happy, satisfied kind of noise that comes from a bunch of people having a great time. Kids were running around with their faces painted, laughing like crazy, while the grown-ups were busy chatting and enjoying the food. Everywhere I looked, there were people just soaking up the good times, making the most of the afternoon.

Doing my rounds, I couldn't help but feel a mix of happy and sad. This tour had been a wild ride, and finishing up these last bits of work made it all feel so final. But even as I ticked tasks off my list, my mind kept drifting back to Wyatt. It was like even though this chapter was closing, we were on the brink of something new and exciting, just waiting to start. The air around me was electric, all laughter and music and the kind of good vibes you wish could last forever.

Standing there, in the middle of it all, I knew I was right where I was supposed to be. It had been fun and exciting and had been an adventure like nothing I'd ever experienced before. It was a strange feeling, balancing on the precipice of change, the familiar mix of anticipation and nostalgia swirling within me as I looked around at the faces of our crew and cast and their families. This had become more than a job; it was a family, a collective of individuals who had shared in this unique journey across the country, bringing music and joy to countless fans.

But when my thoughts shifted to the future, this was definitely not something I could see myself doing full time. Instead, I pictured spending my days at The Yellow Rose Inn, pouring coffee and welcoming guests to a place where I'd found safety, a refuge, that I now called home. I even let my mind wander to the possibilities of starting those days with Wyatt waking up next to me and kissing me goodbye, telling me to have a great day at work.

I sighed audibly as I wished for that future to come true but was startled from my wishes when a pair of strong arms wrapped around my waist and lips found my shoulder. Six months ago, I would have likely screamed or passed out if this had happened to me. Now, though, I leaned into the embrace letting the warmth of the body behind me consume me.

"I think I heard you sigh from a mile away," Wyatt's voice came from behind me. "What did it mean?" he asked, spinning me to face him.

My clipboard and arms were sandwiched between us as I gazed up into the face I had just been imagining. "It means, I'm very happy and very sad to see this day come and go."

His eyes searched mine, a mix of concern and understanding lighting them up. "I get that," he said softly, his hands still on my waist, holding me steady amidst the fading day's chaos. "Endings are hard, especially when things have been as good to us as this tour has."

The music from the stage had given way to the sound of people packing up, the metallic clang of equipment being dismantled mingling with the laughter and farewells of our newfound friends. The scent of the barbecue had grown fainter, but the warmth of the afternoon sun still lingered, like it was reluctant to say goodbye to the day as well.

"Yeah," I admitted, allowing myself a small smile. "But one ending means a new beginning, right? Something maybe even better." My words hung between us, filled with the hope and uncertainty that the future held.

Wyatt's smile in response was like a burst of sunlight, dispelling any shadows of doubt. "Absolutely."

Our conversation was cut short when my radio buzzed with the voice of a crew member calling for me to meet him at the stage. His grip on my waist loosened reluctantly as I grabbed the radio on my waistband. "I'll be right there," I responded, a tinge of professional urgency in my voice.

After a quick kiss on my forehead, Wyatt gave me an understanding nod. I turned to leave now wishing more than ever this part of the day was done.

As I made my way back to the stage, weaving through groups of people still lingering in the fading afternoon light, the reality of my role snapped back into focus. The buzz of activity around the stage was a stark contrast to the quiet moment Wyatt and I had just shared. Crew members hustled back and forth, coordinating the teardown of the stage with practiced efficiency. The metallic clangs and shouts of direction filled the air, a symphony of closure to the day's events.

I met the crew member by the stage, his face flushed from the effort and the heat. "We've got a bit of a snag with the sound equipment," he explained, pointing to a tangle of cables that mirrored the complexity of dismantling a tour that had become a part of our lives. As we worked together to sort out the issue, I couldn't help but feel a pang of nostalgia. Each piece of equipment, each cable and mic stand, was a reminder of the countless performances and moments that had defined our journey.

Once the problem was resolved, I started rounding up the cast and sending them to the hotel to change and get ready for the evening's wrap party. Heading back to where Wyatt and I had parted, I found him talking with Nash and Cassidy.

I heard Wyatt saying, "I know it's not exactly halfway between L.A. and Nashville, but there's a fantastic inn with a breakfast menu that could make you slap your grandma. And probably the best bar in the country is just up the road from it."

Nash was clearly liking the idea by the look of excitement on his face. His arm around Cassidy pulled her a little closer to himself. "I think that sounds like a great meeting spot," he said wiggling his eyebrows at Cassidy who gently swatted his chest with the back of her hand.

"Thank you, Wyatt. That does actually sound really nice," she said.

As I walked up I added, "And, I might just have an in with the owner's son who could get you a discount on your stay."

They all laughed and Wyatt threw an arm over my shoulder and squeezed.

"Also," I continued, "you all need to go ahead and head to the buses that will take you to the hotel so you can change and get ready for the evening's events."

Nash and Cassidy said their goodbyes but Wyatt lingered.

"Will you be here much longer?" he asked, his hand now holding mine.

Shaking my head I said, "No, not much longer. The crew is doing their own thing tonight and my job is officially done once I get the eleven of you to dinner."

Wyatt's eyes softened, the corners crinkling with a smile that reached deep into his soul. "Then, I'll wait for you in the room. We can head to the party together," he offered.

I nodded, feeling a wave of gratitude for his support. "Thanks. I just need to do one last sweep to make sure everything's set for tomorrow's remaining breakdown, and then I'll take the car to the hotel."

He squeezed my hand gently, a silent promise that he was there, no matter what. As he joined the others heading towards the buses, I turned back to the now nearly empty venue. The sun had dipped lower, bathing the scene in a soft light. It was as though a curtain was gently closing on this chapter of my life.

The work was familiar, a routine I had come to know well over the past months, but tonight it felt different. Each step I took, each task I completed, was heavy with a sense of finality but also accomplishment. I'd managed something I never thought possible—to live in every moment without being afraid the next might never come. The growth I'd experienced personally and professionally would stay with me forever. And navigating the complexities of tour life, all while building relationships had changed me in ways I was only just beginning to understand.

As I finished my last task, a sense of relief washed over me. My role as tour manager had come to an end, but the experiences, the lessons learned, and the friendships formed were mine to keep.

Wyatt was waiting for me, just as he said he would be. Every time I was near him, it felt like coming home. As we made our way to the dinner, hand in hand, I couldn't help but feel excited about the next chapter. Liberty, with its familiar streets, The Inn, and the promise of new beginnings, was calling us back, but for now, the night was ours to enjoy, a celebration of everything we'd achieved and a toast to the adventures yet to come.

The evening unfolded with laughter, stories, and sad goodbyes— a fitting end to an unforgettable journey. And as Wyatt and I looked ahead to our return to Liberty, I knew that this was just the beginning. The tour might have ended, but our story, filled with love, hope, and endless possibilities, was only just beginning.

56

KENSI

While I had enjoyed every minute on the road experiencing life like I never had before, there were no words to describe the sense of relief I had when I saw the sign welcoming us back to Liberty. With its familiar streets and friendly faces, Liberty was a haven that I hadn't realized I'd been craving until that moment. The open fields rolled past us, expanses of green that whispered of homecoming and simpler times because it had become home to me. Wyatt caught my hand, his fingers entwined with mine, and I glanced over to see that shared sense of contentment reflected in his eyes.

The journey back had been a relatively quiet one, filled with reflective silence and exhaustion. Words were few and far between as we rode in the back of the car we'd scheduled to drive us home from the airport. It was as if we were both soaking in the last moments of our shared adventure, knowing that stepping back into Liberty meant stepping into a new chapter.

Our relationship, which had flourished on the road, was about to be put to the test back in the real world. Living in the small house behind The Yellow Rose Inn had always been a temporary solution, a place of refuge in a time of need. But now, as we drove past the familiar landmarks leading into Liberty, I couldn't help but wonder about the permanence of our places in each other's lives. I knew where my heart landed on the subject and while I wanted to say I knew Wyatt's feelings, too, I didn't dare set my heart on something we hadn't even talked about.

Moreover, there was the undeniable truth of Wyatt's career. Our shared ordeal had highlighted the unpredictable nature of his work in private security. The realization that his commitments could, at any moment, whisk him away to some distant corner of the globe filled me with a mix of pride and trepidation. It wasn't just about the danger inherent in his job; it was the potential distance it could put between us, physically and emotionally, at a time when we were just beginning to uncover the wonders of who we were together.

These thoughts swirled in my mind as the miles rolled by, a tangled mix of excitement for the future and concern for the unknown variables that lay ahead. Our relationship had proven its resilience under extraordinary circumstances, but the real world, with its everyday challenges, was a different battlefield. The reality of integrating our lives in Liberty, each of us with our own routines and responsibilities, presented us with a new set of hurdles.

As we neared our destination, I looked over at Wyatt, his profile set against the setting sun. In his silent presence, I found a reassuring calm. Perhaps it was true that our relationship had yet to be really tested in the "real world," but the foundation we had built was rooted in more than just circumstance. When he noticed me staring he met my gaze.

"What?" he asked, a smile playing at his lips.

"I love you," was all I said, letting the words hang between us, a declaration made all the more significant by the journey behind and the uncertainty ahead. Wyatt's smile widened, the gentleness in his eyes easing the edges of my apprehensions. He squeezed my hand, a gesture filled with promise and reassurance.

"I love you too, Kensi," he replied, his voice steady and sure.

After a moment, I mustered the courage for the question that had been dancing at the edges of my thoughts. "Have you thought about what comes next? For us, I mean?"

Wyatt's response was immediate, his tone laced with a light teasing that was so characteristic of him. "All the time."

The simplicity of his answer, coupled with the playful glint in his eyes, brought a smile to my face. "And?" I prompted.

"And," he continued, "I think I'd like to keep you forever," the light teasing still present but underscored by a depth of sincerity that reached right through to my heart. "If you're up for that, of course."

The thought of a forever with Wyatt, after everything we'd been through, felt like the most natural progression in the world. It was a future I hadn't dared to fully imagine until now, but hearing him voice it made all the pieces fall into place.

"I think I'd like that," I responded, my voice a mix of laughter and emotion. "Very much."

"Good," was all he said.

* * *

The car delivered us and our belongings to The Anchor, where we were greeted by the community's joyous welcome, complete with music and laughter. Missy and Stephen were there to greet us, their smiles wide and welcoming. Missy threw her arms around me in a hug, while Stephen clapped Wyatt on the back.

"Oh my gosh, you're finally showing!" I exclaimed as Missy stepped back.

Placing her hand on her small but noticeable bump, Missy's face lit up with a radiant smile, a mix of pride and a touch of shyness in her expression. "Yeah, it's starting to become pretty obvious," she said, her voice carrying a tone of wonder and excitement. "We have so much to catch up on but I know you have a lot of people wanting your time so let's make time this week once you've recovered, OK?"

"Absolutely," I agreed, feeling a wave of affection for my friend. "I want to hear everything, especially about this little one," I added, gesturing to her bump with a smile.

Stephen, ever the protective partner, wrapped an arm around Missy, his pride in their growing family evident in his beaming smile. "We'll have plenty to talk about," he chimed in, his gaze softening as he looked down at Missy. "But tonight, let's just enjoy having y'all back home."

The whole bar was abuzz with energy, a testament to the tight-knit community that had become my family. Stories were exchanged, laughter filled the air, and the feeling of being home was overwhelming, but I knew it would never get old. As I moved through the crowd, greeting friends and acquaintances, the happiness of the moment was tinged with the realization of how much I needed this feeling of connection and security.

The evening at The Anchor eventually wound down, the crowd thinning as people began to say their goodbyes, their faces alight with the joy of the reunion. It was then, in the quieter moments that followed, that I finally had the chance to catch up with Evelyn. She approached me with her familiar, maternal smile, the kind that always seemed to say she knew more than she let on—but only ever out of care.

"I'm so glad you're back, Kensi. We've all missed you around here," she said, her voice carrying the familiarity of home.

"Thank you, Evelyn. It's good to be back. Really good," I replied, feeling ready to get back into a familiar routine. "I'll be at The Inn bright and early tomorrow, see if I can start catching up on everything."

Evelyn shook her head, her smile taking on a gentle firmness. "Actually, I was thinking you should take the next week off. Catch up on your rest, adjust to being back home. There's no rush, and everything at The Inn is under control."

I started to protest, feeling the need to contribute, to return to some semblance of normalcy, but she held up a hand. "Speaking of The Inn, I wanted to run something by you," she continued, her expression shifting to one of contemplative seriousness.

I nodded, curiosity piqued as I waited for her to continue.

Evelyn beamed, her gaze meeting mine. "Ed and I have been doing a lot of talking, especially after seeing how you and Wyatt have handled everything... it inspired us. We've decided we want to travel, see more of the world while we still can."

Her words were unexpected, and I could only nod, encouraging her to go on.

"So," she said, a mixture of excitement and solemnity in her voice, "we were wondering if you're still interested in taking over the management of The Yellow Rose. Full time, I mean."

The offer took my breath away, a surge of emotions overwhelming me. Honored, surprised, a little apprehensive, but above all, touched by the trust and faith she was placing in me."I... Evelyn, I would be honored," I managed to say, my words tumbling out in a rush. "And I can start looking for a new place to live, make sure I'm not in the way—"

Evelyn's laughter cut me off. "Oh, Kensi, don't you worry about that. You can stay in the cottage as long as you want, or as long as it feels like home to you."

The tour executives had asked if I'd consider signing on for the next season's tour, and as much as I had loved the experience, it wasn't where my heart was, so I'd declined. But this? This was right.

"Thank you, Evelyn. Truly," I said, the depth of my gratitude making my voice thick. "I... I don't even know what to say, except that I'll do my best."

Evelyn hugged me, a sweet, motherly embrace that said everything without having to say anything. As we pulled away, her eyes were shining with unshed tears, but her smile was bright.

"I know you will, dear. I have every confidence in you."

Wyatt joined us moments later, his presence immediately bringing an added layer to the already emotional moment. He wrapped an arm around my shoulders, pulling me into his side.

Wyatt glanced between his mom and me, a curious look on his face like he was trying to piece together what he'd just walked into. Evelyn beamed up at him, her pride impossible to miss. "Your girl here just agreed to take over running The Yellow Rose Inn," she announced, her voice warm with happiness and just a hint of mischief.

Wyatt's grin came instantly, wide and bright, his eyes shining with surprise and joy. "That right?" he asked, looking at me like he couldn't quite believe it, like he was seeing me in a new light.

I nodded, the weight of it all settling on me in a way that was both exciting and terrifying. "Yeah," I said, my voice quieter than I intended. "Looks like I'll be sticking around for a while." The words were heavy with meaning. I searched his face for any sign of hesitation or doubt. I didn't find any of it. Instead, I found hope.

"That suits me just fine," Wyatt drawled in a low rumble, sending a shiver down my spine.

Evelyn gave a knowing smile. "I figured it might. Now, you two are probably exhausted or your adrenaline is going to give out pretty soon. Why don't you take her home, Wyatt, and we'll make sure everything here is taken care of."

Wyatt nodded in agreement, his gaze softening as he looked at me, an understanding passing between us. The day had been a whirlwind of emotions, reunions, and now, life-changing decisions. The adrenaline that had carried us through was indeed beginning to wane, replaced by a gentle exhaustion and the contentment of being home, truly home.

"Sounds like a plan," he said, offering his mother a grateful smile.

Turning to me, he asked, "Ready to head home?"

Home. I could only nod, my heart full. As we said our goodbyes and thanked Evelyn for her incredible generosity and trust, I couldn't help but feel overwhelmed by the turn my life had taken.

Wyatt's hand found mine as we walked to his truck Stephen had brought to The Anchor for him. The spring night air was warm against my skin, a gentle reminder of the changing seasons and the new beginnings that lay ahead. The peaceful quiet of the evening settled over us as we drove.

As we pulled up to the small apartment behind The Yellow Rose Inn, I smiled, remembering Evelyn's words to me. You can stay in the apartment as long as you want, or as long as it feels like home to you.

It wasn't the apartment that felt like home so much as it was who was with me.

The night passed in peaceful quiet, the kind that speaks volumes. And as I drifted off to sleep, wrapped in Wyatt's arms, I realized that I didn't just have a place in Liberty. I had a home, a purpose, and a future that was brightly unfolding before me. And it was all mine.

57

WYATT

Liberty, Texas, had never felt more like home to me than it did these past eight months since Kensi and I returned from the tour. Even though I grew up here, having Kensi here cast everything in a new light. She brought a sense of renewal, making every sunset we watched together from the porch of The Yellow Rose Inn feel like a spectacle we'd never witnessed before. The town, with all its routines and rhythms, danced to a different tune, one that resonated deep inside my soul.

With Kensi by my side, Liberty wasn't just the place where I grew up; it was a home in a way it had never been before. She turned the familiar into something extraordinary, grounding me in a life I'd always wanted but never thought I could have. Every day with her was something new, but today... today carried a different kind of weight. One I felt every time I reached into my pocket and brushed my fingers against the small box inside.

Walking into The Anchor, my chest tightened with nerves that had nothing to do with the usual hustle of the bar. Stephen was behind the counter, wiping down a glass, but his attention shifted the second I walked up. I didn't bother with small talk. Instead, I reached into my pocket, pulled out the box, and flipped it open.

The ring inside caught the bar's soft light, the faint gleam dancing across the surface. It had belonged to my grandmother, a piece of history that felt right in my hand now. "I'm doing it," I said, my voice low but steady, the weight of my words grounding me even as my pulse quickened.

Stephen glanced at the ring, then back at me, a slow grin spreading across his face. "You sure about this?"

"It's the only thing I've been this sure about in my entire life," I replied, my resolve firm. There was a brief pause as the image of what I was about to do formed in my mind. The seriousness of the moment made me think about all the steps that lead up to something like this, about the conversations that needed to happen and the understanding that had to be shared between two people.

Thinking about it, I turned to Stephen, a thought crossing my mind. "Have you guys talked any more about getting married? I mean, since the last time you asked her?" I ventured, knowing this was a sensitive topic but also one that Stephen needed to navigate if he and Missy were to move forward.

He shook his head. "No, not really. It's like we're stuck in this loop. I love her and our kid more than anything, but this... this hesitance of hers is tough to get around. Tim really did a number on her." Stephen's voice trailed off, the pain evident in his expression.

I took a moment before responding. "Have you thought about maybe flipping the script on her? Like, if she changes her mind about marriage, maybe she should be the one to ask you." The idea was a bit unconventional, but given their unique situation, it might just be the key to moving forward.

He paused, his gaze drifting to the array of bottles behind the bar as he considered my words. A new kind of light ignited in his eyes—hope.

"Well, no, I hadn't thought about that. But, giving her the control to make that decision might just ease some of her fears. She knows I'm not going anywhere, but maybe this way, she'll feel safer about it all. That's a good idea, man." Stephen's smile, hesitant at first, grew wider, a sense of relief emanating from him.

"Yeah, she deserves that much, right?" I encouraged.

Stephen nodded, a look of determination settling over his features. "Right. It's not the traditional way of doing things, but then again, when have Missy and I ever been traditional?" He let out a short laugh, the sound breaking the tension that had hung between us.

"Exactly," I agreed, clapping him on the shoulder. "You two have always done things your way, and it's worked out pretty well so far."

The conversation drifted to fatherhood, and Stephen's face lit up with pride and love. "It's incredible, man. And seeing Missy carrying our baby and now as a mom? It's just..." His words trailed off, filled with emotion.

As I listened, I couldn't help but imagine Kensi in a similar light, loving our child with that same love and tenderness I knew she possessed. The thought ignited a deep longing that surged through my chest, a future I was now determined to bring to life.

With curiosity and excitement, Stephen asked, "So, when are you planning to do it?"

The details of my plan were already laid out in my mind, ready to be shared. "I booked a cabin in Montana for a few days. Told Kensi it's a getaway before the Christmas rush really sets in. We're heading out tomorrow," I explained. The idea of escaping to somewhere quiet and breathtaking with Kensi to ask her to be mine forever made every nerve in my body buzz with anticipation.

Stephen's eyebrows raised in approval, a knowing smile creeping onto his face. "That sounds perfect."

"Yeah, I wanted it to be somewhere special, away from everything and everyone. Just Kensi and me," I said.

Stephen nodded, his expression softening with a sense of brotherly pride. "She's going to love it, man. I mean, how could she not? You, a cabin in Montana, the stars... It's like something out of a romance novel."

I chuckled, the tension of the moment easing with his words. "That's the plan. Something just for us."

"Man, I'm so happy for you two. You've got this," Stephen encouraged, his confidence in me bolstering my own.

Everything was aligning just as it was meant to. Now I needed to pack and pray everything would go as smoothly as I'd planned.

58

KENSI

The Yellow Rose Inn had been booked solid for the last six months and it didn't appear to be slowing down. Christmas was two weeks away, and I had let Wyatt convince me to take a few days off since it had been almost eight months since I'd taken any kind of break. At first I was thrilled at the idea and immediately agreed, but the closer the time came to hand the reins, even temporarily, to my assistant manager Gemma, the more convinced I was that the timing was terrible and I was making a mistake. I actually tried to convince Wyatt on the way to the airport that we needed to reschedule and try for a less busy time. He'd laughed and asked when I thought that might be, seeing as how business continued to grow fast enough that Evelyn, Ed, and I'd had a very serious conversation recently about adding some rooms onto the house. I knew Wyatt had been right, but I hadn't realized it until we were standing in front of the most picture perfect cabin surrounded by a white blanket of snow in the middle of a secluded wooded area.

"It's beautiful," I whispered, my breath forming a misty cloud in the chilly air. Wyatt squeezed my hand, his smile wide and infectious.

"I'm glad you like it," he said, leading me up the steps to the cabin door. "I wanted to find somewhere away from everything, where we could just be together."

The cabin was cozy, the perfect blend of rustic charm and modern convenience, with a crackling fire already warming the living room. It had been like stepping into a Christmas card with one of those picturesque scenes you wish you could live in, and here we were, doing just that.

Wyatt took our coats and hung them up before pulling me close. "I know you were worried about leaving The Yellow Rose Inn," he said softly, "but I promise, Gemma's got everything under control."

I nodded, leaning into his embrace. "I know, I just... it's hard to let go sometimes. But I trust you, and I trust Gemma. And this," I gestured around the cabin, "is just what I needed."

We spent the evening exploring the cabin, finding a well-stocked kitchen that promised meals cooked together, a collection of board games for playful competition, and a stack of blankets perfect for cuddling by the fire. Dinner was simple but delicious, and afterwards, Wyatt surprised me by pulling out a guitar.

"I thought maybe I could teach you a few chords," he said with a grin. "Consider it a continuation of your country music education."

I laughed, delighted at the thought. Music had become another language between us, a way to share pieces of ourselves and our stories. Wyatt motioned for me to sit between his legs, back against his chest, as he reached around to guide my hands onto the guitar. The light of the fire flickered across our faces, casting shadows that danced along the walls of the cabin. It was clumsy and filled with more laughter than music, but it was perfect.

"OK, your turn," I insisted, letting my hands fall to my lap, leaving his arms around me.

There was a moment of silence, a peaceful pause, as Wyatt's hands resumed their position on the guitar. The melody he began to play was soft and slow, a slow tune that filled the cabin. I leaned back into him, feeling the vibrations of each note through his fingertips and into my very being. I could feel his breath against my neck with every chord he strummed and word he sang.

. . .

Baby, you're not broken
It's okay to be scared
Let me be your hope, be your light, help you repair
The hurt from the words that were spoken
All the things he did wrong
When he told you you're nothing
And he wished you were gone

Girl let me love you - I know a thousand ways
You don't have to try or to be or to do or to say
You don't need to change a thing
Just let me love you. Let me love you.

Let me hold you close, I'll keep you warm
I'll be the calm in your storm
He tried to break you, but you're still here
You don't need to hide your scars
I'll chase away the fears, just let me hold your heart

Girl let me love you - I know a thousand ways
You don't have to try or be or do or say
You don't need to change a thing
Just let me love you. Let me love you.

As the last chord faded into the crackling sound of the fire, the silence that followed was deep, filled with emotion that words could barely capture. I remained still, my heart beating a rapid rhythm, moved by the beauty of the melody and the intimacy of the moment.

"Who was that by?" I asked, my voice barely above a whisper, not wanting to break the spell that the music had woven around us.

Wyatt's arms tightened around me for a moment before he replied, his voice equally soft, "I wrote it... for you."

The revelation sent a shockwave through me, a mix of surprise, humility, and a deep joy. I turned slightly to look at him, needing to see his face. His eyes shone with a vulnerability and an honesty that made my heart skip a beat.

"For me?" My voice was a mix of awe and disbelief.

"Yeah, for you," he confirmed, his smile tender. "Every word, every note."

I turned fully now to face him, forcing him to set the guitar to the side, my heart in my throat. "It's beautiful, Wyatt. So incredibly beautiful. Thank you," I said, my voice thick. The song's lyrics echoed in my mind—words of love, healing, and acceptance that reached deep into the parts of me I had thought were beyond repair.

Wyatt's hand reached up to gently touch my face, his thumb brushing away a tear that had escaped. "You've given me so much, Kensi. I wanted to give you something that made it clear what's in my heart. To tell you that you're not alone, that you never have to be again."

Surrounded by the warmth of the fire, the coziness of the cabin, and the depth of Wyatt's love, a new kind of healing began. Not just from his words, but from the knowledge that here, in his arms, I was safe, cherished, and loved for who I was. The burden of the past was lighter, replaced by the promise of a future filled with love and understanding.

With a slight shift in his posture, Wyatt carefully reached into his pocket, a move almost too smooth to notice. But I did notice the slight distraction in his eyes as he fumbled to grip something small. His deliberate actions unveiled a tiny box, his nervous excitement adding to his appeal.

"Kensi," he started again, his voice barely above a whisper, filled with emotion, "will you marry me and let me love you forever?"

Every detail in that moment of pure, unadulterated love sharpened. And as I nestled closer into his embrace, feeling the earnestness of his heart through his quivering hands holding the ring box, I whispered, "Yes," completely and utterly certain that my answer was, and always would be, a resounding yes.

59

KENSI

A year to the day after Wyatt proposed, the crisp December air in Liberty, Texas, was filled with a sense of anticipation that had invaded every corner of the town. One might think an important dignitary or some celebrity was coming to visit but that was not the case. No, it was just the fact that Wyatt and I were getting married. And despite my wishes for a small, intimate ceremony, the entire community had other ideas. The love and support we'd received had been overwhelming, which was honestly a testament to how deeply ingrained my life had become with the entire town. So after fighting several losing battles, our wedding was set to be a grand affair, one that would accommodate not just our families and friends but practically the entire town.

From the moment I stepped foot in Liberty, escaping a past I'd rather forget, I never imagined I'd find myself at the center of such a loving and eccentric community. But here I was, planning my wedding with more "helpers" than a royal bride. We'd kept the news between the two of us until we could share it with Evelyn, Ed, Missy, and Stephen. The moment it became public knowledge, the floodgates of offers to help and be part of the wedding opened. Every morning, as I opened The Yellow Rose Bed and Breakfast, the townsfolk would start trickling in with offers to contribute to our big day.

Mrs. Harper from the bakery insisted on baking our wedding cake. "Three tiers," she declared with a twinkle in her eye.

Then there was Bob, the barber, who volunteered his garage band to play at our reception. "We've been practicing Can't Help Falling in Love all month," he boasted, his enthusiasm barely contained. Wyatt leaned over and whispered, "They were banned from the town festival this year for causing a feedback loop in multiple hearing aids that scared off half the audience." We decided it was best to let them play—after the elderly guests had left.

Even the local police force and fire department wanted in, offering a joint 'safety escort' for our wedding procession. It sounded more like a parade than a solemn event, complete with flashing lights and sirens. I had visions of saying "I do" over the sound of a fire truck horn.

As the wedding drew nearer, every detail had been commandeered by someone in Liberty. The local art store owner, Maria, was hand-painting our invitations. The Thompsons from the dollar store were somehow responsible for decorations, promising a mix of elegance and "good ol' Texas flair," which I feared translated to cowboy boots filled with wildflowers on every table.

Through all this, the one constant was Evelyn and Ed. Evelyn, with her ever-present smile and boundless energy, had taken on the role of wedding planner, orchestrating the chaos with a grace that left me in awe. And Ed, dear sweet Ed, had been the father figure I'd longed for, offering his arm for that all-important walk down the aisle —a moment I insisted remain untouched by the town's enthusiastic meddling. Though the local Boy Scout troop had offered to provide a multi-person escort down the aisle.

Wyatt and I spent evenings on the porch of my small apartment, looking out over the town that had adopted me, laughing over the latest wedding "update" that inevitably came our way. Despite the craziness, there was a profound sense of belonging and love that I had never expected to find.

The morning of the wedding arrived with a bustle of activity. All of Liberty seemed to be in motion, everyone rushing to put the final touches on what was being touted as the event of the year. As I stood at the entrance of the local church, transformed beyond recognition by the townsfolk's efforts, I couldn't help but smile.

The walkway leading up to the grand wooden doors was lined with delicate, frost-inspired luminaries that would be lighted and make it appear as if the path was sprinkled with starlight, guiding guests to the celebration within.

Stepping inside, the transformation filled me with awe. The pews were decorated with garlands of silver and white, intertwined with soft, twinkling fairy lights that gave the interior a magical feel. Instead of traditional floral arrangements, each garland was dotted with delicate paper snowflakes, each one unique, handcrafted by the children of Liberty's elementary school under Evelyn's watchful eye. It was a beautiful nod to the community's involvement, and seeing those snowflakes flutter slightly in the heated air brought an unexpected tear to my eye.

The altar was a masterpiece of understated elegance. A backdrop of sheer white fabric was draped gracefully behind it, with strands of fairy lights woven through, mimicking a cascade of falling snow. In front of this ethereal scene stood two large, winter-bare trees, their branches dusted with a shimmering frost effect, flanking either side of the altar. It was as if the very romantic essence of winter had been captured and brought indoors, creating a sanctuary that was both intimate and grand.

Evelyn had orchestrated every detail to perfection. The floral arrangements were a mix of white roses, lilies, and frosted greenery, echoing the winter theme while adding a touch of color amidst the cooler tones. Bouquets and centerpieces were strategically placed around the church, on windowsills, and at the end of each pew, their fragrance subtle but unmistakably present, making the space feel even more welcoming.

Even the lighting had been thoughtfully considered. With fairy lights providing a soft illumination and strategically placed spotlights creating a gentle cascade of light down the aisle, every step I took towards Wyatt would be perfectly lit.

As I made my way to the small room assigned for my final preparations, I passed by the members of the town, each busy with their last-minute tasks, yet all of them stopped to offer me a smile, a hug, or a word of encouragement. It was in this moment, surrounded by the love and effort of the people of Liberty, that I truly understood the depth of what we were about to celebrate.

The room was a cozy nook, usually reserved for the choir's robes, but today it was my private dressing room. The walls, typically bare, were now draped with soft, flowing fabrics in shades of white and silver, lending an air of elegance and calm. In the center stood a large, full-length mirror, flanked by two vintage dressers adorned with all the essentials for today's preparations.

Babs, Liberty's go-to hairstylist and unofficial makeup guru, was already there, her kit spread out like a treasure trove of beauty secrets. Her presence settled me. "Ready to become the most stunning bride Liberty has ever seen?" she teased, her smile infectious.

Just as I was about to reply, the door creaked open, and Evelyn peeked in, her eyes sparkling with unshed tears and excitement. "Oh, Kensi," she breathed, stepping inside, "everything is coming together beautifully. You should see the look on Wyatt's face; that boy is positively beaming."

Evelyn moved closer, her hands clasping mine. "I just wanted to say," she paused, her voice thick with emotion, "how proud I am of you. Of both of you. Wyatt is my son, but you, Kensi, you've become the daughter I never had. Today isn't just about joining two lives; it's about expanding our family."

The word family hit me harder than I expected. A lump formed in my throat, and before I could stop them, tears welled in my eyes. I wasn't someone who cried easily—at least, not until recently. But something in me had softened, and Evelyn's words spoke directly to that part of me.

I tried to blink the tears away, but Evelyn only smiled knowingly, her grip on my hands tightening as if to steady me. "Now," she said, her tone shifting to one of cheerful command, "let's get you ready. We've got a wedding to celebrate!"

I nodded, laughing softly as I brushed at my tears. "Thank you, Evelyn," I whispered, my voice trembling. "For everything."

Babs sprang into action, her skilled hands working through my hair, weaving it into an elegant updo that somehow managed to be both sophisticated and effortlessly beautiful. As she applied makeup, Evelyn busied herself with laying out the dress and accessories, each piece chosen with care and a deep understanding of my style.

The early afternoon's calm was briefly interrupted as Missy came rushing through the door, her breaths short and her apologies flying faster than her entrance. "I'm so sorry I'm late!" she exclaimed, her hands instinctively moving to her slightly protruding belly, a visible sign of her sixth month of pregnancy. Behind her hurried words lay the unspoken chaos of managing life with her eighteen-month-old, Ella, who had decided that today of all days was the perfect moment to showcase her burgeoning independence.

As Missy settled into the room her apologies were met with laughter and understanding, the bonds of our friendship allowing no room for reprimand. "I'm just glad you made it," I reassured her, my smile aiming to ease the flurry of her arrival.

Evelyn offered a chair and a pat on the back, her motherly instincts kicking in as she guided Missy to sit down and catch her breath. The room, once a quiet space of preparation, now hummed with the energy of shared lives and friendship.

As the morning wore on, the room transformed into a space of laughter, storytelling, and occasional bouts of advice from Evelyn, who had seamlessly taken on the role of matriarch for us all. Missy, now more settled, shared tales of Ella's latest escapades, her stories a welcome distraction from the nerves that ebbed and flowed with the ticking clock.

The dress, a stunning creation that hung waiting by the door, caught the light in a way that reminded me of the new beginnings that today represented. Evelyn, with a gentle nudge, signaled that it was time to step into the gown that would mark my transition from fiancée to wife. As the fabric settled around me, the room fell into a reverent silence, the significance of the moment not lost on anyone present.

As the final touches were added, Missy stepped back, her work complete. "There," she announced, a proud gleam in her eye, "Perfect."

The fabric whispered against the floor as I stepped forward to examine the reflection in the mirror. The image that greeted me was one of radiant happiness, a bride ready to step into her new life with confidence and joy. It was in this moment of quiet reflection that a gentle knock echoed through the room, pulling my attention away from the mirror.

"Kensi?" The familiar, warm voice of Wyatt called softly through the door, laden with a mix of excitement and a hint of nervous anticipation.

Instantly, the room filled with a flurry of whispers and admonishments about bad luck and old wives' tales. "Wyatt, you know it's bad luck to see the bride before the wedding!" Evelyn's voice was playful yet firm, echoing the sentiment of tradition that clung to moments like these.

From the other side of the door, Wyatt's chuckle was audible, carrying with it the ease of our shared understanding. "I promise, I won't look. I just... I needed to hear her voice. Make sure she's okay."

His words melted my resistance. With a collective nod of understanding, Evelyn, Babs, and Missy quietly excused themselves, their exit filled with smiles and knowing looks, leaving me to share a moment with Wyatt.

Moving towards the door, I paused for a brief second, overwhelmed by the significance of the gesture I was about to make. As I reached out, my hand brushed the cool air of the hallway, only to find Wyatt's warm hand waiting on the other side of the slightly open door. His hand was familiar, strong and reassuring, enveloping mine in a gentle squeeze that spoke volumes.

"Hey there," I whispered, the door still separating us.

"Hey yourself," Wyatt replied, his voice soft, carrying a smile I could hear and feel in my heart. "I just wanted to check on you. Make sure you're doing okay."

His concern, always so tender and genuine, brought a smile to my face. "I'm more than okay. I'm... I'm happy, Wyatt. Really, truly happy. Everyone's been amazing, and everything's so beautiful. I can't wait to see you at the end of that aisle."

There was a pause, a moment charged with the emotion of our impending vows, before he responded. "I can't wait either. You know, standing here, talking to you, not being able to see you... it's making me realize just how much I can't wait to spend the rest of my life with you. To see you every day, to be there for you, and to share every moment, good and bad."

The depth of his words, spoken through the barrier between us, only served to deepen the connection I had with him, to this town, and to the life we were about to build together.

"Me too," I murmured, squeezing his hand tighter.

After a moment more, we reluctantly released each other's hands, knowing we'd see each other very soon. As I heard his footsteps retreat, a sense of peace washed over me.

The calm inside me lingered as the room returned to a state of bustling activity, the final touches being applied with meticulous care. Amidst the flurry, the faint strains of music began to filter through the walls, a melodic signal that the moment we had all been waiting for was drawing near.

As the music swelled, a soft knock at the door heralded Evelyn's return. Her eyes sparkled with excitement, and her smile was contagious as she opened the door, peeking in with an air of official business. "Five minutes, Kensi," she announced with a gentle authority that brought an immediate hush over the room.

The hive of activity settled into a quiet hum of anticipation. Missy, Babs, and I exchanged looks of solidarity, their smiles offering strength and encouragement before they headed for the sanctuary.

Left alone in the room, the soft strains of music filtering through the walls became my sole companion. Standing there dressed in the gown that symbolized so much more than just a bridal attire, gratitude filled my heart. Gratitude for the strength to leave a past that no longer served me, for the courage to embrace the unknown, and for the serendipity that guided me to Wyatt, to Evelyn, to Ed, and to a community that had become my family.

The door creaked open once more, and Ed stepped inside. His eyes met mine, and in them, I saw not just the kindness and wisdom that had always characterized him, but also affection.

"Kensi, my girl, you look beautiful," he began, his voice carrying a timbre of solemnity, "I remember when I first stepped into Wyatt's life, after his father passed. It wasn't easy for him, or for me, trying to find our footing. But I never saw Wyatt as anything but a son." He paused, his gaze unwavering, ensuring his words sank in.

"And just the same," he continued, a smile softening his features, "you've become a daughter of my heart. Life has a way of bringing us to where we're meant to be, not by erasing the past, but by building on it, learning from it. What you've brought to our lives, the joy, the resilience, the love... it's more than I could have ever hoped for him, for all of us."

The moment those words hit, I came undone. Ed's words served as a reminder that I had found this family, these people, who had chosen to love me despite everything.

"Oh my God," I choked out, fanning my face furiously as if that would somehow stem the tide of tears I was trying to hold back. "You're going to ruin my makeup," I managed with a watery laugh, dabbing at my eyes with trembling fingers.

Ed chuckled softly, stepping closer and placing a reassuring hand on my shoulder. "Good makeup can handle a few happy tears," he said with a wink. "Now, go on, get yourself together. Wyatt's waiting for his bride."

I nodded, taking a deep breath and clasping my hands together to stop their shaking. "Thank you, Ed," I whispered, my voice breaking.

He extended his arm, a gesture both protective and empowering, ready to guide me to the beginning of a new journey. As I wrapped a hand around his offered arm, a symbol of acceptance and trust, the music crescendoed, a signal that the time had come to step forward.

With Ed by my side, I took a deep breath, the air filled with the promise of new beginnings. The path ahead, once fraught with uncertainty, now lay clear and bright, illuminated by the love and support of a family chosen by fate and bound by heart.

Together, we walked towards the door, each step a testament to the journey that had led me here, to this moment. And as we stepped into the light, the faces of those who had become my world smiled back at me, a sea of acceptance and welcome, ready to bear witness to the vows of love and commitment that would weave Wyatt and me into the fabric of each other's souls, forever.

60

WYATT

As I stood at the altar, the hum of anticipation from our friends and family filled the air, but my world narrowed to the memories flashing through my mind. Kensi, with her strength veiled by vulnerability, had walked into Liberty—and my life—as a mystery wrapped in pain. Her journey from the shadows of her past to the light of today was nothing short of miraculous. It was a testament not just to her resilience but to the unforeseeable path Fate had charted for us.

When I looked into the audience I saw members of the Stealth-Wave Security team who had been there and had my back through countless missions. Nash and his fiancée Cassidy had made the trip to celebrate with us and in a few months we'd be headed to West Virginia to stand with them as they tied the knot.

Stephen, my best man and brother in all but blood, stood by my side, a steady presence as always. Missy, radiant in her role as Kensi's matron of honor, was the picture of happiness. She'd finally broken down after she found out they were expecting their second child and told Stephen they needed to get to the courthouse and make some things official. Two days later, they were married. I wasn't sure if it was possible for Stephen to be any happier, given the permanent smile on his face these days.

The room went silent as the ceremony began. The only sound was the soft rustle of fabric and the piano. It was as if time itself had slowed, waiting for this moment to unfold. As the music swelled with a soft melody, everyone rose to their feet, their eyes riveted to the entrance. Kensi appeared, arm in arm with Ed, her smile radiant.

When Kensi walked down the aisle, every worry and every doubt I'd ever had melted away. She was a vision, and as she stood before me, my world fell into perfect alignment.

My hands were shaking as the pastor directed us to share our vows. The shaking quickly stopped when Kensi's own trembling hands landed in mine.

"Kensi," I began, my voice steady despite the hurricane of emotions within me, "from the moment you bravely stepped into Liberty, you turned my whole world upside down in the best way. You didn't just show me what it means to be strong—you showed me what it means to be brave. You've faced things most people couldn't imagine, and instead of breaking, you've built something beautiful— something I'm lucky to be a part of.

Today, I'm promising you more than just my love. I'm promising to stand beside you, no matter what comes our way. To be the place you can always come back to. I'll push you when you need it, catch you when you stumble, and remind you every day of just how incredible you are.

You've made me a better man, Kensi. You've taught me that strength isn't just about holding it all together—it's about knowing when to lean on someone else. And I promise, for the rest of my life, you can lean on me. Together, we've faced some of the hardest moments, and I know we'll face more. But I also know there's nothing we can't handle, as long as we're together. I love you, Kensi. And I always will."

Kensi's eyes shimmered with unshed tears. Her voice was clear and resolute. "Wyatt, I love you. In you, I found safety, love, and a belief in myself that I thought was lost forever. You stood by me when shadows loomed large, offering me a light I dared not hope for. Today, I vow to stand beside you as your partner, your ally, and your greatest supporter. You've encouraged me to dream, to step beyond the confines of my past, and to embrace a future filled with hope. You've shown me that true love challenges us to be better, to do things we never thought possible. With you, I've found not just love but a home. I want to be the same for you. I promise to be the calm in your storm, the joy in your heart, and a constant in this ever-changing world."

Kensi's words hit me like a force I wasn't ready for. They weren't just words; they were a promise, grounding me and lifting me all at once. As I held her gaze, something shifted. That moment, her voice, the look in her eyes—it all became a part of me, like a mark left on my soul that I'd carry forever.

61

KENSI

As we sealed our vows with a kiss, the whole atmosphere shifted seamlessly from solemn promises to a full-blown celebration. Laughter, whoops, and hollers mingled with the chatter, as the seriousness of our ceremony transitioned into the party waiting for us.

The walls of the reception hall were strung with lights that twinkled like stars, casting a cozy glow on the rough-hewn wood around us. It smelled like Christmas, with a blend of vanilla and cinnamon. Tables were decked out with holly and mistletoe, and a massive, decked-out Christmas tree stood proudly, like it was also celebrating our new beginning.

The room erupted in cheers when we walked in, our friends and family's faces glowing with joy. The flashes from cameras caught every laugh, every impromptu dance move, every real, unguarded smile that spread without effort.

The reception was pure magic lifted straight from a storybook. The dance floor was always buzzing, alive with the sound of festive songs and those tunes that tugged at our hearts, reminding us of the journey that led us here. We shared stories that made us laugh until we cried, clinked glasses in toast after toast, and soaked in the electric thrill of being surrounded by everyone we loved. It was a celebration of love in its purest form, filled with the kind of moments that remind you that you're exactly where you're supposed to be.

The highlight of the night for me was Wyatt joining Bob's garage band when they sang their very well rehearsed but unique rendition of *Can't Help Falling in Love*. This wasn't your usual reception performance; it was filled with a happy kind of chaos that only Bob and his motley crew could conjure. The song sounded like a mash up of Garage Rock and Country with an odd smattering of the occasional ukulele.

Wyatt beamed as he joined right in as though this had been a song he'd sung with the group every Thursday night in Bob's garage. I'd laughed and been unable to stop smiling no matter how badly my face hurt.

As soon as the song ended, Wyatt exited the stage and caught my hand, his eyes sparkling with a mischievous glint.

His voice barely a whisper in my ear, he asked,"Want to escape for a bit?" His look held a knowing glint, hoping for a stolen moment away from the prying eyes of our guests.

I hesitated, a laugh escaping me. "We can't just leave our own party, can we?" The thought was tempting and the idea of sneaking away felt a tad rebellious.

He grinned, a mischievous sparkle lighting up his gaze. "We'll come back. Just think of it as...borrowing a moment for ourselves." His suggestion, whispered so only I could hear, sent a thrill through me, the audacity of it all both shocking and exhilarating.

The idea of stealing away, even just for a little while, was irresistible. Nodding, I let Wyatt wrap his tuxedo jacket around me then lead me by the hand, slipping quietly away from the heart of the celebration and into the serene Texas night. Stepping outside, we were greeted by a cold breeze, a welcome change from the lively atmosphere of the church hall where music and laughter echoed behind us.

We found ourselves wandering to the side of the church, where the shadows stretched long and the world outside the celebration was quiet. Hidden from view by the ancient oak trees that dotted the church's grounds, we stumbled into our own secluded hideaway. The stars above us shone with an intensity only seen far from the city lights, a sparkling canopy in the wide Texas sky.

Turning to face me, Wyatt's hands found mine, his touch both grounding and electric, sending a shiver of anticipation through me. The night air was sharp and cold, but the heat radiating from him set my skin ablaze. "This is perfect," he murmured, his voice low and rough-edged, the sound wrapping around me and making my pulse skip.

The intensity in his eyes held me captive, pulling me closer until the world around us blurred, leaving only the two of us under the endless stretch of the Texas sky. His arms slid around me, strong and sure, pulling me against him until I could feel the steady beat of his heart beneath my palms. When his lips met mine, the kiss was soft, tentative at first, like we were savoring the moment. But then it deepened, a current of emotions and the thrill of the day pouring into it, igniting something between us that couldn't be ignored.

The chill of the air faded, replaced by the heat of his body, the press of his mouth against mine. Our breaths mingled in cloudy puffs of vapor, the only reminder of the cold night surrounding us.

"I needed this," he sighed against my lips, the words a whispered confession, warm and raw in the stillness.

Wyatt's hands traced the outline of my back, pulling me closer, and I lost myself in the sensation, in the overwhelming love that saturated the very air we breathed. It was a moment of intimacy, a celebration of our love that wasn't meant to be shared.

There, in the shadow of the church, surrounded by the quiet of the night and the soft whisper of the wind through the trees, everything else melted away. It was just us and the future shining as brightly as the stars overhead.

With a mixture of reluctance and amusement, we pulled apart, still breathless and sharing soft laughter, as though we couldn't believe our audacity. I shivered as the heat surrounding us began to fade and the cold mingled with the light sheen of sweat I'd formed under the coat.

"We should head back," Wyatt said, his expression mirroring my own reluctance to leave.

Hand in hand, we made our way back to the church, the sounds of the reception growing louder with each step. Our brief escape into the night had been a shared secret, a private declaration of our love and desire. As we stepped back into the light and warmth of the hall, greeted by the smiling faces of our friends and family, the memory of our moment in the shadows lingered, a promise of all the moments we would steal together in the years to come.

62

WYATT

Dawn broke over New York, but in our boutique hotel room, time moved differently. The world's chaos was muted. Lying next to Kensi, my wife, in the cocoon of our bed, I was keenly aware of the gentle rise and fall of her breathing, the way her hair cascaded over the pillow, and how the first hints of sunlight played across her skin. I traced the back of my fingers gently down her arm, marveling at the softness of her skin, the way she shifted slightly closer to me in her sleep. This quiet moment, rich with the promise of shared secrets and whispered dreams, felt a world away from the bustling city that awaited us.

I'd offered to go back to the cabin where I'd proposed in Montana for our honeymoon, but she'd been adamant that I needed to experience New York City at Christmas. It had been just over three years since Kensi first left New York and I couldn't help but wonder if she also had a simmering desire to face her past and maybe make new memories in a place she'd once loved.

She'd been right when she said the city was something to behold at Christmas. Texas does everything big, but this was a different kind of big. The streets were a spectacle of lights and decorations, creating a canvas that was almost surreal. Kensi took my hand as we ventured out, her excitement contagious. She guided me through her city, each step a story, each turn a memory. It was like watching a flower bloom in real-time, witnessing Kensi reconnect with her roots, the places that had shaped her.

We stopped at a small, unassuming café that Kensi claimed had the best bagels in the city. As we sat, sipping coffee and sharing a cinnamon bagel, she pointed out various landmarks, sharing memories or stories she'd held onto over the years.

The cold of the December air was mitigated by the warmth of our intertwined fingers as we continued our exploration. Kensi's vibrance was infectious, and I found myself caught up in the magic of the city that had once been her home. As we joined the queue for ice skating at The Plaza, a voice sliced through the holiday cheer, freezing us in our steps.

"Rose?"

It sounded unsure, almost lost amid the sounds of the season, but it struck a chord.

As Kensi's grip on my hand tightened, a clear signal of her distress, I instinctively moved to stand slightly in front of her, my body positioning itself as a barrier between her and the unknown. Releasing her hand, I gently but firmly took her elbow, guiding her a step back, ensuring I was the first line of defense if the need arose. My eyes, sharpened by the urgency of the moment, flicked across the faces in the crowd, searching for any sign of threat or recognition. This subtle shift in stance wasn't just about physical protection; it was a silent vow that I was there, ready to shield her from anything and everything.

Then, amidst the throng of faces wrapped in scarves and caps, a man emerged, his face lighting up with recognition and something like relief when his eyes landed on Kensi. The moment hung between us, thick with unanswered questions and the weight of a past Kensi had left behind but was now staring back at her, in the middle of a New York City teeming with holiday spirits and ice skaters.

"Marco," she breathed as I felt her entire body relax before she let go of my hand and surged forward to hug this stranger.

Even as Kensi's body relaxed and she moved to embrace the man named Marco, my senses remained on high alert. My gaze shifted from him to the woman and child who followed in his wake, studying their faces for any sign of threat. The woman's expression was open, her eyes filled with a kind of understanding and kindness that slowly began to ease the tension coiling within me. The child, a girl who couldn't be more than eight, looked on with a mixture of curiosity and shyness, clutching her mother's hand tightly.

As Kensi and Marco separated from their embrace, her laughter and tears mingling in the cold air, I took a cautious step closer. The protective part of me couldn't fully recede—not yet—not until I knew for certain that Kensi was safe. But watching the genuine affection in their reunion, and seeing the open, honest faces of Marco's family, my defensive stance began to soften.

Kensi turned toward me, her eyes shining with more tears and a radiance that came from the release of pent up fears. With a gentle tug, she brought me closer into the circle. "Wyatt, this is Marco," she introduced, her voice thick with emotion. "He's the reason I'm here today."

Marco, with a modest nod, shifted his attention to me, and it was in that moment, standing amidst the whirl of New York's Christmas hustle, that the gravity of what he had done truly hit me.

I extended my hand, and as Marco took it, I found myself locked in a gaze filled with mutual understanding and respect. "Marco," I started, but had to clear my throat as it had clogged with emotions. "I can't even begin to express my gratitude for what you've done. You saved Kensi. You gave her a chance at a life she deserved, and for that, I will be forever grateful." My words, sincere and from the bottom of my heart, hung in the cold air, a testament to the depth of my gratitude.

Marco's response was a humble shrug, his eyes reflecting a sense of duty and kindness that needed no thanks. "I did what anyone would have done," he said simply, but his actions, the courage it must have taken, spoke volumes beyond those words.

After Marco's modest dismissal of his heroic actions, he introduced his wife, Sheila, and daughter, Lacey.

Kensi turned her attention to Sheila, her eyes gleaming with a mixture of gratitude and admiration. "Sheila, I don't even know where to begin," Kensi said, her voice quivering slightly with emotion. "Thank you, for everything. I know Marco says he did what anyone would have done, but we both know the risks he took to help me."

Sheila smiled graciously. "It was all Marco," she said, her voice soft yet firm, reflecting the strength it must have taken to stand by Marco through it all. "He has a big heart. I just supported him."

But Kensi shook her head gently, her gaze shifting between Sheila and Marco. "Marco might have been the one to help me directly, but he couldn't have done it without your support. The risk you both took..." She trailed off, perhaps realizing words couldn't fully capture the depth of her gratitude.

I stood by, a silent observer to this profound reunion, feeling an overwhelming sense of gratitude for the man who had played such a crucial role in Kensi's journey to freedom.

As we said our goodbyes, I offered Marco another handshake. "I'll always be in your debt," I told him earnestly. "For rescuing Kensi before I knew she needed me." His response was a humble nod, an acknowledgment of a deed done simply because it was right.

* * *

Sliding into our skates, memories of our first laugh-filled attempts on ice back in Texas flashed through my mind. Back then, I was anything but graceful, leaning heavily on Kensi for support.

"I might need to keep a grip on you. You know, so I don't end up on the ground," I half-joked, squeezing her hand a little tighter. Truth be told, these moments of being close, sharing laughs, and just being us was like a heartbeat—natural, necessary, and life-giving.

Kensi gave me that look, the one that says she's onto me, and chuckled. "Or you just want an excuse to hold my hand," she shot back, her eyes twinkling with mischief. As we stepped onto the ice, it was clear my skating hadn't gotten much better, but that wasn't really the point. Holding onto Kensi, feeling her laugh and guide me, was everything I wanted and more.

Weaving through the other skaters, with Christmas tunes setting the scene, I found myself asking, "Is it everything you remember?"

She stopped for a second, looking at me with so much love it made my heart swell. "It's so much more," Kensi said softly, her words hitting me deep. "With you here, it's like I'm living a dream." Her confession, so full of heart and truth, made everything else fade away.

In the heartbeat of the city, amidst a sea of skaters and a chorus of holiday songs, I drew Kensi in close. The noise around us blurred into a distant hum, and for a moment, it was just us—two hearts beating as one in the glow of New York's Christmas lights.

"Kensi," I whispered, the words floating between us like the snowflakes above, "You've filled my life with magic and hope like I've never known. Thank you for letting me love you."

Her eyes lit up, mirroring the festive lights that surrounded us, a universe of love and promise in her gaze. "Thank you for loving me," she whispered back, her eyes alight with every twinkling light around us, "and I love you, too."

Then, with the city as our witness, I kissed her— a silent vow stretching into forever. For a brief, perfect moment, the world paused, wrapping us in its embrace as we sealed our love with a kiss. A love like ours was meant to be celebrated, so we did just that right there on the ice. It was more than just a moment; it was our forever, wrapped up in the magic of Christmas in New York.

EPILOGUE

Six Months Later

Kensi

The room was brightening with the glow from the morning sun peeking through the curtains. Wyatt was still peacefully asleep next to me. Today was Nash and Cassidy's wedding day, and the excitement that had been building up for weeks was now mingled with an unexpected bout of nausea that had me clutching my stomach.

I tried to get up quietly, not wanting to disturb Wyatt, but the moment my feet hit the cold floor, the room seemed to spin. "You okay?" Wyatt's voice, groggy with sleep, filled the room.

"I'm not sure," I replied, my voice barely a whisper. The world tilted once more, and I rushed to the bathroom.

Wyatt was by my side in an instant, his concern palpable. "What can I do? How can I help?" he asked, his voice filled with that protective tone I had grown to love.

I couldn't help but find amusement in his worry, despite my

current state. "It's okay. I just need a minute," I managed to say before the nausea overwhelmed me again.

We were staying in a quaint homestay cottage, surrounded by the serene beauty of West Virginia's mountains—a peaceful scene compared to the turmoil inside me. As I leaned against the cool bathroom wall, trying to catch my breath, Wyatt's brow furrowed as he watched me, his protective instincts kicking in. "Do you think you caught something? Or maybe it's something you ate?"

I shook my head slowly, the puzzle of my discomfort assembling piece by piece in my mind. "I don't think so," I said, the realization dawning on both of us at the same moment. We locked eyes, a silent communication passing between us. Could it be? We weren't even trying.

Before we could vocalize the thought, another wave of nausea washed over me. As I knelt there, Wyatt was right behind me, holding my hair back and rubbing soothing circles on my back. Once the wave of nausea passed, I sat back, feeling exhausted but strangely exhilarated.

He threw on his joggers and hoodie that had been discarded by the bed the night before and kissed my forehead before saying, "I'm going to run to the pharmacy in town. Just rest, okay?"

Left alone, I sat on the edge of the bed, wrapped in a blanket, processing the possibility. Anxiety should have been gnawing at my insides, but instead, a wave of happiness, contentment, and excitement washed over me. The thought of a tiny life growing inside me, of Wyatt and me starting a family, filled me with an indescribable joy.

When Wyatt returned, he dumped four different boxes of pregnancy tests on the bed, each boasting its own promise of accuracy. "I wasn't sure which one to get, so I got a few," he said, a sheepish grin on his face.

We followed the instructions on each box, then waited the longest five minutes of our lives. One by one, the tests confirmed what we had begun to suspect. I was pregnant. The room quickly filled with the sounds of laughter accompanied by tears and kisses. We were ecstatic, our hearts bursting with a love that grew with every passing second. This moment was ours, a precious secret we held close as we prepared for the wedding.

The day passed in a blur of joy and celebration. Nash and Cassidy's happiness was infectious, and while we were over the moon about our own news, we chose to keep it to ourselves for now. Today was their day, and our little miracle could wait a little longer before being shared with the world.

As we danced under the stars, Wyatt pulled me close, his hand resting gently on my stomach. "I love you, Kensi Turner. I love you more and more every single day. And I already love this little one more than I thought possible," he whispered, his voice filled with emotion.

"I love you too. Today, tomorrow, and forever," I replied, my heart full. In that moment, surrounded by friends and enveloped in love, I knew that no matter what the future held, we were ready to face it together.

A NOTE TO THE READER

If you or someone you know is experiencing domestic violence, please know that help is available, and you are not alone. No one deserves to live in fear or be subjected to abuse, and there are people and organizations ready to support you.

In the United States, you can reach out to the National Domestic Violence Hotline at 1-800-799-SAFE (7233) or visit www.thehotline.org. They provide confidential support 24/7.

For those outside the U.S., similar services are available worldwide. Organizations like the Hot Peach Pages (www.hotpeachpages.net) offer resources and contact information for shelters and hotlines in multiple countries.

Taking the first step to reach out can feel overwhelming, but it is a step toward safety and healing. You are worthy of love, respect, and a life free from violence.

Thank you for reading Kensi and Wyatt's story. Their journey is fictional, but the issues it touches are real. If this book has inspired you or someone you know to seek help, please remember that hope is always within reach.

With love and care,

Jen

RUN TO HOME BASE

The 9K Wyatt runs in chapter 53 of *Let Me Love You* is real. **Run to Home Base** happens every year through the streets of Boston to "home base" at Fenway Park.

Countless Veterans and their Families bear the daily weight of visible and invisible wounds—trauma that doesn't always end on the battlefield. From physical injuries to PTSD, depression, and the devastating ripple effects of suicide, these struggles touch not just the individuals but entire families and communities. These are not just statistics; they are lives, stories, and legacies that deserve our deepest respect and unwavering support.

At the heart of hope stands Home Base, an organization committed to addressing these wounds with compassion and expertise. They provide life-changing clinical care to Warriors and their Families across the globe, supporting over 40,000 individuals to date. Whether treating physical scars or the hidden pain of mental health challenges, their work offers healing where it's needed most. And they do it all without any out-of-pocket costs—because no one should face the burden of recovery alone.

The **Run to Home Base** is more than just a fundraiser. It's a call to action, a celebration of resilience, and a tribute to the brave men and women who have given so much. Every step taken, every dollar raised goes directly toward the critical care that saves lives and restores hope for Warriors and their Families.

Learn how you can be part of this mission and make a difference by visiting runtohomebase.org. Together, we can honor their sacrifices and ensure no one is left to fight their battles alone.

ACKNOWLEDGMENTS

First and foremost, thanks be to God, whose grace for this and every journey is wholly necessary and sufficient.

To my husband, Rob, your unwavering support and love have been the foundation on which I've built every word of this book. You are my favorite person. I love you.

Ashley, my sister and editor, your sharp eye and endless patience turned draft after draft into something I'm proud of. Thank you. I love you, Seester.

Kearstin, you were one of the first to take a chance on my book, and I was honored to be among the first to support your growing platform. Having our paths cross has been a gift, and I'm so glad we're friends!

And to my incredible ARC team: Thank you for your patience, your enthusiasm, and your encouragement!

Stanley 🐻, once again I "bear-ly" made it through, but you make it a much more enjoyable experience.

To anyone who has dared to pick up any one of my books and asked me when to expect the next one. YOU are the true hero. Thank you for your support, your excitement over the stories that pop into my head, and for spurring me on to write the next one.

～

ABOUT THE AUTHOR

Jennifer Carr is a romance author, lifelong daydreamer, and psychology nerd turned author.

A degree in Psychology, a Master's in Marriage & Family Counseling, multiple certifications in life/wellness coaching and brain health, and years teaching AP Psychology gave her a deep understanding of people—but it was writing that finally gave her a way to share their stories.

What started as a curiosity ("I wonder how that dream was going to end?") quickly turned into something bigger. One book became several. Passion became purpose. And a new career was born.

Married to her childhood best friend and raising a creative daughter on their quiet Alabama farm, Jennifer writes emotional, character-driven fiction with heart, healing, no spice, and just the perfect amount of swoon.

When she's not writing, you'll find her reading romance novels, listening to music, baking something delicious, or sipping strong coffee with her cat nearby.

Learn more or get signed books: jcarrwrites.com

Independent authors NEED reviews in order for their work to be discovered. If you have the time, please consider leaving your honest review on any platform for others to find.

ALSO BY JENNIFER CARR

Real American Country Series

Fall When You're Ready, Jordan & Rachel (Book 1)

Wrapped Up in You, Nash & Cassidy (Book 2)

Let Me Love You, Wyatt & Kensi (Book 3)

Still Holding Out for You, Austin & Willow (Book 4)

A Little More You (Book 5)

Who I Am With You (Book 6)

No Matter What Series

No Matter What

The Lost and Found

Available on Amazon, Kindle, Kindle Unlimited

Signed copies can be found at jcarrwrites.com